# THE WALKING DEAD

On a bright spring morning, the paths of two men cross. One is a policeman, tasked with neutralising the growing threat of terrorism to London's safety. The other is a man who has travelled from a dusty village in Saudi Arabia, hoping to go to his God as a martyr, taking many innocent lives with him . . .

# ABOUT THE AUTHOR

Gerald Seymour spent fifteen years as an international television news reporter with ITN, covering Vietnam and the Middle East, and specialising in the subject of terrorism across the world. Seymour was on the streets of Londonderry on the afternoon of Bloody Sunday, and was a witness to the massacre of Israeli athletes at the Munich Olympics.

Gerald Seymour is now a full-time writer, and six of his novels have been filmed for television in the UK and US. FIELD OF BLOOD is his eighth novel.

For more information about Gerald Seymour and his books, visit his Facebook page at
www.facebook.com/GeraldSeymourAuthor

# FIELD OF BLOOD

'Seymour keeps all in doubt up to the last gasp . . . streetwise with a difference' – *The Sunday Times*

'Action is what Seymour does best . . . terse, clipped, brutal' – *The Times*

'Brilliant . . . moments that explode with heart-stopping suspense' – *New Yorker*

'The three British masters [of suspense] Graham Greene, Eric Ambler and John le Carré have been joined by a fourth – Gerald Seymour' – *New York Times*

# HAVE YOU READ . . . ?

## AT CLOSE QUARTERS

Lebanon's Beqa'a Valley is home to many of the most revolutionary groups in the Palestinian guerrilla war against Israel. To be captured in this territory means torture and certain death.

British diplomat Peter Holt and his guide, Israeli sniper Noah Crane, plan to enter the midst of the valley's fortifications to find one man – an assassin whom only Holt can identify. But when their cover is blown and Syrian Intelligence is alerted to their presence, it is too late to turn back . . .

## RED FOX

Beautiful, seductive and extremely dangerous, Franca Tantardini is one of Italy's most ruthless political extremists. When she is captured in a shoot-out, her fanatical young lover Battestini vows to set her free.

In Rome, political wrangling takes hold as British businessman, Geoffery Harrison, is taken hostage by a ruthless organised crime syndicate. Battestini seizes on the opportunity to secure the release of his beloved Franca and decides to capture Harrison, intent on bargaining his life for hers.

## THE HEART OF DANGER

A mass grave is uncovered in a devastated Croatian village, and the mutilated body of a young Englishwoman, Dorrie Mowat, is exhumed. When the authorities show no interest in the case, Dorrie's mother turns to private investigator Bill Penn, a former MI5 agent. Penn anticipates a short trip to Zagreb, but once there his search becomes an epic journey into a merciless war where the odds are stacked high against him.

# Field of Blood

## Gerald Seymour

HODDER

First published in Great Britain in 1985 by Collins

This paperback edition first published in 2014

1

Book ISBN 978 1 444 76015 6
eBook ISBN 978 1 444 76016 3

Typeset by Hewer Text UK Ltd, Edinburgh
Printed and bound by Clays Ltd, St Ives plc

Hodder                                            are natural, renewable
and re                                      and grown in sustainable
forest                              manufacturing processes are expected to
confo                                    regulations of the country of origin.

Hodder & Stoughton Ltd
338 Euston Road
London NW1 3BH

To Gillian, Nicholas and James

Then Judas, which had betrayed him, when he saw that he was condemned, repented himself and brought again the thirty pieces of silver to the chief priests and elders, saying, I have sinned in that I have betrayed the innocent blood. And they said, What is that to us? see thou to that. And he cast down the pieces of silver in the temple, and departed, and went and hanged himself. And the chief priests took the silver pieces, and said, It is not lawful for to put them into the treasury, because it is the price of blood. And they took counsel, and bought with them the potter's field, to bury strangers in. Wherefore that field was called, The field of blood, unto this day.

Saint Matthew XXVII, vv. 3–8

# FIELD OF BLOOD

## *Introduction by Tom Bradby*

Gerald Seymour was always something of a legend at ITN. When I arrived as a trainee in 1990, he was still much talked of as the guy who had managed to make a massive success of two quite different careers. He had been admired as a reporter of great skill and integrity who travelled the globe over many years and found himself at the heart of major historical events on more than one occasion (he was the ITN man covering Bloody Sunday, after all). But to have gone on from that to write a thriller that was a bestseller all over the world; wow, that was cool. So, even many years after its publication, HARRY'S GAME was the talk of the ITN bar.

To say that Gerald was something of an inspiration for me would be a great understatement. I read all his books and enjoyed each and every one. They may have very different settings and plots, but they do have the same authenticity, style, structure and pace. In his book *Adventures in the Screen Trade*, William Goldman wrote that 'screenplays are structure,' and the same is even more true of thrillers in general. As any writer in this genre will tell you: get the structure right and everything becomes easier, get it wrong and you will be labouring frustratingly in the dark for a very long time. Every Gerald Seymour novel is a master class in structure.

I don't know how many times I have read Gerald's three Northern Ireland novels, but let's just settle for 'numerous.' Both HARRY'S GAME and THE JOURNEYMAN TAILOR are brilliantly atmospheric and gripping and reek of authenticity, but somehow FIELD OF BLOOD has always been my favourite.

Partly, it is the time and place in which it is set. The intelligence officers who came up with the idea of using informers to put hundreds of IRA men on trial must have thought they had finally cracked the Troubles. Membership of the IRA was in itself illegal, don't forget, so the idea of using secret agents of the state inside the organisation to give evidence in court about their colleagues seemed like an imaginative way to break Irish Republicanism.

And, for a while, it looked like it would work. The so-called super-grass trials sent a wave of fear through Belfast. One IRA leader daubed a slogan on a mural as a warning to others: **Remember Christopher Black.** Underneath, one wag added with black humour: **I hope to f\*\*\* he doesn't remember me.**

This is the world that FIELD OF BLOOD brings to life so brilliantly. Rarely can any individuals in any community have been loathed as much as those agents who gave evidence in the supergrass trials. Not for the first time and not for the last, you could have scraped the hatred off the walls in those courtrooms.

But the success of FIELD OF BLOOD is about so much more than setting. In terms of characterisation, pacing and, yes, structure, it is pitch perfect. When I came up with the idea of writing *Shadow Dancer* (my own Northern Irish novel), I worked out fairly early on that it would be a good idea to spend some time studying thrillers I really admired. I figured that if I could work out why these worked so well, I would be able to compare and contrast my own structure.

I looked at a pretty diverse range of the great thrillers of all time, from *Silence of the Lambs* to *Presumed Innocent*, but the novel I came back to most often was FIELD OF BLOOD, and not just because of the similarity of setting.

It is a gripping tale and yet it all unfolds with such effortless ease. You'd think writing a thriller like this was simple. But every writer knows different.

I said at the start that Gerald was an inspiration to me and he probably has no idea just how much this is true. I have now had parallel careers as a writer and television reporter for almost two decades and it was the path Gerald forged that convinced me this might be possible. And I have needed that, because there have been plenty of people along the way who have told me I was quite mad to even try.

When *Shadow Dancer* came out in 1998, Gerald sent me a lovely note of congratulation and a first edition copy of HARRY'S GAME.

It meant a huge amount.

So the truth is that he is not just a genius, but a gent, too.

Tom Bradby, London, February 2014

Tom Bradby's bestselling thrillers include *Shadow Dancer* (for which he also wrote the film starring Andrea Riseborough and Clive Owen), *The Master of Rain*, *The White Russian*, *God of Chaos* and *Blood Money*. Tom is also ITN's Political Editor and presenter of ITV's The Agenda.

# PROLOGUE

It was a good plan. The Chief and his Brigade Officers had worked at it for five weeks.

They knew in which car the target would travel, and which routes his escorts could take between the detached suburban house and the Crown Court. They had the timings on the car, and they knew that all the routes used the same final half mile to the Court buildings.

The weapon was in the city. The weapon and its single projectile were available and waiting. The marksmen were available and waiting. The strike was fixed by the Chief for the Thursday of the following week.

It was a good plan, too good to fail. That it seemed to have failed was a matter of dismal luck, the luck that had haunted the Organization in the last months.

Eammon Dalton and Fran Forde were stopped on the Glen Road at a randomly placed police road block. On another evening the two Volunteers might have carried off the Person Check with indifference, given their names and addresses quietly and calmly, spilled the fictitious every-night story of where they were going, and been cleared and sent on their way. They were heading, when they were waved down, to a final briefing from Brigade. They were nervous and strung taut and they aroused the interest of the heavily armed constables peering down at the two young Catholics' torch-lit faces. Dalton wouldn't speak, and Forde gave, in the heat of the moment, an alias which was found a minute later to differ from the name on his driving licence. Dalton swore as soon as Forde had opened his idiot mouth. At first, of course, the policemen didn't know what they had, but they guessed they had something. Dalton and Forde were pulled out of the car and their hands were spread on the roof and their legs were kicked apart, and they could hear the sergeant feeding the registration of the car into his radio's microphone – and that was bad luck because the car was a Datsun and the plates had been lifted off a Sierra. They were covered by an M1 carbine and a Sterling SMG, and they stayed very still because they knew the policemen would dearly love to have them break and run, and they knew the fingers were stroking the triggers. The report on the plates came back to the sergeant's earpiece and the handcuffs clicked on Eammon Dalton and Fran Forde's wrists. They were hustled to the dark interior of the police Land Rover.

For these two Volunteers the war was over, for some years at least.

The Chief and his Brigade Operations officer were brought the news of the arrest by courier.

The Chief reflected. The plan was too good to fail just because a piss-arse Volunteer couldn't remember the bloody name on his driving licence. The weapon was good, but bloody damn useless in the fists of a man who hadn't been trained for it. He'd learned how useless this prize weapon was in untrained hands when a projectile had overshot an Army Pig vehicle and blasted a Primary classroom, and when a projectile had missed a Pig and hit the front axle of a coal delivery lorry. Dalton and Forde had been trained to use the weapon. They had had the luxury of test firings in a remote Donegal quarry over the border, into the south.

The plan was too good to waste. He had the weapon, but only one projectile. No bastard could make it work on a live first time firing.

The Brigade Operations officer read his mind.

'I'd do it myself, but . . .'

' 'Course you would, 'course I would and we'd be lucky to hit a bloody wall, let alone a bloody car.'

'In this city you had two boys only who could use it, both gone . . .'

The frown cut into the Chief's forehead. 'What of the old teams, the old boys who used to be trained on it?'

'One's shot, one's in the Kesh, one's buried for blowing himself away with his own bomb. And one went down south, way back.'

'Could he still fire it?'

'Too right, but he went over the border, quit.'

'Get him,' the Chief said.

'He walked out on us – he was good with it, but he quit on us.'
'Get the fucker back.'
'He could fire it, if we could get him here.'
'It's too good to waste. Get him back.'

# I

He rubbed at the condensation on the window and peered out at the slow-moving car.

It was the second time it had cruised past the caravan.

A grey, misted morning. The cloud fog softened the greens of the grass on the canal's bank and brightened the yellows of the collapsing weed beds and darkened the tarmac of the roadway running beside the straight line of the canal. He had first seen the car when the bird had flapped fast away from the perch he had placed for it in the grass. He always fed the bird at that time.

He moved quickly from the end window to the side window and stretched across the small Formica-topped table and his stomach wobbled the sauce bottles he had left out for his tea. His fist smeared against the window so that he could better see the car as it went up the narrow road towards Vicarstown. His vision was obscured by a wild hedgerow but he made out the red flash of the brake lights, and he knew that the car had stopped. He darted back across the caravan and switched off his radio and strained his ears in the new-found quiet. Very faintly he could hear the drive of the car's engine as it turned in the roadway and skidded on the verge beside the canal. He saw the bird, apprehensive in a tree across the water, watching.

Then silence. Only the wheeze of his own breathing. His eyes were against the window. He saw no movement from between the hedgerow branches where the brake lights had shone.

He cursed and hurried the three strides back to the end window of the caravan from which he had first seen the car. He looked both ways up the road and he saw nothing.

He went to the door at the back of the caravan, the end away from the road, and opened the door carefully and looked out over the fields to the squat farmhouse two hundred yards away. Smoke from the chimney climbed straight to the cloud ceiling. No sign of life. Again he strained his ears and heard nothing. He closed the door behind him.

For two years the caravan had been his home. It had a single bunk, a table, a chair, a gas ring, a sink. Behind a curtain near the door was a chemical bucket lavatory. On the wall above the table was a photograph of his wife and one of two of his children. The photographs were fastened to the wall with old, dried out Sellotape. His breakfast plate and mug lay in the small sink. Across the width of the caravan, at eye level, hung a string carrying two pairs of pants and some socks and a shirt. Because a cable reached from the farmhouse to the caravan he had the electricity to burn a single-bar fire. The caravan was his home.

He had made out the blurred outline of two men in the front seats each time that the car had passed. He wondered why they waited. Perhaps they worked to a schedule and waited on their watches; perhaps they allowed themselves a cigarette before coming to him.

It was more than a year since he had been visited at the caravan. It had been two detectives then. They'd said they were Crime and he'd known they were Special Branch, and they'd come down from the station at Monasterevan, and they'd looked around and talked gently with him, and said it was only routine, and that if he stayed clean then he'd be left to himself, and that if he went dirty that they'd fucking smash him. The one had looked quietly around the caravan, and the other had spoken with a twinkling eye and a soft Cork brogue. All right for a Belfast man to live down south, but Jesus had he better be clean ... Because if he was dirty, if he was Provo dirty, then he was in a heap of shit. And they'd shaken his hand, and called him by his first name and closed the door behind them and gone on their way. He had been clean before they came to the caravan, and clean ever since.

That was the last time that the young kestrel bird had been frightened away at feeding time.

He rubbed again at the window, and tried to see the car and could not.

It was two years since he had taken up the offer of the caravan on the farm of his mother's cousin. The cousin lived on his own, and

6

didn't look for a stranger's company. There was the caravan at the end of the lane, beside the roadway, and it was available for a distant relative who was a refugee from the north. In the summer if there was hay to be cut then he helped, or if there was repair work to be done on a roof of an outhouse then he would do it. Mostly weeks went by and he only saw the old man at a distance across the fields. It was a lonely life and Christ for all that it was better than the life he had lived before two years back. Only on a Saturday evening would he take the bicycle into Vicarstown and drink some stout in a bar. He knew that his accent betrayed his origins and wondered what the local men said of him. He was lonely because he did not seek the locals' company, nor was he given it. When he drank he'd have a plastic carrier bag beside his knee that was filled with sliced loaves and packets of margarine and a pound of rashers and a pound of sausages. He took his milk from the farm, he took his money from a Thursday morning ride to Monsterevan and the 'brew' from the Post Office.

The bird was his only companion. The farmer had taken the fledgling kestrel from an abandoned nest a month after he had come to the caravan, and fed it on bread and milk and meat scraps to maturity. The bird wasn't tame, not so it could be touched, but it nested within sight of the farmhouse and the caravan, and it came most days for food. He talked to the bird, softly so as not to frighten it, and it had his bacon rind and slices of raw sausage. The bird wasn't a prisoner, no clipped wings, no thongs. The bird was free, as he was free since he had come to the new life two years back.

He loved the bird.

Before he had come south he couldn't have imagined himself as pansy enough to love a pink-tailed kestrel bird. He loved his wife, too, but she was in Belfast. The kestrel bird was with him, and was all the company he had.

Through the window of the caravan he heard the dulled bang and knew it was the slamming of a car door.

If his wife had travelled south with him then he might possibly have wriggled a lasting escape from the life of before two years back, but she said there was no way she was going to exist in a soddin' field. She said Belfast was bad but it's where it's familiar. He'd told her it was a mobile home they could live in, she said it was a soddin' caravan, and no place for the wee ones. She said she'd prefer to be with her Ma and her Da, and his mates and her friends, and not hidin' in a soddin' bog down south. She said she knew why he'd gone, because he had to go, she didn't think the less of him for going. He went back three times the first year, four times the second year. Back to Belfast to be with her, to be with the kids. He hadn't been for two months, but he'd be back up with her and the kids for Christmas. He often had the radio on inside the caravan, and when the reporters broadcast of house searches and lifts and aggro and shootings in the area where his wife lived, where his kids were, where his Ma and Da were, where her Ma and Da were, then he would suffer a little in his helplessness. But she always said that she understood why he had gone away. She never blamed him. Christ, it would have been easier if she had.

He wiped once more at the window glass. There were two men walking up the centre of the road towards the caravan.

He saw their pale town faces. The taller man wore a cap and the shorter man's hair was long to his shoulders and his beard covered his throat. The taller man bent and picked a stone off the side of the road and threw it hard and high into the tree where the bird perched and watched the bird fly swiftly away. He grinned as if it pleased him that he had disturbed a picture that had been at peace. The kestrel flew frightened away down the length of the canal. The shorter man retched and coughed and spat and dropped a half-used cigarette into the road where it burned on after he had walked past. They came to the hole that was cut in the hedgerow.

He saw them cock their ears, he saw them turn their heads and swivel their eyes down the road in front of them and behind them.

There was no weapon in the caravan. Weapons were Belfast. He had no need of a weapon to keep him safe in a caravan beside the canal near Vicarstown. The taller man's jaw was cartwheeling as he chewed at a mouthful of gum. When they were satisfied they came fast through the hole in the hedge. They crossed the long grass that bordered the vegetable patch square that he had dug out in the summer. He saw the grimace of annoyance from the taller man as the wet grass splayed over his shoes. He grew the vegetables for the old man in the farm to sell to the store in Vicarstown, lettuce in the spring, carrots and parsnips now that it was winter. He saw that they said not a word to each other, and nor did they look up at his face in the caravan window.

He knew it would come and yet he was jolted upright by the rap at the caravan door. His eyes closed. His teeth bit on his lip, and he felt a moment of pain. He dragged a gulp of air down into his chest. He stared at the door, and he saw the inexact outline of the two heads beyond the glaze glass.

The shorter man was standing on the step and was lighting a cigarette and smiled as the door was opened. The taller man showed no visible expression.

'Yes?' He tucked the thumb of one hand into his belt, and the other hand was in his trouser pocket. The strangers should not see the tremble in his fingers.

'McAnally?' The shorter man spoke with the raw accent of West Belfast. 'Are you McAnally?'

'Yes.'

'Sean Pius McAnally?'

'Yes.'

'And your home, up there, is 63 The Drive in Turf Lodge . . .?'

'What have you come for?' He snarled the question because that way his nerves were hidden from them. He disliked them because they had frightened him. He was not a man who should easily have been frightened. No man who had led an Active Service Unit in Turf Lodge, Ballymurphy and Whitcrock would admit to fear.

'Easy, boy.' The taller man spoke.

'Come to take you back,' the shorter man said.

'Better talked about inside, pissing cold out here,' the taller man said.

'Nobody tells me where I'm going.'

'Like he said, easy . . .' The shorter man smiled a second time.

McAnally stood aside from the door, made way for the two men to climb up into the caravan. Suddenly the inside of the caravan was crowded, bursting. It was his place of refuge, and it was invaded. They looked around them, they stripped the privacy from the walls. In turn they bent to look at the photographs, at the sink, at the

9

curtain that hid the chemical lavatory seat. The taller man leaned his bottom against the table-edge. The shorter man sat on the chair and stretched out his legs. McAnally closed the door.

'What do you want?'

'What I said . . .' The shorter man dragged far down on his cigarette, went to the door, threw the stub outside, coughed and spat, shut the door, went back to the chair. 'What I said, come to take you back.'

'Who says?'

'It's what we've been told, take you back.'

McAnally thought they might as well have crapped on his floor, on the linoleum, or they might have pissed on his walls, on the photographs. Between the two of them they suffocated the privacy of his refuge, the privacy of the caravan.

'What's your name?' McAnally asked the shorter man.

There was a smile without amusement, without pity. 'You've been away too long . . . we don't like names.'

McAnally laughed, shrill, excited. 'Because you're all riddled with touts. Weren't any touts in my time.'

'Your time's not done, Gingy,' the taller man said.

McAnally rocked slightly on the balls of his feet. That was his name when he was in the war. He was always called 'Gingy'. All the men liked a name that was short and sharp and familiar. All the men had their nicknames. Ducksy and Cruncher and Puffer and Bronco and Buster and Bluey and Fitzy and . . . He was Gingy because the moustache that was now shaved away had once been redder than his hair. He was Gingy in the Turf Lodge, and Gingy in the ASU. He had been Gingy for five years in the Long Kesh prison camp, and Gingy in the Remand Wing of the Crumlin Road gaol. Gingy was his name before two years back.

'Who wants me back?'

'The Chief wants you back.' The shorter man grinned. There was a gap in his front upper teeth. Now that the shorter man wasn't smoking, McAnally could smell his breath and his armpits. 'You won't be asking his name?'

McAnally said softly, 'And what it's for . . .?'

'We wouldn't know, would we? Cop on, Gingy. You'll be told when you've come back.'

'I'm out, I quit.'

'You took an oath, you swore your oath,' the taller man said.

Eleven years before Sean Pius McAnally had made his oath to the Organization. He had made it in his own home. They couldn't use the front room because his Da was watching telly, couldn't use the kitchen because his Ma was dishing the supper. He had made his oath on the upstairs landing, and they'd all had to whisper because his sister was trying to get her baby to sleep in the back bedroom. He had made his oath, he had offered his allegiance to the Provisional wing of the Irish Republican Army.

'An oath's an oath. An oath's a lifetime,' the smaller man said.

'An oath doesn't get torn up just because a boy wants to sit on his arse in the south ... and let others do what the boy swore to do himself,' the taller man said, and McAnally had to lean forward and strain to hear the words.

An oath whispered on the landing of a three-bedroomed Housing Executive semi-detached. An oath made while a sister crooned to a baby, while the telly blared a comedy, while Ma crashed the saucepans.

'We're wasting time, Gingy,' the smaller man said.

McAnally wondered if they were armed. Didn't matter, because there were two of them. And two of them could wreck him, and wreck the caravan. As he stared into their faces his thoughts were totally lucid. If he expelled them from the caravan, if he damaged them, then they'd be back, and others would be back. The smaller man lit another cigarette and looked into McAnally's face and then down at the dead match in his fingers and dropped it onto the lino-leum. They were squatting over him, crapping on him, pissing on him. He shrugged.

'I'm not promising anything.'

'You're not being asked to promise anything,' the taller man said. 'You're being told to obey an order from Belfast Brigade.'

McAnally crossed to the bunk, stepping over the outstretched legs of the shorter man, insinuating himself past the taller man. He crouched down and reached into the space underneath the mattress for a canvas grip bag. There was always a pain in his right knee when he bent low where the rubber bullet had ricocheted up from the pavement in the Motorman fight. He winced, and stood up. He collected the clothes from the drying line and folded them into his bag.

'If they want me, then it's something special,' McAnally said to the taller man. He looked him in the face, eye to eye. 'If they want me then it's for a job that's too big for the likes of you fuckers.'

He thought the man would have liked to belt him. He watched his fingers tighten on the seams of his jeans. The shorter man was making a play of grinding his cigarette out on the linoleum as McAnally zipped up the bag.

'All I hear on the radio down here is about the touts up there . . . Am I safe from touts if I go back with you?'

The taller man shouted, 'You call me a tout, McAnally, and I'll break your neck. You can be a fucking Battalion Officer, a fucking Brigade Officer, you call me a tout, I'll break your fucking neck.'

McAnally saw the sweat on his forehead. 'No-one ever informed in my day. You could beat the shit out of a man, and he never told. Whatever the 'tecs did in Castelreagh and Gough and Strand, a man never touted . . .'

'Touting isn't something you make a crack about,' the shorter man said, and the smile was gone from the white chubbiness of his cheeks.

'I want to go up to the farm.'

'What for?'

'To see the old man.'

'To tell him you're going back to Belfast, to tell him the boys came to fetch you back to Belfast?' The sneer of the shorter man.

The taller man asked, 'What have you to tell him?'

McAnally hesitated. He would have told his Ma's cousin that he'd be away for a few days, that the kestrel needed feeding. He couldn't tell them that, not these bastards. He shrugged.

'Doesn't matter,' he muttered.

From the hook behind the door McAnally lifted down his anorak, slid his arms into the sleeves.

'Will I see my wife?'

'You'll be dropped there tonight,' the taller man hissed.

McAnally unplugged the electric fire, and then the connection to the single bulb that hung down from the ceiling. He took what remained of a loaf and a packet of margarine and the bacon and the sausages from the one cupboard and handed them to the shorter man to hold.

When they were out of the caravan he busied himself fastening the padlock on the door, and then they walked together through the gap in the hedge and onto the road. They let McAnally walk in front, as if they were an escort to him. From the roadway he threw the margarine and the bread into the grass by the canal, and the bacon and the short string of sausages to the place where the kestrel fed. He reckoned the bird could peck into the margarine carton.

It was mild and there was a fleck of rain in the air and already the light was sliding over the bare-branched elm trees that were mirrored in the canal.

They went up the road, towards the rusted Cortina that was parked flush to the hedge.

McAnally looked around him, into the still canal and into the thin stretching roadway and into the small fields and into the deep blanket of cloud. He saw the kestrel a long way off, watching from a diseased elm branch. He stared back one last time at the roof of the caravan. He remembered when he had decided to quit the Organization and go south. He climbed into the back of the car and slumped against the seat and closed his eyes and heard the gunning of the engine.

The taller man drove. Going north and three hours to Belfast. Three hours for Sean Pius McAnally to reflect that two years of escape was gone.

He was born into the Falls, screamed his first baby shouts in the front bedroom of a brick terraced house that was without a bathroom, without a flushing lavatory. His eldest sister helped the mid-wife with the delivery.

The early memories were of the van that came to move the cheap furniture from the old decay of the Falls to the new decay of Turf Lodge. Turf Lodge was a sprawl of a housing estate out to the west of the city of Belfast, and well away from any comparable Protestant housing estate. The memory of the loaded van competed with the memory of his father coming back to the new house in Turf Lodge within a week of the move, and his father's lip was bleeding and his front lower teeth were missing or chipped, and the scurrying words between mother and father were of intimidation and that the buggers said they wouldn't have a Taig working in a Prot butchers. The memories slid easily into the groove of a father who sat the days away in front of a fireplace that burned scavenged wood, a father who no longer believed in the possibility of work. The memories drifted through a three-bedroomed house that was home for a family of Ma and Da and five sisters and Sean Pius McAnally. The memories eddied into the wearing of a cast-off blazer carrying the badge of St Peter's Secondary School, Whiterock Road, a good walk from Turf Lodge but Ma liked the priests there, and of the misery of homework in the quiet of the box bathroom that was the pride of a Turf Lodge house; a bloody waste of time, that homework, because there wasn't any work after school for half of the St Peter's leavers. Gone from school at sixteen, and no exams passed – exams were for the Protestants in their Academies and Institutions, exams weren't for kids from Turf Lodge.

Those were the distant memories. Sharper were the memories of the times since the war began.

He was recruited when he left school. The second year of the war.

At first the stoning and the petrol bombing of the Pig armoured cars that patrolled Turf Lodge, the night watch at the end of the Drive and the Avenue and the Parade with the whistle in his hand and ready to blow the warning if the foot patrols came through. Aged seventeen he had seen his first soldier die. A file of soldiers, spaced and on both sides of the Drive, patrolling in Turf Lodge. One echoing crack of the Armalite, one belt from the widow maker. The teenage boy had joined the other teenage boys and the teenage girls of the Drive as they chanted at the tops of their voices 'If you see a Brit soldier die, clap your hands, clap your hands, if you see a Brit soldier die . . .' and he had hated the boy whose blood was spilling in the road's gutter, and he had loathed the bitter-faced troops who bent over the boy and who trained their rifles on the crowd. And he had worshipped the unknown man who had fired the single shot.

When things in Turf Lodge were hot then Sean Pius McAnally, the teenager, was on the streets. When they were cold he was lounging on the street corner, or flopped in the chair by the fire at home, always bored when it was cold, always restless.

Two days after his twentieth birthday, ten long years ago now, when he was combing his hair in the bedroom that he shared with two of his sisters, when he was thinking about his supper, when he was wondering how far he would get with Roisin O'Rourke behind the garages when it was dark, two men came to offer Sean Pius McAnally membership of the Organization and the rank of Volunteer in the movement. The oath on the upstairs landing. A binding oath, an oath of a lifetime. Onto an ASU, a member of the new cell system. Into action against the Brits and the pig police. Quick learner, wasn't he? No bloody exams at school, but good with the American M16 rifle. His eyes were quality, and his hands were steady, and he was told that if he kept going well they'd give him a job with the sniper gun, with the Remington Woodmaster M742. He had money now from rolled banks and held-up Post Offices and a twenty-first birthday wedding to Roisin O'Rourke, and a week's screwing, and back to Belfast and her Ma's small bedroom, and the first time out with the Remington Woodmaster. She was a great girl, his Roisin, a great kid, and the crack in the Drive was that he was one hell of a lucky bugger to have had her.

Crystal-clear memories now. Memories of a road block manned by the fucking Fusiliers with the fairy pom-poms on their berets, of the driver spinning the wheel, of the rifle shots impacting into the driver, of the North of England voices yelling commands, of crawling out of the car with his hands held high. Memories of the Castlereagh Interrogation Centre, and of the beatings. Memories of not touting, of enduring the pain. Memories of the trial at the Crumlin Road Court House, and of a judge in red robes who looked down on him as if he were a bad smell. Memories of the H blocks, and of the stink of the shit protest, and of the weapons classes in Long Kesh. Memories of mastering the theory of the RPG-7 rocket launcher that was armour-piercing and death to the Pigs and the Saracens and the reinforced Land Rovers. Memories of crying his frustration at the cell walls because he would have to wait to use the rocket against the bastards.

Memories that were fresh as yesterday, of release, of handling the RPG-7, of firing it three times in fourteen months, of seeing the devastation on the telly news, of watching a funeral on the evening round-up. Two more kids conceived in the trembling aftermath of a firing. Targets getting harder, police Intelligence getting better. The RPG wasn't fired from behind a wall, the RPG had to be lined up, aimed, held firm. The risk getting worse, the chance of success getting poorer.

Memories of the day that was a sledgehammer, the day that a Volunteer in the Turf Lodge was turned, became a grass, touted on the rest of his ASU. Shit, that day was sharp in his memories. Not Sean Pius McAnally's ASU . . . If it had been his ASU then he would have been away to the Kesh as a lifer. No fucking way, not him doing a life stretch. He hadn't asked their permission, he had told them he was going. He didn't reckon a man who was expert in the use of an RPG needed to get bloody permission.

Memories of the first week in the caravan. Memories of lying in the narrow bunk bed and knowing that he was safe, knowing that the life sentence in the Kesh was another bugger's and not his own, and of the day when he had first coaxed the bird onto the grass beside the caravan door, and it had plucked at the bacon strip.

All the memories of the times before he quit.

They had come across country to join the main road north of Drogheda, then through Dundalk and over the border where the Customs men of both the Republic and the north were warm in their huts, and up the fast drag to Belfast.

Off the motorway at Stockman's Lane, up Kennedy Way, over the roundabout and onto the Glen Road. He felt pleasure coursing in him as the car took him closer to Roisin, and to Young Gerard and Little Patty and Baby Sean. He sat hunched forward with his arms tight across his chest, and he was smiling. The sight of the soldier crouched with his rifle at his shoulder in a garden gateway was momentary.

They were past the church, towering in the darkness, short of the Andersonstown RUC station, almost onto their turnoff left into Turf Lodge, when they came to the road block.

McAnally shivered. He always shivered and sweated at a road block, and would do to his dying day after what had happened at the block eight years before. The soldier he had seen in the gateway was positioned to pick up those who spun to make an escape. The taller man, the driver, would have heard the spurts of McAnally's breathing, he gave McAnally a single sharp glance, then was changing down through his gears, feeling the brake pedal.

'Easy, Gingy, nothing to fret on, the plates are clean,' the shorter man said quietly.

They had stopped. They waited their turn in the short queue of cars. The soldiers were as young as the one spitting towards death while McAnally had sung his triumph thirteen years before, as young as the constable who had been killed in the flame-flash of the RPG missile three years before, as young as the soldier blinded by a missile's shrapnel two years before. The soldiers were young and cold and bored.

He watched their faces. He saw the roving of their eyes. He saw the rainwater dribbling on their cheeks. He knew the wicked hitting power of their rifles.

A corporal bent down to shine his torch on the number plate of the car, and then he straightened and spoke into his radio. He was feeding the computer at headquarters. McAnally sat very still. He peered at the corporal who walked a slow circle with the radio held against his ear, waiting on the computer.

From the corner of his eye, McAnally saw the face that was now close against the rear door window. A different face, firmer and stronger than the faces of the young soldiers. He saw the embroidered pips of a first lieutenant on the shoulder flaps. He saw a quick brittle smile that the lieutenant aimed at him. He responded without thinking. Meaningless, short smiles. The lieutenant's face was daubed in dark cream. McAnally saw the flash of ordered white teeth, he saw the dark hair that lay underneath the beret, he saw the eyes that beaded on him and stripped him.

'Clear, Mr Ferris . . .' the shout from the corporal.

The lieutenant stepped back from the car. He nodded to the driver.

'Have a good evening, gentlemen.'

The car surged forward, then went left into Norfolk Parade. McAnally was twisted round, staring through the back window of the car.

'Smug shits . . .'

The shorter man laughed. 'You'll get your chance, Gingy. That's what we brought you back for, so you'll have the chance to damage the smug shits.'

The taller man spoke softly. 'You'll hear when you're wanted.'

The car had stopped. He had come home. The lights were on upstairs at Number 63. He could hear a baby crying. He walked towards the front door and did not look back as the car drove away.

# 2

He was on his back and he was asleep and again he screamed his protest.

'I won't do it . . . you can't tell me . . . I'm outside, you can't make me . . .'

Roisin lay awake on her side, her back to him. After the first and the second time she had cuddled him and tried to comfort his torture and had lulled him back to a calmer sleep. She could see the clock beside her head and knew that she had another hour before she must get up and begin preparing Young Gerard for school.

'You've no fucking right to tell me what I have to do . . . I'm not having my fucking arse shot off just on your say-so . . .'

The bed heaved as he bellowed his dreaming fear around the small front bedroom. She could smell the sweat scent that his stomach had spread on her belly when he had loved her earlier in the night; when he had loved her before sleeping, before dreaming, before screaming.

'Find some other bugger, I've done my time, let another bugger share what I've done . . .'

To Roisin her marriage to Sean Pius McAnally was a miracle of survival. When he was over her, covering her, pounding her, then she could play at a fantasy that her life was a kingdom, that she was a queen. To her Ma the fantasy was a lie, to his Ma the marriage was catastrophe. Her husband, the king in her realm, had never worked in his life and now lived in a dirty caravan box away from her. He was a stranger who came back in a guilty blurt of excuses to share her bed in the leaking house provided by the Housing Executive. He could be no support to her, not now that he had run, nor before when he had been active, nor before that when he had been locked away in the Kesh. The support for her existence and the life of her

19

children came from the Green Cross donations for prisoners' dependents, from the occasional charity of the Organization if she showed a favour to a big man, from the Social Security and the Supplementary Benefit and the Children's Allowances. Only a dribble of Republic bank notes came in the post from the letters marked Monasterevan. From the start the marriage had been a disaster to her Ma and his Ma . . . A week on the seafront at Bray in the south's County Wicklow in a guest house where they reckoned they were doing you a favour if they made the room up before lunch, and where it had rained on each and every one of the six days, and where he had humped her so frequently that he had run out of the Johnnies by the fourth night and not known how to replace his stock in good old Catholic Twenty-six County Ireland, and got her in the family way on the fifth or the sixth night. And on the seventh morning in the hotel, the morning they were leaving, the dawn they were going back to Belfast, that morning and that dawn the bastard Special Branch had paid a call. In the first early morning light, three SB men had crowded into the tiny bedroom that was a double and a wardrobe and two chairs and hardly more room for a cat to stand upright. The SB men had taught her that they were of the same breed as the northern peelers, that a fighter for the unity of Ireland was as much a piece of dirt to a Republic policeman as he was to a Six County policeman. There had been a brusque, thorough, intimidating search of their two bags, the spilling out of her new underwear, and her in tears and him never opening his mouth. A marriage that started with the stamp of disaster, and gone on as a disaster when he was lifted at the road block one week after their return, and yet she loved him.

She had loved him through the months of taking the prison bus through the morning sickness, and through the bulging pregnancy . . .

'You can't fucking order me to do it, that's fucking suicide what you're saying . . .'

She had loved him through five years of taking the prison bus with a pram, with a push chair, with a toddler, with a growing boy who did not understand why his father was always on the far side of a heavy wood table, why a man in uniform and a shined peak cap stood at the side with his arms folded and contempt smirking his lips. A small boy going to his first Infant school, and coming home and chorusing in a tinkling parrot voice, 'Is my Da a Provo? The priest says the Provos have spat on Jesus, has my Da done that?' To Roisin McAnally, née O'Rourke, there was no disaster, only a strengthening love, and his Ma told her she was bloody mad.

She did not turn her head. She hissed into the pillow.

'Don't bloody tell me you're not going to do it, tell whoever's bloody asking you. If you're outside, then you're outside, don't tell me, tell them. If you don't want to do it then why did you bloody come back?'

She felt him heave, and the bed shook, as if he convulsed in waking. She heard the new panting speed of his breath. He would be lying on his back, he would be staring up at the dark ceiling. Perhaps the bugger could make out the damp patch in the right-hand far corner. The day he had come home she had spent four hours with her children in tow trying to interest the Housing Executive in the damp patch in the ceiling. Some bastard manager with a house in Dummurry and a salary and a pension scheme who didn't give a shit that a front bedroom in Turf Lodge had water running from the ceiling of the front bedroom.

'Did I wake you?' He spoke gently.

'Me and half the bloody street.'

'I'm sorry, love . . . must have been dreaming.'

'Bloody nightmaring, more likely.'

He took her shoulder and pulled her down onto her back and his hands were warm on the flesh of her thighs and the skin of her small slack breasts.

He hadn't used anything the night before, he'd said the machine down in the Bar's jacks was broken. The bloody priests who said you shouldn't use anything, they didn't know what it was like to be dropping kids. A bit of labour pain wouldn't be lost on *them* . . . She laughed out loud. She saw in her mind a flash picture of Father Mulvaney lying on a bed on his back with his spindle legs up round his ears, groaning in delivery agony.

He'd stopped.

'Not at you, Sean, wasn't laughing at you . . .'

She put her hand over his hand, the hand was down at her thighs. She usually guided him. He was always a bit fumbling when he came back from the bloody caravan, so she knew he hadn't a woman down there . . . If he would only cut his nails . . . He loved her, she knew that. What ever he'd done, why ever he'd gone south, when ever he came back, she knew that he loved her. She had other men, not often, not out of habit, only occasionally when the loneliness was too great to bear. Just sometimes she needed a man, just needed a body with no strings and no-one beside her when she woke in the morning afterwards. The children were hers, more than they were his. His kids wouldn't tell their Da that sometimes a man stayed late. She hoped he didn't know.

'What did they want you to do?'

His second day back two men had come to the house. She had been doing the kids' tea, beans and toast and a mug of Bovril. They'd gone upstairs with Sean. They'd have sat on her bed, and after they'd gone, when she went up to bed there was the smell of cigarettes in her bedroom and ash on the floor. She'd heard the raised voices.

'Something big . . . Shit, that's lovely . . . I said I wouldn't.'

'Because of me, that wasn't why you said you wouldn't?'

She blamed him for nothing. If the house leaked then that was the fault of the Brits who refused to come and repair it. If her man hadn't work then that was the fault of the Brits who wouldn't provide employment for the work force in the Nationalist housing estates. If Sean Pius McAnally was in the Provos then that was the fault of the Brits for putting their fucking soldiers on the streets of Turf Lodge and the 'Murph and Andy' town, and Whiterock. She would have thought the less of her man if he had not been in the Organization. She had nagged him once into going for a job at the De Lorean, and he'd been taken on, just after coming out of the Kesh, and the day he should have started he'd chucked it and gone with the ASU – that was somebody's fault, not her man's fault.

'It wouldn't be because of me that you said you wouldn't?'

She was glowing, she was wet. His hand was strong, good, brilliant. She had never argued when he'd said that he was going south. He'd sat that night, more than two years before, on the end of the bed and he had said that if he stayed he was either dead or he was in for a 'lifer'. He'd said that after a time any man had the right to quit. He'd said that staying alive and staying free was luck, that a man in an ASU used up his store of luck. The bloody Brits with their army and their police and terror gangs of SAS murderers would take him. He'd said he wasn't a coward, he'd said he was just being smart. He'd said that some other bugger should do his turn. She hadn't blamed him.

His chin was on her shoulder, the nipple of her breast was swollen hard between his fingers, his lips were beside her ear.

'Not because of you. Perhaps it should be, but it's not.'

'Why won't you do what they ask?'

'Shit, I don't mind helping . . . What they want isn't helping, it's fucking kamikaze . . . Fuck, you're lovely . . .'

The bed sang as he climbed onto her, spread her, wriggled inside her.

Baby Sean had begun to cry, a clear sharp wail through the thin partition wall. Young Gerard was shouting at Baby Sean to shut his face. Young Gerard was the son of the night's loving in the hours before the southern SB came to the honeymoon room in Bray. Little Patty and Baby Sean were both conceived after he had run the risk of standing clear on a street corner to aim the RPG at a Pig or at an armoured Land Rover. After that the risk of getting Roisin in family had seemed pathetic, unimportant. Baby Sean crying and Young Gerard shouting at him.

She pushed him off her. She swung out of the bed and he saw the gleam of damp on her legs. He lay on his back. He thought he saw tears in her eyes. She went out of the bedroom and through the wall he heard her speak to Young Gerard and croon to Baby Sean. She came back into the bedroom and laid the baby in the crook of her husband's arm. She started to dress.

'So you've said you won't do it, so what's going to happen?'

'I'm to be taken to see a man.'

'What man?'

'The Chief.'

'And when he asks you to do it, what'll you say?'

'I don't know,' he said.

'I'll make some tea.'

She wore jeans and a sweater and she was shivering in the chilled room as she pulled on her socks. She combed her hair perfunctorily, rich and lovely black hair that fell to her shoulders. She was tall, as tall as him, and he thought she was beautiful. He was blind to the worry bags under her eyes and the pallor of her cheeks. She kissed him on the forehead and went out of the bedroom and down the stairs. He heard her stumbling in the darkness of the downstairs front room for the packet and her first cigarette of the day. Beside him Baby Sean gurgled in delight and tugged at his Da's hair.

He had had bread and jam for breakfast and more tea, and he had cleared his pockets of Republic currency that his wife would change at the bank in the Andersonstown parade, and he was listening to the radio news, when the knock came at the door.

Not much on the radio, a quiet night it had been in the war. Three aimed shots at an army patrol in the Derry Bogside, all missed. An R.U.C. constable cops on that there's a bomb under his car when he does his morning check, defused. Waste of fucking effort . . . The boy at the door was straight out of school. Roisin stood at the bottom of the stairs and watched.

'In thirty minutes, Mister, you're to be on the corner of Westrock Gardens and the Parade. You'll be told then where to go.'

The boy didn't wait for an answer.

'Is you going out, Da? Can I come?' Young Gerard stood behind his mother, and two stair steps higher.

'It's a school day, 'course you can't go with your Da.'

McAnally took his anorak from the hook behind the door.

'You won't be knowing when you'll be back?' his wife asked.

'No.'

McAnally went out through the door, pulled it noisily shut behind him. The wind caught his face and he felt the light rain on his cheeks. He should never have come back, but he had not known how to refuse. His hands were buried deep in his anorak pockets, chin down on his chest.

His home might be a caravan in a soddin' field down south, but it was better than Turf Lodge. He saw the decay of the pavement and the roadway of the Drive; he saw damp rotted windowframes of the houses, he saw the neglect in the overgrown front gardens. The house in the Drive in Turf Lodge was a prison when set against the freedom of his caravan in a field beside the canal at Vicarstown. There were no trees here for his companion the kestrel. At the far end of the Drive he saw the foot patrol approaching, four on each pavement, moving warily. He saw the hackles on their berets, and thought it an act of insolence by the soldiers to wear the red and white feathers that would make a splash of colour for a sniper to aim at. He had never wondered where the soldiers hailed from, whether they had been kids in another faraway rotting estate that was no different to Turf Lodge. He had never imagined the soldiers as being anything other than cold bastards in uniform with a Self Loading Rifle tight in their khaki-gloved fists. He knew that sometimes the soldiers were frightened, that sometimes they were arrogant; he knew that always the soldiers were his enemy. A woman came out of Number 11, and was pushing a pram and had three more kids with her. She set off towards the patrol and when she came to the lead soldier she walked straight on as if he didn't exist. The soldier hesitated and made room for her. The woman didn't see the soldier, nor the other three behind him, and she walked straight ahead, and the last soldier in the stick gave her a sign that wasn't for victory, but he stepped out of her way.

As McAnally walked down the slope of the Drive, he closed on the approaching patrol. The soldiers had a stuttering movement. Jogging, crouching, lying flat and splayed in the aim position, up again and sprinting. Trying to create an absence of a pattern. Sniping wasn't McAnally's job, never had been, so he reckoned it wouldn't have been easy to take one of them out, difficult to bead on the ducking, bobbing, weaving figures. He took his cue from the woman with the pram. He passed the first soldier without a glance. He stared straight in front of him. He smelled the stale damp sweat of the soldier play at his nose.

'You, here . . .'

McAnally heard the officer's command. Bastard Brit officers always had the same voice, always bloody shouted. He thrust his hands deeper into his pockets and walked on.

The second soldier in the line was bent low against a lamp post. His face never turned to McAnally as he covered the rooftops and the upper windows of the street. The soldier spoke from the side of his mouth. North country England, and a snarl from the side of his mouth.

'You. Fart face. My officer's calling you.'

McAnally stopped, looked around him. The officer was on the other side of the Drive, standing with his arms folded, waiting for him. The soldiers in the patrol had scattered and taken cover. The officer carried a rifle. He was distantly familiar to McAnally.

'Here, please . . .' A voice of authority. McAnally bit at his lip, and started across the roadway.

The officer looked at him. Not hostile, just careful. Examined him.

'My name's Ferris, Bravo Company 2 RRF. My platoon works Turf Lodge . . . I don't know you.'

'Sean McAnally.'

'Roisin McAnally, of 63 . . .'

'That's my wife.'

'And where are you when you're not at home, Mr McAnally?'

'Down south.'

He remembered the name and he remembered the face. The road block of two nights before. McAnally shivered, his breath was spewing in front of his face. Under his tunic and his flak jacket Ferris wore a heavy knit sweater. Bastard would be warm enough. Bastard wouldn't be hurrying.

'Work down south?'

'Kind of.'

'I hope you'll be able to stay with us till Christmas, be nice for the lady and the children.'

'Suppose it would.'

'It's a cold morning, Mr McAnally. You should have wrapped up better. Nice to have met you . . .'

The officer, Ferris, walked on. The patrol materialized from their hiding places. McAnally set off again for the end of the Drive. He loathed himself for his fear, and the bastard officer had seen it and had cracked his little private joke about a cold morning. When he turned round the patrol had almost reached the bend in the Drive.

On his way to his rendezvous he went past the barricade at the

Andersonstown RUC station. Shit, the place had been well drubbed since he had been active. Smashed up and patched. Dirty, shitty place behind the screens and the wire netting and the concrete sentry boxes and the high tin gates. The wire netting was for him. The wire netting was to explode the armour-piercing charge of a rocket propelled grenade.

But he had said no to the men who had come to his house to get him back into the Organization. And because he had said no, he was on his way to meet with the Chief, with the Commander of the Belfast Brigade.

He walked past the sentry box. He wondered if it was a rifle or a stub-barrelled carbine that covered him from behind the aiming slits. It was one thing to turn down a messenger. It was a different thing to spit in the face of the Chief.

The gates of the Milltown cemetery on his right were open wide. Inside were the stones, and far away on the reverse slope and hidden by the stones of crosses and Jesuses and Marys was the Republican plot. That's where they all were, in that plot, all the Volunteers and the Company Officers and the Battalion Officers and the Brigade Officers, all the martyrs of the Organization. He knew what the Brit squaddys called it, they called Milltown the 'home for retired gunmen'. Fucking young, weren't they, all the boys in the Republican plot. Sean Pius McAnally hadn't wanted to join them, so he'd run down south. He still didn't want to keep them company, but he was going to see the Chief. Hands deep in his pockets, chin hard on his chest, cold, and shivering.

Halfway up the Whiterock Drive he saw ahead of him the boy who smoked and sat on the bonnet of a car. He reckoned the boy was twelve or thirteen years old, and he was wearing the local uniform of close-cut hair, a windcheater and jeans and high laced 'Docs'. He reckoned the boy four or five years older than Young Gerard. The bugger was playing truant. He wondered whether his Gerard would be running messages for the Organization in four or five years. And if in four or five years his son was out of class and on a street corner for the Provos, then would his Da be shouting? Like father, like son. And if his son grew up and shot a Brit, or smashed a peeler, then would his Da be shaking his head and telling him

'Fucking well done, boy'? He wondered what future his son had that was beyond the walls of the Kesh and the stones of the Milltown cemetery. He didn't think like that often, only when he was down. But a man who had blinded a Brit and taken out a constable could hardly cuff his son on the ear if the kid wanted to follow his father into the Organization.

McAnally saw the frank admiration in the boy's eyes. He felt better, stronger.

'Into Westrock Gardens, take the left, on the left-hand side the second from the end.'

'Thanks.'

The boy grinned, pleased, and ran. McAnally saw that he had a school bag with him. Shit, couriering for the Provos before playground time. He saw Young Gerard's face and bit the flesh of his thumb to shift the pain.

The door of the small red-brick house was opened for him by a grandmother. She was old enough to be a grandmother, and in the hall was a playpen with a baby trapped in it. The woman had curlers in her thin hair and a Sweet Afton blowing a cloud from the side of her mouth, and she wore fluffy slippers that had once been pink, and she shouted over the noise of her vacuum cleaner. 'In the back room. You'll take a cuppa?'

He sat in the back room for half an hour. He cleaned his nails, he pinched hairs from his nostrils. Over and over again he planned his refusal to the Chief.

Through the thin walls of the house he heard the front door's bell.

He was standing when they came in with his hands held across his crotch, and he felt he was a bloody felon.

'Morning, Gingy. Good to see you. Long time.'

McAnally knew him, not well but he knew him. A cold, hard fucker, those that knew him well said he was. They'd met in the bars after McAnally had come out of the Kesh. They'd known each other when McAnally was a big man who was on the RPG-7 ASU. This was the Chief. There were three men behind him. None of them kids, none of them the prison fodder that were the Volunteers. Brigade men. Men that the *Mirror* called the Godfathers. The Chief wore a black donkey jacket with the collar up and round his cheeks, and he had a flat cap down over his eyes. His fingers were fidgeting, couldn't help himself. McAnally smiled. He had on the end of his tongue the name that the Chief was called. He was called 'Windsy'. Not to his face, but behind his back. It was said that he lived off Chinese takeaway, noodles and rice and spare ribs, and that was why 'Windsy'. Be a brave bugger, or a daft bugger, who would call him that to his face. A fierce face, power and authority jutting from the little that McAnally could see of it.

'Yes, it's been a long time.'

'When was it you went away, Gingy, how long?' A grating nasal voice.

'Two years.'

'They all need a rest . . . those that can get it. You'll be well rested now.'

McAnally put his hands on his hips. He stood at his full height, and he was three inches shorter than the Chief. He smelled the soya.

'I quit . . .' McAnally said.

'No, Gingy, you rested.'

'I said that I'd quit . . . that's what I meant, you know how it is.'

'I don't fucking know how it is. You rested. There's boys here, brilliant boys, who'd give a lot for two weeks resting, not two years but two weeks. It's *tiring* fighting the war, Gingy, more tiring than resting for two years.'

The Chief smiled. What showed of his face was pale except for the ruddy scar across his nose. A soldier's baton had done that back in '71. The story had it that seven soldiers had been needed to hold him down, and all swinging batons, and him alone with his fists. A bit of myth was needed by a man if he was to make CO of Belfast Brigade.

'The boys came to see you, Gingy, you told them to piss themselves. They spelled out the plan. They tell me that you said it was a crazy suicide plan . . .'

McAnally blurted, 'To stand in the Crumlin, daylight, with the RPG, too right that's suicide.'

'My plan, Gingy, you farted on my plan,' the Chief said, and his voice was little more than a whisper.

Christ . . . McAnally saw the cold smile on the Chief's mouth. A little joke between the two of them, not shared by the three men behind the Chief. Bitter, pinched faces, hard, killing faces . . . Christ.

'Perhaps the plan wasn't explained that well, Gingy.'

'Perhaps it wasn't,' McAnally said bleakly.

'Missus . . . Missus . . .' The Chief's voice bellowed in the room, and his face never turned away from McAnally. 'Tea for five would be nice.'

There was a muffled reply. 'I'll leave the tray at the door.'

The Chief lit a cigarette, and belched with the first drag.

'You're going to do it, Gingy, because I'm going to ask you to do it.'

'Why me?'

'Gingy, there was a time when we had ten RPGs up here, five in Belfast. When you went for your rest two years ago there were three RPGs here. Now we have one. One for Belfast, Derry and South Armagh. You know how many projectiles we have now? Right now I've got one projectile in Belfast. I've got Chief of Staff and Army Council breathing on me. If I don't use it, then I'll be ordered to ship it out, send it where it can be used. It's not like your day any more, the RPG isn't for police wagons and Brit pigs, the RPG's too precious for that. Are you listening to me, Gingy?'

'I'm listening.'

'My plan, the plan you said was a bad plan, is to use the RPG so's the bang's heard across the Six Counties, and across the Twenty-six Counties, and right across the bloody waters to the States. My plan says that the biggest bang comes in the Crumlin Road tomorrow morning. My plan says that you, Gingy, you make that bang.'

McAnally saw the bright diamonds of the Chief's eyes under the shadow of his cap. He saw the spittle at the sides of the mouth that was close to his.

'Why me?'

'That's what you said when the boys came to see you. You said, why did it have to be you, why couldn't it be some other bugger, that's what you said. I tell you. You were the firer on the RPG. You were the Belfast RPG team. You had four shots of practice across the border in Donegal before you took the army Pig, before you took the police Land Rover. You had the training, and you delivered. Bloody good you were, Gingy. Two firings, two hits.

'There were four on your team that had the training. Now I've got one warhead, one firing chance, and no chance of training a team like you had. My last two got lifted, you were told that ... What happened to the four on your team, Gingy, the team you had when you quit? Tell me what happened to them?'

McAnally said, 'Shay got himself shot, peelers had him. Chicko's in the Kesh on a tenner. Gerry blew his face off, mixing ...'

'And you were the fourth, Gingy, and you were the best.'

'I quit,' McAnally said.

'And you changed your mind,' the Chief grinned.

There was a light knock at the door.

'Thank you, Missus.'

One of the men who stood behind the Chief opened the door and lifted in the tray and kicked the door shut behind him. He set the tray on the table, and began to pour. The baby was shouting happily in the hallway.

The Chief took from his jacket a folded Ordnance Survey map of Greater Belfast, spread it out on the floor and knelt beside it.

'Come on down, Gingy, inch to 300 yards. When I've talked you through it, tell me then if it's still a crazy plan.'

McAnally sank down on his haunches. The soya smell was foul. He swallowed hard.

'You're the only one who can do it for me, Gingy. That's why it's you.'

The Chief slapped his fist across McAnally's shoulders and one of the others put a mug of tea in his hand.

'Come.'

The Intelligence Officer was sitting in his usual posture, chair tilted on the back two legs, shoes on his desk. He nearly always managed to spend his day in shoes, as if it were a perk of the job along with staying in his office with the gas stove on while the likes of Ferris were out tramping the streets of West Belfast. Battalion Headquarters worked out of the back of the Springfield Road RUC station. Captain Jason Perceval had done well for himself. Intelligence

Officer was a good number. He had an office big enough for his desk and chair, plus an easy chair, plus his VDU, plus a table for his portable television set. His walls were papered with the photographs of escaped prisoners and activists gone underground, what he called the OTRs, those On The Run.

He had been reading, and he placed the papers upside down on his desk, as if Ferris represented a security risk.

'What can do, David?'

The telephone rang. The Intelligence Officer grimaced as if to explain the pressure of work, picked up the receiver.

'Wait one, David . . . Yes, yes . . . There's someone with me. Call me back, please. Five minutes . . . Now, what can do, David?'

Ferris often wondered where Jason Perceval had learned his language, and where he had learned that toothy smile that was meant to charm.

'Just came across a new face today, thought you might like to have it.'

'Very conscientious . . . What new face and where?'

The majority of the Battalion officers were Grammar School or Comprehensive, different to ten years back, sign of new times. The minority had been privately educated. Ferris thought the minority were bloody anxious to point up the difference.

'Gave his name as Sean McAnally, address as 63 The Drive, Turf Lodge . . .'

'Doesn't ring with me.'

'If you're not interested.'

'I didn't hear myself say I wasn't interested. No need to scratch. Tell.'

'Sean McAnally, aged about thirty, fair hair, ginger really, says he works down in the Republic. Wife is Roisin, she's full time up here with the kids. My platoon hadn't come across him before. He was in a car we stopped at a VCP two nights ago, the car was cleared. That's all.'

'Kind of you, squire.'

The Intelligence Officer lifted his chair across the room to the table and the Visual Display Unit. He flicked the switch, animated the screen, and started to type.

Ferris watched as the Intelligence Officer eased his chair back, waited for the Headquarters computer to throw them some information, and lit himself a black-papered Sobranie.

'I'm all for HumInt,' the Intelligence Officer said easily. 'EllInt's got a place in things, but HumInt's what scores . . .'

The screen began to fill. Ferris disliked the military's jargon. Human Intelligence in Ferris's book was simply observation, and Electronic Intelligence was mechanical surveillance.

'Bit of a bullseye, David. Very good. McAnally, Sean Pius. Born 1955. Fianna Youth cadre. Aggro brat. Thought to be ASU member in Turf Lodge and Ballymurphy through to mid-seventies. Done on possession of firearms in '76. No statement, written or verbal. Five years in the Lazy Kay. Wasn't on the dirty protest, didn't wipe his shit on the walls. Wasn't on the list of those wanting to slim for Ireland, not a Hunger Striker. Came out and went back to his old ways, but sharp enough never to have been incriminated, never found in flagrante, and never informed against either. Two years ago he went south. The law have checked him out down there, the word came back that he'd cut his links. Probably just back to give his lady a touch of the tickler . . .'

'Are they able to cut their links, do you think?'

'Perhaps, perhaps not . . . That's why it's useful to hear your news.'

'He looked as if he could have messed his pants when I had him over.'

'You're not starting to feel sorry for the vermin, David?'

'He was pretty pathetic.'

Jason Perceval looked keenly at David Ferris. 'Your job's soldiering, laddie, not feeling sorry for them.'

'I only said that he looked pathetic.'

'Have you ever seen an armed terrorist, David?'

Ferris hesitated. 'No . . . well, I've seen prisoners.'

'Have you ever seen a terrorist with an Armalite or a nail bomb or an M 60 machine gun?'

'No.'

'Well, I fancy that if you had then you wouldn't be talking about him looking pathetic . . .'

'That's twisting what I said.'

'I'm telling you, once you feel sorry for them, then the next step is saying that if you'd been brought up in Turf Lodge that you'd be a terrorist, that sort of drivel.'

'I don't have to take that.'

'What I'm telling you is this, you muttering about known terrorists looking pathetic doesn't exactly move along our war effort. They're vicious psychopaths, and recognizing that is the first step towards grinding them down.'

'You know what . . .?' Ferris flared. 'That's precisely the attitude that has kept us here fifteen years, not winning . . .'

'They're vermin.'

'They're human beings, and when we start realizing that we might stop losing.'

'What utter shit . . . If you weren't a damned good officer I'd see this conversation went further.'

Ferris spun on his heel and slammed the door behind him on his way out.

It was dark when he came home, and he had no front door key for his own house. He pressed the bell, he heard the shouts of the children inside, he heard the slither of his wife's slippers. The smell of soap was still on the palms of his hands from when he had sluiced away the traces of weapons oil.

They had worked on the plan, they had taken him to a lock-up garage where the RPG was stored and he handled it and cradled it and checked the projectile, and after that they had taken him to a bar. He had been told to wash his hands. Two years ago it would have been second nature. He had flushed because he had had to be reminded.

Roisin opened the door. He hurried past her. He was bursting. She followed him to the half-closed door of the lavatory off the landing.

'You just missed your Ma, she waited all afternoon for you. She says for you to go round tomorrow morning.'

'I'm out early tomorrow morning,' McAnally called over his shoulder, and pulled the chain.

There was a flatness in her voice, not approval and not criticism. 'They talked you into doing what they want.'

34

He was at the top of the stairs. He nodded. 'They talked me.'

'You want me to wish you luck?'

'I want you to love me.'

'You're jarred.' But she was smiling.

'Love me.'

'You'll get your love when the kids have had their tea, and washed, and are in their beds . . . You'll get your love then.'

He came down the stairs, loud and clumsy. He held his woman in his arms, and the strength with which he clung to her squeezed the grin from her cheeks.

She kissed him under the ear and she whispered, 'You'll go careful.'

'I told them it was a suicide plan. They didn't listen to me.'

Her eyes were closed. Her face was hard against her man's.

'Go careful, Gingy.'

# 3

There were three men with him, and the car was behind them against the wall of the backyards of the flats, its engine throbbing quietly and the exhaust fumes pouring from its tail. He didn't know the names of the men. He knew that one would drive and that two would ride shotgun with Armalite rifles. He knew that the mission was controlled by a Citizen's Band radio.

It was raining. A dreary soft Belfast morning . . . The rifles were on the back seat of the car, covered by a coat, loaded and cocked. The RPG was in the boot of the car, laid diagonally because the projectile was attached and it had to be laid that way to fit inside.

The CB radio would give him two minutes' warning. Two minutes to extract the launcher from the car, to drape the coat over it, to walk across Regent Street, to take up a position alongside the dark, derelict walls of the Methodist church, to look down busy Clifton Street at the cars approaching the Carlisle Circus.

He knew the target car would be a black Rover.

The car would not be difficult to identify; the armour-plating in the doors would weigh it down low on its wheels; sometimes, he had been told, they made it easier, the driver and the car's escort, by flashing the headlights of the Rover and the back-up as they approached the roundabout.

Shit . . . blasting the car wasn't the aggro bit, the bad bit was the clearing out afterwards.

He knew how to use the optical sight on the RPG. He'd studied a translation of the Soviet manual, provided years back by a Russian language student down in Dublin. He'd used the optical sight on the police Land Rover. He wouldn't use the optical sight that morning. From the edge of the church wall to a car manoeuvring left on the roundabout was point blank range, so he'd use the iron sights, aim up on the forward leaf on the tube and the rear V above the grip stock. The three men talked occasionally in low voices behind him. They ignored him, as if he were separate from them.

The Chief had told why the target had been chosen, why the firing had to be in the shadow of the Crown Court House, why it had to be within earshot of the gaol that was across the road from the yellow and honeysuckle of the Court's façade. The Chief had said it had to be a one-off because he had only one fucking projectile.

He stamped his feet. The driven rain was on his face. He badly needed to piss.

He heard the click of the boot being opened. He spun. He saw one man thrusting the earpiece cable for the CB into his anorak pocket. He saw the launcher being lifted out of the boot, a crude, heavy shape under a raincoat. He saw the driver slip behind the wheel of the car.

'On his way . . . Two minutes, boyo.'


David Ferris was in a rare good humour. A patrol from his platoon was accused of shoplifting from a Sweets and Fags lock-up on the Falls. Bravo's Company Commander had advised a hard, defensive line. Take it on the chin and give them a blunt denial. Ferris was to attend Hastings Street RUC station and there make a statement denying all knowledge and gilding the character of his Fusiliers. Actually he didn't believe the charge. They were tough little buggers, his Fusiliers, from the workless zones of the north-east of England. If they had gone in for shoplifting they would have stripped the lock-up bare, and probably lifted the knickers off the proprietor's wife for good measure.

He travelled by Land Rover. The Battalion's Sunray didn't believe in closed Land Rovers. Sunray had taken his style from the commandos and the paratroopers. Open Land Rovers offered more visibility to the riflemen. Great way to travel when it was raining, marvellous when you were stuck on the traffic lights. Ferris sat beside his driver, his rifle on his thigh, watching the front. There were two Fusiliers behind him covering the side and rear.

So Ferris was getting wet, but that was a damn sight better than footing it around Turf Lodge.

With a bit of luck, if the policeman wasn't too quick with a long-hand statement, he would spin this into coffee and biscuits time.

They were out into the traffic. The gates of Springfield Road were squealing shut behind them. Ferris smiled at the banter around him.

'I hear, Nobby, they've got women old Bill down where we're going.'

'Bollocks, it's chaps, you have a grope, see what you find.'

'Had to be women there, that's why a good-looking fucker like me's on the escort.'

'What's a woman look like, Nobby?'

'Not like anything you'll see here, fucked if I can remember . . .'

'Eyes peeled, lads, and concentrate,' Ferris said.

'You ever seen an actual Provo, Mr Ferris?' the driver asked.

'Provos are to me what women are to you, Fusilier Jones,' Ferris said. 'All photographs . . .'

'Good one, Mr Ferris.' Laughter from the back.

'That's enough, lads.'

Ferris's eyes raked the taxi stopped in front of him at the red light, and the van in front of the taxi that had a dark interior because the rear doors were off, and he switched his attention to the pavements and the early morning drifting crowds. Divis Street in the Falls. All wire-meshed windows and cement-blocked doorways and daubed slogans of sometime's victory and petrol bomb scars and blast scrapes. Famous throughout the Western world for its hatred and its killers . . . and so damned ordinary.

His thumb was close to the safety catch of his rifle, and his fingers rested hard against the trigger guard.

They stood beside the church wall. His legs were tight, stiff muscled, as if the walls across the deserted narrow Regent Street had been a bloody marathon. He hadn't seen the dog mess that he'd walked through, smeared. Shit, and he was naked. One of the men stood in front of him and was able to see down Clifton Street to the place where the slip road came off the Westlink. The other man was behind McAnally, sheltering the loaded launcher against his legs. Five past nine in the morning, bloody daylight, out in the open for any shit to see. Out in the open and squeezing his bladder back into his bloody stomach. The Court House with all its armed peelers was about a quarter of a mile up the Crumlin from the roundabout. The gaol with all its armed squaddy Brits was a quarter of a mile up the road. The North Queen Street RUC station was three hundred yards to the north. It was still suicide . . .

The man in front of him raised his hand, hesitated for a moment, dropped it smacking against his thigh.

McAnally's hand snaked behind him. He gripped the launcher. He pressed it against his leg and stomach. He took the pace forward.

'Make it fucking count . . .'

'Fuck off behind me.'

He stood at the corner.

He saw the black Rover eighty yards from him. He saw the face of the driver, and of the front passenger. He saw the pale blur of a head against the back seat. He saw the headlights of the back-up car. His mouth was set, his face was contorted as if in rage. He thought, just the right bloody weather, peeing rain, and the 'tecs in the back-up have the windows up . . . can't shoot out . . . because the 'tecs would see him, see him as soon as he took the last step forward and heaved the launcher onto his shoulder.

The Rover was up to the roundabout, slewing left. Thirty yards. He saw the red flash of the brake lights. He didn't look any more for the back-up car. He drew air down into his lungs. The launcher was on his shoulder. The V of the rear sight and the leaf of the forward sight were locked onto the back window of the Rover. Twenty yards. His finger found the chill metal of the trigger. He thought he might piss himself. He squeezed the trigger.

Fucking judge, fucking bastard. He saw the bald crown of the target's head silhouetted in the back window.

He felt the shuddering jolt that tore at his shoulder bones. He felt the hot air blast that flared back from the church wall. He felt the bitter smoke smell at his nose. He felt the thunder of the impact of the projectile with its armour-piercing high explosive warhead against the window of the Rover.

A catastrophe of noise burned in McAnally's ears.

He turned. He was running for his life along the side of the church wall. An arm tugged at his, half-halted him. The launcher was

39

snatched from his grasp. Momentarily he saw the face of a boy he had never seen before. As he reached the car he saw the boy and the launcher disappear in a headlong scramble over the wall and into the backyards of the Unity flats.

The car doors were open. The driver was nudging forward. The man who had given the signal dived for the front passenger seat. The man who had held the launcher for McAnally now shoved him hard into the back, across the seat.

The car was skidding, spinning, ripping at the waste-ground earth, before the tyres gripped.

They went the wrong way round the circus. McAnally lay face down on the seat. They went down Clifton Street and surged hard and screamed right for the slip road and the Westlink.

They were halfway along Divis Street, past the Library and the Baths when they had heard the explosion. If it had been a closed Land Rover they might not have heard the distant, thudding report. All ears were cocked. The smoke-grimed pigeons wheeled squawking to the north.

'About a mile, Mr Ferris, like an anti-tank, sounded like a Milan,' the driver said confidently.

'Or an RPG,' Ferris said grimly. The driver had slowed. They were waiting on his decision. He felt very cold. He felt totally alone.

'VCP procedure, coming towards us,' Ferris snapped.

With a mirthless grin on his face the driver heaved the Land Rover across the centre of the road. He straddled the spaced white line. Ferris's men in the back jumped clear and split. One forward of the Land Rover as a block to a vehicle that spotted them and turned back. One behind the Land Rover to take out a vehicle that crashed them. The driver took a firing position low beside the front wheel. Ferris stood behind the Land Rover peering down the length of Divis Street.

Cars, taxis, lorries wafted past them. They were ignored by Ferris. A getaway car would be different.

There was no pursuit from the roundabout.

The detectives from the back-up had first spilled out of their seats and sprinted to the wreckage of the Rover. The one in the back was young, new to plain clothes. He held a Sterling sub-machine gun in his right hand and aimed it at pedestrians who sought to come forward towards the raging inferno that was the Rover, and was shrieking obscenities and weeping. The front seat observer of the back-up sprayed the flames with an extinguisher.

Hopeless, bloody waste of time. When the extinguisher was virtually empty he realized that all his efforts to damp the fire had been at the front of the car, where his friends had been. He carried on with the foam, spraying until the black seat-belted shapes were closed in a white shroud, until there were no more flames in the charred interior of the Rover. He dropped the extinguisher into the roadway. He walked over to the new boy, still yelling.

'Do us a bloody favour and shut your face.'

There were more sirens in the air, converging on them. He had lost his colleagues, he had lost his charge.

He went to his transport.

'What have you put over?'

The back-up driver said, 'Just a Contact. That it was an RPG, that it was a hit . . .'

He took the microphone, stretching the length of its cable away from the window. In front of him the Rover was smouldering dark smoke. He could see the police and the troops who had sprinted down from the Court House.

'This is Foxtrot Zulu 24. Time zero nine zero seven. We have lost Jupiter. RPG direct hit. Jupiter is dead . . . so are my bloody mates . . . out.'

He walked away from the car and was sick on the raised stonework of the roundabout.

Each man in the car had a critical role in the execution of the plan.

All the previous week the lookout man who had given the signal had tracked and tailed the judge's transport. The man who had stayed with McAnally was regarded as an expert in the use of a folded stock M16, he was responsible for the safe escape. McAnally was the marksman, and he had scored. Crucial now to the escape from the hit scene was the driver.

The driver of the getaway had first come down Clifton Street, then taken the sunken dual carriageway of the Westlink under the bridges that led to the Shankill Road and Divis Street. When the Westlink surfaced to ground level at the Grosvenor Road he had gone hard right and right again to insert himself among the modern terraces of Cullingtree. He was doubling back as he swept past the kids playing outside the crumbling escarpment of the Divis flats. The description of the car would by now have been broadcast over the police and army nets, and the car would have been identified as heading south-west along the fast road that hooked onto the motorway.

His only participation in the Organization was as a driver. He reckoned he was the best, and there weren't many who told him otherwise. Always the need to shift the first car at speed away from the scene. The car wheels screeched as they curved and bounced over the rough broken ground in front of the flats. There was a sharp confident smile at the driver's face. It was what he was good at. The car lurched onto Divis Street. The plan called for him to drive most of the length of Divis Street, as far as the Library, go right into Sebastopol, left into Odessa, right into Clonard, right into Kashmir, left into Bombay. In Bombay Street there would be two cars waiting for the break-up of the team.

They were in the traffic stream. The smile wiped from the driver's mouth. They were slowing. Fucking lorry in front winking its back brake lights. Not the time for the driver to settle back in his seat and pick his bloody nose, not before the first car switch, not before the split. He swung the wheel, he jerked the car out onto the on-coming lanes. His foot stamped down on the accelerator. No power in a bleeding Ford. He ground past the lorry.

'There's a fucking block . . .' McAnally screamed.

McAnally had seen the Fusilier who was positioned furthest down Divis Street. The red and white feathers of the hackle had caught his eye.

All together the four men in the car saw the Land Rover parked across the centre of the road.

'Shit . . . Christ . . . Fucking Jesus . . . Bust the bastards . . .' Curses swimming in the ears of the driver.

The driver saw the tall upper body of the soldier behind the Land Rover. He felt the frightened pants of McAnally's breathing on his neck. The man beside him was dragging the rifle from under his knees. He heard the unison clatter of two rifles being armed.

The driver saw for a fleeting moment the staring young face of the soldier who was low at the front of the Land Rover.

There was a hospital outpatients' van heading towards him. Fuck it, let it look after itself. He was back into the on-coming lanes. With all the impetus he could kick out of the clapped-out Ford he swerved past the tail of the Land Rover. The rifles in the car were on automatic. A stink of cordite in the car, and the hammer sounds of the firing. McAnally was shouting behind him, the driver couldn't understand the words. The driver saw the soldier who had been behind the Land Rover hurl himself down onto the road.

'Down . . . down . . .' the driver yelled. He saw the solitary soldier who had been placed in a doorway behind the Land Rover. He was the wrong side for his riflemen. The driver took the car straight towards the soldier and when he cowered away, the driver wrenched his car back onto the track of the road. He heard the scream of the van's horn . . . Fuck you, mate . . . he heard the single report of a rifle shot that had missed.

They swept on up Divis Street, and took the right into Sebastapol. They were all yelling, laughing in the car, and slapping the driver's back.

Ferris climbed to his feet, spared a moment to wipe the wet dirt from his camouflage trousers. He looked in front of him and behind him. He saw his Fusiliers sprinting back to his position. His driver stood by the bonnet of the Land Rover and his face was creased as if he had been presented with a puzzle to which he could not fathom the answer. Already a crowd had gathered on the two pavements to watch him.

A child with a shrill, cutting voice called out. 'Heh, Mister, the Provies wiped you on the ground. The Provies made an arsehole of you, Mister.'

Ferris depressed the Speak button on his radio. His hand was shaking. He could barely hold the button down.

The Secretary of State for Northern Ireland had once been considered an ambitious member of Cabinet. Too ambitious, had been the verdict of certain colleagues in government. They were highly placed, these colleagues, high enough on the ladder of influence to speak into the Prime Minister's ear when they stood on tiptoe. So this ambitious man had been given responsibility for the United Kingdom's warring province some eighteen months earlier. It was a pretty damned awful job. He gained very little credit when the violence diminished, the laurels went to the Generals and the Chief Constable. When the wheel turned, the media splashed gory headlines and the Secretary of State took the brickbats. He was no longer ambitious.

He had flown into Aldergrove that morning and then been lifted by RAF helicopter to his residence and office at Stormont Castle. Questions in the House of Commons and a dinner for American industrialists had taken him to London. A barrage of accusations of incompetence from the Protestant MPs, and vague promises of economic commitment had been the order of the previous day. Now, back to the treadmill. Back to the misery.

On the castle lawns he smilingly shook hands with the helicopter's pilot. His face was masked in a fraud of confidence. It was part of his work to seem unmoved by catastrophe, to appear saturated in optimism. His bodyguards flanked him as he walked briskly towards the Castle's side door. He always walked briskly, not because he was an athletic man, but because that was the instruction of the Detective Inspector from Scotland Yard who headed his security detail.

Waiting on the steps at the Castle's side door was an Ulsterborn civil servant, a gaunt and cheerless man.

When the civil servant was on the steps it only added to bad news. The Secretary of State was without an overcoat, the rain was flapping on his jacket, staining his tie.

'Morning, Fred.' The Secretary of State liked to call his advisors by their first names, to create a team atmosphere.

'Morning, Secretary of State.'

The civil servant had fallen into step beside him, taking precedence over the two secretaries who had come over from London.

The Secretary of State smiled loosely. 'I've had a good night's sleep, I've had a good flight, I'm as ready as I'll ever be. Give me the gloom.'

44

'It's been a bad morning for the Province.'

'My memory doesn't stretch back to a good one.' The flippancy was a disguise.

They went into the Secretary of State's office, palatial and yet comfortable. A warm and friendly room, subdued lighting, new-cut flowers on the table by the window that was screened with blast-proof glass.

The Secretary of State said abruptly, 'Well, don't hang around, Fred.'

'They've murdered a judge.'

The Secretary of State looked at the floor. He saw the blades of wet grass at the side of his shoes. His lips pursed. A judge . . .

'Details.'

'Half an hour ago. PIRA have already claimed it, that's in the last five minutes. Mr Justice Simpson, Billy Simpson. Always gave ten years for conspiracy or firearms possession . . . You know, "Tenner" Simpson.'

'Wasn't there any damned protection?' the Secretary of State flared.

'He had five with him, three in the escort, two in his own car. His car took a direct hit from an RPG-7 rocket. There were two detectives with him, and they died with him.'

'And no arrests.' The Secretary of State tried to be angry. 'Of course, no arrests.'

'No arrests.'

The Secretary of State stared into the lined, fleshless face of his civil servant. 'So what do I do?'

'I suggest you speak to the Prime Minister . . . sorry, but that's what you ought to do first. Then a statement to camera for the lunchtime bulletins. Then a meeting with the Chief Constable . . .'

'I'm turning into a bloody parrot, you know that? I haven't the faintest idea of what I'll say that I haven't said before. I detest this place, Fred. I detest it because it has rubbed all sense of shock and outrage from my mind.'

The Secretary of State sagged into an easy chair. He heard his civil servant let himself out of the room. When he was alone, when he had calmed his thoughts, he was able to remember Billy 'Tenner'

45

Simpson. One of a golfing four at Shandon Park, a pretty good player and near to scratch. A small, round, unsmiling man with a detective to caddy for him, who had not had much that was nice to say about the Secretary of State's game. All the usual phrases cavorted into the Secretary of State's mind ... Senseless murder ... bestial cowards ... determination of our government ... all decent minded people ... personal loss ... never be deflected ...

He reached for the telephone. He asked the switchboard for Downing Street.

'I thought you should know, Prime Minister, it's been a bad morning for the Province ...'

Ferment in Springfield Road barracks. Always the same after a major incident. Local commanders always saturated their areas after a nasty one. Road blocks, foot patrols, and mobiles. No local commander would have it said that his response was lacking. Saturation in the Falls and Clonard and Springfield and Beechmount and Ballymurphy. Kick the backside of a platoon lieutenant or a uniformed RUC sergeant who ventured to ask what they were searching for. Good reaction time was what mattered.

The Ford had been found, and collected from Bombay Street. It had been towed into the yard at the back of the barracks. It was surrounded by traffic warning signs and a scrawled notice that read DON'T TOUCH – WAITING ON F-PRINTING.

Fusilier Jones stared at the car. Nobby's bullet hole was there to see, side of the boot entry, not too far from the back passenger seat, but just too far, worst fucking luck. He could see into the back seat through the open window.

'Bugger me ...'

Fusilier Jones spun away from the car and doubled towards the Ops Room to find his lieutenant.

'He's sure?' asked Sunray.

The coded radio callsign of the Commanding Officer was Sunray. He enjoyed it, he encouraged its use. He had been heard to remark that it emphasized the Battalion's active service and operational role.

He would be the Commanding Officer again when they left the Province, but in Belfast he could be Sunray.

'He's positive,' Ferris said firmly.

'Has to be watertight.' Sunray sat at his desk.

'Can't afford a mistake, on a thing like this.' The 2 i/c was by the door.

'If it's a Roger it's something of a coup.' The Intelligence Officer held in his folded hands the VDU print-out concerning Sean Pius McAnally.

'He's absolutely positive,' Ferris said again.

'He'd have to be.'

'He'd have to swear to it in court.'

'SOP would be to bring in our friends in bottle-green . . . but we just might lift him ourselves.'

'Fusilier Jones will swear that the man I questioned yesterday in the Drive, Turf Lodge, and gave his name as Sean Pius McAnally, was the same man that he saw in the back seat of the car that we failed to stop in Divis Street this morning,' Ferris said. 'That's the beginning and the end of Fusilier Jones's statement.'

'Steady, David, you did damn well this morning. Fast professional thinking, damn well done.' Sunray's accolade.

'It's identified from the RPG attack location as the getaway car . . . It would be a hell of a thing for the Battalion, sir, if we nailed a Johnny for murder. Could be the high spot of the tour . . .' The Intelligence Officer's enthusiasm.

'Not a lot of thanks we get from RUC these days, they'd be on their bended knees for this one.' The 2 i/c's cunning.

Ferris thought of the moment when he had seen the Armalite barrel spitting from the window of the Ford, the moment of terror, and the moment he thought he would die. He could feel the scrapes on his knees and elbows. He hadn't seen the face in the back seat of the car, he had only seen the black barrel of the Armalite.

'Right, Standard Operating Procedure's that we inform RUC of our suspicions concerning McAnally . . .' Sunray was lighting his pipe.

'Police presence isn't essential for the arrest.'

'We can do it under Section 14. There's no problem.'

47

The face of the man burgeoned into Ferris's mind. The scrappy ginger hair, the nervy eyes, the slack chin, the mouth in the half-smile that tried to please.

'Your platoon'll do it, David, 0200 hours tomorrow morning. It'll be an excellent show for your platoon . . . and bloody well done.'

'Are we going to have a surveillance detail on the house, sir?' Ferris asked.

'What for?'

Ferris blinked, seemed so obvious. 'So we know he's there, sir, when we go in.'

'No surveillance. We don't have that capability, not in Turf Lodge. Stand a damn sight better chance of lousing it if I put men into the Drive, kicking dustbins over. We go in cold because that's best.'

'Yes, sir.'

'And bloody well done, David.'

They had left their transport, two Pigs and a Land Rover, at the junction of the Drive and the Parade. They would leg it to Number 63. Blackened faces and hands. Rifles cocked, one up. Quiet padding feet. The glow of the image intensifier night sights carried by the marksmen. Twenty men briefed on their positions in the outer perimeter and the inner perimeter, four more with Ferris for the snatch. Always bloody raining, and the haze of mist cloud sneaking in from the fields at the foot of the mountain to blanket Turf Lodge. No street lights; the street lights had been knocked out in '71, Internment, and replaced; knocked out again in the Queen's visit rioting, and replaced; knocked out again in the Hunger Strike fighting of '81, and abandoned.

A pace behind Ferris was Fusilier Jones, loping along like he was heading for Wembley, like he had a Cup bloody Final goal on the end of his boot.

Only it wasn't a game in Ferris's book. It was going to snatch a man out of his house in the dark of the night, strip him from his bed, tear him away from his wife and kids. It was going to put a murderer into a cell for a life sentence. Some bloody game. If it was a game then it was a dirty bloody game.

Number 63. His platoon sergeant was beside Ferris.

Ferris heard the whisper. 'All ready . . . let's get the shit out of his wanker.'

He had woken the moment before the explosion of the front door caving in. He had sat up, straight up, the moment before the screech of the front door's lock being smashed clear of the door post. He felt Roisin stir beside him. She'd four Bacardi cokes in her to his six stouts, she moved drowsily.

McAnally heard the oaths from the foot of the stairs. Baby Sean's pram was always outside the door in the day, brought into the hall at night, no other place for it . . . Mother of Christ, fucking English oath.

He wore a Marks vest, nothing else. He heaved himself out of the bed, dragging the sheets and blankets with him. He saw the white blur of Roisin's thighs, and her stomach. He crashed into Baby Sean's cot and was out of the door before the baby had screamed. From the landing he saw the torch at the bottom of the stairs, and a dark shadow figure wrestling with the pram. He saw the torch beam dive forward towards the stairs.

'Freeze, McAnally . . .'

The yell blasted at his ears. He charged into the back bedroom, jumped on Young Gerard's bed, stumbled on Little Patty's body, reached the window, ripped at the cotton curtains. He had no thought but flight, to run and to survive. He heard the thunder of boots on the staircase, sounds amplified and magnified by the tininess of the back bedroom.

His fingers found the window catch, he heaved it up, pushed the window open. Night air closed on his gut and his privates. Light flooded into the room. He saw the terror shape of the soldier charging into the room. He saw Young Gerard rise up from his bed and grapple with the soldier. He saw the soldier cuff the boy away. As the soldier lunged for him, McAnally jumped.

He was dazed, stunned.

He hit the small flat roof of the kitchen, bounced, scraped his shins and thighs and stomach on the roof guttering. He toppled down onto the concrete slabs beside the kitchen door. A leg was caught between the frame of Young Gerard's bicycle. He could see the bicycle, see its colours. The light from the back bedroom lit the small square backyard. He was clear of the bicycle when he saw the soldiers materializing from the shadows, from behind the coal bunker, from behind the kids' swing, from the shadow by the back fence.

McAnally kicked the first soldier who reached him. The bare instep of his foot hacked into the soldier's groin. Above him he saw Roisin dark-framed in the back bedroom window and flailing at a squaddy with Baby Sean's yellow plastic pot. The soldier bent double in front of him. Scream, cunt . . . but the soldier only moaned. He lashed with his fist at the soldier who came from the side and his knuckles caught the rim of a helmet. A rifle stock hammered into the back of his skull. A boot cracked into his shin. A soldier dived on him as he fell, and McAnally groped and found the man's cheeks and eyes and raked them with his nails. He fought with his hands and with his teeth and with his feet as the blows fell on him, clubbed down on his body. He heard the pain shouts of the soldiers, and further off the screams of Young Gerard and the anger of his Roisin. He fought only for survival. He lost the feel of pain. He lost the sight of the soldiers. He lost the sounds of the voices of Young Gerard and his Roisin.

A numbness in his body and a mist in his eyes and wads in his ears.

He saw the indistinct shapes of the legs that stood over him.

'For Christ's sake, pack it in . . .'

He felt the blood on his head and running from his lip.

'That's a prisoner, for Christ's sake.'

The officer stood over him.

'He is a prisoner and he will be treated as a prisoner . . .'

The soldiers were in a ring beyond his reach. And he now was beyond theirs.

'You're soldiers, you're on active service not in a bloody pub brawl. Sergeant, this man is not to be touched. Come here, Jones.'

The officer had taken hold of McAnally's wrist, held it securely. He shone a torch into McAnally's face, blinding him.

'That's him, Mr Ferris, that's the one I saw.'

The torch was switched off.

The officer said, 'Sean Pius McAnally, I am arresting you under Section 14 of the Northern Ireland (Emergency Provisions) Act, 1978. You are not obliged to answer any questions other than those relating to your identity ... You'd better get some clothes on, Mr McAnally. You won't be hurt, you're in my custody.'

After what he had done the morning before, they could have beaten the life out of him. He had seen the car on the telly before he had taken Roisin to the bar, seen the car wreck and the photographs of 'Tenner' Simpson and two detectives. He had heard the tributes ... they could have battered him to death for what he had done.

The officer led him back into the kitchen. McAnally covered his groin.

# 4

A little before three Ferris was back in the Mess.

He had been on the go for close on twenty-one hours, but he'd had to tell his story, laconically in the old style of the Regiment, to the IO and the Bravo Company Commander and separately to Armstrong and Wilkins with whom he shared his room. He could have done without the accolade treatment after he had checked his prisoner into police custody and the Springfield Road cells.

There was a handwritten note from Sunray. 'Excellently done, a most creditable night for the Battalion, fast professional soldiering. Congratulations, Townsend.' He'd have to go through it all again in the morning for Sunray.

He had two glasses of orange juice, and then the IO told him that there was a detective coming up from Castlereagh, a chap called Rennie, and would he wait up for him.

He was left to wait in the Mess, stretched out on the sofa, able to doze.

The Company Commander had been gushing, the IO had been cool, Armstrong and Wilkins had been jealous as tomcats. He hadn't spoken of the sledgehammer attack on a wet rotten front door, nor of being snagged in the hall by a pram that stank of nappy urine, nor of pounding up the carpetless stairs, nor of a kiddie of seven or eight years who had taken on the soldiers to help his father, nor of a proud woman who had spat her hatred at his men. He didn't think they'd want to know.

Sam might want to know. When he'd finished with the detective, and had a hell of a sleep, and a bath if he could find any hot water, he'd write to her. He was thinking of Sam, drowsily and happily, when the ceiling light billowed across the Mess.

'Are you Mr Ferris?' The scrape of the Belfast accent.

Ferris sat up. 'That's me.'

It was a huge man that towered over him, his size accentuated by Ferris's position on the sofa.

'I'm Rennie . . . Detective Chief Inspector Rennie . . .'

He spoke the words slowly, as if the rank gave him pride. Ferris sat up, rubbed his eyes.

'Howard Rennie, Castlereagh . . . I hear you buggers have been fart-arsing with us . . .'

'I beg your pardon . . .?' Ferris yawned. The Mess was bloody arctic. He stood, and tucked his shirt down into his trouser waist.

'The police lift men in Belfast these days, if you didn't know. The military provide support, if requested. I can do without clever buggers.'

'You've no right to come in here, into our Mess, with that sort of language on your face.'

'I like a man out of his bed, into the Land Rover, down to Castlereagh, while he's still asleep. I like him stripped and weighed and checked and in his cell before he's had time to think. I have to work on him, young fellow, and I've shit all time to do it, as you'd know if you took the trouble to read the P. of T. Act, and what doesn't help me is him sitting in a cell here getting used to the fact he's in the cage. As I see it, young fellow, getting my friend into the Interrogation Room in the right frame of mind is more important than your fucking Colonel getting a back slap from his General. Got it?'

Ferris thought he liked the man. He was laughing quietly. 'Got it . . . round here, Mr Rennie, you might believe that the capture of old McAnally added up to the final victory.'

It was a big weathered face that confronted Ferris. There was no crack of a smile. The hairs of the moustache were splayed out. There was a nick from a fast shave on the throat. The breath was of cigarettes and gin. The ceiling light glowed on the high forehead. 'Tomorrow, if I can take the time off from "old McAnally", I'll have two funerals to go to, good friends, so I'm not in the mood for a laugh in your Mess. I want McAnally now, I want you and the lad who identified him down at Castlereagh in the afternoon for statements.'

'He's already in police custody, why don't you just bloody take him?'

'There's a form for these things. He's going to appear in court, long after you've been ferried out and back to war games in Germany. Long after you've gone some smart lawyer will be putting the arrest procedure under a 'scope. You won't be here but I will, so I say that everything has to be right, and I'm taking him from *your* charge. Got it?'

Ferris led the way. Out into the night air and across to the police cells, down the corridor, escorted by a constable. The crash of the keys, the swish of the door. McAnally sat on the iron bedframe. His knees were clamped close together, his arms were hard against his chest. His lip was swollen. Ferris was behind the shoulder of the detective, but he could see McAnally stiffen, straighten, at the sight of Howard Rennie. Ferris reckoned it the defiance of a trapped rat.

'Morning, Gingy . . .'

McAnally stood up. He tried to lift his chin. He walked to Rennie and then turned his back, reached his wrists to the base of his spine, and was handcuffed. He turned back to face Rennie.

'The injury to the prisoner's mouth, Mr Ferris, that happened during his arrest?'

'Correct.'

'Just getting it right, Mr Ferris, like I said. Come on, Gingy.'

Detective Chief Inspector Howard Rennie strode away down the corridor. His shoes were iron-tipped, reverberating. His quilted, open anorak seemed to fill the corridor. Ferris followed, walking alongside McAnally. The constable was behind them. Rennie was hurrying, as if the whole visit to Springfield Road had been a bloody liberty taken at his expense. Ferris felt the light kick at his heel. McAnally was close to him. The prisoner looked up once into Ferris's face. He spoke quietly, almost a whisper, out of the side of his mouth.

'I know what you did.'

'What I'm paid to do.'

'You stopped them kicking the shit out of me.'

'Safe journey, Mr McAnally.'

McAnally was bundled into a police Land Rover. The engine was already running, spewing smoke across the yard. Rennie was unlocking the door of his car. Ferris saw him take off his anorak and sling it into the back seat, and then produce his pistol from a shoulder holster under his jacket, and cock it and place it in his waistband. The convoy of the Land Rover and Rennie's car swept out through the gates, out into the early morning darkness.

Ferris headed off in search of a cup of tea and then bed.

'You go easy with it, I'll fix it proper later.'

The neighbour stepped back to let Roisin McAnally out through the front door of Number 63. All the neighbours had called on Number 63 in the hours since the military raid. The first had come in their sleeping clothes, in their dressing gowns and slippers. As the light had come up, they had come dressed for the day. Some came to comfort, some to help, some to witness the scene. This neighbour had come with his tool kit to repair the front door.

'That's a terrible bloody way to be coming into a family's wee home . . .' The neighbour shrugged. He had come with his drills and screw drivers because his own woman had told him that he must. He wouldn't have said that he liked Roisin McAnally. With drink taken he would have called her a stuck-up cow. But his wife had told him to come and so he had made a job of mending the hinge fastening on the door. And the bitch hadn't even thanked him, just looked through him, and stamped off down the pathway to the front gate that was already hanging slack from a long time before. He was buggered if he'd fix the front gate . . . To himself the neighbour reckoned that all the Provo widows were the same, stuck-up cows. Not that he would have ventured that opinion in public, wouldn't have said that down at the bar on a Saturday evening. They were always called 'the widows', whether their man was dead or running or walled up in the Kesh, and he reckoned they all wore their widowhood with a sort of bloody arrogance. So, she hadn't thanked him for fixing her door, and he simpered a smile behind her back as she stalked away. In a right paddy temper, the neighbour thought. Could see it in her chin and in her mouth and in her eyes, like she's going to kick the arse off the first man that crosses her.

'You go carefully with it, Missus,' the neighbour called at her back . . . and more quietly . . . 'or you'll be doing the fucking thing yourself, if you bust it.'

The neighbour had read Roisin McAnally right.

55

She smouldered in a ferocious anger as she set off down the broken pavement of the Drive. She walked with her back straight, and her head up, and knew that the curtains all the way down the slope of the Drive would be flickering back. They would all be watching her, all of them in 61 and 59 and 57 and 55 . . . and all the curtains on the other side of the road would be twitching, and those that couldn't see her because there was a car parked in the way would hustle up their bloody stairs to get a grandstand view . . . They'd been there in the night, whining their sympathy, and asking the sly bloody questions. 'What had he been at, Missus McAnally? . . . He's not one for stepping into trouble, is he, Mrs McAnally? . . . Doing well down in the Free State, isn't that him, Missus McAnally? . . .' Her mother was now in the house, and fretting, and minding the kids, and the kids were all quiet as if they'd been thrashed. Young Gerard hadn't opened his mouth since the soldiers and his father had gone, and Little Patty had cried in her bed and wet the sheets which she hadn't done for a year, and Baby Sean had screamed because his mother was cold and numbed and couldn't offer him love.

And the coldness had changed to fury.

She knew where to go. She knew in which house she could let rip her temper. A quarter of an hour's fast walking on a chilled damp morning.

She knew her man's speciality was the RPG launcher.

She knew what he had done the previous day. She had known he was on a hit from the time he had crept out of the house before dawn, and from the time when he had come back home and made a joke and laughed and his chin had shaken as if the muscle-wires were loose and uncontrolled. She had known from the way that he had paced the little front room and picked up the kids and made too much noise and not been able to settle. From the way he had smoked half a packet of cigarettes and stubbed each butt down. From the way he had loved her in their bed . . . He had been silent only once the previous day, when the telly news was on, when he had seen a blackened car and a chorus of politicians and churchmen keening a litany of condemnation. And she had never referred to it. She hadn't pretended that she knew. That wasn't the way of the widows. The

56

widows did not expect to be told. The widows expected to serve up the food on the table and the comfort between their legs. Deep down, hard down, she supported her husband's involvement in the Organization. Down in her guts she saw herself as a prop to her man. She had a brother and a first cousin in the Kesh. She accepted that her husband was involved. She had not cared to understand why her man had gone south, and turned his back on the war. She knew the strain of fighting the war. She carried the same strain. Roisin McAnally was no quitter. She believed in the war, she was committed to the armed struggle. She wept no tears for the enemy's fallen. If she could have killed one of the soldiers who came into her house in the small hours of that morning, she would happily have done so.

Her raven black hair streamed out from her head as she walked into the teeth of the wind. She wore jeans and a sweater and a bright red nylon shower-proof jogging jacket. Her clothes, and her children's, she gathered from jumbles and from relatives' cast-offs. And with her head up, and her chin jutting, and with her eyes burning in her anger, Roisin McAnally was beautiful.

The man opened the door to her knock. He was Battalion staff. He had not shaved. She knew him because in the old days he'd brought her money. He wore his socks and his trousers and a vest. He had his kids round his legs, jam and crumbs at their mouths. He had once tried to bed her, but he'd been pissed and she hadn't counted it against him. He would have seen her anger, and he made way for her and hurriedly opened the door of his front room that reeked of old smoke and smelt of cold damp, and he cuffed the kids out of the door and closed it on their protests.

'They took my Sean, the army came this morning and took him.'

She saw the shock spreading on his face and the shadows forming in his frown.

'They took Gingy . . . ?'

She roared at him. 'They took Sean. He's back two days, and they came for him. First job in two years, and he's lifted. How did they know to come for him? He's been informed on . . . he's been fingered by a bloody tout . . .'

57

The man ducked, as if attempting to deflect the accusation. 'Informer' and 'tout', they were the obscenity words of the Organization. His teeth were biting on his bottom lip. Nicotined teeth on the pale pink of his lips.

'You can't say that, woman.' Said as if he hardly believed his denial.

'I can say what's the truth . . . He comes back, and he goes out, and he's lifted. It wasn't a routine lift. My house was half filled with bloody soldiers. Who touted on my Sean?'

The man squeezed his eyes closed and shook his head. 'How can I answer . . .?'

'You find the bloody answer. You find who touted on Sean.'

'You best go home . . . You're better at home.'

'Don't you want to talk to me? Won't you face me?'

'If Gingy's been touted on then I've work at hand.'

'Kill the bastard. Kill him for me.' The blaze in her eyes was misted.

'If there's a tout, we'll find him.'

'And kill him . . . What sort of bloody army is it when a man doesn't know whether the boy with him is a friend or a bloody tout?'

She was sobbing, and the man took her in his arms. He thought she was a great girl, he thought she was one of the best. He held her against him and felt the ripple movements of her crying.

'If there's a tout then we'll find him. That's a promise, Missus.'

'Bloody good for me,' a small voice, choking. 'My Sean's on a lifer . . .'

She went out onto the street still crying. She stumbled once on the broken pavement where the slabs had been lifted to be smashed into missiles. As far as she looked there were narrow roofs and spirals of smoke and grime-laden façades. In that moment she hated Turf Lodge. In Turf Lodge a man had touted on her Sean. She saw the graffiti . . . 'Provos Rule' and 'Brit Bastards Out' and 'Smash the H Blocks' and 'Touts Will be Shot'. Shooting was too good for a tout.

It did not enter her mind that there could be any other reason for the arrest of her husband. He was in the cage because a tout had put him there. She saw a lifetime ahead of her, from youth through to

58

middle age and through to old age, of traipsing to the stop for the prison bus . . . because of a bastard tout.

All around her was the emptiness of the early morning. A lifetime of waiting for the fucking prison bus. A lifetime without a man. A lifetime of scrimping and saving her pounds.

She began to run, and her tears hastened her. She ran back to the Drive and her home, back to her children.

The word would spread, like the scent of foul air, like the drift of a winter wind off Divis Mountain. The word said that Roisin McAnally had claimed to a Battalion Staff Officer that her husband had been touted. The Organization cringed at the word. More than all the soldiers and all the policemen ranked against them, the Organization feared the tout. The tout was a dark shadow swimming as a germ in the bloodstream. The tout struck at the core of the Organization. The tout was to be tortured, hooded, executed, dumped.

Within an hour of Roisin McAnally's reaching home, the news of Gingy's arrest had reached the Housing Executive maisonette in Andersonstown that was the current refuge of the Chief. He called for a conference in the early afternoon. He summoned to the meeting those who were closest to him, those that he trusted absolutely. But the doubt gnawed in his gut. The men who were closest to him were the same men who had known of the arrival of McAnally in Belfast.

The Chief had a way with touts. Cigarettes on the balls and the stomach, for the confession. Then the hooding. Then the noisy cocking of the pistol against the ear of the tout. Then the shot into the ground beside the tout's foot, so that he pissed himself and messed himself. Then the barrel against the back of the neck. Then the killing.

It had to be a tout, and a tout who knew only of McAnally's role in the Crumlin Road hit. A tout who didn't know the names of the man who had driven the car, of the men who had ridden shotgun, of the youth who had fled with the used launcher.

The girl he lived with, Mary, stayed in the bedroom, abandoned him to his angry pacing of the living room.

'You stay in your bed when they come.' He shouted at her as if she was just something to be kept in a cupboard, put away when there was business. He felt a flicker of regret . . . There had been a man once who had told him earnestly and sincerely that his Mary was a risk to his security, and he had smashed the man's chin. Now he had shouted at her as if she was a danger to him and his closest lieutenants.

'You are not obliged to say anything, unless you wish to do so, but what you say may be put into writing and given in evidence . . . You are Sean Pius McAnally?'

'You know my name.'

There were two detectives with him in the Interrogation Room. He knew there was a father-mother of a row over his arrest. He knew that if they had been expecting him then the detectives would have gone straight to work.

'63 The Drive, Turf Lodge?'

High on the wall and facing him in the bare room was the camera. In the old days they would have beaten him, half knocked hell out of him. He knew that the camera ensured that the detectives wouldn't touch him. He knew all the rules under which the detectives operated.

'You know where I live.'

'We'll call you Gingy, right?'

'You call me what you like.' McAnally sat on a chair at a table. The detective who asked the questions was behind him, standing. Across the table from him was the detective with the notepad.

'Would you like to tell us where you were yesterday morning, Gingy?'

Don't reply. That's what the big men said. Think of your woman, think of your kids, don't ever listen to what they say to you.

'Yesterday morning, Gingy. Tell us where you were.'

He looked at his finger nails. He saw the wrinkles in his hands, and the little cuts that came from the farm work down by the canal in the south.

'Prefer it if we told you where you were?'

Before the new rules were enforced in the Interrogation Rooms, he would have been on the end of their boots and their fists, straight up, no messing. That's what they'd done to him way back, when he was married a week.

'Prefer it if I said you were in Crumlin Road yesterday morning, how about that, Gingy?'

He hadn't broken the last time, not for all the slapping and the punching and the kicking. The bastards knew how to do it, so there weren't bruises. Just so there was the bloody pain.

'Gingy, you're in bad shape. You're identified. You're placed at Crumlin Road on the RPG team. That's murder three times. You're placed in Divis Street in the getaway. That's attempted murder. That's a life sentence, Gingy. There isn't a way round that. Sitting on your bum and saying nothing, that's not a way out of it. It'll be a life sentence with the judge's recommendation that you serve a minimum of twenty-five years. That's a bad scene, Gingy.'

He knew their trick. The trick was always to pretend they knew more than they did.

'Twenty-five years, Gingy, that's a hell of a bloody stretch. Is that what you came back from the south for, to serve twenty-five years?'

He thought of Young Gerard twenty-five years from now, and Little Patty, and Baby Sean. In twenty-five years Roisin would be a grey-haired widow. In twenty-five years the kids would be grown up, left and married.

'Gingy, my book says that the man in the back of the getaway is the jewel. The man beside him and the front passenger, they're the back-up, and there's the driver. My book says that the jewel is the laddie who was on the RPG. My book says that you're the jewel, Gingy McAnally . . . and my book says that a big precious jewel like you goes down for twenty-five years.'

Difficult for him to imagine Young Gerard as a grown man. A grown man who might travel to the Kesh to see his father, aging in an H Block. Young Gerard had fought the bloody soldiers, bloody child and he had the loyalty to his father to fight the soldiers.

'Great future, isn't it, Gingy? You inside for twenty-five years. What's the old woman going to do, Gingy? Good girl, is she? Keep herself good and clean and wait for you? What do you reckon, Gingy?'

He clamped his teeth together. He could smell the aftershave of the detectives, and he could see their laundered and ironed shirts. They wore well cut jackets and slacks with creases and shoes that were polished. He thought that when they had finished with him then they'd go and take a cup of coffee and a sandwich, and at the end of the day they'd have a few beers, and they'd be pissing themselves laughing about Gingy McAnally.

'Please yourself, Gingy. This is just getting to know you, and you getting to know us. This is just for you to know where you stand ... you'll be standing for twenty-five years, Gingy. That's all ... for now.'

They went to the door. They didn't bother to look back at him. The detective who had asked the questions whispered something that McAnally couldn't hear to the detective with the notebook, and they were chuckling as they went out.

A uniformed constable was framed in the open doorway. His face was expressionless, cold. He nodded curtly for McAnally to come to the door.

From Rennie's office the information was fed to the Press Office at Police Headquarters on the Knock Road. From the Press Office the information was dispersed on the Not Attributable basis.

Lunchtime's local television news and the Belfast evening newspaper first editions carried the report that 'according to senior police sources a man is in custody following an anonymous tip-off, and is being questioned in connection with inquiries into the murders yesterday of Judge William Simpson and his two police bodyguards.'

Roisin McAnally watched the lunchtime news and felt vindicated.

The Secretary of State was handed a transcript of a radio broadcast, and was seen by an aide to sigh with relief.

David Ferris was given a digest of the news story carried in the evening newspaper. He had slept, he was rested, but he shook his head as if in confusion when the Intelligence Officer drily explained the sophistications of 'psywar'. And he hadn't time to stand around when he and Fusilier Jones were already late for their Castlereagh appointment.

The Chief heard the radio, and was convinced, and waited for the men he had summoned to gather at the maisonette.

62

And Belfast went about its business. The shops were full in Royal Avenue, and the bus stops were crowded by the City Hall. The city breathed and continued with its life. And the disgust at a triple murder waned with the daylight.

'It wasn't the boys who brought him back from the south. I'd stake my life on them,' said the Brigade's Adjutant.

'It's not any of those who were with Gingy at the Crumlin Road, or it wouldn't have been just Gingy who was lifted,' said the Brigade's Quartermaster.

'And all of us, we knew that Gingy was up from the south, and we knew what he did.' The Chief spoke with a mock lightness, an ice tinkle in his voice.

'That's fucking ridiculous . . . if one of us is a tout, then the whole fucking war's finished . . .' The hoarse response from the Brigade's Intelligence Officer. 'If that's meant as a crack . . .'

'I tell you what I'm thinking, this is what I'm thinking . . .' The Brigade Quartermaster was tugging at the Chief's sleeve for his attention. 'I'm thinking, is Gingy McAnally one of us?'

'What's that mean?'

'It means that he quit. He walked out over the border.'

'You've not told me what you mean.'

'How's he going to be in there, that's putting it flat.'

'What's you saying?'

'Shit, do I have to spell it?'

The Chief stared him out. 'You have to spell it.'

The Brigade Quartermaster looked for the support of Intelligence and Operations, didn't win their encouragement. 'I just wondered how Gingy would stand up in Castlereagh, because he'd run once . . .'

The accusation died on his lips.

'I brought Gingy McAnally up from the south, that's down to me,' the Chief said. 'If I brought him up then he's not a man to tout. And you're talking out of turn. It's a liberty, diabolical, for you to be talking about Gingy McAnally, whether he'll turn, when some shit's just dropped him.'

'It was worth saying.'

'And I've answered it . . . There was the boy that couriered him to the meeting with us.' The Chief's voice was a wind whisper.

'That's Mattie Blaney's . . .'

'I know who he is.' The face of the Chief was settled, as if everything before had been preamble.

'Mattie Blaney's as true a Republican . . .'

'I was at Mattie's wedding.'

'It would kill Mattie, to think his kid touted.'

'The boy who brought Gingy, when Gingy wasn't so keen, he saw only Gingy.' The Chief smiled, a sad crisp smile. 'Only Gingy's been lifted.'

'Mattie's boy's only fourteen fucking years old.'

'A tout's a tout.' The Chief slapped his hands together for effect. 'Touts destroy us. People have to learn that there's no future in touting.'

They went their way in silence. They went their way to hand out the order to those whom they could trust. They left their Chief to cross the landing to Mary and his bed. They left to find the men who would pick up Mattie Blaney's boy, the boy who had been sitting on a car smoking and waiting to direct Sean Pius McAnally to a rendezvous before going to school.


Rennie walked with David Ferris and Fusilier Jones down the corridor that ran the length of the ground floor Interrogation Rooms.

A far door opened. Two detectives spilled out. Hard on their heels came the prisoner and his escort.

The prisoner saw Rennie. His head had been down, his face was strain-torn. He saw Rennie and managed to snarl at him. A captured man with no chance of fighting to freedom.

The prisoner saw Ferris. The moment had been created by Rennie for a formal identification of the prisoner by Fusilier Jones. The prisoner saw Ferris and for an instant his defiance dissolved. Perhaps his mouth moved as if to speak, Ferris could not be certain, and he heard nothing, and Ferris couldn't help himself and he smiled quickly.

Rennie saw this silent exchange. They flattened against the corridor wall to let the prisoner and escort pass.

Rennie was pondering.

'Well?'

'That's him, sir. That's Sean Pius McAnally, who I positively identify as being in the car in Divis Street,' Jones replied.

'Very good. We'll get you onto paper. Sorry for the performance, but it's necessary.' Rennie's voice died. He was watching Ferris's face, and he was watching Ferris's eyes that followed the prisoner away down the corridor.

# 5

In the old days of the Troubles, the days of Army supremacy, a military intelligence officer had once remarked of Howard Rennie, 'Get blood out of granite, that one.' The remark had been thought amusing by a more junior officer, and over a glass in the Lisburn HQ Mess, it had been passed to the major who acted as RUC Liaison. Through the major's daily contacts it had travelled to Police HQ. The title of Granite Rennie was now embedded in the lore of the police force. There were some senior officers who flitted in and out of the front line of the war. There were some who served two years in Criminal Investigation in Andersonstown or Crossmaglen, before a transfer to the safer Protestant recesses of County Antrim or County Down. Howard Rennie had never left the sharp end. He was now serving his ninth year in Criminal Investigation, and before that he had endured six years of Special Branch work.

He was now forty-nine. He had enough years behind him for a reasonable pension, and there were many commercial groups in the Province who would have paid him handsomely to come onto their staffs as a security consultant. He had never entertained the thought. Nor had he considered requesting a posting to a desk job. Howard Rennie was a front-line fighter.

His size and the intimidating cragginess of his face had fashioned him for a formidable reputation as an interrogator. Amongst the PIRA ranks, amongst men locked up and at liberty, he was a man marked down for killing.

His strength lay in the force of his belief in an ultimate victory. Not a victory tomorrow, or next week, or next year, but a sometime victory. He believed in the day when the opposition would be drowned in their own filth, the day when their ability to retaliate would finally have been destroyed. It was not a view shared in high places, either in Police HQ, or amongst the politicians from London who administered the Province. The opinion of Howard Rennie was reckoned to be out of step with upper echelon thinking, and so he had stayed as a Detective Chief Inspector and been many times passed over for promotion to the rank of superintendent. His war was that of attrition. He could not contemplate an end to the war that involved appeasement to his enemy. If there was to be a some-time victory then it would have to come on Howard Rennie's terms.

The puffiness at the jowls was evidence of his fierce off-duty drinking. He would have denied angrily that he was an alcoholic, he would have said that he drank as much as the next man, and no more. Because of that high profile police work he was under perpet-ual strain, and some comfort from the strain came from the gin bottle. To the Organization he represented a considerable threat, a threat they had attempted twice to eliminate. The living room of his cul-de-sac house in the quiet Dunmurry suburb of the city was replastered and repapered but still showed the indentations of a burst of Armalite on automatic when the animals had made it inside his house to wait for his return home. More recently they had tried to car bomb him. A Ford Fiesta loaded with fertilizer mix and parked on the main road at the junction past which he must drive on his way to work, and the remote controlled detonation a split-second late, and the force of the blast taken by a young housewife out shopping. The housewife had died, and Rennie had survived untouched and drunk a half-bottle before lunchtime. He was supported by his wife, who had spent one ever-to-be-remembered Sunday evening cuddling her children and facing the Armalite barrel and the pinched, hating face of a Provisional marksman. She never questioned her husband nor urged him against his prosecution of the war. She accepted that on the table beside their marriage bed there would always be, at night, a loaded PPK pistol. She was Gloria. She lived behind blast-proof windows, she lived in a house that was bathed in light at night. She helped with the outings for the RUC Widows and Dependents, and with the tombolas that paid for them. Her husband left the house most mornings before eight, and returned fourteen or fifteen hours later . . . and through the day she listened to each and every one of the local radio news broadcasts. She thought Howard

Rennie was a grand man, and she knew she had no chance of changing him.

In the war, the Interrogation Rooms were his chosen battleground. In the twenty-one Interrogation Rooms at Castlereagh he was a familiar figure. He could be hunched and confidential and kindly, his elbows splayed on the table, his face close to that of his prisoner. He could be angry and pacing and shouting and threatening. The camera watched him, but there was no microphone in a Castlereagh Interrogation Room.

It was the middle of the evening.

Rennie had eaten his tea in the canteen. Sausages and chips and a smear of brown sauce, and a mug of tea with two sugars. From the canteen he stamped his way over to the Interrogation Block. He rarely strolled. It was his habit to hurry. McAnally was up for the third time. And the third team of detectives was working on him. Rennie knew they had been brief and cursory the first time. That was often the tactic. Let the implications of capture swim in the prisoner's mind. The second session was always tougher, more direct, attempting to exploit those implications . . . but, of course, since the bloody Amnesty fellow travellers and the European Court creatures had had their pennyworth, then the likes of Howard Rennie were no longer permitted to slap and tickle a prisoner – that was the camera's job, to make certain the likes of Howard Rennie didn't take a fist to the chin of a horrible little bastard whose only talent in life was sniping with a Woodmaster Remington rifle, or mixing fertilizer for a beer keg bomb . . . Shit, and if you couldn't belt the bastards, then there was sod all hope of getting them to talk.

Rennie knew that in the second session, McAnally had not opened his mouth. Not one bloody word from the little beast that was useful.

He shouldered past the uniformed policeman patrolling the corridor, into the fifth room from the end on the right. He nodded for the younger of the detectives to get himself up from his chair and out. Bloody regulations, regulations said that no more than two detectives should be present at any one time for interrogation . . . bloody regulations tying the hands of the men who tried to keep the Province safe for decent people, that was Howard Rennie's anthem.

McAnally was looking up at Rennie.

'I'm obliged to give you my name. I'm Rennie, DCI . . .' Rennie spun the chair back to front. He sat heavily down, elbows resting on the chair's back. He belched, all the bloody chips. He was leaning forward.

'Being helpful are we, Gingy?'

Behind McAnally's head the detective shook his head.

'Are we going to be sensible, or are we going to be difficult? Are we going to have a life sentence without a minimum recommendation, or a life sentence with twenty-five years written in?'

McAnally flopped his head down onto his fists.

A cold grin from Rennie. 'I'm not allowed to offer you an inducement, McAnally, but all the big boys know the form. Help us, and there's a life sentence without a recommendation, that's a bloody sight easier than a Twenty-five . . .'

McAnally closed his eyes.

'McAnally, if you're not daft you'll examine your position. You were informed on . . . that's how rotten your organization is, it's rotten from floor to ceiling. Your own people grassed on you.'

McAnally opened his eyes, glowered at Rennie. His lips trembled, but he said nothing. Fighting to say nothing.

'Couldn't have been many who knew you were coming up from down south. Well, one of them that knew was friendly enough with us to grass on you. Are you going to spend a bit of time working out in your head which one it was? 'Course you'll spend a bit of time, you'll have twenty-five years of time to think which one it was . . . if you're not sensible. You've been inside, Gingy. You know how long twenty-five years takes inside.'

McAnally rolled off his chair.

He lay on the floor of the Interrogation Room.

He was face down on the floor, and he covered his ears with his hands.

'Getting the message, Gingy?'

Rennie was now off his chair and dropping to his hands and knees, and then straightening his legs as if about to make a press-up, and he lowered himself down, down onto the floor, down beside McAnally.

'You should be getting the message by now, Gingy. They grassed on you. They brought you up for a one-shot, and that was the end of their use for you.'

Little Gingy McAnally and big Howard Rennie both stomach-down on the floor, and McAnally squeezing the palms of his hands against his ears, and Rennie whispering into the cracks between his fingers.

'Nasty cut that one on your lip, Gingy.'

McAnally's tongue slipped between his teeth, rolled over the swollen lip.

'Don't you like a beating, Gingy? You're good at handing it out. You gave a bit of a beating to Billy Simpson. There's plenty in here would like to kick your stomach through your arse.'

Rennie saw McAnally try to bury his head down against his chest, as if that way he could better shut out the tap-drip of the voice in his ear.

'I would have thought the soldiers would have half killed you, Gingy . . .'

He saw McAnally's head move in the barest and quickest acknowledgement. Rennie crouched over McAnally and his hands were either side of McAnally's head, and his mouth brushed against the nape of McAnally's neck.

'The officer saved you, didn't he, Gingy, saved you from a bloody thrashing, didn't he?'

McAnally nodded.

'The officer stopped them from belting the shit out of you, Gingy?'

'Yes.'

'That officer showed you a bit of kindness?'

'Yes.' A tiny, reedy voice.

'A bit of kindness where you didn't expect any kindness?'

'Yes.'

'You'd trust that man, that officer, would you, Gingy?'

'Yes.'

'You'd trust him because he was a good young man, because he wasn't a bastard like me, because he saved you from a beating. Right, Gingy?'

'Yes.'

'And that officer's name is Lieutenant Ferris?'

'Yes.'

All of interrogation was a chance. Each day when he went into the Interrogation Rooms it was without a clear idea of how he would respond to his suspect. He played his hunch, sometimes he won, many times he lost. Rennie's head dipped, his forehead was against the floor. His mouth was close to McAnally's ear.

'I reckon that officer feels sorry for you.'

Rennie reached up. His fingers found the table's edge, and he levered himself to his feet. 'I must be about my business now, Gingy. I'll be back. And in the meantime you just have a wee thought on your friends,' Rennie said. 'No great urgency, of course,' he added, as the door closed behind him.

Past nine in the evening and the inside lights glowing through the thin curtains of the Turf Lodge streets. Wet streets, glistening in the Land Rovers' headlights. Empty streets, because the Social Security was not paid till the next morning, and there was no money left for the bars. The Land Rovers cruised slowly, engines whining. Ferris and his driver and two squaddys, in the lead vehicle.

Ferris was thinking of Sam. He hadn't had a letter from her that week, but then he hadn't tried to ring, so it was quits. When he did write to her, or telephone, he never had much to say about Turf Lodge, about night patrolling. If he didn't write often and he didn't ring often, it was because there was nothing to say that he thought she ought to know, not because he didn't miss her. A girl who lived with her parents in a six-bedroomed stone house with a paddock and an orchard in rolling Somerset wouldn't have too much in common with patrolling the Turf Lodge estate – so he didn't tell her about it. He'd tell her about Sean Pius McAnally, but only enough for her to know that his platoon was getting the Glorygrams from Sunray. She'd like that, and she'd tell her father. Sam's father was a retired half Colonel. Effectively he had made Major and Company Command in the old Somerset Light Infantry, but he'd been upped to half Colonel to oversee the local schools' Cadet units. Not a bad chap, Sam's father, and he didn't stand in the way of what Sam did when David Ferris was down on leave. Trouble was he'd forgotten he hadn't made General, forgotten it clean out of the window when he'd had the Falklands map pinned up in the study during the South Atlantic affair.

She was lovely, his Sam, but thinking of Sam on a cold, wet night in Turf Lodge was enough to get himself sniped. Safer to be thinking that there might be a marksman in a snipe hide between the Drive and the Parade. She had bloody good thighs because she jogged three times a week, and bloody good breasts because she drank a pint of milk each morning and she was a bloody good girl because she kept herself for David Ferris all the time he was cruising through the Turf Lodge estate. If a chap had to be sniped then so much the better if he had a clear picture of Sam's very beautiful body in his head when the bead was on him.

'What are you thinking of, Jones?'

'Fanny, sir. What are you thinking of, sir?'

'Military tactics, Jones, what else?'

In the faint light Ferris could see Jones holding a straight face. He smiled. He heard the snigger of the squaddys behind him.

'. . . DELTA FOXTROT COME IN OVER . . .'

His head spun with the cry in his earpiece. He found the button on his radio, twisted the volume down.

'. . . Delta Foxtrot Receiving Over . . .'

'. . . DELTA FOXTROT THIS IS 49 . . . S.A.P. PARADE STROKE AVENUE R.V. . . . OUT . . .'

Ferris said quietly to Jones: 'Soon as possible to the junction of the Parade and Avenue.' He turned to his squaddys behind him. 'Sharp lookout, lads . . .'

Fusilier Jones knew the Turf Lodge like a local. Three right turns and a left.

The headlights swung along the street and caught a squaddy crouched against an overgrown hedge, and then the corporal who was bent down against the wall of a lock-up garage. Ferris saw what seemed to be a bundle of rags, perhaps a sack, beside the corporal before Jones killed the lights. Ferris swung his legs out of the Land Rover and scurried to his corporal.

The corporal's masked torch shone down into a small white face. Ferris saw the terrified, staring eyes and the blood-drained cheeks that were smeared with tears.

Ferris's thoughts were racing. Bloody hit and run driver, no bloody lights in the street . . . But the corporal's torch was moving down the short length of the boy's jersey . . . Ferris saw the hole at the elbow, worn through . . . and the torch moved on down the boy's thigh. He saw the blood-soaked knee of the boy, and the dark bullet hole set in the spread of crimson.

'But it's a bloody child . . .'

'It's a child, Mr Ferris, and he's been knee-capped,' the corporal said grimly.

'God Almighty . . . I don't believe it . . .'

'He's Liam Blaney, he's thirteen years old. Father's in the Kesh . . . Want to see his stomach?'

The corporal didn't wait for Ferris's reply. He pulled back the boy's shirt, lifted his jersey. Ferris saw the burns and the bruises.

'Must reckon him an informer, sir,' the corporal added.

Ferris knew the corporal's own children from back at the depot in England. He knew the dry, flat answers to be a sham.

'I'll run him down to the barracks, have an ambulance rendezvous there. Snap them up on the radio . . . Come on, son.'

He lifted the boy up in his arms. He felt him struggle, and then wince from the pain. He heard him cry out. He could sense what it would mean to the child, to be held in the arms of a British officer, and he thought he could sense the agony that would follow a bullet fired at point blank range through the bone and muscle and tissue of a knee-cap, and that was after the cigarettes, and after the beating. He held the child against his chest, tight so that he couldn't fight him. He walked to the Land Rover and climbed in, and the boy was cradled in his lap.

'They wouldn't do this to each other if they lived in a bloody zoo, Mr Ferris,' Fusilier Jones observed, and slapped his hand onto the gear stick.

'Just get the thing moving, Jones . . .'

He didn't know what to say to the boy. He did not know how to comfort a child who had a shattered knee-cap and whose stomach was burnt. He wedged his rifle between the seats and held the boy closely and tried to protect him from the lurching journey of the Land Rover.

\*      \*      \*

73

'So what sort of a lad is your Ferris?'

Rennie, thank God for it, had been given a gin by the Commanding Officer.

Sunray had a Scotch, and the Intelligence Officer had a half-pint silver beer tankard cupped in his hands.

'A very professional young officer, proved that by his actions yesterday.' Sunray sat at the desk of his office, his fingers played with a paper knife.

'I'm not interested in his professional abilities, sir. What's his personality. Frankly, please.'

'Pretty much the same as everyone else,' the Intelligence Officer said cautiously.

'If he was pretty much the same as everyone else I wouldn't have bothered to come. If he wasn't *different* I'd be at home now in front of my bloody fire. If you can't be straight with me then I'm wasting my time, and I'll leave you in peace . . .' Rennie drained his glass, slapped it down on the polished table at his elbow. 'If you are able to be straight with me then . . . then Mr Ferris might just be very useful to me . . . Colonel, if it wasn't important, then I wouldn't be here.'

Sunray had little time usually for policemen in the Province. This man he could respect. A rough-cut stone, and a hard, tired face.

'Tell him, Jason.'

'There's no family tradition in the army, he's not the sort we usually get. He tried for a University commission, but he didn't get the college marks so he went to the Royal Military Academy, came to us that way. He's in our Regiment, but I wouldn't say he's part of us. Tried to leave us last year when we'd finished in Crossmaglen. He went for the Special Air Service selection course. Understand me, it's not against him, but SAS evaluation of him was that he lacked the necessary cutting edge for that outfit . . .'

Sunray cut in. 'If the army was confined to graduates and SAS qualifiers it would be a pretty small army. Wouldn't have me for a start.'

'He's a quiet man, Inspector Rennie, doesn't put himself about. If we have a Mess thrash, then he won't be there, not his scene. He'd regard the likes of me as a black and white merchant, therefore a bit stupid.'

Sunray said, 'His men are quite obviously fond of him. Which may not always be a good thing.'

'He has a pig-obstinate streak. If something's stuck in his head then it's time wasted to try and talk him out of it. And he's a doubter, if you know what I mean.'

'What does he doubt?' Rennie asked.

'What we're doing here, what else? ... Example, he bawled me out the other day after he'd P-checked this McAnally creature, before the RPG hit. I said he should wake up to the fact that we were fighting psychopaths, he was jabbering about human beings. We had a bit of a stand-up.'

'It's what I hoped to hear,' Rennie said. 'I'd like to borrow Mr Ferris from you, Colonel.' Rennie smiled. He held out his glass. 'And I'd be obliged for the other half.'

The ambulance was already waiting inside the barracks yard when Ferris brought in Mattie Blaney's boy. The tears had stopped. Ferris thought it must be the shock setting in.

His squaddys hadn't talked on the drive back to the barracks. It was as if a message had sunk through to all of the soldiers in the Land Rover; if the enemy would do this to a child, to one of their own, then what would they do to a soldier if they were ever able to lay their hands on him, what would they do to a plain clothes soldier of SAS or Mobile Reconnaissance Force or Intelligence Corps . . .? And the thought was enough to make Ferris shiver.

The priest had arrived at Springfield Road. The squaddys called him 'F Two' or the Fucking Friar. He was Father Francis . . . It was said that he spoke the Gaelic language as a first choice, and was more fluent there than in English. Whenever there was an incident he was always fast down to the barracks from Turf Lodge. He was young, not out of his twenties, and wore short-cut hair and heavy pebble glasses over pink cheeks that were hardly ready for the razor. The officers in the Mess all reckoned that he prayed on bare knees each night for the ground to open up and swallow all of the British army in Northern Ireland and then close over and suffocate them. The priest made a point of brushing against one of Ferris's soldiers as he went forward to watch the boy being lifted into the rear of the ambulance, and he could have walked round the soldier. He seemed to whisper in the ear of the boy before the doors were closed.

Ferris felt the anger rising in him. They were told always to be polite to priests. Headquarters laid down that the priests were a moderating influence on the community and were a necessary vehicle by which to detach the population from the clutches of the Provisionals. Headquarters only talked to the bishops.

'Quite a nice class of parishioner you have, Father Francis . . .' Ferris said.

'Mr Ferris, isn't it? I presume it's what you wanted, Mr Ferris, a boy knee-capped, or a man executed.'

'What I wanted? . . . Absolute bullshit.'

The priest glared at Ferris. 'Obscenity is usually the hallmark of a second-rate vocabulary. You lifted Sean McAnally, a good family man, a man living in the south and trying to renounce violence, you lift him when he comes home to see his wife, and then you make your vicious insinuation in the media . . .'

'What the hell are you talking about?'

'You let it be known that an informer had led you to Sean McAnally. You know what happens to informers, Mr Ferris. That's why I say with confidence that the mutilation of this child is what you wanted.'

The priest turned to walk away.

'That's just not bloody true,' Ferris called after him.

The priest swung to face Ferris. 'I haven't the time to stand around, Mr Ferris. I have to go to the Royal Victoria Hospital to offer consolation to a small hurt child while the surgeons rebuild his knee-cap. They do a good job, but he'll never run again. Then I have to go to his mother. Someone has to try to sweep up the filth left by your dirty tracks.'

The priest was gone, out from under the arc lights, out into the night. The high iron gates closed behind him.

Ferris shook his head, as if there was a bad taste in his mouth and a pain in his forehead. He had heard the phrase 'anonymous tip-off' on the radio, and he'd wondered, and he'd had a laugh to himself about it when the Intelligence Officer had explained the ploy. Christ,

76

what a bloody awful place. He had used his sleeve to wipe the tears off the child's cheeks.

The Intelligence Officer was standing in a doorway, watching. He would have heard the exchange.

'Sunray's office, David.'

Ferris went to the Weapons Pit, aimed at the sand, cleared his rifle, and headed for the Intelligence Officer. He felt betrayed. There was a sort of a truth in the accusation of F Two. 'Psychological Warfare' the Intelligence Officer called it. 'Dirty Tricks' the priest called it. And both *knew* they were right . . .

He followed the Intelligence Officer to Sunray's office.

He saw Rennie sitting in an easy chair, with a glass in his hand, and comfortable. Sunray didn't offer Ferris a drink. He went straight to the point. Detective Chief Inspector Rennie had made an unusual request that Ferris be from time to time available at Castlereagh. There was nothing frivolous about the request, and he had been convinced of the urgency of the matter and so had waived the normal etiquette of consulting with Lisburn Headquarters. Ferris should put himself at Detective Chief Inspector Rennie's disposal. Ferris looked at his watch. Near to ten o'clock.

'Let's shift ourselves, young man.' Rennie acknowledged the drink with a nod to the Commanding Officer, and led the way out.

Ferris travelled in Rennie's car. Hell of a job holding a Self Loading Rifle in some state of readiness while sitting in the passenger seat of a saloon. There was a police Land Rover behind them. Rennie drove fast, eyes alert and scanning the road ahead and the pavements. There were occasional bar crawlers meandering on the streets' sides. Generally the pavements were deserted.

The silence was broken by Ferris as they came off the Grosvenor Road to cross the centre of the city. He wouldn't have spoken while they were in 'hostile' territory, wouldn't have distracted the driver.

'It wasn't true that we were acting on a tip-off for McAnally . . . whoever put that out should be bloody well ashamed of himself.'

'I put it out,' Rennie said. 'And, Mr Ferris, it'll take a lot more than that to shame me.'

'It was a kid.'

Rennie looked away from the road, looked into Ferris's face.

77

'I've been fighting this war for more than fifteen years. In that time a few things may have happened that I regret having happened. But I don't need a lecture on mistakes from someone who's been here eight weeks . . . there's a war going on here, Mr Ferris. You want some victims of the war? Try the Pentecostalists hymn-singing when they're shot down, try the nurses who're going to bed when the hostel's bombed, try the folks having a meal out at the La Mon when they're incinerated. I care about those victims, worshippers, nurses, folks having their dinner. I care about them more than I care about a Provo kid getting his knee blown.'

'And the kid isn't what I've been dragged out for?' Ferris said brusquely.

'Don't tell me you're knackered, lad, we're all knackered. And don't tell me it's unfair, because everything that happens in this God-forsaken place is unfair. Listen, my mates are buried here. That's why I care about winning this war. That's why mistakes don't keep me awake.'

'I'm listening.'

'So listen, and don't interrupt.'

Ferris grinned. 'Let's have it, Mr Rennie.'

'First the logistics. We're allowed four interviews with a prisoner in any one day, and the day finishes at midnight. We'll be at Castlereagh at eleven, and we've had three sessions with our laddie . . .'

'With McAnally?'

'Do us a favour, young man, shut up . . . I have one more hour with McAnally before I have to tuck him up for the night, and I don't get back to him until he's had his cooked breakfast in the morning. That's the logistics. Now the history . . . In the old days, when the police role was upgraded to primacy over the army, we were given the job of criminalizing the paramilitaries. We had to get them into court and win a conviction on a criminal basis – murder, attempted murder, possession of firearms, membership of a proscribed organization. No witness'll dare to come forward, can't blame them, so we used to be a bit physical in persuading the "freedom fighters" to sign away their liberty. They confessed and the courts locked them up, and the politicians across the water got faint-hearted and started screaming. We were filling the Kesh up, putting the bastards away . . . That's history. Castlereagh's wired for cameras now. There are uniforms crawling up the bloody corridors. Confessions don't come easily any more. Got the picture?'

They went out into the south-east suburbs. Tree-lined roads, solid family houses. Home for the Protestants to sleep safe in while the war was fought in their name away in the ghettoes, away to the west of the city.

'Got it.'

'So, we had to find another way. We have one thing going for us here, it's the only bloody thing. We have money, we have as much money as we can spend. We had to stop thumping the confessions out of them, and we started to buy the information we required. We bought informers . . . Twenty-five a week in old notes, or fifty, or up to a couple of tons if the leak was good and sharp. PIRA doesn't like informers, so the bodies started showing up on the wasteground. Our informers were getting the message that it wasn't a pensionable job. We moved on, we started to work on those we already had safe in custody, those that were safe from a kangaroo court and a bullet. We called it the Converted Terrorist policy . . .'

'Supergrass.'

Rennie was bent over his wheel, talking quietly into his dashboard.

'The Brits have to anglicize every bloody thing. "Supergrass" is your word, from the East End of London. "Converted Terrorist" is mine. To the Provos, he's a "tout" . . . Even the bloody man in Stormont Castle calls them "supergrasses" . . . if that's what you want, David, we'll call them that, we'll keep it British. It's a genius trick . . .'

'When it works.'

'It's genius because they don't know where the risk comes from next. They have to spend half their bloody time wondering whether they're going to be shopped by their own crowd.'

'I read the papers, I'm not a damned idiot, you've had some that have worked, you've had more that have reneged on the deal.'

Rennie ignored the interruption. He had a cigarette in his mouth and was lighting it with a match and turning left and changing up through his gears. Expert hand and eye.

'We've found something of a pattern for the man who might go supergrass. He's in the twenty-five plus age group. He's beyond the aggro corner stuff, petrol bombs and stones, he's too old for that. He's got a woman, probably he's got kids. He's got a fixed address. He's done a stretch inside, knows what the Kesh is like. He's come back out and returned to his old ways, and he's been lifted, and this time he's going away for a lifer, or as near as makes no difference. He's on a treadmill because with his record and his new offences he's going away until he's an old man. That's the one we convert.'

'That's McAnally,' Ferris said softly. He saw ahead of them the high brilliant lights of the Castlereagh perimeter. He felt the trembling of his hands on the stock of his rifle.

'When you lifted him he was still wearing his vest, silly bugger, and very considerate. They don't learn. Forensic's done the work on the vest. Forensic puts McAnally on the RPG. Your Fusilier puts McAnally into the getaway car. McAnally's away for twenty-five years, that's what I've told him.'

'Why me?' Ferris knew the answer.

'For a man to turn, he has to make a hell of a decision. He's chucking over his shoulder everything that he knows, every single bloody thing except, perhaps, his family.'

They had come to the gate. Rennie held up his I/D for the police sentry to see from the gatehouse window.

'Why me?'

'He's turning his back on everything he's ever relied on before, and he has to have a hell of a trust of us.'

'And he trusts me, is that why it's me?'

'Something like that.'

Rennie accelerated into the Castlereagh car park. He stopped, switched off the engine.

'Once they start there's no stopping them. It's getting them started that's the hard bit. Get Gingy McAnally started tonight, and I'll kiss you on both bloody cheeks of your arse.'

Rennie climbed out of the car; when he looked back he saw that Ferris was still sitting in his seat, staring ahead through the windscreen, expressionless.

'I told you. I haven't all night.'

'I don't know whether I want to do it.'

Rennie climbed back into the car, his knee was on his seat. He lowered over Ferris. 'Don't fucking tell me what you *want* to do. You can't choose what you *want* to do . . . you just bloody get on with it.'

Ferris slammed the car door shut behind him. He went to the gatehouse and accepted a chitty for his rifle. He followed Rennie through the inner gates and into the cell block.

He had been briefed in the canteen over a tired cheese sandwich and a beaker of coffee. He knew what he had to say. He knew the time that had been given to him.

McAnally was sitting cross-legged at the head of the bed. He wore his trousers and was bare from the waist up because he had taken off his shirt, and they had taken away his vest.

Ferris sat on the floor, his back to the wall. The cell was dimly lit from the ceiling. The cell was warm. McAnally said nothing.

Ferris talked, and sometimes McAnally seemed to listen, and sometimes he was a year away, and sometimes a mood away, and sometimes he reacted and squirmed, and sometimes he screwed down his face as if the emotion was too great to bear. Ferris could see that McAnally was exhausted, twenty-two hours since he had been lifted, desperate for sleep. Ferris thought that if McAnally had not been so tired he would have to have seen through the clumsiness of the subterfuge.

Ferris said that he happened to be at Castlereagh at that time because he had been out on patrol and this was the first opportunity for him to make a formal statement, hadn't had the time when he was down before. He had drifted on, a rambling monologue.

'. . . we were patrolling Turf Lodge, round your home. The lights were on upstairs, I suppose they'd gone to bed, didn't see anyone, we didn't knock on the door. It's three kids, isn't it? I'd have liked to have spoken to your wife. If the lights were on upstairs, I suppose she was putting the little ones into bed. That's a hell of a boy you've got . . .'

Drifting on, just as he had been told.

'I'm a bit upset tonight, actually. We saw a pretty horrible thing in Turf Lodge. I had a call-up from one of my foot patrols that was out in tandem with us. They found a boy who'd been knee-capped. I'd never seen a knee-capping before. I think he's thirteen, the boy they knee-capped, and they'd burned his stomach with cigarettes. I took him down to the barracks and packed him off in an ambulance. He couldn't really talk. Shock, I imagine. He was really brave . . . God, I can't imagine what the pain would be like. It seems that your friends reckoned he'd informed on you. His name's Liam Blaney . . . I suppose you know him. I was told they can fix these things up pretty well in the Royal Victoria. He was really gutsy . . .'

Ferris could not take his eyes from McAnally's face. He saw when he scored, and he saw when McAnally was able to deflect him. But the face was more rested, not in such turmoil. The eyes were less haunted.

'The policeman who took you away from us, I was talking to him this evening. He told me that you'd made it out of the Organization. From my side of things I shouldn't say it, but that must have taken a damn great effort. He said you were down south, that you'd gone down there to live. It must be really difficult to break out . . . Well, it must be difficult, but I suppose it's wonderful that you can go to bed at night and know that you'll sleep through to the morning, that you won't have the likes of my platoon heifering in on you . . .'

There was a weak, poor smile on McAnally's face.

'You were the first Provisional I'd ever seen, you know. I'd seen guys up for screening, that sort of thing, guys that the IO said were in the Organization, but you were the first real live one . . . They've told me now that you're implicated in the Crumlin Road thing. That's bloody dreadful . . . I mean, you made the effort and went down south. I suppose they brought you back for this, for the RPG job . . . sorry, don't say anything, I'm not a detective. When I say that's bloody dreadful, what I mean is that it's dreadful that the buggers couldn't leave you alone. There's you, building a new life, and then this happens . . . To me, not leaving you alone down there is worse – yes, I reckon it's worse – than what was done to the Blaney boy . . . God, I can't get that kid out of my mind, can't get away from knowing that after what was done to him he'll never run again, never kick a football . . . I know my squaddys turned you over a bit, you got one of them in the goolies, but what they did to you, that's nothing like what was done to Liam Blaney . . .'

Ferris looked at his watch. McAnally's eyes seemed to plead with him as he stood up.

'Sorry, I have to be off, look at the bloody time. They took your watch, of course . . . it's close to midnight. If I see the wife about I'll speak to her, tell her you're in good shape.'

He went to the cell door. He rapped his knuckles on it. When he looked around he saw that McAnally faced the wall.

'Good night, Mr McAnally . . . Try to find a way to help yourself . . . after what the bastards have done to you, after the shit they've dropped you into, see if you can help yourself, and your wife, and your kids . . . God knows what's possible now. If anything's possible, hang onto it . . . Good night, Mr McAnally.'

Ferris looked for a last time at the face in profile against the wall. He felt soiled. Rennie had decided that a serving officer of 2 RRF was soft enough to strike a chord with an RPG marksman of the PIRA who faced a triple life sentence. And the shit had decided right. McAnally bit at his lip and muttered at the white-painted bricks of his cell wall. Rennie had known his chemistry.

'Do you know anything about kestrels, Mr Ferris?'

'No, sorry. I don't,' Ferris said.

The constable had opened the door, made way for Ferris to step out of the cell.

Standing by the protected door at the end of the cell block, Rennie watched Ferris come towards him. He saw Ferris pass under a bright ceiling light. He looked for the mood. His cheeks broke into a smile. He sighed deeply in relief. He saw the trouble in Ferris's face.

'Well done, David . . . and if you didn't know it, the war's bigger than that little rat.'

'Your little rat asked me if I knew anything about kestrels.'

'What did you say?'

'That I didn't know anything.'

'Then find out.'

'Why?'

'Because a kestrel's freedom, that's what I want him talking about, thinking about.'

# 6

When he was active, before he had gone south, in the time that he was on the RPG team, the Volunteers and Battalion men were briefed on the tactics employed by the interrogators, and on the countermeasures to confound those tactics. The men who gave the briefings were those who had been with some frequency in the solitary cells and the Interrogation Rooms of Castlereagh in Belfast, in Gough in Armagh, or Strand away in Derry. The first twenty-four hours weren't the hardest, the briefers said, because the prisoner was still close to his home and his family and his muckers, but the isolation was clawing at the prisoner by the second twenty-four hours, and was worst for the third twenty-four hours. After three days, the briefers said, then the isolation slipped. They could only hold you for seven days. After seven days they had to charge you, or release you. After seven days the prisoner was either turfed out to make his way back to his family, or he was booked and shipped off to the crowded Remand Wing of the Crumlin Road. Seven days was the length and breadth of the isolation. For seven days the prisoner saw only the escorting policemen and the interrogating detectives. And the second and the third days were the worst, because after the third day the prisoner was on the downhill road and heading for the company of his family or the Remand Wing. The briefers said that if a man was to implicate himself or himself and his friends then he would do so on the second day of solitary or on the third day. The briefers said that it was the easiest for the man who could stay silent ... Shit, McAnally had tried to stay silent, he'd even laid down on the floor to get away from the water-drip of their voices, and the bastard Rennie had followed him down to the floor. The briefers said that it was the worst for the man who tried to argue the facts put before him. The briefers said that it was good if you could get a small stone or a sliver

84

of glass into your shoe and under your toes, if you could squeeze your toes down and hurt yourself and turn your mind from the questions. The briefers said that the detectives would always pretend they knew everything. The briefers said that the detectives would try to turn you, and they'd offer money, money and immunity from prosecution and safety for a lifetime in return for a statement that betrayed the Organization.

Sean Pius McAnally had six more days of resistance.

And after the six days? After the six days there was a year of remand. And after the year of remand? After the year in the Crumlin Road there would be a sentence with the recommendation that the prisoner serve a minimum of twenty-five years.

He thought he could remember each day of his five years served in H Block 7 . . . Shit, this was a five years' sentence times five. This was every day of five years times five. Every day in a two bunk cell times five, every strip search and cell search times five, every visit from Roisin and her mother and his mother and Young Gerard times five, every sneer from the screws times five . . . and every year when the victory wasn't closer times five. After five years times five his mother and her mother would be dead, and Roisin would be age lined and – shit –Young Gerard might be in another cell in the block.

Day after day in the caravan near Vicarstown he had sworn to himself that he would never go back, never reinvolve himself in the Organization . . . because he would disintegrate under the weight of another five years times five.

He had told the bird about the Kesh. When the bird had the freedom to fly, and when it perched in the branches over the caravan door for the bacon rinds, he had told it about the compounds and walls and cell blocks and keys and bars and watch towers of the Kesh. The bird knew what the hell it was about. The bird could fly from the trees by the caravan and soar in the winter winds high above the canal. He had once gone into the library in Monasterevan and he had found a book on Falconry on the shelves – first time in God knew how long that he had taken a book from a shelf – and he had read about the equipment used by people who kept tamed birds of prey. He reckoned it was all shit. He reckoned the hoods and jesses and the leash and the bells were the same words as compound, wall, cell

85

block, key, bar. To trap that bird and tame it would be to sentence his kestrel to the Kesh. In his mind he could see the bird, and he wondered if the farmer, his mother's cousin, had come to the caravan to feed it. He wondered if the bird waited for him, or if the bird had flown.

The cells were sound proofed. He was alone and stifled in his own silence.

They wouldn't hurt him, not like they had the last time. Who needed to be slapped and kicked and punched when they had six more days of him in Castlereagh, and a year on remand, and twenty-five more years in H Block 7? Jesus Christ . . . and he had sworn an oath, an oath of loyalty on the landing above the stairs of his Da's house, and never had a doubt that he could handle the bloody oath.

The cell door opened. McAnally hadn't heard the footsteps approach down the outer corridor.

The policeman looked at the prisoner curiously, like he was a bloody freak.

'You all right, McAnally?'

Why shouldn't he be all right? Only got six more days and then a year on remand and then twenty-five years in H Block 7.

McAnally nodded his head. So bloody tired, and a pain behind his eyes, and the figure of the policeman in the doorway was blurred. The policeman in the doorway spoke with an English accent, one of the bastards who had come across the water to do a dirty job. They were always the worst, the English ones. They had a bolt to run to, back home.

'Bring your tray here, McAnally.'

Without thinking he picked the tray off the cell floor and carried it to the policeman. There was a trolley in the corridor, and another policeman who eyed him with distrust and dislike.

'What time have you, sir?' McAnally asked.

'What time? Breakfast time, of course.' And the policeman was laughing with his mate as he closed the door, locked it.

He hated them, because they were the enemy. And when he had the RPG in his hands, then the bastards wouldn't be laughing at him. He tried to remember the feel of the RPG. So bloody long ago . . . Two days ago.

★    ★    ★

86

'What happened last night?'

Armstrong passed the marmalade to Ferris. He had been on Ops Room duty when Ferris had returned from Castlereagh.

'Not a lot.'

Wilkins slid the butter dish across the table. 'You slunk in last night like the world was on your shoulders.' From the Chaplain's room, enjoying a coffee, he had seen Ferris returning to their room.

Armstrong persisted. 'Something must have happened for them to want you down at Castlereagh.'

'I was put in with McAnally.'

'What on earth for?'

'To turn him,' Ferris snapped. 'What else could it be for?'

'Shirt on, old chap, just asking.'

'And now you know.'

Wilkins said, 'Hope of a supergrass, eh? That's the big time for a platoon commander.'

Armstrong said, 'I suppose he's all wet round the privates now he's in the cage.'

'I'm trying to eat my bloody breakfast.'

'Is this going to happen often?' Armstrong was filling his coffee cup.

'What's it to you?'

'If you're going to be swanning off to Castlereagh then George and I are the buggers who're going to be covering your rosters, that's what it's to do with us.'

'My advice, David,' Wilkins said deliberately, 'don't get involved.'

Ferris clattered his chair back. A triangle of toast was buttered on his plate, untouched. He stormed to his feet.

'I didn't bloody ask to be involved. I was told it didn't matter a toss what I wanted.'

'Supergrass is police work.'

'Pity nobody said that last night, when I was hijacked.'

'Not a chance, not if he's like he was when I had him yesterday.' The detective, McDonough, had done five years in Criminal Investigation, was reckoned a good interrogator.

87

'You weren't there for the last session, I was,' Rennie said harshly. 'And he had his soldier friend for Horlicks before we tucked him up . . . There's a good chance.'

'He's going down for triple murder. What's on offer for him?' Astley was younger than McDonough, more obviously keen.

'Nothing specific's on offer, but McAnally's a shaky boy right now, and needs to be kept shaking.' Rennie closed his file.

'You're on hand this morning, Mr Rennie?' McDonough asked.

Rennie hesitated. 'Not this morning, got some business. After lunch I'm here.'

'Nothing on offer then?' Astley was polishing his spectacles. More of a schoolmaster than an interrogator.

'For a few names, for jumping up in the witness box, there might just be no recommended minimum,' Rennie said.

'Out in seven years, fifty bloody per cent remission.' McDonough's lips twitched in disgust.

'Like I said, for a few names.'

The Secretary of State stood bareheaded in the light rain. This once he had contradicted the Detective Inspector who was responsible for his personal safety. The Detective Inspector would have had him stay in the church after the service, and avoid the graveside because there was a crowd gathered at the church gate, and they had jeered the Secretary of State on his way in, and when the body was down and covered their inhibitions would be slight. He had insisted that he should go to the graveside whether or not the threat existed of kicks and fists and stones.

William 'Tenner' Simpson was being buried in a village church-yard north of Ardmillan, within sight of the dark islands littering the inshore waters of Strangford Lough. It was Protestant country. It was the country of people loyal to the Crown.

'Yet, O Lord God most holy, O Lord most mighty, O holy and most merciful Saviour, deliver us not into the bitter pains of eternal death.'

Not a wet eye in sight, the Secretary of State thought. These were not whining folk. They stood straight-backed, straight-faced. They ignored the Secretary of State as an unwelcome interloper. He would not be ignored at the church gate. When he left the consecrated ground the crowd would angrily show their gut feelings for the security policy over which he presided.

'Forasmuch as it hath pleased Almighty God of his great mercy to take unto himself the soul of our dear brother here departed, we therefore commit his body to the ground.'

The Prime Minister had been on the telephone before he left Stormont. Prime Minister's Questions in the House that afternoon, and a question down calling yet again for the Secretary of State's resignation and demanding to know what action was being taken against the Republican gangs who could assassinate a judge in broad daylight . . . He would dearly like to have told the Prime Minister that a Sean Pius McAnally was to be charged with Billy Simpson's killing. He had only replied that a man was helping police with their inquiries, and heard the whistle of impatience on the scrambled line.

'Earth to earth; ashes to ashes; dust to dust.'

The soil scratched the coffin wood.

The Secretary of State felt the light tap on his shoulder, and turned to his civil servant.

'Bit soon, Fred,' the Secretary of State mouthed.

'No-one here will miss shaking your hand,' the civil servant said. 'You've been photographed here, that's good enough.'

He flushed. He walked away from the mourners. The civil servant was at his side. There were eight detectives in a wall around him. They went out through the gardener's gate of the churchyard to where his car and the back-up were parked alongside the grass cuttings and the compost heap. Uniformed policemen were holding back a knot of sullen-faced men and women. The widow was still at the graveside. He might get away without an incident. The detectives were hurrying him, almost forcing him to run. The crowd loathed him because they held the man from Westminster responsible for the atrocities of the Provisionals . . . The back door of the car was open for him. The civil servant nudged him forward, pitched him down into his seat. The cars surged forward. For a moment a woman's face was pressed against the armour-plated window by the Secretary of State's head. He heard her howling at him, couldn't understand what she told him. A constable heaved her back, and the car and the back-up were away.

'What did she say, Fred?'

'She said, "You'll be making him a supergrass, the rat that killed our Billy, and giving him immunity", that's toned down a bit.'

'The man who killed a judge get immunity for grassing? Over my dead body.'


McDonough smoked a pipe. Astley lit a cigarette. McDonough was pacing. Astley lounged against the wall.

McAnally sat at the table.

'So you haven't an offer to make to me?'

Astley shook his head.

McDonough said, 'What's on offer, Gingy, is three life sentences . . .'

'What about a bloody offer?'

'With a recommendation of a minimum number of years to be served.'

'We reckon the judge'll recommend twenty-five, Gingy,' Astley said. 'He's hardly going to go easy when it was one of his own.'

The breath sighed in McAnally's mouth. Sometimes he could see Astley's watch. He had been in for an hour. There had been long, aching silences. They didn't seem to be interested in talking to him, they seemed prepared to let him sit at the table and brood on twenty-five years.

'You've got a problem, Gingy,' McDonough said earnestly.

'Twenty-five fucking problems.'

'That's quite witty, Gingy.' Astley chuckled.

McAnally scratched his forehead. He thought of his oath. He thought of Roisin and Young Gerard and Little Patty and Baby Sean. He thought of the men who had been on the hit with him, and the men who had brought him up to Belfast from the caravan. He thought of a life sentence in H Block 7. He had no stone in his shoe, no splinter of glass to press against his toe. They always called him 'Gingy'. Whether they shouted at him, whether they whispered at him, he was always 'Gingy'. His friends called him 'Gingy', his friends on the RPG team, and the men he had known in the Kesh who were still in the cells there, behind the wire there. Who were these bastards to call him 'Gingy'?

The quiet was broken by Astley's hacking cough, a smoker's cough. Then, after he had cleared his throat and snorted into his handkerchief, the quiet was back again and simmering through the room.

'What's the best that could happen?' He heard his own voice booming back from the walls.

'That "Tenner" and his two 'tecs could walk through the old door, that's about the best that could happen . . . but they won't come through the door.' McDonough was beating his pipe bowl into the tinfoil ashtray on the table. 'So I don't know what's the best that could happen.'

'Don't piss on me.' McAnally's eyes raced between the two men who watched him without passion. 'What are you offering me?'

'We're not in the offering business, Gingy,' Astley said.

'We don't have to offer you anything, Gingy,' McDonough said.

'We've got three life sentences on you,' Astley said.

'With a minimum recommendation,' McDonough said.

'What I'd suggest, Gingy . . .'

'Listen carefully, lad.'

'. . . is that you have a little think, on your own . . .'

'Try and think what we might be grateful for.'

'There's just a possibility, Gingy . . .'

'No more than a possibility.'

'. . . that we might get a judge to forget the minimum recommen-dation,' Astley said.

'If we were to say that we were really gratful,' McDonough said.

'Why don't you have a little think, Gingy?' Astley's hand was on McAnally's shoulder. He jerked him upright, and frogmarched him to the door.

'Some quiet thinking, Gingy,' McDonough said.

Middle morning in Turf Lodge. The patrol moved circumspectly through the estate. Upstairs curtains were drawn in 31 and 35 and 39 and 47 and 53 of the Drive. Ferris noted the drawn curtains. He knew the men in those houses had no work. The wife would have been up early to see the children to school with their sandwich boxes, the man would have stayed in his bed. The man would get up before lunchtime, and in the afternoon he would take his place on the corner of the Drive and the Avenue if it wasn't raining and gossip with his cronies, or stand in silence beside them to watch the slow-moving life of Turf Lodge. Ferris knew that there was fifty per cent plus unemployment amongst the men of Turf Lodge. He supposed there were estates on the fringes of English towns where the workless rate was as high. What he did know was that there were no estates in English towns through which soldiers walked with so great a caution.

David Ferris's father was a bank manager living on the outskirts of the Lancastrian town of Preston. He firmly believed in the advice offered by an English politician, that the unemployed should get on their bicycles and set off in search of work. David Ferris's father knew nothing of the life of Turf Lodge, and less than nothing about what his son did in the Turf Lodge Estate.

The middle of the morning was a bad time for the patrols ... Earlier, there would be the children and their mothers going to school, and at lunchtime there would be the mothers collecting the smallest children, and in the afternoon there would be the older children coming home. The soldiers were always more relaxed when the pavements and roads were filled with children. The risk of bombs was always greatest when the streets were empty; the car bomb, the bicycle bomb, the culvert bomb, the pipe bomb, the booby trap bomb. The bomb could be resting in the boot of the rust-damaged Ford Cortina parked half on the pavement and half on the gutter, it could be laid in the strapped-down bag on the back of the bicycle seat, it could be placed under the man-hole cover in the pavement, it could be stuffed into a length of builder's plastic piping, it could be under the wood stairboard of a derelict house. The bomb could be detonated by remote command, by wire control, by contact.

David Ferris thought that his father, sitting in the manager's office in his bank, would not have been able to comprehend what it was like for his son to walk through Turf Lodge mid-morning in early December. He knew his mother and his father went to church now, he knew that they prayed each week for his safe return from that barbarian place, and would do until his sixteen weeks were done.

He saw Mrs McAnally, with her push chair and with the little girl beside her legs, come out through the broken gate of 63. She was on the same side of the road as Ferris, coming towards him.

The soldier in front of Ferris made way for her to squeeze between him and a front garden hedge. She had her eyes down when she passed the soldier. When she looked up, Ferris was in front of her. For a moment she stared at him, recognizing him.

'Mrs McAnally . . .'

He saw her lip curl in dislike, the tired prettiness of her was wiped away.

'I saw your husband last night.'

For a moment her chin quivered, as if she were about to reply to him, then she thrust the push chair forward and the wheel bounced on his boot and a wing bolt caught at his trouser legs, and she was past him.

He felt a sense of despair. For a few seconds, the time it took him to move a dozen yards, his mind was clouded by the disgust in her mouth and eyes.

And she would have seen him dead, he knew that, and if he had been dead in the Drive it was a good bet that she would have clapped.

Sean Pius McAnally lay face down on the mattress of his cell bed.

His hands covered his eyes. His wrists protected his face from the bedding material.

The thoughts bellowed in his head, and tortured him. The thoughts were of opting out, of going south again and turning his back on the Organization, the thoughts were of a lonely life in the caravan beside the canal. He hadn't asked to be brought back. He hadn't asked to have the bloody RPG put into his hands . . . and he hadn't asked to be dumped in a cell in the Castlereagh Holding Centre, staring twenty-five years in the Kesh in the face.

In his agonies, lying on his stomach, Sean Pius McAnally resolved to fight to win his freedom. He didn't concern himself with the morality of the decision, nor with the consequences. His thoughts were simple and immediate. They were of the echoing cold wings of the H Block, and of his children crawling over him, and of the warmth of Roisin against him in the night, and of the bird in the tree above the caravan, and of the clean night mists rising from the canal.

Abruptly he sat up and faced the door of the cell and waited for the policeman to lead him back to the Interrogation Room.

The police band was far to the front, crying out the death march. Howard Rennie walked in the tenth row of mourners behind the hearse. In the first rows of mourners were the family of the Detective Sergeant who had died in the Crumlin Road, and behind the family were the Security Forces' public faces – Chief Constable, Deputy Chief Constable, GOC NI, GOC Land Forces who had helicoptered in from Billy Simpson's burying. Rennie was back amongst the 'tecs, with the men who had worked with the Detective Sergeant and who faced the fair old risk of following the same trek into the Roselawn cemetery.

She was a great girl, the widow. She'd not let herself down, not in the church, not at the graveside.

Rennie knew the Presbyterian Minister who was burying his friend. He'd heard him at the last police funeral for a parishioner, heard what'd he'd said about the killers of a policeman. If the Minister came down to the Interrogation Room at Castlereagh, and sat in on the questioning of murder suspects, then he'd wipe the waffle about conscience from his funeral addresses. Rennie had yet to discover remorse in the Interrogation Rooms. Regret at being caught, yes. Conscience, never.

He would be going straight back from Roselawn, with the grave earth on his shoes, to Castlereagh, to the murderer of his friend.

'Don't go biting my head off, I'm just telling you there's a powerful anger at what happened to Blaney's boy. That's all I'm saying.'

'Who's angry?' The Chief sat in the snug of the bar on the Falls down at Beachmount. There was a man on the door of the snug. The drinkers in the main bar could not see in. That morning the Chief was holding court for two members of his Brigade staff and the Falls Provie Battalion Commander. It was a dark recess of a room, with the small window's light diminished by the heavy protective mesh outside the glass. 'Who's bloody angry?'

'People are angry, people from the Blaney boy's street.' It was rare for the Provie Battalion Commander to take on the Chief.

94

'Gone soft on touting, have they, in the Blaney brat's street?'

'They're angry because they say he's not a tout, they say no boy of Mattie Blaney would be a tout.'

'There was a court martial . . .'

'He didn't admit to nothing.'

' 'Course he wouldn't bloody admit it. It was legit . . . I'll not have fucking touts, who's ever son they are.'

'That's my place up there, Turf Lodge, that's my swim . . .'

The Chief leaned forward across the table. He hiccupped sweet and sour breath. 'Touts kill us . . . got it? Touts kill us, so we kill touts. The Blaney boy was lucky he wasn't killed . . . got it?'

'What if he wasn't a tout?'

The Chief's fist darted across the table, caught the collar of the Provie Battalion Commander and twisted so that the collar bit into his throat. 'I don't want to hear about the Blaney boy. I don't give a shit for Mattie Blaney's boy. I care for Gingy more than Mattie Blaney's boy . . . and Gingy's in fucking Castlereagh . . .'

The fist loosened its hold.

'I was just telling, you, that's all . . .' The Provie Battalion Commander was a window cleaner. He was good with a rifle, and poor with words. He wished that he had kept his mouth shut. In the subterranean areas of his mind he cut off the thoughts of Mattie Blaney's boy and the cigarette burns on the kid's stomach, and the screaming, and the blood from the smashed knee-cap. He cut off the thoughts because he was aware in all his waking moments of the Chief's principal fear, the fear of touts.

There was a knock at the outside of the door to the snug. The door was opened a few inches. A paper bag was passed in. The Provie Battalion Commander thought he might be sick at the stench of the Chinese cooking.

'I'll be away.'

The Chief was dragging the tinfoil caps from the food bowls and the plastic fork from the bottom of the bag.

'If we don't hit at touts, then the touts will destroy us,' and the Chief was busy with his food.

★    ★    ★

95

He was brought into the Interrogation Room, he sat down, and he heard the door close behind him, and he said, 'If I make a statement, what'll you do for me?'

Behind him Astley smirked. In front of him McDonough sucked at his pipe.

'What's for me if I talk.'

McDonough's expression was a mask. 'I am Detective Sergeant McDonough, this is Detective Constable Astley. Sean Pius McAnally, you are not obliged to say anything unless you wish to do so, but what you say may be put into writing and given in evidence . . . Can we have that again, Gingy?'

'If I make a statement, what do I get for it?'

McDonough played indifference. 'If you make a statement implicating yourself, a little bit. It might count for a bit, not a lot. If you make a statement that implicates others, then a little bit more . . . but this is the wrong way round, Gingy. The way it happens is that you make the statement, and then the Director of Public Prosecutions has the say in what happens to you. I don't make deals . . .'

'That's not done at our level, Gingy,' Astley said.

'It has to be a matter of trust, Gingy,' McDonough said. 'You have to trust us, because there's no other bugger for you to trust. I'll put it frankly, Gingy, we'd need an awful lot from you to count in the smallest way against what you've done. What I'm really saying, lad, is that I can't see that you could give us enough to do yourself any good . . . I said I'd be frank.'

McAnally was trembling. His body shook and the legs of the chair on which he sat tapped out a beat on the floor as he rocked the chair backwards and forwards.

'Can't I say anything that'll help me?'

'Have to be a terrible lot said to help you, Gingy.' Astley's voice was quiet, soothing. 'And we don't make the offer, we don't give any inducements. You have to ask, Gingy.'

His fingers were pattering on the table. He was breathing heavily. There was a sweat sheen at his throat.

Smoke clouded from McDonough's pipe between them.

McAnally looked into McDonough's face. He saw the hard,

uncaring mouth of his enemy. He saw the pitiless eyes of his enemy. The words seemed to croak from his throat.

'I want immunity.'

'Immunity, Gingy?' McDonough whistled his surprise. 'Two 'tecs blown away, and a judge, and you want immunity?'

'Immunity from prosecution.'

McDonough shook his head, theatrically slowly. 'I can't see it ... Can you see it, Detective Constable Astley? I mean, how do you get immunity from three murder charges?'

'That's all I'll talk for, for immunity.'

'Going supergrass, Gingy, is that what you're saying?'

''Course it's what I'm saying ...' The words rattled from McAnally.

'Are you talking about going the whole hog?' McDonough spoke as if to a child.

'Into the box, Gingy? Into the witness box to give evidence?' Astley asked quietly from behind.

'Into the box, if I get immunity ...'

The words hung in the air, hung with the smoke of McDonough's pipe. McAnally glared at McDonough.

Why did everything have to be repeated again and again? And why didn't the bastard smile and look pleased?

McDonough sighed. 'Wouldn't it be lovely, Gingy, if it were so simple. Two 'tecs killed, and a judge, but Gingy McAnally's going to go supergrass and inform on a few of his horrible mates, and we're going to pull in a handful of PIRA Volunteers, and he's going to get immunity. Wouldn't it be lovely, Gingy?'

'What do you mean?'

'Cop on, Gingy ... What have you got to offer that's equal to two 'tecs and a judge ...? Sorry, wrong, not equal ... What have you got to offer that's bigger than a conviction of an RPG man for three murders?'

'There's another matter, Detective Sergeant McDonough,' Astley said.

'What's the other matter, Detective Constable Astley?' McDonough asked.

Astley said easily, 'Why did they bring Gingy back from the south? They brought him back because they knew he was good on the RPG. Where did he get to be good on the RPG? Got to be good when he was using it, stands to reason. Stands to reason that Gingy's so damn good on the RPG that he's the man they have to have . . . Stands to reason he's used it before. Stands to reason there are other charges of a very serious nature that we haven't even come round to thinking about yet.'

'Gingy, I'm corrected by Detective Constable Astley. I should have said . . . What have you got to offer that's bigger than a conviction of an RPG man for three murders, and for crimes that we haven't even come round to thinking about yet . . . It really isn't going to be easy. You do see that don't you, Gingy?'

McAnally felt the sweat drip from his neck to the small of his back. He felt the damp in the fold of his stomach, and running to his groin. He seemed to hear the clanging of the cell doors in the H blocks, and the laughter of Young Gerard. He seemed to feel the wet cold of the Kesh exercise cages, and the fire heat of Roisin. He seemed to know the loneliness of the prison wings, and the peace and freedom of the caravan beside the canal. The hysteria was rising in Sean Pius McAnally.

'The guys who were with me in the Crumlin Road . . .'

'Volunteers in an ASU . . . ? Not enough,' McDonough said.

'The ones who brought me back.'

'Couriers, nothing . . . they're rubbish.'

'The guys who briefed me.'

'Battalion Ops, Battalion Intelligence, can't see that being enough, Gingy.' McDonough's voice fell to a whisper.

'The fucking Chief briefed me,' Gingy screamed at him.

McDonough smacked the bowl of his pipe into his hand, dropped the remnants into the ash tray. He was reaching in his pocket for his tobacco pouch.

'Come again, Gingy?'

'The Chief briefed me.'

'Belfast Brigade Commander?'

'He briefed me.'

'Who was with him when he briefed you, Gingy?'

'Brigade staff – Quartermaster, Intelligence, and Operations.'

McDonough was filling his pipe, filling it like a blind man, by touch. His eyes never left McAnally's. 'When you were briefed it was by the Belfast PIRA Brigade Commander, and Quartermaster and Intelligence and Operations of Brigade, that's right?'

'That's what I bloody said.'

'And that's what you're offering us?'

'For immunity.'

'And you'd make a statement, and you'd go into the witness box?'

'For immunity.'

McDonough struck a match. It was a moment before his flame found the filled bowl of his pipe. 'Would you get Rennie in here?'

The door closed behind Astley.

'Is that enough, for immunity?'

'I don't know,' McDonough said, and stood up, and stretched himself. 'I don't make the decision, thank God.'

Astley followed his knock, strode into Rennie's office. He was beaming with excitement.

'McAnally's going to cough . . . He's going to give us the Brigade staff . . .'

Astley saw the black tie pulled loose on Rennie's throat below the unfastened top button.

'For immunity, he'll give us the Brigade staff in Belfast.'

Rennie clasped his hands, rested his chin on his fingers. 'Little bastard,' he said.

'It's what you hate, isn't it, Mr Rennie, seeing them go free after what they've done?'

'The comfort I get, young man, is in the knowledge that it's a rough sort of freedom.'

He closed the file on his desk. He thought of the widow who had stood tall and proud at the graveside. He leaked a quick half-smile at Astley. Rennie walked out of his office, and towards the Interrogation Block, to begin the process of turning the man who had made that girl a widow.

# 7

The uniformed policemen who patrolled the corridors of the cell block and the Interrogation Block at Castlereagh knew the signs. There had been enough of them in the previous two years for them to read the signals that heralded the turning of a prisoner.

On that afternoon the uniformed policemen saw Howard Rennie and Astley stamping down the corridor on the ground floor of the Interrogation Block . . . Another little shit had changed sides to save his neck.

The uniformed constables always saw the plain clothes detectives as the cowboys, the mavericks. They liked to smile behind their hands when the 'tecs came pounding out of the Interrogation Rooms in search of a senior man. They shared something of the excitement now when they heard that Blackbush bottles were being opened up in the Administration offices, but they liked to smirk with each other when the deflation set in, when a convert turned the rest of the circle and retracted.

It was one thing, the uniformed policemen would have said, to get a Provie to make a statement implicating his former friends, and quite another thing to build into the bastard the courage to go, weeks and months later, into the witness box to testify. The uniformed policemen had seen and heard the celebrations. Also they had seen and heard the wakes of the detectives when word slipped through that another supergrass had retracted.

Astley closed the door of the Interrogation Room behind himself and Rennie, shut out the interested eye of the uniformed policeman who hovered in the corridor.

'Let's get the formalities through,' Rennie said. 'I am Detective Chief Inspector Howard Rennie. You have already been cautioned by Mr McDonough and Mr Astley. Now let's hear what you've got to say.'

McAnally sat limp in his chair. The presence of Rennie seemed to crowd the room around the prisoner. McAnally slowly straightened, as if the movement exhausted him.

'I want immunity. If you give me immunity I'll make a statement . . .'

'What's the statement going to tell me?'

'Who was with me, when I was on the hits . . .'

'That's not good enough.'

'Who briefed me. I was briefed for Simpson by Brigade.'

'Names?'

'Yes.'

'You're offering that for immunity?'

'That's a hell of a lot, that's more than you've ever had.'

'And you'll go into the witness box, into court?'

'I've said I will.'

'And you're asking for immunity?'

'And I want my wife out, and my kids. I want to be shipped out.'

'I don't know that I can deliver, Gingy,' Rennie said.

'You've got to deliver,' McAnally's voice was rising. Big eyes, staring eyes, beading onto Rennie. 'I can't go back in there, not into the Kesh, not for twenty-five . . . I can't.'

Rennie's hand snaked out. He patted McAnally's shoulder gently. 'Easy, lad.'

'Everything I can bloody give you, I'll give you, but don't put me back in there.'

'Easy, lad, because it's not that straight.'

'I've said I'll go into the bloody court, I'll finger them, the whole of Brigade . . . What more do you bloody want?'

'Gingy, listen . . .' Rennie was bending over McAnally, and his hand had secured a father's grip on McAnally's jersey. 'Listen . . . last year, and the year before, we were into chucking immunity about in return for a promise of going into court and giving evidence. We got to look a bit silly, Gingy. Too many chickened out, too many retracted . . .'

'I'll go the whole bloody way, I swear I will.'

'All the ones who retracted, they all swore they wouldn't.'

'What does that mean?'

'It means that it's a bad time for me to promise immunity, and for you to promise to deliver.'

McAnally's head lurched forward onto his hands. Rennie wondered whether he was about to weep. He reckoned that he had seen them all, all the marksmen and the bomb-makers and the executioners. Bloody awful figure they cut when they were alone, without an Armalite to cradle.

'You won't do it?'

'Did I say that, Gingy? Listen to me. What it comes down to is a matter of trust. We both have to trust each other. You have to trust me, and I have to trust you. Trust is a two-way thing. Are you listening, Gingy?'

McDonough watched, and shook his head slowly. Jesus, and you had to hand it to the old man. Winding the bugger up, wasn't he?

'Trust, Gingy . . . You have to trust me, as I'm going to trust you. You have to talk to me and trust that I'll do the best I can for you. It might be no minimum recommendation, it might be immunity, you have to trust me. That's one side. There's another side. I have to trust you. A statement from you, naming names, naming dates and places, that's no use to me unless I get you into court, unless I have you under oath and standing up to cross-examination. Two sides to the coin, Gingy. The trouble is, Gingy, can I trust you?'

'Trust, you and me, you're fucking joking, Rennie,' McAnally snorted. 'Forget it. It's immunity or it's nothing.'

McDonough choked. Astley had stiffened straight, no longer leaned against the wall. Rennie was flushed, angered.

'I'm one man,' McAnally said, spitting. 'I'm sod all use to you in the Kesh. The Brigade staff, that's useful to you, that's more bloody useful than me. I want an answer.'

Rennie bit at his lip. His fingernails were driven into the soft part of his hand. He controlled himself. 'I'll get you an answer, Gingy.'

Rennie spun on his heel, strode out of the Interrogation Room.

'If it's a joke, Fred, it's a joke in the poorest taste.'

'The Chief Constable isn't given to jokes.'

The Secretary of State pushed back the tray on his desk. The civil servant helped himself to a sandwich, and wiped his lips carefully with his handkerchief.

'I can't make a decision on immunity.'

'The Director of Public Prosecutions makes the decision. The Director is answerable to the Attorney General in government. The Attorney General is in Cabinet, as you are. If you were to recommend to a political colleague that he should take a certain course of action . . .'

'The Prime Minister would have to sanction it.'

'The Prime Minister would, you are quite correct.'

'Can you imagine . . .'

'What the Prime Minister would say? I've a fair idea. The Chief Constable's taking an unusual course. He's bringing with him the Detective Chief Inspector handling McAnally.'

'To confuse me with security jargon?'

'To put you in the picture.'

'When's he coming?'

'Half an hour.' The civil servant reached again for a sandwich. They were potted shrimp. He fancied the Secretary of State's wife had made them up in the flat. They were quite excellent.

'I've got the Moderator then, to hector me about the security of his flock on the Border.'

'He's on ice, you're fine to see the Chief Constable.'

'Damn you, Fred. I detest letting a beast like this McAnally go free, whatever he does for us.'

The civil servant smiled. 'Principles are a luxury, sir, in wartime . . . I'll sit in on the Chief Constable and his hatchet fellow.'


Ferris's Land Rover arrived at the supermarket with the first of the ambulances. The street in front of the supermarket windows that were festooned with cut-price advertisements suitable for dole customers was filling with Pigs and police wagons. The shoppers who had been inside at the moment of the raid and the shooting were spilling out onto the wide forecourt of the supermarket. He saw the shock and white numbness on the faces of the housewives. Bloody amazing, wasn't it, that fifteen years into the Troubles these folk could still manage a snatch of shock? Bloody daily occurrence, wasn't it, a hold-up that went wrong?

He saw the Company Sergeant Major. Ferris went to him.

'You want a Sit. Rep., Mr Ferris?'

'Just what's happening will do.' Ferris saw the CSM pucker his mouth in amusement. All the Battalion NCOs knew they couldn't lure Ferris into the army shit talk.

'A couple of heroes went in after the Christmas Savings fund box. There's a pay-out this afternoon. Assistant Manager said it was in the safe and he hadn't the key, got himself shot as encouragement to fish in his pocket. An RUC mobile trotted past as the heroes were bunking. The old Bill put down a barrage like it was Port Stanley, they've managed a grannie, the heroes managed to leg it. They're off into Andy'town now.'

'Descriptions?'

'Good laugh, Mr Ferris . . . Deaf and dumb brigade here.'

Ferris watched as the first stretcher was carried out. There was a young man, on his back, with his mouth wide open and his breath coming in short bursts. His shirt was blood-soaked . . . What a vile place, what a bloody awful place to spend a bloody awful afternoon. He saw the old lady who lay at the far end of the forecourt. They'd covered her head with a blanket from the back of the ambulance, a warm scarlet blanket. Her ankles protruded from the blanket and Ferris saw that she wore thick stockings and sensible shoes, and the blood seeped from under the blanket by the bulge that was her head. She'd be there until the police photographer arrived.

He walked away from the CSM. He'd go through the routines. He went to a crowd that had gathered to watch the casualties and the ambulance men and the milling police and the crouched soldiers in their fire positions. Jones, his driver, was close behind him.

'Anyone see what happened?' Ferris managed a good, authoritative voice.

'The peelers shot Mrs Murphy.'

'Only just out of hospital, and the fucking bastards shot her down.'

'She'd a hernia, murdering pigs.'

'Mrs Murphy wasn't thieving, didn't stop her getting shot.'

Perhaps he should have laughed in their faces. Perhaps he should have laughed until his stomach hurt.

'There was a robbery . . .' Ferris said.

'And the peelers came and killed Mrs Murphy, out for her week's shop.'

'Did anyone here see the robbers?' Ferris tried to be deliberate and spelled out his question as if talking to backward children. 'Did anyone here see the two men who carried out the robbery on the supermarket?'

'I's seen Mrs Murphy shot . . .'

'Bloody murdered, more like.'

'I's seen the peelers do that.'

'But you didn't see the thieves . . . ?' Ferris stared at the faces of the crowd. 'You didn't see the Freedom Fighters . . . ? You didn't see the bloody freedom fighting ASU attacking the legitimate target of your own bloody Christmas box . . . ?'

'Don't you fucking swear at us, you fucking Brit cunt face.'

Ferris turned to his right, sought out the voice. She was quite a pretty girl. She was about seventeen, and she wore a tight sweater under her open anorak and tight jeans, and her mouth was twisted in a savage arc.

'Pithily put, Miss.'

He went back to the Land Rover. Ferris and his escorts and Jones mounted up. He told Jones that they would tour round the Andersonstown sidestreets, away behind the supermarket. It was a case of finding something to do.

They drove off the main road, into the maze of small streets flanked by red-brick houses.

'She needed a good fuck, that cow . . .' Jones observed. 'Ever get the feeling you're wasting your time here, Mr Ferris?'

'That's not the kind of thought permitted to an officer, Fusilier Jones.'

They drove through Andersonstown for half an hour. Since they had no idea of what their fugitives looked like or were wearing, it was a wasted effort.

When their radio called them back to barracks they drove past the supermarket. A smaller force of police and soldiers were still in position and white ribbons marked the area of the incident. The shoppers were streaming round the ribbons, in and out of the supermarket. Ferris couldn't see the bloodstain from the old lady's wounds, washed by the rain.

'Fusilier Jones, if we weren't here then it would be even worse than it is,' Ferris said. 'That's why it's worth us being here.'

Fusilier Jones kept his eyes on the traffic in front of him. 'If you say so, Mr Ferris.'

McAnally had eaten his lunch in his cell. The uniformed policeman had given him a cigarette when the tray was taken away. The uniformed policeman knew McAnally was special, and had given him one of his own Bensons. He sat on his bed. McAnally was an oasis in the cell block. All the cells were occupied. He was the one who had turned, who had asked for immunity. In the other cells were men from the Provos and from the INLA and from the UVF and from the Ulster Defence Association. Castlereagh was not sectarian. The Prod paramilitaries had the cells beside the Taig paramilitaries. He drew on his cigarette. He rarely smoked. Roisin always had a fag in her mouth, even when the baby was on her knee . . . It might have been the strength of the cigarette, it might have been the fact of his asking for immunity, but he felt light-headed, like he'd sniffed glue. All the cells were taken, but his was different. In his cell was a man who had turned, a man who had offered to break the oath of the Organization. And it had all been so easy . . . Sean Pius McAnally was not a man to examine his own navel, but he chuckled to himself when he considered how easy it had been. And he had the bastard Rennie running every bloody which way, had him sprinting up his arse. He'd make a statement. He'd give evidence. What was the big deal about giving evidence? No big bloody deal . . . He'd give evidence. Then there was the new life. There was a life outside Belfast, a life outside Ireland . . . All so bloody easy, all so bloody simple.

He would be living a new life with Roisin and Young Gerard and Little Patty and Baby Sean, while the H Blocks were full, while the courts were full, while the bloody cemeteries were filling.

They'd reckoned Gingy McAnally was a pushover when they'd come down to the caravan beside the canal, they'd bloody learn what it could cost them.

Supergrass . . . Super Gingy . . . Super McAnally . . . Super hit man on the RPG . . . Supertout.

He was laughing. His laughter cracked back at him from the cell walls. He felt no remorse at the treachery. He felt no guilt at the betrayal. He felt an ecstasy because he believed he had avoided three life sentences with a recommended minimum of twenty-five years to be served.

Super Gingy McAnally, and no bloody pushover for any bastard.

'Every instinct, Chief Constable, every instinct I possess points to the moral and political dangers of granting this man immunity.'

The Secretary of State was fighting his corner, and losing.

The Chief Constable was a brusque short man, glorying in his reputation of direct aggression when confronted with politicians.

'Your instincts are wrong, Secretary of State.'

'It's a dirty business, the supergrass business, and shown to be fallible.'

'The policy of the Converted Terrorist has provided us with a greater fund of intelligence than we've ever had on the PIRA.'

'Every retraction after the granting of immunity makes us a laughing stock.'

'That's the worst, Secretary of State, the retractions. Even if there's a retraction we have still gained valuable information.'

The Secretary of State believed the Chief Constable to be a non-drinker. He never took a drink when they met socially. He believed there to be a direct link between monumental pomposity and alcoholic abstinence.

'I've been in this job three years, for the first time in that three years I believe I am close to dealing a very considerable blow to the mainstream effectiveness of the PIRA ... political dangers are not my concern. As to moral dangers, I would regard myself as being as aware of those as any other man. I want to hit the Godfathers. I want immunity for McAnally.'

The Secretary of State fidgeted on the settee. That had been his first error, sinking down into the soft cushions while the Chief Constable sat on a high-backed chair, on the raised ground where he could dominate. And Fred was no damned help, kept his mouth shut. And all the time there was the towering figure of the detective that the Chief Constable had wheeled in, and who stood behind his master's chair as if he was struck dumb.

'McAnally's a murderer.'

'We'll have a dozen men charged with murder, and we'll have the Brigade staff for conspiracy.'

'Cabinet won't agree to it.'

'You have to make them agree to it, otherwise there are many people alive and well at this moment who will lose their lives, if those Brigade staff men go free.'

'That's rhetoric, Chief Constable.'

The Secretary of State heaved himself up from the sofa. The room was too hot, he was perspiring. He went to the window. He felt as if his room was invaded.

'What do you want of me?'

The Chief Constable's voice softened with the fruits of victory. 'I want you to speak with the Attorney General, and I want you to listen to Mr Rennie. Mr Rennie is one of two officers based at Castlereagh who head the Converted Terrorist programme. He is a formidable opponent of the Provisionals, who have twice tried to murder him. I want him to tell you at first hand of the importance of the Brigade staff of PIRA.'

'Tell me, Mr Rennie.'

'I went to a funeral this morning, Secretary of State, as you did. I carried the coffin some of the way. He was an old friend, a good friend. He was killed by Sean Pius McAnally . . .'

Such a stern, strong face, the Secretary of State thought. God, would he ever be rid of these suffering, intense faces. He was an intimidating man, this Rennie. The Secretary of State rarely met the men who fought the war in the middle echelons. He met the Generals and the Chief Constables at conference, and he met the private soldiers and the constables for fast casual conversation.

'I spend my time locking away Volunteers. I never get my hands on the men who control those Volunteers. Brigade staff don't carry weapons, they don't carry target maps, they don't carry my photograph. The rubbish kids carry the weapons and the maps and the photographs. Brigade stays above incriminating evidence. If I can get a man into court to give evidence against the Brigade staff then

I will have severely damaged their movement. I need McAnally to have immunity, I need McAnally to know that he's not going down. I have to win his trust, perhaps even his affection . . . and he killed my friend. The Brigade men believe they're safe from us. I don't want them to feel that any more.'

The next weekend the Secretary of State would be at his English home, on his Yorkshire acres, and while he was out on the moors with his dog, this man would be in the Interrogation Rooms at Castlereagh. He saw Rennie hesitate, question to himself the wisdom of speaking again.

'No, Mr Rennie, I want to hear everything.'

'The ghettoes in this Province, sir, are maintained by two factors, fear and loyalty. By breaking with his people McAnally has cut his loyalties. They'll work the fear on him. It's a fear that it's difficult for an outsider to comprehend, because it's the fear of a bad death at the hand of your own people . . . What I'm getting to is this. If we're to use McAnally against the Brigade then we have to show trust in him. If we try and kick him into the witness box, or trick him in, then we'll fall on our faces . . . Sir, he's gone further down the road than I'd dare go. Myself, I'd rather do the twenty-five years.'

'And for us to win his trust you want immunity?'

'Yes, sir, I want immunity for McAnally.'

The Secretary of State said, very quietly, 'So be it.'

'Thank you, sir.'

Rennie's eyes roved over the room, as if hunting down a whisky decanter. Not a drop in sight. The Chief Constable stood with his briefcase and looked ostentatiously at his watch. The civil servant showed relief, because the Moderator could still be fitted into the schedule.

The Secretary of State smiled, the public smile. 'What sort of fellow is this McAnally?'

'A disgusting little wretch, sir,' Rennie said.

Disappointment clouded the Secretary of State's face. 'If I'm to argue for his immunity I'd like to have heard him spoken better of . . . You won't fail me?'

'You'll have my best effort, sir.'

*　　*　　*

Ferris was tumbled off his bunk by the shout of the adjutant. He was led to the Commanding Officer's room.

A telexed order from Lisbon HQ was handed him. The GOC's office instructed Sunray to make Lieutenant David Ferris available at all times possible for liaison with Detective Chief Inspector Howard Rennie, RUC Castlereagh.

'It's not of your doing?'

'No, sir.'

'What's being cooked?'

'I don't know, sir.'

'I don't like clever games that get in the way of professional soldiering.'

'It seems I don't have much choice, sir.'

'You've no choice, and neither have I, which is why I don't like it. What's so special about you and this McAnally man?'

'Nothing that I know of, sir,' Ferris said.

Sunray looked curiously at Ferris. 'The battalion's an open family, David. The battalion doesn't have secrets.'

'I'm as much in the dark as yourself, sir.'

A police Land Rover was standing ready to take Ferris away from the Springfield Road barracks.

The identity of the Chief, who had taken over responsibility for the running of Belfast Brigade two and a half years previously, was known to only a small handful of men in the city. As a figure in the background of public events, the Chief had seen off the threat of informers that had threatened to strike at the very intestines of the Provisionals' Organization. One after the other, the supergrasses had copped out, backed down, retracted. The Organization had survived, but was now warier. He reckoned the Organization was tighter than at any time since he had grasped the rank of Belfast Brigade Commander. He operated on the need to know philosophy. Through a labyrinthine chain of command he controlled the activities of the ASUs, their weapons' systems supplies, their financial support through the robbing of banks and Post Offices and businesses, and the discipline of the movement. This chain was well disguised. No Volunteer could finger him, nor a Company officer, nor the men who ran the skeleton staffs of the Battalions. Those who formed his Brigade companions were friends from the beginning of the war. He liked to read of the frustration of the Prime Minister, expressed in British newspapers, at the inability of the Brit forces to trap and capture him.

The Chief was a militarist. He had studied the history of the freedom wars. He fought a battle of attrition. It was the attrition of his own comrades that had brought him to the command of the Belfast Brigade. He believed in no sudden stroke that would collapse the British administration and the Protestant resistance. He rarely made speeches, but when he talked late at night to his cronies, and they sat around him in a respectful silence, then he talked of striking at the defenceless base of the powers of occupation – hitting the policeman overseeing the school road-crossing, the headmaster who was a part-timer in the Ulster Defence Regiment Reserve, the unarmed prison officer coming off duty. The Chief would have preached to his faithful that if the ordinary man walks alone in the shadow of death while the big men of the community are cluttered with bodyguards, then the ordinary man will lose confidence in the Brits' ability to protect him. 'Tenner' Simpson was an exception. 'Tenner' Simpson was a good target, a popular target with the boys, good for the boys in the Kesh doing their tenner handed down by Simpson. The Chief would fight until he was captured or shot dead by the Army's SAS or MRF squads or the police Support Units. He had a deep contempt for the former fighters who had discarded the Armalite and taken to electioneering as candidates for Provisional Sinn Fein. He despised them because he reckoned they'd sold out of the only game that mattered, the fighting game. He was contemptuous of them because he reckoned that campaigning for housing conditions and drains and bus routes was the poorest substitute to beating the Brits where it mattered, on the street battlefield. What was relevant was sending Brit soldiers home in boxes, and having the police band play the death dirge into Roselawn.

He was a lonely man. When he had been a street aggro organizer he had been able to swim with the crowds. When he had been rated as a marksman, one shot only and that a killing shot, he had moved with the companionship of the Volunteers. When he had led the First

Battalion, he had still moved with a kind of freedom. He was lonely because the commander of the Belfast Brigade had to be. And lonely, too, since the death of his wife. Mary was an indifferent replica of his wife, younger and prettier but nothing in comparison. The Brits killed his wife, that was what he said . . . On the afternoon after a dawn army raid on his home, she had taken an overdose. He had been away, down south, negotiating with the Army Council for a shipment of weapons. The army had come and wrecked his house, they had torn up the floorboards, ripped open the thin Housing Executive walls. She had emptied a bottle of Nembutal down her throat. The Brits had killed her . . . It had never crossed his mind that any responsibility for her death lay with him, that the OC of the First Battalion had in fact brought the soldiers into his home.

A lonely and desperate man sought by thousands of troops. A ruthless and skilled man hunted by thousands of policemen.

Because the Chief had dedicated his life to the campaign to drive the Brits at barrel point from the Province, he was a man of rare calibre in the Organization.

Beyond the windows of the maisonette in which he stayed the afternoon was going and the evening closing down on the street outside. The downtown radio headlines had told him of the unsuccessful raid on the supermarket in Andy'town. The headlines in the morning would tell whether there had been success for the sniper ASU in Clonard. The war went on, in failure and success, the war of attrition.

Rennie had met Ferris at the entrance to the Interrogation Block, taken him from the escorting constable.

'What am I here for?' Ferris said aggressively.

'You're here because I said I wanted you here.'

'That's not a reason.'

'You're here because what you can do in Castlereagh is a damn sight more important than anything you'll do traipsing the streets,' Rennie said.

'Are you going to tell me?'

They went into the Interrogation Room. Bare walls, no decoration. A table and two chairs. Ferris faced the two detectives already there.

'This is DS McDonough ... this is DC Astley ... David Ferris, Lieutenant.'

They shook hands, Ferris and McDonough and Astley, with caution.

'Sit down, David.'

Ferris sat at the table. The policemen all stood. He felt the damp in his clothes from the day's rain, he felt the twelve-hour stubble on his chin.

'You have a line into McAnally, and that's a line we're going to hang onto. Trust is the name of the exercise, and McAnally trusts you. You're going to believe me when I tell you that we are doing our damndest to get McAnally immunity ... in return for the full works ...'

'How full's that?'

'PIRA Belfast Brigade, and going into court to give evidence. It's a hell of a chance that we're taking, David. What I'd say to you is that without your co-operation the chance isn't worth taking.'

And the damned Intelligence Officer had advised that he shouldn't get involved ... Jesus.

Ferris remembered the faces of McAnally. The face in the back of the car, nervous. The face in the P-check on the Drive in Turf Lodge, frightened. The face in the yard at the back of 63, broken. The face in the cell block the previous night, despairing. He wondered what the face would have been at the moment of firing the RPG, at the killing of a judge and two policemen.

'You'd better bring him in,' Ferris said grimly.

McAnally was at the table. He knew it was different. More than two 'tecs in the Interrogation Room told him the rule book was out of the barred window.

Ferris was opposite him, sitting as well. The big 'tec, Rennie, was behind Ferris. The other 'tecs were behind him.

It was hard for McAnally to concentrate. All the good news was spilling out of Ferris's mouth and into his ears. All the bloody good incredible news.

'You're *going* to get immunity, Mr McAnally ... the problem is that we can't say that for definite, not now, not at this moment, but we know you're going to get it. It's got to go to the DPP, and then to the Attorney General, and he'll have to clear it in London. Because of who you are, and what's involved, you're going to get immunity but the nobs in London have to give the green light. That's going to take a few days . . . Before we get it for definite you've to trust us, Mr McAnally. We've five days left, and then the police have got to lift the men you've named. You see, under the Prevention of Terrorism Act after seven days you're either to be charged or released. After seven days you go into protective care, and the lifts are on. If you're not released and you're not charged then everyone'll know that you've turned and they'll run. They'll vanish. And your evidence will be of no use. You've got to start talking to Mr Rennie and his colleagues *now* . . . I know that you're going to get immunity. I really believe that, Mr McAnally . . .'

'And a new life?'

'A new life for you and Mrs McAnally and for your children.'

'Out of here?'

'Right away from here . . . It's going to happen, Mr McAnally. You believe me, Mr McAnally?'

'I believe you.'

'And they're going to trust you, Mr McAnally, that you'll go through with it.'

'I'm going to do it, Mr Ferris. I bloody swear I'll do it.'

'Stand up in court, Mr McAnally.'

'You can trust me, Mr Ferris, as I trust you.'

There was no weight on his soul. He arced his neck back as if that was the way to prove to himself that the weight was gone from his back. He thrust out his hand. He saw the officer hesitate, and then respond. Their hands met. He felt only the sense of the freedom.

And McAnally was laughing, laughing back at the officer, and gripping his hand. He didn't see the slow satisfied smile on Rennie's face. He was laughing fit to bust, he was laughing so that his shoulders quivered, and his hand and the officer's hand banged on the table as he laughed.

He was still laughing when he heard the rasp of Rennie's voice.

'Very good, Gingy, now let's start earning that immunity.'

*       *       *

No-one had been to visit her, not through the whole day.

But then Roisin McAnally had been out and away from the Drive until the late afternoon. Her Ma had been in the house, her Ma didn't always hear the door knock. Her Ma had been there from lunchtime looking after Little Patty and Baby Sean, and Young Gerard had been at school. She had been into the city. She had sat for more than an hour in the waiting rooms of Mr Pronsias Reilly. She had spent a black taxi fare both ways because she couldn't wait for the buses. Most times Mr Pronsias Reilly acted as defending solicitor for men from Turf Lodge. She hadn't an appointment, hadn't found a telephone in Turf Lodge that was coin box and working ... and over her dead body would she have gone crawling to a neighbour to use a phone and know they were all listening from the front room to what she said in the hall ... she'd sat for seventy minutes in the waiting room outside Mr Pronsias Reilly's office, and been told first that he was in court and expected back, and then that he'd gone across to Crumlin Road Remand Wing for a prisoner interview ... He wouldn't be back. She had never before met Mr Pronsias Reilly. He was just a name that she'd heard of until she had seen his photograph on the wall of the waiting room – fat and sleek and doing well from Legal Aid, doing bloody well from the boys who were behind the wire. She had to have a solicitor. She had to have a solicitor to bang on the gate at Castlereagh and demand access to Gingy. He was her man ... She'd packed her Ma off and protesting that she'd help with the tea ... What bloody tea? Sausages and spaghetti hoops ... She couldn't stand Ma fussing her, and fussing the kids, not when Gingy was in Castlereagh ... There was a sale of clothes at the church in the morning, she had to go to the sale, had to find shoes for Little Patty, had to get the shoes before she could think of going back to the city on another day in search of an interview with Mr Pronsias Reilly.

'Ma ... Ma ...'

She was in the kitchen. She was frying the sausages slowly. If she fried them too fast they burned and the goodness was wasted. She heard the piercing voice of Young Gerard.

'You come here, Ma.'

She was in time to see on the television the familiar flashback pictures of Judge Simpson's car. She stood in the doorway. She could hear the sizzling of the sausages on the ring. Young Gerard turned to her.

'They showed two peelers getting buried . . . did our Dad blow the fuckers out?'

She turned, and went back to the kitchen.

'Bring Patty, Gerard,' she called. 'Your tea's ready.'

Rennie paced the Interrogation Room, never speaking.

McAnally talked.

McDonough sometimes prompted, mostly sat quiet at the table facing him, nodding encouragement.

Astley sat at the table that had been brought in and placed behind McAnally and filled the pages of a notebook.

Always begin at the beginning, Rennie taught his interrogators. They had started with Sean Pius McAnally's release from Long Kesh four years before. There were no time limits set against them now, they would talk deep into the night. The bastards always amazed Rennie. The matter-of-fact description of a killing with an RPG. A constable's life swept away, and told like it was the scoring of a goal on a Corporation soccer pitch, and names named like they were the other boys in the team. Later, he would slip out of the room to telephone his wife and warn her that he would be late home, again.

He had sent Ferris back to his barracks before the note-taking started.

'. . . Shay was on lookout, Shay saw the Land Rover turn into Whiterock. There was this gap between the garages. I couldn't see the Land Rover, not till after Shay shouted . . . Eug passed me the RPG when Shay shouted. We'd been there three times before in two weeks. I fired. Dommy took the RPG off me. We didn't stop about, we just pissed off. I knew I'd hit it . . . We ran to Flaherty's place. He'd got some cans in the fridge. We had a few cans, then we went home. It was really good, the RPG, went a dream. Eug drove me home from Flaherty's . . .'

Stroke of luck, latching onto the Ferris boy, Rennie thought.

# 8

While Sean Pius McAnally gushed his recollections to his interrogators, Belfast spluttered and coughed and existed through the winter days.

Every morning and every afternoon and every evening the rain dripped down onto the streets outside the high fences and the tin walls and the locked doors of Castlereagh. Alone with McDonough and Astley, in oil-fired warmth, lit by bright fluorescent strips, McAnally talked. He wore clean socks that they had brought him, and new underwear, and he was allowed a razor for his personal use, and he was cocooned from the breathing and dying of the city.

A comedian from cross-Channel played at the Opera House, and told the BBC Northern Ireland interviewer that he always liked to play in the Province because the audiences were the best in the United Kingdom, and the interviewer gave him a tired grin and wondered why the star needed to be so patronizing.

An industrialist from Germany came and looked at the dead De Lorean car factory and talked to the Chamber of Commerce of a thousand chemical plant jobs, and the businessmen clapped him and wondered why he had lied.

A Royal cousin-in-law journeyed to the Province and planted a tree and opened a children's wing at a hospital, and spoke from a prepared text of the courage of the civilian population, and the nurses wondered what option anyone had but to show courage.

As the Secretary of State flew to Heathrow he mused to his civil servant whether back-bench oblivion might not be preferable to the running of Northern Ireland.

The flowers were dying on William 'Tenner' Simpson's grave.

A young part-timer in the Ulster Defence Regiment was outside his mother's house in Finaghy cleaning his car when the assassins came for him, travelling by motorcycle, and sprayed at him with a Mauser and missed and decapitated his mother's cat, which was probably why the incident rated space in the English newspapers.

A man was shot dead in his house in Newtonabbey, but the police press desk told the journalists not to concern themselves because it was only family, which was why the killing didn't go cross-Channel.

A boy of sixteen years, five months out of school, appeared before the city magistrates charged with writing down police number plates as they left Andersonstown RUC station.

The Chief Constable issued a warning that men prominent in public life should take especial precautions against Republican gunmen ... A Guards battalion completed their tour and sailed home on the Liverpool boat, and more than a hundred were sick with relief and alcohol before they docked ... A priest issued a statement to the *Irish News* complaining of army brutality in Ballymurphy ... A Protestant politician called a news conference to denounce the Security Forces' softly softly approach to terrorism.

Outside of the perimeter of Castlereagh, the days slipped by, unmemorable and unremarkable.

Each in his differing way, McDonough and Astley were good at their work.

They were trained to show no animosity to the informer. They listened to the catalogue of hits and attempted hits and aborted hits without ever revealing their disgust. They had both been on the course with the English psychiatrist who had talked of body language communication with the informer. Nothing that they heard appeared to shock or horrify them. Not the death of a constable, not the blinding of a soldier. McDonough always probed for the information. Astley always wrote the verbatim at the second table. Through the passing days they saw the growing cockiness of McAnally, as if he revelled in the attention given him. They let it ride, they made no attempt to deflate that cockiness ... Soon enough Gingy McAnally would be put to the test, and then the louse would need all his cockiness.

'... I wanted to get the Pig in the middle. I reckoned if I got it in the middle that I'd do the squaddys inside. If there's a Pig out then there'll always be half a dozen squaddys in the back. A Pig's a sitting duck arse for an RPG. We were down in Beachmount, there's plenty of Pigs come up the Falls through Beachmount. We took over this house . . . There was just an old gasser in the house, Fatsy watched him, I went upstairs with a young lad . . . didn't have a name, not to me. It didn't bloody work like it should have done. We had the window open, of the front bedroom . . . Shit, it stank in the old gasser's bedroom, he slept on bloody newspapers . . . It didn't work because the Pig braked just as I was on the trigger. Once you start on the trigger you can't help yourself, it's like pissing. The squaddy braked just as I was firing, when I was still on the engine. The engine went up, only did a bit of damage to the driver, didn't even kill him. I went down the bloody stairs, like I got the claps. You know what Fatsy was doing? I'm hitting a Pig with a bloody RPG, and Fatsy's supposed to be minding this gasser, and Fatsy's got the back off his telly and he's fixing the line hold for him. You know what, Fatsy went back and finished the job three days later. That's rich . . . The lad and I and Fatsy, we got out the back of the house, and belted . . .'

'Fatsy was who?'

'Fatsy Rawe . . . we belted down Iveagh Parade to where the motor was. Bugsy was on the motor. We went down Broadway. I reckoned we got out just before the blocks went in. It was a real bad one because the kid didn't show who was to take the RPG. We had to keep it with us. Couldn't hang about could we . . . ?'

'Who's Bugsy?'

'We call him Bugsy, he's Eamonn Malone . . . You know what . . . I pissed myself in the car. I pissed myself down my leg. I went home to my woman and I had to go straight upstairs and change my pants, so she wouldn't see. I got a load of stick for that one, they said I should have held the fire, or got the Pig in the middle. Those bastards, they don't know what it's like on the RPG. You have to line the RPG up, and if you fire it in a room you're dazed afterwards, I know. You try telling the bastards . . .'

'Who were they, Gingy, who gave you stick?'

'Jimmy Flanagan, Noel Connelly, Brennie Toibin, they were Battalion . . . They gave me some stick because they said the RPG warheads were gold dust, they said I only wounded the squaddy and didn't get all the rest with him. But they split their heads when they heard the kiddie hadn't turned up to take the RPG. At least he got a beating. It was gold dust, the RPG. Because we hadn't dropped it, Bugsy took the RPG home. It was behind his sofa for a week . . . That's a bloody laugh, his missus was screaming blue about it, so he told her to fuck off and cracked her. The whole thing was a shambles . . . I mean, we got one squaddy, but one squaddy isn't worth an RPG round. Well, it isn't, is it? It was just bloody cowboys . . .'

The Secretary of State was rarely invited to Downing Street other than for Cabinet. He was in London every week of the year, whether the Commons was sitting or whether in recess, but he seldom received the summons.

Inflation was down, the pound sterling was steady, unemployment was at last bottoming. Central government's posture was buoyant and aggressive. It was trumpeted that the nation's health was improving. Only Northern Ireland cracked the mould of success.

The Secretary of State had not raised the matter of immunity for McAnally at Cabinet. On the aircraft over he had decided to broach the issue in private to the Attorney General. And callow fellow that he was, the Attorney General had slipped the word to the Prime Minister. Sometimes the Secretary of State, from the distance of his pro-consulship in Belfast, believed that his colleagues in the Cabinet only broke wind if they first received the Prime Minister's permission. An hour after his conversation with the Attorney General, and barely back at his desk in the Northern Ireland Office, the Secretary of State had received the call.

They met in the Prime Minister's personal office, with a Principal Private Secretary taking notes. The walled garden outside took his attention for a moment before he was waved to a chair. It was well cut down for the winter. Because it was warm and damp the songbirds were in force on the lawn. Nice little things . . .

'The Attorney General, quite rightly, brought this matter to my attention. You are asking for immunity for a man who slaughtered a courageous judge and two dedicated police officers. You are suggesting that the man who took three fine lives should be allowed to walk free, and given the chance to begin a new life at the expense of our taxpayers.'

'Putting McAnally away, Prime Minister, would win us a skirmish. Giving him immunity provides the opportunity for us to win a battle . . .' The Secretary of State quite liked that. Fred had fed it to him in the drive across Whitehall.

'The idea of this man having immunity is one I find repellent.'

'The reality of Northern Ireland is often repellent, Prime Minister, as I'm sure you've found from your visits.' Good one . . . the Prime Minister came at Christmas to be photographed with the troops, particularly enjoyed being photographed while wearing a Marine beret or a flak jacket.

'I don't think public opinion would stand it, and I for one . . .'

'We can handle the public opinion side. There's enough chaps at Army and Police Headquarters to handle that.'

'And what if you don't deliver?'

'That's the gamble.'

'What's to stop him accepting our immunity, and then retracting, and going free?'

'There's nothing to stop him.'

'That's a dreadful answer.'

'It's the truth.'

'If that's your final word then my mind's made up, no immunity.'

The Secretary of State stood up. His arms were folded easily across his chest. 'Very good. Thank you for the decision. Let's hope there are no leaks . . .'

He knew the Prime Minister. He knew the neurosis on the leakage of confidential information. He saw the angry frown settling on the forehead.

'. . . Let's hope there are no leaks from Castlereagh or from Headquarters. I'd hate to have it thrown back at me that by sending one man down for a life sentence we had passed over the chance to put away the nucleus of the Provisional Brigade staff along with elements of Battalion command and a bus full of Volunteers. I'll do my damndest to see that doesn't leak, and to see that it doesn't come back to your door, Prime Minister. Thank you for your time.'

He turned. He wondered if he would have reached the door before he was called back.

'Your job depends on it, on him not retracting.'

'People's lives depend on him not retracting. Thank you for the decision. To give this creature immunity hurts me as much as it does you, but you've made the right decision. Good day, Prime Minister.'

'There are too many getting lifted. I says, I says Gingy McAnally's not going to be one of them. It was just after I'd done the Pig. There was guys getting lifted every bloody morning round West Belfast. I'd had one go in the Kesh, and I wasn't going back inside, not just for hanging about and waiting to see who was going to tout next. If it hadn't been for the problem with the RPG then I might have stayed. I went to see Joey – that's Joey Mulvaney. Joey says to me that I'd used the last of the warheads they had for the RPG. He said they'd get some more, that they were down south. He said they had a stack of them down south, but he said that South Armagh wanted them, and Derry had chipped in for them. He was pretty good to me, Joey Mulvaney, he didn't bullshit me. He said it would be weeks before Army Council's Quartermaster let them go. He said that I'd had two firings and that the boys down in Armagh and Derry were bleating for a bloody go at it. He said they'd need warheads to train with. He said we were bottom of the list . . .'

'Joey Mulvaney was . . . ?'

'Two Battalion, OC . . . I wasn't a marksman . . . well, I'd been out with an M16, but I don't reckon I hit the wall behind the squaddy. Marksman's a different thing . . .'

'Date, place, who were you with?'

'Christ . . . September, must have been the eighth,' cos it was the day before Roisin's birthday . . . I didn't want to go, I said I had to buy her something, I went then and had to leg it down to the Avenue and get her something. I didn't get to Royal Avenue, I went to Smithfield, I bought her a new iron . . . well, it wasn't new, it was seconds . . . We had three rifles. We were behind the wall at Milltown boneyard, waiting for the squaddys to come out of the Andersonstown barracks. That's when it was, where it was . . . Joey was one of the rifles, Dusty was the other . . .'

'Dusty?'

'O'Hara . . . Damien O'Hara. Billy Clinch took the shooters off us at the bottom of the graveyard. Dusty nearly shot him, he fell over a stone and he hadn't gone to Safety. Fierce bloody language Billy used on him. I was no marksman . . . I wasn't anything on the explosives. All our bombs came up in kits from Monaghan. The feller down there made them up, and they came in pieces to be assembled up in Belfast. I wasn't going to touch no bloody bomb. He was a watchmender, the man that made the bombs, so he always used old watches for the timing that had been left with him and not collected. The lads always used to say that the Jap digitals would put him out of business. I never heard his name, but he was somewhere behind the market in Monaghan city. So, I didn't do any sniping and I didn't do bombs. I was RPG and they'd no warheads. And the lads were being lifted, every bloody day . . . So, I went south. Roisin didn't fight me. She didn't say I was yellow, nothing like that. She didn't say I shouldn't. She's wonderful, my Roisin. She never gave out, just packed my bag. I went down south . . . Shit, I didn't know life could be so bloody perfect as it was down south.'

'We have to know everything. Every single thing.'

'There was a Post Office. There was two cars I hijacked. There was a punishment shooting, I didn't actually shoot him . . .'

'One at a time, in order, and the names.'

'Am I doing all right?'

'You're all right so far. We'll start with the Post Office . . .'


'It is indeed a lovely thought, Mrs McAnally. It's a beautiful thought but it just doesn't work that way. In theory I can drive down to Castlereagh and announce at the gate that you have instructed me to take your husband's case and that therefore I have come to seek a visit to him. And if they let me in, and they give me access to your husband then that would indeed be lovely and beautiful. As I say, it doesn't work that way.'

Mr Pronsias Reilly's desk was deep with briefs. He had the briefs on his desk of four men who had been up before the Magistrates in the morning, and more briefs for two more who would be up the following morning. He had the briefs of six more clients who had been on all day in the Lord Chief Justice's courtroom on the Crumlin Road, and that was a counsel trial with a chance of acquittals. He had his preparation reading to do that night before the morning sitting.

'If I had all the hours of the day to devote to your husband, Mrs McAnally, then I just might get into Castlereagh, and they might just have to produce him. They know my work schedule, they know what time I have available, so they'll keep me kicking my heels while the clock goes round. That's the way it works.'

He thought she was quite a good-looking girl. He thought that if she wasn't running a house in Turf Lodge on Social Security then she could have made herself into a really good-looking girl. Bony round the hips, and a little slack on the chest, but a smashing face on her. Hell of a sight better than half of the slags that came and parked in his office looking for help in keeping the husband out of the Kesh.

'With your husband's, er, antecedents, he'll know to keep his mouth quite shut for seven days . . . after that he's home, or he's in court and charged. If he's charged I'll be in court to take his brief . . . It's Mr Justice Simpson, isn't it? I hear, round the corner information, that his clothes didn't do too well at Forensic. Believe me, Mrs McAnally, even if I were to camp at Castlereagh and finally get access, I don't think that I could keep him out of court.'

He saw her chin quiver, and her lips were thin and pale and tight, and her fingers clasped a small handkerchief. She was a tough one, she'd screw like a steam engine . . . He smiled, held out his hand to be shaken, and to indicate that the interview was terminated. He often thought that if the PIRA men were as tough as the women they left behind then the war would have been won many years before.

'Thank you for dropping by, Mrs McAnally. You should look on the best side of things . . . I'm sure Mr McAnally is much too sensible to incriminate himself.'

Dropping by. He knew the poor wretch would now have a fight on her hands in the black taxi queue, and then the trudge from the Glen Road back into the depths of Turf Lodge.

'. . . I used to come up from the south every three, four months, but only for a few days, and to see Roisin and the kids. You get a bit hungry for the woman, you know it's like that. You have to have a woman, if you're not a bloody monk, and you have to see the children. The boys left me alone when I came up . . . They must have known that I was up, you don't bloody cough in Turf Lodge without the boys knowing, so they'd have known that I was up and with Roisin, but they let me be. I reckoned they left me alone because they hadn't a launcher, or if they had a launcher they hadn't any warheads for it. I'd go down the bar sometimes when I was with Roisin, and I might see someone that I knew, and I'd wave, and they'd wave, but they left me to myself. I guess it was kind of understood . . .'

The confidence of Sean Pius McAnally was full grown. And in front of him McDonough was nodding earnest encouragement, and behind him Astley was writing furiously. The fifth day was slipping by, and McAnally was now a favoured creature, part of another man's army. He told himself that what he did was for Roisin, and for Young Gerard and Little Patty and Baby Sean.

'. . . Then these two came to the caravan.'

'Names, Gingy.'

'Never had any names, and I'd never seen them before. They didn't give me their names. They brought me back. They didn't ask me to come, they just brought me back, like I'd bloody deserted. They didn't have the right to treat me like I was some sort of filth.'

'We'll work you through the snapshot book.'

'They'd no call to treat me like I was rotten. They brought me back, they seemed to think I'd just cut and run when I went to the Free State . . . Bastards.'

'When you've finished with them, Gingy, they'll wish they hadn't treated you like filth.'

'I was a good man, I was one of the best men in the Organization. When I was with them I never let any bugger down. I did what was bloody asked of me, I did it good and well . . .'

'We got the message, Gingy. They'll get the message.'

'Too bloody right they will.'

Each evening the typists took dictation from Astley, and the statement file of Sean Pius McAnally grew fatter. And the statement file bred other files and the cross-indexing and the computer searches

125

splayed outwards. There was a cross-index and a new file for every name mentioned by the new tout. And each night, after the typists had finished, the new files and read-outs from the P-Band computer ended on Rennie's desk.

It was brilliant, magic.

He knew it was just for starters. Turning them was one thing, keeping them turned was the devil's own work. Howard Rennie was a methodical man. By the fifth evening he had started to plan the lifts and swoops that would follow the seventh day of McAnally's incarceration at Castlereagh, and he let it be known that he would require the entire cell block to be cleared and waiting empty for a new intake. And a message had come down from on high, from the Castle at Stormont. The message said that he, Howard Rennie, was responsible, that his career depended on McAnally's statement.

The platoon had been on 'Immediate', so they were scrambled first from Springfield Road.

Two Land Rovers and two Pigs, and bursting out of the barracks with the headlights on and the horns blasting and the traffic scattering, and bellowing off down the Falls.

The report that had tumbled the platoon out of the quiet of Springfield Road was as vague as all of the initial call-outs. The reports said there was a crowd on Divis, gathered outside a chipper, that shots had been fired. There would be nothing clearer until Ferris and his platoon were on location, and back on the radio. Not much talk in the Land Rover. All tensed because they were off and riding into the unknown. Tensed and hushed because no man in the platoon could wipe from his mind the thought of a come-on, the ruse to lure the Security Forces into the field of a sniper's fire, or within range of a hidden mine.

They came across the junction of Falls and Springfield.

Ferris saw the crowd, halfway down Divis, spilling from the pavement onto the street. He heard the baying of angered voices.

There were three single shots, and for a fraction the crowd was silent and scurried back, and then surged forward again, as if the shots were insufficient to frighten it. Behind Ferris there was the metal scrape of the escorts arming their rifles. If there was any slight reassurance it was in the heavy engine whine of the Pigs behind Ferris. Nearer to the crowd now and the voices were sharper and belting out hostility.

The platoon had a drill for such an occasion. Nothing for Ferris to say, the drill would be automatic. His Land Rover and the rear Land Rover came right to the edge of the crowd before scratching to a stop. The first Pig swerved past them and then slewed across the road fifty yards ahead to block the oncoming traffic. The second Pig would do the same behind them. The cordon was immediate.

Hate filled the faces wherever Ferris looked. The women were at the back of the half-moon crowd, their voices braying at the upper windows of the brick building, screaming and finger pointing at the twin windows above Fiori's chipper. It was a silly thought, but Ferris briefly entertained it ... World's worst urban guerrilla battlefield, and the place was chosen by Signor Fiori to open a chipper and flog hamburgers and sausages and rock salmon ... Christ, it must have been bad in Naples to get Signor Fiori to try his luck in the Falls of Belfast ... A bloody daft thought ... The women were at the back, and in front of them were their menfolk. Ferris saw what they called in the Mess the aggro yobs who threw themselves against the closed street door like there was no tomorrow. It was the door at the side of the chipper that was their target. The door would lead to a staircase and a self-contained flat above the chipper. Ferris could see the upper windows were broken, and were curtainless ... a derelict flat.

The voices were a cacophony around him as Ferris and his escort and Fusilier Jones came out of the Land Rover. The noise was ringing in his ears, but in those first moments he seemed to hear no single and distinguishable voice, only a reeking babble of alien accents. The soldiers prised their way through the crowd and to the front of Fiori's chipper, and used their rifle butts to chop the crowd back from the door. When Ferris looked up he fancied he saw a shadow pass close to the window. His nose puckered at a sharp, acrid, smarting smell.

'Rear's secure, Mr Ferris ...' The shout of Ferris's platoon sergeant. 'But there's no back exit.'

Ferris was close to the side door. There was deep grey smoke filtering from underneath the door and through the old post slit. He felt the irritation at his eyes. Bloody gas ... CS gas ... The faces of the crowd were close to him, twisted in their anger as if a prize was escaping them. At last he understood the venom of the words.

'Fucking SAS bastards . . .' 'Come to keep your fucking spies safe, have you? . . .' 'Bloody killer squads . . .' 'Found out, you bastards, because you're not as fucking clever as you think you are . . .'

Ferris understood.

The derelict flat was a covert observation post occupied by the Special Air Service, and not covert any longer. And the mob had gathered for them, and the SAS troopers had fired warning shots and tipped CS grenades down the stairs to hold the crowd back. Not bloody laughing gas, but Ferris was grinning. He'd heard once, down in the country on his first tour, of a shop owner who'd reckoned he'd rats in the rafters, and who'd called in the Pest man, and that fellow had crawled through a ceiling hole with his tin of poison paste and confronted a long-stay surveillance squad . . . some rats. The SAS getting themselves rumbled was enough to bring a grin to any soldier, especially to Ferris, passed over by that Regiment.

'Back the Pig up, right up to the door . . . Don't take all bloody day.' A whining Brummie accent squeaking through the post slit.

Ferris gave his orders. His Fusiliers patiently worked the crowd back, but the fury was gone because the chance of success was lost. The Pig was driven close to the door, and its back doors opened to make a shield, to separate the crowd from the doorway.

The gas had now caught at Ferri's eyes. You weren't supposed to wipe your eyes with your sleeve, you weren't supposed to blink and try and squeeze the irritation out. He did both.

He bent to the post slit.

Ferris shouted. 'You can come out now, it's safe . . .'

Ferris felt himself reeling. And his balance was frayed at the hands of the men from the Regiment that had turned him down. He could hear voices raised in laughter against him as he struggled to stand straight.

The door was wrenched open.

'Took your time, cocko . . .' The Brummie came out through the door. He was short, squat, like a well fed spider. He wore a navy boiler suit, and a week of beard growth and a wool stretch hat. He carried a rifle, a pair of bulbous night-sight binoculars and a rucksack. He came through the door fast and jumped easily into the Pig. There were two more following, laden down with surveillance equipment and personal weapons.

Ferris stared into the Pig.

'What blew you?'

The last man out replied. He was Glasgow. 'I got leg cramp, swung my leg straight, kicked our shit bucket . . . Get us out.'

He didn't expect politeness, not from the clandestine heroes. Ferris went to the front of the Pig, gave the driver his instructions.

He watched the Pig drive away. He thought to himself that he was enjoying a soft war in comparison with men who squatted in the damp cold roofing above Fiori's chipper for days on end.

He heard the jeering of the crowd as he gave the order for the pull out.

'. . . The morning after I came back there were two men who called up at the house. They just came in, like it was public . . .'

'Names, Gingy.'

'There was Phonsie McGurr and another fellow, Devitt, I don't know his first name, big fellow with a tricolour tattoo on his wrist. They didn't give their names, but I knew them before I went away. They seemed to reckon they just had to snap their fingers and Gingy McAnally was jumping. They said I was on a job in the morning, I said I wasn't. They said there was a job in the Crumlin all set for me, I said it was for someone else. They said that everyone had sweated to set it up, and it was going to happen at early morning tomorrow, I said they could bloody think again . . . I said I wasn't standing out in the middle of the Crumlin in daylight firing an RPG . . . We'd gone up to the bedroom, we were sitting on Roisin's bed . . . They said it was going to be the biggest belt in Belfast that year, they said it was going to have the Brits screaming all the way to London. They said it was a one-off, that I'd go home after it, and that the next day I could be away down south again like nothing had happened . . . I said I wouldn't do it. Every time I said I'd quit, they just kept talking like they weren't hearing me. They were right pigs, they just wouldn't hear me. They said there was no-one else that could use the RPG 'cept me. They said it had been a hell of a business to get the RPG into town and to get a warhead for it . . . They said it had to be me.

We were all shouting together . . . I'd come back to see my wife and my small ones, and I'm ending up in the bedroom shouting whether I'm going on a hit. They said that I'd see the Chief . . .'

Astley's eyes flickered up from his concentration on his notepad. McDonough bit hard on the end of his pencil.

'The Chief . . . ?' McDonough was a good experienced detective. He had the commendations from the Chief Constable, but there was a hoarseness in his echoing of the words.

McAnally smiled, cheeky now. 'The Chief . . . Belfast Brigade's big shot.'

'And you saw him?'

The grin was spreading on McAnally's face. 'You said we were working from the beginning, you said we wasn't to jump . . . I didn't see the Chief till the morning.'

'Sorry . . .' McDonough tried to match McAnally's fun. 'Fair cop, Gingy. My fault . . . when we come to the morning we'll come to the Chief.'

For a moment McDonough's hand rested on McAnally's tight fist, on the table. Astley watched them.

Astley felt a slight, fast chill of fear. If the Provos identified the detectives who had successfully twisted a man into the supergrass system, then they shot those detectives. Done it in Londonderry, done it in Belfast. They slaughtered the detectives, if they could name them, who had converted a man to touting. And the man sitting at the table with McDonough and Astley was the best 'grass, the biggest tout, the most considerable informer yet to have been through Castlereagh. If they ever identified the 'tecs who had turned McAnally, they'd put them top of the list. He could have worked in a bank, he could have sold insurance, he could have gone across the water to England. Astley breathed deeply, concentrated again on the written page.

McDonough was still grinning. 'Right, Gingy, so they said to you that you'd better see the Chief . . .'

'What's with Gingy McAnally?'

The Chief and Frankie Conroy walked a wet evening pavement. The Chief liked Frankie. It was rare for the Chief to form friendships inside the Organization, few friendships since he had muscled his way to commander of Belfast Brigade. Frankie was loyal and subservient, and he did what he was told, didn't question what he was told. Frankie had a good record, for the Organization . . . and he had a good record with the Director of Public Prosecutions.

They walked in Andersonstown. Coat collars up, flat hats on their heads, duffle bags on their shoulders. To a passing mobile patrol they would have seemed like two workmen returning home in the dusk.

'You feel bad about Gingy?' There was a sibilant whistle in Frankie's voice. Way back he had been shot in the throat by a Brit undercover man, and he'd done half of a twelve stretch for attempted murder, possession and membership.

Each time the Chief saw the puckered hole in Frankie's throat, then he reckoned the man was lucky to be alive.

'I feel bad about any bugger that's lifted.'

'He was special, didn't want to be in, that's what I heard.'

'You met the joker who wants to get lifted, Frankie? What's the word on him?'

'The word is that he's playing stone statues in there.'

'Where did you get that?'

'My cousin's boy, he's a scribbler on the *News*. He meets the big 'tec, Rennie, at a club, a bloody rugby club. My cousin's boy's a good player or they wouldn't let him in the bloody place, it's a Prod's club. Rennie told him that Gingy hasn't opened his mouth since he's been there. He's like a fucking dumb man, that's what my cousin's boy said Rennie told him.'

'Have they enough on Gingy to charge him?'

'They charge him tomorrow, or he's out. My cousin's boy didn't say about a charge.'

Frankie heard the wind breaking from the Chief, the scent was at his nostrils. He was too long in the Chief's company to react.

'There's a nice one coming up, Frankie. The Brit battalion at Springfield use open Land Rovers, always open. When they're at the lights on the Falls, when they're stopped, there's a hell of a chance of getting some petrol out of a top window onto them . . . like it, Frankie?'

'Like it . . .' Frankie looked into the Chief's face. 'That kiddie, Mattie Blaney's boy, the kiddie that was 'capped for informing on Gingy, that was right, was it?'

He saw the distant glint in the Chief's eyes. He was over the line. He was always frightened of the Chief when he was over the line.

'I was asking you, Frankie, how you'd like it, warming up some Brit squaddys in an open Land Rover.'

'Yeah, I'd like it,' Frankie said, and looked away from the Chief's face.

'So, who was in the room?'

'The Chief . . . and Brigade QM, and Intelligence, and Operations.'

'Names, Gingy.'

'The Chief, that's Kevin Muldoon . . . QM is Ollie O'Brien . . . Intelligence is Joe McGilivarry . . . Operations is Tom McCreevy . . . They were all in the room when the Chief told me his plan.'

'No second thoughts, Gingy.'

'I told you I'd do it.'

'When the going gets rough, Gingy . . .'

'I said I'd bloody do it.'

'It'll get really rough, Gingy.'

Sean Pius McAnally stabbed his ferret glance at McDonough. 'But I'm getting immunity, aren't I? And you're going to keep me safe, me and the missus and the kids, aren't you?'

It would be a frantic evening for Howard Rennie.

Into Central Belfast as the offices were closing for a session with the Director of Public Prosecutions, to confirm the issuing of immunity to a self-confessed killer, and to drop off a seventy-eight-page statement of confession and implication.

Afterwards to Police Headquarters for the briefings on the lifts of twenty-eight men and three women.

And later, very late, five minutes of the Chief Constable's time.

'You'll get him into court, Rennie?'

'If I have to carry him there, sir.'

# 9

He sat in the back of an armour-reinforced police Land Rover.

Over the shoulders of the driver and the forward seat observer he could see the nightlights of the deserted city.

Rennie was on one side of him. Hemming him in on the other side was a police sergeant, uniformed and huge in his bullet-proof vest.

It had been explained to Sean Pius McAnally that he was no longer a prisoner, that he was no longer in custody. Rennie had told him that he was a free agent, that he was in police care. If he had been in custody he would have been handcuffed as the convoy swept out of the gates of Castlereagh. Because he was in care he was merely sandwiched between Rennie and the sergeant. There was a difference between custody and care . . .

And Sean Pius McAnally needed care because he had become a traitor to his own.

There was no talking in the back of the Land Rover. McAnally and Rennie and the sergeant and two constables sat in deep silence. There were the flashes of their matches and their lighters, and the glow of their cigarettes. When they dragged on their cigarettes, McAnally could see the faces around him. They were the faces of the men who had been his enemies. There wasn't much thinking in him. He had been up late, and woken early in his cell. They had come for him, at four. They'd given him a mug of tea and a Penguin biscuit, and he'd felt the beard on his face and the dirty cold in his crutch. They had taken him to Rennie and the car park. Rennie had said, 'I've taken a chance with you, Gingy. I've taken one hell of a risk. I've chanced that you've the bottle to see this through. I've chanced getting immunity for you. You're now a free man. You can turn your back on us and walk out on us. But you won't do that, Gingy, because you know that after today you're dead if you do that. Don't get me wrong, Gingy, I'm not making threats. What I'm saying is this: after your statements, after our lifts, you're dead without us looking after you. That's facts.' They had stood, Rennie and McAnally, in the car park, out of earshot of the uniformed men. They had been wrapped in the cold in their own shadows. When Rennie had said his fill he had cuffed McAnally hard on the shoulder, as if that were the end of the private talk for all time, and McAnally had known the force of Rennie's fist, and they had gone to the Land Rover.

Too early in the city even for the Corporation's cleaning carts. Wide, wet streets. A convoy of three Land Rovers. McAnally crammed between two men, and his Land Rover between two others.

The Land Rovers swung past the roundabout at the bottom of the Grosvenor Road. He was coming to his own territory, and coming in protective police care. He felt against him the warmth of Rennie and the angles of the sergeant's armoured vest. He was coming back to collect his wife, and to gather up his kids. He was shivering and not cold. He tried to remember what he would say to Roisin, and his mind was vague, and the words were lost.

They passed the Royal Victoria Hospital. The soldier he had blinded long ago with the RPG had gone to the casualty at the RVH. The policeman he had injured when he had killed another had been rushed to the same rear entrance of the old hospital. No traffic on the Grosvenor, and the Land Rovers went over the junction traffic lights on red. Not hanging about, were they, the Land Rovers traversing Provoland, not when they were carrying a traitor? The convoy slowed on the approach to the Springfield Road barracks. McAnally sensed the tension of the men around him. Eyes on the upper windows, a pair of hands tight on the wheel, other hands on cocked Stirlings. Christ . . . and he had to find the words for Roisin.

They turned into the gates.

The barracks was a staging post. When the rear doors opened McAnally was gestured out, and he saw the scores of men and their vehicles in the barracks yard. Soldiers in combat gear, uniformed police, and Saracen armoured cars with their engines whining and the fumes coughing out of their exhausts. He stayed close to Rennie.

He was a dog in a strange street and he kept himself close to his master. He couldn't help himself. He saw the eyes on him. The sharp eyes of the young uniformed policemen, and the eyes of the soldiers set as bright jewels in the camouflage cream on their faces. Every bugger in the yard knew he was on duty at five in the morning because Gingy McAnally had gone supergrass. The eyes followed him, tracked him.

There was a hand on McAnally's sleeve. He spun. He saw Ferris, the officer. And in the moment of recognition Rennie had abandoned him. Pass the bloody parcel, Rennie off to talk to the big shots, and Gingy left with Ferris, the officer.

'Well done, Gingy . . .' Ferris's quiet voice close to McAnally's ear, private.

'What's you mean?' The snapped question. McAnally searching for his answer and looking up at Ferris's blackened cheeks.

'For doing the right thing.'

'I'm not doing this because . . .'

'Doesn't matter why you're doing it.'

'It's for my missus, and the kids, you got that?'

'Got it Gingy. And good luck.'

Ferris walked away. Rennie was striding back to McAnally, testing a personal radio against his ear. McAnally lost Ferris amongst the mess of uniforms as the soldiers made for their vehicles. There was the shouting of orders, and the Saracens and the Land Rovers were filling fast.

The police sergeant was behind McAnally and holding his Stirling readied, as if safety was from now on a dubious matter. Rennie took McAnally's arm and led him back to the Land Rover.

The long column of vehicles spilled out into the Springfield Road.

Going fast, going for surprise. Through the road blocks that were already in position to seal off West Belfast.

The column was splitting, dividing, hiving off its parts.

He couldn't remember the bloody words. It had been easy enough to remember the bloody words when he was in his cell. He wouldn't have long. They'd told him that. Just long enough to get the missus dressed and the kids into their clothes and the cases packed. Not long enough for a bloody debate.

Hammering up the Springfield Road, heading for Turf Lodge. A traitor coming under the cloak of darkness with the soldiers and the policemen, coming back to his home.

Bravo Company and Charlie Company of 2 RFF and some two hundred policemen were on the move, out on the streets.

Thirty-one names shared out amongst the soldiers and the police for lifting.

Ferris rode in the front of his open Land Rover, behind him was a Saracen and two police Land Rovers.

In the breast pocket of his tunic was a 4" × 2" photograph of a middle-aged man, features indistinct from magnification, with the over-stamped name across the base of the picture of Kevin Muldoon. In the pocket, against the photograph, was his notepad and the pencil-written address on the top sheet where Kevin Muldoon was thought to be sleeping.

'What have we got, Mr Ferris?' Fusilier Jones asked cheerfully. 'A good fat cat?'

'Do you think they'd tell the Poor Bloody Infantry, Fusilier Jones, if we were going for a fat cat or a bottle washer?'

He could see and hear again the evening when he had been in McAnally's cell at Castlereagh. He had willingly joined the conspiracy to turn a fighter . . . Bugger what the fighter had done. He had upset the flywheel of a man's soul. He shook his head, to Fusilier Jones he seemed dazed, because he wondered how Gingy McAnally would be when he had to stand face to face with what he had done.

'You all right, Mr Ferris?'

When he reached Number 63, the Drive in Turf Lodge then Gingy McAnally would know what he'd done.

'I'm fine, thank you.'

The Land Rover stopped at the cordon that was halfway up the Drive. Beside McAnally, Rennie leaned forward and talked urgently through the driver's window to a uniformed Inspector. There were voices, urgent and hushed, sweeping into the back of the Land Rover, Protestant voices of the Province and faraway English voices. Rennie was satisfied. He tapped the driver's shoulder.

He saw his own home in the Land Rover's lights. He felt sick. He saw his own curtains and his own door and his own front gate. The headlights were cut. There were the shapes of men running as shadows past the windscreen of the Land Rover. His eyes were closed as Rennie pushed him firmly towards the back doors. He opened his eyes. Rennie was pressed against him, crouched under the low roof of the Land Rover. There was the smell of Rennie's breath and of old cigarettes and of the exhaust fumes. The doors opened.

Rennie led McAnally up to the front door. Only the two of them going up the path.

'Knock her up.'

Rennie had taken his place behind McAnally.

Almost diffidently McAnally rapped on the door. Behind the door was the quiet of a sleeping home. He tugged savagely at the short crop of his hair. He heard Rennie breathing impatience behind him. He hit the door with his fist, then craned forward to lift the letter box flap and listen. An upper room light fell onto the front garden. There were policemen cursing softly and scurrying to new shadows when before they had been hidden. A noise upstairs, an opening door. He pressed his mouth to the letter box flap.

'Roisin, it's me, Gingy.'

More lights, and a fast footfall on the stairs, the drumming on the boards, the squeak of the pram's wheels, the growl of the bolt being drawn.

She wore a nightdress of pink flannel. There was a dressing gown slung over her shoulders that she held secure at her throat. She looked full into his face, and her chin was loose and her mouth was wide and her eyes were staring in astonishment. There were a hundred questions on her lips, and each one stifled. Her arms were rising up, to take her man against her, and then she saw the hulking shape of Howard Rennie, and the beam from the opened door caught the policeman crouching with a rifle at the front gate. There was a small choke in her throat, a waking from a dream. Her arms fell to her side, and the dressing gown slid to the floor.

Rennie shoved McAnally inside the door.

'Get on with it, Gingy.'

She backed into the pram, winced. She was going for the stairs. McAnally surged forward, caught her with his hands. She was looking back past him as Rennie led the stream of uniforms and weapons into the hallway. There was no part of it that she understood. McAnally's hands were on her hips, feeling the bones of her body through the nightdress. He forced her onto the first steps of the stairs and held her when she stumbled, and drove her up, and all the time she was gazing, dumbstruck, back at the police in her hall.

They reached the top of the stairs. He led her to their bedroom. He heard the catarrh cough of Little Patty. He saw their bed, and Baby Sean asleep under the ceiling light and half covered by the bedclothes.

'I've done it for you.' A desperation in McAnally's voice.

Her lips were apart, she was shivering as if in shock.

'I've done it all for you.'

There were low, muffled voices rising from the hallway, and the static scream of a radio set.

'It's all for you, and for the kids . . . That's why I've done it.'

Through the thin wall, Young Gerard's bed sang as he turned in it, and again the hacking throat of Little Patty.

'We're going to be all right. It's going to be a new life. We're going to have a new life . . . that's what they're going to give us.'

Now she understood. Her hair was across her face, ignored. She pushed him harshly from her. He could see the shapes of her body. He could see the anger settling on her forehead.

'It's what's best for us,' he said aloud.

'You've touted?' she accused.

'For all of us, for you and me and for the kids . . .'

'You've gone supergrass, you've gone tout . . .? Jesus . . . Sean, tell me that's not true.'

He might as well have smacked his fist across her face.

'Get yourself dressed, get the kids dressed, get your clothes in a case.'

'Have you gone tout, Sean, not really . . .?' And no more doubt on her face, only a world collapsing.

'I was going down for twenty fucking five years,' McAnally shouted. 'Is that what you fucking wanted? Did you want me away for twenty-five years? Did you want me away till I was old, you were old, till the kids were gone. It's us first, it's no other bastard first in front of us.'

His words blasted at her. She seemed to sag as if her strength had gone from her.

'You bloody damned fool, Sean.'

'Get the kids dressed. Get yourself dressed.'

'What did you do it for?' Her voice was a murmur. She slipped down onto the bed. Her fingers were at her mouth. Her nightdress had tumbled from her shoulder.

McAnally caught his wife's chin, pulled it up from her hands. 'I did it for twenty-five years of my life, and that should be good enough for you.'

Her head fell onto her fists, the tears began.

'Mrs McAnally . . .'

Rennie was framed in the doorway.

He spoke brusquely. His words cracked through the room. 'Mrs McAnally, there are certain facts about your husband's situation that you should understand. Your husband has made a full statement concerning his criminal activities while a member of the Provisional IRA. Your husband has implicated many of the senior members of the Organization. In return for your husband going into the witness box and giving sworn evidence against close to thirty men, he has been guaranteed personal immunity from prosecution. He has also been promised the chance of making a new life for himself with you and your children at a place where you will be safe from the Provisional IRA. You should do as you're asked, Mrs McAnally. You should get yourself and your children dressed.'

She sobbed, 'You've turned my man into a bleeding tout.'

'Converted terrorist, we call it.'

'I hope you're proud, of what you've done to us.'

'He's more than lucky to have had the chance to turn. You've got less than ten minutes to shift yourselves.'

'And if I won't . . .?'

'Then you never see your husband again, as long as you live, Mrs McAnally,' Rennie said. 'And your children will never see their father again . . . I can't see the point of argument.'

Her glance, loaded with anger, slashed past McAnally and rested on Howard Rennie. He stared her out. She heaved the nightdress over her head, and tossed it behind her. For a moment she was still on the bed, naked, white, defiant. Then she shook with her crying. She took her underclothes from the chair and dragged them on automatically and without thought, and her jeans and her sweater and her socks and her sneakers.

'It'll seem better later on, Mrs McAnally, and it'll seem a hell of a lot better than you staying on.'

'We've never had a tout in our families before.'

'Probably because there's never been anyone before with the guts.' Rennie closed the bedroom door silently behind him.

'Roisin, a life elsewhere for all of us has to be better than you here and me in the Kesh on twenty-five.' McAnally's hands were fidgeting uselessly in front of his stomach. She tossed back her head, fastened her hair ponytail with an elastic band. He turned for the door.

'Where are you going?'

'To get the kids up.'

'Don't you bloody go near my children.'

He stalked to the wardrobe. He remembered the door was always stuck because the wood was warped from the damp. He wrenched it open. Baby Sean had started to cry. There was only one suitcase in the wardrobe. It was the suitcase in which she had packed her sparse trousseau for the honeymoon in Bray. He pulled out the suitcase and unzipped it. There was pale green mould inside. He was wiping it furiously away with the sleeve of his anorak.

Six minutes later they were gone from Number 63.

Two white-faced, button-lipped children and a baby who was crying fervently and Roisin McAnally, and Sean Pius McAnally who had turned supergrass, were hurried through an avenue of armed policemen down their front path, through their front gate, across the rough pavement and into the back of the Land Rover.

All along the Drive the upstairs lights were on, and the upstairs curtains were heaving. The neighbours saw a policeman lift Little Patty up into the Land Rover, and saw a suitcase passed in after her. The neighbours would like to have seen the faces of McAnally and his missus, that would have been gilt on the ginger, but the early morning darkness denied them that pleasure.

Over his radio Rennie broadcast to the Ops Room at Springfield that the trawling in of the McAnally family was complete.

The Land Rovers revved their engines. The street was bathed in moving headlights, and then the night quiet fell again on the Drive in Turf Lodge.

Roisin McAnally allowed her husband to hold her hand in the back of the Land Rover. Her ankles were against a police constable's boots, and Little Patty was on her knee and Baby Sean was gurgling on her shoulder and Young Gerard was clinging to her elbow. He held her hand. She made no attempt to hold his. She was dead to the comfort of his hand. She was not crying any more. She would not let the constable sitting opposite her, with the Stirling on his knees, see her crying.

Over the radio came the coded message to announce that the lifts were in progress.

The squaddy in the centre of the three hung by his arms from the shoulders of the other two men. His legs swung free as they stampeded across the inner hallway of the maisonette block. He jack-knifed his knees up and thrust the soles of his boots into the lightweight door. The door caved in. Ferris was behind the squaddys with a uniformed Inspector. The light from the landing half lit the hallway, showed them the closed doors leading from it. The first door they tried was the kitchen, the second door was the living room, the third door was the bedroom.

It took them a moment to find the light switch by the door. It was a tiny room, big enough only for a double bed and a small wardrobe and two wooden chairs. The bed was lengthwise against the far wall. They had come in at a rush and now they were leaden in their tracks because there was only a girl in the bed. She was a pretty little thing, young-faced as if she were just out of school, and she had tousled, curling, auburn hair. She was sitting up in the bed, the straps of her nightdress on her shoulders and the sheet held vice-like over her chest.

Ferris saw the grin on Fusilier Jones's mouth.

'Sorry for the intrusion, Miss, but I have a warrant,' the Inspector intoned. 'I'm here for Kevin Muldoon.'

For Fusilier Jones and his mates, tipping a bare-arsed girl out of bed at 05.35 on a wet December morning made soldiering worthwhile.

'He's not here,' she was defiant, lovely, blazing eyes.

A squaddy opened the wardrobe, touched the Inspector's arm for attention and shone a torch onto a crumpled heap of a pair of trousers and a shirt and a jersey and a man's shoes.

The Inspector's smile was mirthless, not matching Fusilier Jones's happiness. The Inspector pushed past Ferris and the squaddys, he went to the bed, and heaved the bedclothes down onto the floor. All the soldiers in the room saw her legs and the gold below her stomach, and one sniggered, and they all saw the pyjama bottoms abandoned by her feet. The Inspector caught at the girl's arm and pulled her off the bed. Ferris and his Fusiliers took the cue and slid the bed back.

The man lay on his side against the wall. He was naked, he was shivering, his face was livid red. He held one hand over his privates, the other was raised to protect his head.

Ferris stared down at him, fascinated.

Rifle barrels and Stirling barrels were turned on him. Ferris saw the scar across the bridge of his nose. He thought that if the man had worn trousers he would have hurled himself at his captors. A man can't fight without trousers.

'Hands above your head, Muldoon,' the Inspector said dispassionately.

The hands were raised, then snatched by a constable, and the handcuffs clicked into place.

Kevin Muldoon was dressed in the clothes that had been thrown in haste onto the cupboard floor, the shirt and jersey pulled over his handcuffed wrists. The Inspector recited the terms of the Emergency Provisions powers as the trousers were drawn up over the knees of the man.

The crowd of armed men in the room eased back to allow Muldoon and his escort to be run out of the bedroom, away across the hallway and out to the Land Rovers.

142

'What is he?' Ferris quietly asked the Inspector. 'What is Kevin Muldoon?'

The Inspector turned on him a supercilious glare. 'What's that to an infantry lieutenant?'

'I helped pull in McAnally.'

Now the interest sparkled on the Inspector's face. 'He's the top boy. He runs Brigade.'

Ferris looked back and through the open door of the bedroom, and the open front door. He looked out into the night where the street was alive with the sounds of the soldiers and police and their vehicles. He understood why McAnally was a diamond in Rennie's scheme. He understood why McAnally had squeezed his hand tight to confirm the trust. He thought that he had achieved something after all in the weeks in Belfast, and the achievement was the arrest of a naked man who hid on the floor under his bed.

Ferris said, 'That's a great man to put away.'

'If we put him away . . .' The Inspector shouted from the hallway, 'Are you dressed yet, lady? I've not all day.'

'McAnally will put him away.'

'If you think PIRA's going to lie down under this one then you're a green young soldier, Lieutenant. There's going to be all hell over this one . . . Lifting Kevin Muldoon's the easy bit, putting him away is going to be bloody, bloody hard, whatever that creature McAnally says now . . . or didn't they tell you that? Didn't they tell you that going supergrass is no picnic? I tell you this. If McAnally sees this through when it gets hot, then it'll be a bloody miracle.'

The girl stood in the doorway of the bedroom. She was dressed. There was a constable in front of her and one behind her, and still she showed no submission. She looked as though she would spit in the faces of the soldiers and police.

The Inspector said evenly, 'We'll be on our way, lady . . .' He turned to Ferris. 'In my job I don't see much sign of miracles.'

The door of the maisonette was too damaged to fasten shut after them, and they left it open, with the lights on in the hallway and the bedroom, and with a guard outside to await the arrival of Forensic.

The police Land Rovers were pulling away as Ferris came out onto the street. There was the first grey smear of the daylight hovering over the roofs and chimneys of the street. He had seen the man who ran Brigade, and the bastard was in no way different to the hundreds of men of middle age that he saw on the Falls every day that he was out foot-slogging on patrol.

Roisin McAnally sat in the police canteen at Springfield Road.

Her back was to her husband who stood with a powerfully built detective and whispered the names and peered through the small slit he held open in the venetian blind.

She thought she was being smothered with capable attention by the two policewomen who tripped around her and her children. They had found a portable high chair for Baby Sean; they had brought chips and sausages for Little Patty and cut the sausages for her; they had discovered some Space War comics for Young Gerard. She was proud of Young Gerard. Her son turned the pages automatically and showed no sign of pleasure. She was proud of her boy because he gave nothing to the bitches who fussed around him. She could have kicked Little Patty who ate as though this were the first food she had taken in a week. And Baby Sean didn't give a shit, because Baby Sean smiled in wide-faced happiness at the policewoman who made contorted grimaces across the high chair tray, Baby Sean didn't give a shit that his father was a tout.

There were the sounds of the Land Rovers arriving in the yard below the canteen window. Though he whispered, she could clearly hear her husband.

'That's Ollie O'Brien.'

'Brigade Quartermaster, Gingy.'

'That's right, Mr Rennie.'

She had heard many names spoken. She had heard the names of Joey McGilivarry and of Tom McCreevy and Joey Mulvaney and Billy Clinch and Dusty O'Hara . . . She knew them all. She used to neck with Dusty when she was seventeen, used to let his hand into her blouse but not down her jeans. And Billy used to bring her money when her man was in the Kesh. And there had been a night the year before when Joey had called and if it hadn't been curse time she'd known that she'd have taken him upstairs because the kids were asleep in bed. And Tom sang a dream in the bar on a Saturday

144

night, sang of bloody victory. And Joey had gone serious with her sister, till he'd got nicked and she'd gone to Canada.

And more names ... A policewoman had her hand on Young Gerard's arm and asked him if he'd like some food now, and smiled sweetly at him when he dumbly shook his head. It was a dream she couldn't wake from. There were policemen coming into the canteen and making a noise and laughing too loud, because a few minutes before they had been out on the streets and afraid and so they had to crack a big laugh now to show how brave they were. They carried their trays past Roisin McAnally and the two policewomen and the kids, and they all dropped their voices then, and they all looked the other bloody way, and they all pretended there was nothing that was special about the family at the table.

'That's Kevin Muldoon, Mr Rennie.'

'Tell me who he is, Gingy.'

'You know who he is.'

'You tell me, Gingy.'

'He's the Commander of Belfast Brigade, Mr Rennie.'

With both her hands she clasped Young Gerard's head, and she pulled it close to her mouth and she kissed his hair. When she let his head go free he said nothing, and went back to turning the pages of the comic books. Little Patty had tipped the brown sauce on the table and the policewoman said it was nothing and was wiping it with a tissue.

She couldn't cry. If she hadn't cried in the Land Rover, she couldn't cry in the police canteen.

There was a splash of thin sunshine as the rain cleared briefly over the Belfast dawn, and the Land Rovers carried the haul of prisoners from Springfield Road to the Castlereagh Holding Centre. All but two of the men and women named by Sean Pius McAnally had been successfully lifted. Only one of those held had tried to resist arrest and he would have a technicolour eye by lunchtime and two constables would wear facial sticking plaster for the rest of the week.

Mr Pronsias Reilly was woken by the clock radio beside his bed. He always started the day with the downtown headlines. The first news bulletin of the day usually let him know whether he was required early at the Magistrates, whether he could go straight to the Crumlin Court House. It was only after the headlines and the weather that he realized the omission. No announcement of a charge against Sean Pius McAnally. If a man had been charged with 'Tenner' Simpson's murder, and with the murder of two 'tecs, then the Press Office would have been crowing the news like an early morning cockerel to the News Rooms. And he had heard on the vine that the chemical tests on McAnally's clothing would stitch the case tight against him.

For Mr Pronsias Reilly, dabbing on the pre-shave lotion, groping for his battery razor, there was only one conclusion to be drawn from the downtown headlines . . . Sean Pius McAnally had made a deal.

Alone, in his bath, walking on the Sperrins, sailing on Carlingford, alone in his private and most honest thoughts, he would not have regarded himself as a fellow traveller with the PIRA. But he was a Republican, he was a believer in a United Ireland, and he hated the Protestant ascendancy. He had lived too long inside the Catholic minority ever to abandon his roots. He was a self-taught lawyer before gaining his exam passes at Queen's University.

He remembered the woman who had come to his office. He remembered what he had thought of her. He remembered the fierce loyalty of the woman to her imprisoned man, and her faith was in a fucking tout.

He had been, the previous year, calling on a client in Whiterock and his car had been hijacked by some kids. He had shouted and screamed on the pavement and a big man had come to him, a man with a bullet wound in the throat. The man had calmed him and walked away, and twenty minutes later the man had come back at the wheel of his car and not a scratch on it. He had tried to pay the man, and the man had refused. Mr Pronsias Reilly didn't know what ranking Frankie Conroy held in the Organization and didn't ask. Three times since Frankie Conroy had escorted women to see him and consult with him when their man was inside.

One turn deserved another turn.

He rang the number of Frankie Conroy.

He heard the sleep-filled voice repeat the number he had dialled.

He didn't introduce himself.

'You might wonder whether Sean Pius McAnally has gone supergrass.'

He put down the telephone.

The Secretary of State was taking his breakfast of toast and orange juice in the flat over his office in the Castle, when his civil servant brought him the morning's newspapers.

'A bit damned early, Fred.'

'I've been with the police since five. Belfast Brigade in its entirety is currently enjoying the hospitality of Castlereagh Holding Centre.'

'That's damned good.'

'It's gone like clockwork, so far.'

The Secretary of State looked keenly at his civil servant. 'You'll keep that clock wound . . . if we fail with this one we're all for the rubbish bin.'

'And if we win sir, then it's PIRA Belfast that's on the dust cart.'

The civil servant put down the newspapers, smiled briskly, and let himself out.

The Secretary of State reflected that his political and public career depended on a turned Provo carrying through an act of betrayal against the Organization he had sworn allegiance to.

He glanced at the front page of the *Newsletter*. More demands from the Protestant politicians for his resignation. He picked up the *Irish News*. A Catholic leader said he was tainted with bias and should be sacked as a gesture to the nationalist population. God alone knew that he did his best for the bloody place, and God alone knew where he'd find some thanks for his efforts.

Frankie turned into the Drive and braked.

Far up the road he saw the police Land Rovers, and beyond them, parked at the side of the road, was a removal van.

That was all he needed to see. He reversed and drove away.

Frankie Conroy had told the Chief that Gingy McAnally was playing stone statues in Castlereagh, and all the time the bugger was touting . . . Shit Almighty, Gingy McAnally had been briefed on 'Tenner' Simpson by all of the Brigade.

★   ★   ★

He had been strip-searched. His legs had been prised open and a cold dry hand had felt in his crutch, and the cheeks of his arse had been opened for a mirror examination. He had been weighed. He had been asked if he wished to see a doctor. He had signed for his meagre possessions. His signature was his only active co-operation in the Castlereagh reception process. The Chief sat now in a solitary cell.

He had no way of knowing how many men had been lifted with him, but he had seen the numbers of the vehicles in the yard at Springfield Road. The numbers of Saracens and Land Rovers added up to a big lift.

Confusion, anger, frustration, swam in his mind. What had the pigs got on him? What had the pigs got lined up and ready and waiting for him? No detective had yet bothered to talk to him. He was in bloody solitary.

They had taken the Chief's watch. He had been in the solitary cell probably for less than twenty minutes, and it seemed to be for bloody ever. Many times, dates spread over many years, he had been lifted. This was a changed time. Never before had the bastards seemed so confident.

Frankie came within sight of the maisonettes.

There were Land Rovers outside the block, and uniformed policemen, and as he cruised gently forward he saw two detectives coming out of the doorway and carrying a plastic bag between them that was filled with clothes.

Frankie knew the block. He knew it was where the Chief was currently sleeping.

He set off to check the home of Ollie O'Brien and Joey McGilivarry and Tom McCreevy. He knew what he would find. His face was grim set.

When he saw the Land Rovers at Ollie O'Brien's in Andytown, he muttered soundlessly to his chest: 'Gingy McAnally, you're fucking dead. So help me, you're dead, you fucking tout.'

Rennie had said to him that he shouldn't try to talk to Roisin until they were in the safe house. Rennie warned him that she would be in shock, and that he should take it slowly. Rennie played the marriage bloody guidance priest with him. Rennie had talked to him quietly by the window after the men had been brought into the yard. They would have the morning together, what remained of the morning, and after lunch Rennie would come to the safe house and he would explain to Roisin what was happening and then she'd see it easier.

Didn't see it so bloody easy now, did she? Hadn't bloody spoken to him all the time they had been in the canteen, and he'd seen the vicious look on her face when Little Patty had come to sit on his knee.

Rennie had gone when the Land Rovers had left for Castlereagh.

There was a uniformed Inspector at the next table to them, who cleaned his fingernails with a used match, and there were the police-women who'd become tired of clearing up Little Patty's food and of finding new comics for Young Gerard, and there were two constables who sat at tables that were a little away from them and acted as watch-dogs to stop any man using the canteen from coming too close to them.

Abruptly, the Inspector looked at his watch, like it was an after-thought and he was caught by surprise ... Bloody liar ... The Inspector stood, motioned for McAnally to come and waved to Roisin and the kids that they should follow ... acting like he'd get a bloody disease if he spoke to them. Roisin had Baby Sean on her shoulder. McAnally picked up Little Patty. He put out his hand for Young Gerard to take, and the kid stuck his hands down into his pockets. He'd belt the bugger if he did that tomorrow.

The Inspector led, the family following, and after the family came the policewomen and the two constables. They came out into the yard. It was quiet outside. The family crossed the yard. It was as if they were now unremarkable and uninteresting. McAnally couldn't see anyone watching them. He could see soldiers and police going about their work, but he shifted Little Patty higher on his shoulder and tried to walk taller.

There was an escort of policemen and three Land Rovers waiting for them. He couldn't turn, not to face Roisin. He felt Little Patty flinching against his shoulder as he walked closer to the Land Rovers.

'Well done, Mr McAnally.'

He stopped. He swung and saw Ferris. Ferris was coming forward, walking fast, from behind him. He saw the officer smile hesitantly. His face was still smeared with camouflage cream.

'I really meant it when I said it before, well done. I admire what you've done.'

Roisin was at his shoulder. He felt her eyes on him. 'I told you why I did it.'

Ferris said, 'Doesn't matter why, only matters what you're doing.'

McAnally peered into Ferris's face. 'I did it so's I wouldn't go to the Kesh.'

The officer was shaking his head, laughing gently. 'Rubbish, if you'll forgive me, Mr McAnally. You turned your back on something evil, that's why I admire what you've done . . .'

Roisin was staring at him, contempt at her lips, and she seemed to mouth the word 'evil', as if it were an insult to her religion.

'You know fuck all.'

'Try me, Mr McAnally, try me some day. Come back and tell me whether it was just staying out of the Kesh, or helping to destroy something that's rotten in this community . . . You should be very proud of him, Mrs McAnally.'

'Keep her out of it.'

'I read up about the kestrel, Mr McAnally. Lovely bird. Free to every limit. Free as your children should be, free as Mrs McAnally should be.'

McAnally came close to Ferris.

'Why am I important to you?' he said hoarsely.

'You want to know?'

'I want to know.'

'I can't change the course of this war, can't move it an inch. You can change it, you can cut away something that's foul. I can't but you can. Compared with what you can do, I'm wasting my time. I'm insignificant, all of us here are irrelevant, if we're compared with what you can achieve.'

'I've done it for myself, myself and my family only.'

'I don't think so.'

'Why don't you ever listen?'

'Mightn't believe what I'm told.'

McAnally went to the Land Rover. He waited at the back doors to help Roisin climb up inside.

# 10

The Land Rover carrying the McAnally family jerked to a halt. The rear doors opened, flooding the interior with light. The escorts jumped down. They were in the middle of a housing estate. Past the bodies of the constables he saw small front gardens with low white-painted fences, and windows slung with net curtains and decorated with pot plants. The houses were of soft brick and whitewood facing and were semi-detached. A constable reached back into the Land Rover to lift out the one suitcase.

'Let's get you comfortable, Mrs McAnally,' the Inspector said brusquely. 'Always get the ladies comfortable first, isn't that right, Mr McAnally?'

McAnally reckoned it would have hurt the Inspector to call her 'lady', and him 'Mister'. Roisin, beside him, snorted.

She went first, carrying Baby Sean. He went after her, with Little Patty. Young Gerard ignored his father's hand to help him down, and a constable's hand, and wriggled out on the seat of his trousers and dropped onto the roadway.

Just an ordinary estate, if McAnally kept his eyeline low. An everyday estate for everyday people. They were in the end right-hand house of a cul-de-sac.

The Inspector looked sharply round him, as if on an ordinary estate there could be danger. 'Straight in, please, Mrs McAnally.'

McAnally looked for further horizons. On the rising ground behind the houses he saw the corrugated iron screen fencing, and the coiled barbed wire. He saw a perimeter guard tower, blacked and draped in camouflage netting and further protected by a rocket screen. They were on a sloping hillside, the Shorts aircraft factory and the waters of Belfast Lough were below them.

Palace barracks. Every man who had ever sworn the oath to the

Organization knew about Palace Barracks, Holywood. The lore of the Palace Barracks was rooted in the activities of the Special Branch and Intelligence Corps interrogators a dozen years before, and the 'five techniques' used on the Provo suspects in the early years of the war. Hooding, the noise machine, standing against the wall on tiptoe, deprivation of sleep, absence of food, those were the Famous Five that had been imported to Northern Ireland after successful use in Aden, Cyprus, Malaya, wherever any little nationalist runt gave two fingers to the Brits. More than two thousand men had gone through Holywood before the interrogators packed up, locked up, and went to Castlereagh. Palace Barracks had reverted to its previous role, home for a long-stay married accompanied battalion of the regular army. The Palace Barracks into which Gingy McAnally and his family had been brought was base for eighteen months for the Devons and Dorsets and their families.

Across the cul-de-sac a woman was bent and was picking up by hand the last of the leaves to fall on her handkerchief lawn and was placing them one by one into a plastic supermarket bag, and when she saw the flotsam spill out from the Land Rover opposite she put down her bag deliberately and went back into her house and firmly closed the door.

Roisin McAnally had seen the woman. She gazed expressionless at the slammed door. At the entry to the cul-de-sac were two women, one with a push chair and baby, one with a soldier husband, and their mouths moved in unheard talk, and the woman kissed her soldier on the cheek, and they looked one last time at the family and the soldier went one way and the woman with the push chair went another. She saw the young face of a woman at a window, and when she met the stare the curtain fell and hid the face.

She followed the Inspector up the narrow front pathway, and he took a key from his pocket and opened the front door.

She turned her face away from Baby Sean and back towards McAnally.

'You know they think we're shit, don't you?'

He didn't answer.

If the Inspector had heard, he gave no sign. At a brisk pace he led Roisin McAnally around the house. It was furnished, army issue, for a junior non-commissioned officer. A through living room with a worn sofa and chairs around a gas fire, a table at the far end beside the glass doors out onto the back garden, no pictures on the walls and the last of the ducks in flight had a chipped wing.

'It's the best we could do in the time we had, Mrs McAnally ... and it's safe here, that's the main thing. It's a bit bare, but it's quite comfortable.'

Of course, it was beyond the Inspector's reasoning that Roisin McAnally had never felt anything but safe in Turf Lodge, and could never feel anything but danger if she was sleeping in the heart of a Brit army barracks.

Up the stairs, feet padding on the carpet, the Inspector and Roisin McAnally and Young Gerard staying close to her, and McAnally left behind in the living room holding Little Patty's hand and carrying Baby Sean.

'Three bedrooms upstairs, Mrs McAnally. One's a double bed, one's twins, one's single. Bathroom, loo, hot water all the time, much as you want. It's not that bad, is it?'

'How long are we here?'

'That's not for me to say. Mr Rennie'll be down, he'll decide that.'

'And what do we decide?' she snapped.

'Your decision's been made, Mrs McAnally. Your husband's decided for you, that's why you're here.'

The beds were unmade. There were neatly folded piles of blankets and sheets and pillows on the mattresses.

She came down the stairs after him.

'My baby'll want milk.'

'In the fridge, Mrs McAnally.'

Everything organized, everything planned, and the Inspector seemed to tell her that after life in Turf Lodge this must be bloody paradise. She went into the kitchen to find milk from the fridge.

She heard McAnally's voice from the living room.

'Have you chucked someone out? Have you turfed someone out to make room for us?'

She heard the Inspector's voice.

'Came vacant last week. A corporal was shot in Short Strand. The bullet did his spine, paralysed him. They flew him to Stoke Mandeville in the UK, his wife's gone with him, and their kiddies. That's why the house is free.'

She was frozen at the open door of the fridge, her hand was on the milk bottle. She couldn't help herself, she had to hear what her man replied. There was a long silence.

'I'm sorry,' McAnally said.

Jesus, God Al-fucking-mighty. Sean McAnally telling a Prod peeler that he was sorry a squaddy had got himself taken out of Belfast on his back.

'I'll be outside,' the Inspector said. 'Mr Rennie'll be here soon. You shouldn't go out, not till he's been, and the kids shouldn't go out.'

She heard the door close. She took the milk from the fridge, and then opened a cupboard and she saw piles of plates and saucers, and cups, and mugs. There was a mug with rabbits on it, and she reached for it without thinking, and then she wondered if it had been left behind in the panic rush to get to a bedside in an English hospital. She wondered, and she blinked her eyes, and took down the mug. She might have smashed the mug, instead she filled it with milk.

She took the milk into the living room.

She saw pleading on her husband's face.

'It's nice isn't it?' McAnally said. 'It's a nice house . . .'

'You're bought cheap. Running hot water, and a stair carpet and you're happy to bloody tout.'

'It's the best for us, for all of us,' he was shouting. 'It's because I love you, you and the kids.'

Young Gerard ran from the window to clutch at his mother's waist.

'I'm sorry,' she mimicked.

He looked out of the window. He saw the Land Rover, and the Inspector standing by the door and smoking a cigarette. He looked the other way, down the length of the room, out of the glass doors and across the back garden and saw the dark silhouette of a uniformed constable.

'It's a hell of a way to show you love us, Sean, bringing us here.'

*   *   *

Frankie crossed West Belfast many times that morning in his effort to measure the scale of the lifts. He was in Twinbrook and Suffolk, in Finaghy and Beachmount, in Ballymurphy and Whiterock, in Andersonstown and Falls. He checked the homes and safe houses of the big men of Brigade and the Battalions. He saw the smashed-down doors.

He was known in the Organization as a willing helper. He held no Brigade rank, nor any position in a particular Battalion. His friends liked to think of him as a troubleshooter, and that always raised a laugh in a snug bar or an upstairs back room. He floated from the ASUs and the Volunteers up the ladder to the big shots who surrounded the chief. He knew almost every man who had been taken to Castlereagh, and so he knew how grave the damage was.

That morning Frankie Conroy felt the fear of many men in the city. It was the fear bred by a traitor, and the fear was fuelled by the danger of the domino. If one man turned and implicated a cell block full of friends, then would one of those friends go supergrass too? Where did it end?

There was one way, one way only, in Frankie's thinking, to handle a tout. He should be handled at barrel point. The informer should be terrorized into retraction. The long arm of the Organization had to reach to the safe house of the tout. And the bastard could be in any police station in the city, or in any military barracks, or he could be up in Prot country in the north of Co. Antrim, or he could be in the Air Force compound at Aldergrove . . . where to begin to bloody look?

He had called a meeting. Without authority he had taken charge. Who could give Frankie Conroy authority to blow his bloody nose when Brigade staff was in Castlereagh, and half of the Battalion officers with them? The meeting was called for lunch hour in the bar in Clonard where there was a private room, where Frankie was comfortable.

During the morning Frankie had worked hard. He had dug into the background lives of Sean and Roisin McAnally. In Turf Lodge, the Parade and the Drive ran parallel. He parked in the Parade and cut through a garden and climbed the low common fence and came to the back door of a house in the Drive, the back door of Number 12.

He saw the old woman in the kitchen, washing her smalls.

He rapped on the window.

She came to the back door.

'It's Mrs O'Rourke?'

'Who's wanting me?'

'Not to matter who's wanting you . . . You're the Ma of Roisin McAnally? . . . You're the Gran of Gerard and Patty and Sean . . .?'

He saw the nervousness in her face.

'Been to 63 this morning, Mrs O'Rourke?'

'I have.'

'And I'll bet you didn't get much of a welcome this morning, Mrs O'Rourke.'

'What's it to you?'

'Don't ask me questions, Mrs O'Rourke . . . What did you find, at 63, this morning?'

Between his finger and thumb he could have broken her thin wrist, but he held her wrist lightly, like a friend, and he spoke softly, like a saviour.

'Found nothing, found them gone.' There was a dribble glistening at her eyes.

'Gone without telling her Ma?'

'She never said nothing about going.'

'You've a telephone, Mrs O'Rourke?'

'She never rung me. I've a telephone. She never rung me to say she was going.'

'Where's she gone, Mrs O'Rourke?'

The wet eyes dropped. Frankie was inside the kitchen. He closed the door behind him. She didn't answer him.

'Where's your man, Mrs O'Rourke, where's Roisin's Da?'

'He's in bed, with a chest. It'd kill him to know what she's done.'

'You know what she's done?'

'Her furniture's taken, little enough of it, but it's gone.'

'Shall I make a pot of tea for us, Mrs O'Rourke . . . Sean McAnally's gone supergrass . . . Where's your kettle? . . . Your Roisin's married to a tout . . . 'Scuse me for the tap . . . Your grankids have an informer for a father . . .'

Frankie had filled the kettle. He lit the gas ring. He was looking to the shelves for the tea tin, and she pointed to it.

'It's not out yet, Mrs O'Rourke, but it's going to be out. The dad of Gerard and Patty and Sean is an informer. He's buying his freedom with the gaoling of thirty men. He's a paid perjurer. He's going to lie his way through a show trial. The men he's named, they're some of the finest Irish patriots ever born. Mrs O'Rourke ... we'll need some milk ... Mrs O'Rourke, Sean McAnally is going to be hated in this city wherever there is pride in the nation of Ireland. He's going to be hated, along with your daughter, along with your grankids ... The kettle's boiled, Mrs O'Rourke.'

She made the tea in the old teapot, the pot she had been given at her wedding.

She passed Frankie Conroy his mug of tea. She put him in a spoon of sugar, and her hand was shaking, and the grains were spread on the table beside the pile of waiting washing.

'What do you want of me?'

'I want to help you, Mrs O'Rourke. I'm not asking for anything from you, I'm trying to help you, to save you from what's going to hit you when it's known that your Roisin's man's a tout.'

'What do you want from me?'

'You've got it wrong, Mrs O'Rourke, I'm helping you ... it's good tea ... a man's going to come to see you, a law man, he's going to ask something of you. Mrs O'Rourke, we want to get Roisin back to you, back to her home with your grankids, that's all we want. Mrs O'Rourke, if Roisin telephones for you, find out where she is. If she's not to be hated as the enemy of the Irish people then we have to know where she is ... that's a grand cup, thanks ... we don't want her hated like Sean McAnally, do we, Mrs O'Rourke?'

He left his tea half finished. He went out of the kitchen, and back the way he had come.


Rennie held up his warrant card at the gate barrier. The soldier on sentry scrutinized it, nodded him through, and Rennie gestured behind him to draw attention to the two following cars.

He knew the way, after a fashion. It was a dozen years since he had worked in Palace Barracks, but he remembered the layout although the married quarters had been extended since his time.

St Andrew's Close, Number 15. It was a bugger to find because all the Closes and Terraces and Gardens and Avenues were damn near the same. He asked a housewife, deciphered her Plymouth accent, and found the house with the Land Rover and the Inspector parked outside.

He went to the door. There were two men, younger than Rennie, behind him.

McAnally opened the door.

'Alright, Gingy?' Rennie asked, as if there could be no problem.

'She won't speak to me, fucking cutting me out.'

'Leave her to me, Gingy.'

He went through the door and the two men followed him. They were of a type, old slacks, heavy shoes, sweaters and anoraks. They were alert, interested, they were at work as if going through the door was the act of card punching.

The television was on in the living room, soap opera, trivial lives where no-one thought of blasting a judge to his maker with a Soviet-built RPG warhead. Rennie's nose turned. He reckoned the baby must have peed on the carpet. A fog of cigarette smoke. He saw the filled ashtray on the arm of the chair in which she sat. Half the smoke was going up the baby's nose ... perhaps the little bugger peed on the carpet in protest.

Rennie said, 'Let's get the introductions over ... This is John Prentice, this is Andy Goss. John and Andy are the guarantee of your safety ...'

Roisin McAnally looked up at him, there was a sneer on her mouth. 'Are they here to see we don't run away?'

'They're here as guarantees of your personal protection, no more and no less ... Spare me a minute, please, Mrs McAnally.'

He nodded his head back towards the door. It wasn't a request, and she stood and followed him. They went out of the room, and without comment Rennie led the way up the stairs and into the main bedroom. She had not made the bed, she had not unpacked the suitcase.

'Sit down, Mrs McAnally.'

She sat, and she stared up at him and her eyes were bright with pain and suspicion.

'A few facts, Mrs McAnally. Your Sean, in our book, is a Converted Terrorist. That means that we are prepared to give him immunity from prosecution, while he is prepared to testify in court against the men with whom he formerly engaged in criminal and illegal acts. Some men who have taken a similar road have abandoned their families, left them at home to face the music. Sean insisted that you and your children should be taken into our protective care, and we are very happy to provide that care. For the next few weeks we will keep you in Belfast because there's still a hefty amount of ground for Sean to cover with us, after that you may go across the water to England or we may look further away – Cyprus, Gibraltar – but all that depends on the timing of the Magistrates' committal proceedings in which Sean will provide prosecution evidence. When that's done we'll be thinking about something permanent, a new start for you all. After the trial proper we promise to build a new identity for Sean, you, the children, a new identity in a new location. Financially you will be looked after, not luxury, but comfortable . . .'

'Sean's got immunity?'

'Correct.'

'He's guaranteed immunity?'

'Correct.'

'We're not prisoners here?'

'You're free to go whenever, wherever you wish.'

'And you'll not stop us going now . . . going home now . . .'

She stood.

'Hear me out, Mrs McAnally.'

'I'm going home.'

There was a winter smile spreading on Rennie's face. He took a folded sheet of paper from his pocket.

'Thought this might interest you, transcript of the local lunchtime radio . . . Listening, Mrs McAnally?'

Her eyes never left his face. He thought that if Sean Pius McAnally had blown Howard Rennie away, then she'd have given him an extra screw that night, to tell him he'd done well.

'This is what they said on the lunchtime . . . "Shortly after a West Belfast family were taken by police into protective care early this morning, Security Forces launched their largest arrest operation of the year. A Provisional Sinn Fein spokesman has admitted that Sean Pius McAnally of the Drive in Turf Lodge has implicated many leading Republicans after turning supergrass following his arrest a week ago in connection with the RPG attack that killed Mr Justice William Simpson and two of his police bodyguards." . . . Listening, Mrs McAnally? . . . "Police sources were claiming this morning that Mr McAnally's statements had led to the arrest of the entire Brigade staff of the PIRA in Belfast and of many Battalion-ranking officers. One senior detective said, 'We now have firm evidence against some of the most vicious killers who have been preying on our community.' It is known that at least thirty men were picked up in the dawn swoops." . . . Got it, Mrs McAnally?'

Rennie replaced the sheet of paper in his pocket.

'You haven't a home to go back to, Mrs McAnally.'

'You bastard.'

'And you're a sensible woman.'

'What did you do to him?'

'Your baby's crying, Mrs McAnally.'

'You've bloody destroyed him.'

'I didn't destroy him, Mrs McAnally. I didn't kill a judge and two police officers, I wasn't staring down a twenty-five-year stretch . . . I'm bloody Father Christmas to you and your family.'

'He'll be looking over his shoulder for the rest of his life.'

'Not true . . . and even if it were true that's better than the rest of his life in the Kesh. Mrs McAnally, get used to one thing: after what he's told us there's no going back for Sean, there's no "going home". If Sean goes home he's dead in the gutter. Don't tell me you'd prefer that.'

'You *bastard.*'

'We're getting repetitive, Mrs McAnally . . . Thank you for sparing me a minute.'

Rennie went out, and closed the door on her. He heard the first sob in her throat.

He went downstairs.

He called brightly through the door. 'Did you bring those cans in, Andy?'

Inside the living room was his answer. Half a dozen Tennants cans on the low table beside the sofa. McAnally looked questioningly at Rennie.

Rennie said, 'She's had a hell of a day, Gingy. She's going to lie down for a bit, best for her.'

The Cortina car was unremarkable, eight years old, paint scraped and rusted.

There were two men in the car, and in their different ways they were as unremarkable as their transport. Perhaps they were labourers, perhaps they were a farmer's sons.

It was the third time in as many days that these two men had come south of the border and into Monaghan town. On the previous two days they had established the pattern of life inside and outside the workshop of the watchmender. These two men could blend into crowds, onto streets. It was their training. Without drawing attention to themselves they had surveyed the workshop, found the rear ground-level window to the cellar, reckoned how fire would be contained in the cellar, checked the daily movements of the watchmender. They could blend easily, if they didn't speak.

They had left Gough Barracks in Armagh as the afternoon light was dipping and instead of taking the direct road to Monaghan they had gone the long way, through Killylea and Caledon, before turning off the road to substitute southern car plates for northern ones.

Each man was armed with a Browning automatic pistol. It was a chance, a risk, to be armed and to be stopped at a Guarda or Irish Army checkpoint, but nothing to the chance and risk of being blown by the Provos and left without means of defence.

In the boot of the car was a two-gallon can of petrol.

No record existed of their orders. Their initative was to be given free rein. They appreciated that freedom. All the Troopers and NCOs of the Special Air Service working from Northern Ireland appreciated freedom. These two men had been given the information that the watchmender in Monoghan doubled as a craftsman in explosive devices.

*     *     *

Mr Pronsias Reilly had driven in his lunch hour to Turf Lodge. On the way back to the city centre he had mapped out in his mind the statement that he would issue in the name of Mrs Chrissie O'Rourke. In Mr Pronsias Reilly's book it was a scandal that a woman and her kids could be 'kidnapped' by police from her home in the middle of the night at gun point.

He had told Mrs O'Rourke that he would do his certain damndest to get her daughter back to her, and the issuing of her statement would be a positive step.

Was Mr Pronsias Reilly opposed to the Provos? Too simplistic a question for a successful young legal mind. Phrase the question again. Was Mr Pronsias Reilly opposed to violence? Definitely, he was opposed to violence, to the violence of the British army, the Royal Ulster Constabulary, the Special Air Service, the prison staff, the Ulster Defence Regiment, the Protestant paramilitary assassination squads. Was Mr Pronsias Reilly opposed to Provo violence? Ah, but with all the violence thrown against the Nationalist minority small wonder that they turned to their own army for protection.

From his own perspective he regarded himself as realistic. In the eyes of his professional colleagues, he was ambivalent.

And for their opinions he cared not a tuppenny crap.

The word had gone out, the word said that Frankie Conroy had called for a meeting at the bar in Clonard.

There were eight men in the private room, and there was a man on the staircase, and there were two more men in the long bar to watch.

'There's no pissing, no messing, McAnally's to be stiffed. McAnally's dead, from this time he's dead. McAnally will not appear in court. For what he's done, he doesn't just retract his evidence and walk back to us like nothing's different. He's dead. First I want him cringing, then I want him screaming, then I want him dead. They're crowing up there at Headquarters. They won't crow long. Wherever he is, we reach him.'

There were no interruptions.

'We reach him, and we smash him.'

The meeting settled after Frankie's address to set up the command structure that would replace the lifted Brigade organization, and to prepare the necessary intelligence network that would track McAnally to his safe house.

Eight men, drinking and smoking and plotting the death of Sean Pius McAnally, tout.

'Roisin'll take us to him, whether she knows it or she doesn't. She'll take us there, right to him. She's a good girl, she's the way to him.'

The television was on for the children, cartoons.

John Prentice had taken a chair into the hall, he'd left Andy in the living room with the kids. He thought Mrs McAnally was asleep upstairs, and Gingy had just gone up, to leak, because he'd five Tennants in him. It wasn't the first time that Prentice had played minder to a supergrass. He had been on the squad two years. The last one had been a Protestant, UVF thug, who'd done his show in court and been shipped off to Australia, the last one would be good news to the bookmakers in Melbourne or Sydney or Adelaide or wherever. He was a Detective Constable in the RUC, he had been told that he was selected for work of the most exacting nature. Christ, he hadn't known the half of it when he started out. He had learned to play wetnurse, nanny, prison officer, confidant and bully. The first days were the hardest with a new supergrass. The first days were when he had to grope to find the personality of his man, and then learn to respond to that personality, and then to control it. The psychologist who came to Headquarters said that the relationship between a supergrass and a minder should be taken slowly the first few days. No rush, no speed, because it's ball and chain for weeks and months.

There was a PPK handgun in the shoulder holster under Prentice's jacket. He was a trained marksman. There were two sides to the job of minder. There was the personal contact bit, and there was the bodyguard bit. He was three years senior to Goss, three years more service. He was responsible for getting Gingy McAnally into court as a credible witness offering evidence without corroboration. He was responsible for seeing that Gingy McAnally's nerve held up, and he was responsible for keeping the man out of the gutter and out of the sights of an Armalite. A fair old responsibility for John Prentice, aged twenty-nine. The psychologist said that the minder had to build an atmosphere of delicate control and influence. The psychologist characterized it as 'discreet domination'. Fine for the psychologist. The psychologist wasn't going to be cooped up for weeks with a Provo murderer and a Provo murderer's wife and their kids. In a bag in the boot of his car was a spare shirt and spare socks and a plastic razor. He had nothing to go back to that he could call a home. He lived in a furnished flatlet off the Newtownards Road, had been there since his wife had kicked him out of their Glengormley bungalow. Divorce yourself from the police, or she'd divorce him, that had been her ultimatum. He had made his choice. He thought she was young enough to find some other fellow. He would sleep on the sofa in the living room of the safe house, and not think a lot about it. Andy had it coming, he had a fiancée in the Northern Bank, who didn't like the hours, and didn't like the drinking, and wasn't hot on the danger. Andy's time would come too.

He could handle Gingy, he'd decided that. He didn't know whether he could handle Roisin. He wasn't sure if Gingy could handle Roisin.

The toilet flushed. McAnally was coming down the stairs. Behind McAnally the bedroom door opened. The sleep hadn't done her much good. She came fast down the stairs, and bumped past her man and nearly spilled him, and went into the living room running as if she thought Andy might be abusing her kids.

'Alright, Gingy?'

'Not bad.'

There hadn't been any kids in his own marriage. He'd taken his chair into the hallway because he wasn't good with kids. Andy was better. Andy came from a vicarage in County Tyrone that was stuffed with kids. The older boy had problems written all over him, not responding to Gingy, shrinking from himself and from Andy, and too bloody quiet. The girl was alright, the girl was too young, but the older boy knew his father was a tout.

The cartoons were gone, on the television, and the adverts. John Prentice heard the signature tune of the news.

He heard the voices.

Mrs McAnally said, 'Leave it on.'

Andy said, 'Better you don't see it.'

The announcer spoke the name of Sean Pius McAnally.

'Leave it bloody on.'

'You'll only hurt yourself.'

The announcer described Sean Pius McAnally as the most signifi-
cant supergrass the RUC had yet found.

John Prentice came to the door of the living room. Andy had
given way. The little girl pointed in innocence at the screen and
photograph of her father. The next picture showed a house on an
estate, and the boy watched it blankly and said nothing because it
was his home.

Silence in the room because all eyes were on the television, then
Roisin had her hand at her mouth and her fist was clenched tight.

'That's Ma . . .'

A photograph of an elderly lady on the screen. And the announcer
said that the old lady was the mother-in-law of Sean Pius McAnally,
and that the lady pleaded with her daughter to come back home to
her . . .

'That's Gran . . .' the little girl said.

Her daughter should come back to her, because whatever her
man had done, Roisin had done no wrong.

Shit, Andy bloody Goss should have bloody pulled the plug out.

Prentice strode into the room, straight to the television, switched
it off.

'What's you done that for?' Roisin screamed at him.

'Because it's best off.'

'You tell me what I watch?'

'When it's for your own good, yes.'

'You think I shouldn't know what's said about me? . . . That was
my Ma that you switched off.'

'For a bit it's better you don't watch.'

'You tell him,' she turned to McAnally. 'You tell him I'm watching
the bloody television.'

McAnally walked away. He stepped over Young Gerard's legs, he
went past Little Patty, on past the sofa where Baby Sean was sleeping. He went to the back window of the living room. He could see the
line of the perimeter arc lamps circling Palace Barracks.

'Tell him to put the telly back on for me.'

He went away from the window. He was desperate, he was in agony. She stood in front of him. Her hands were on her hips, her head was tossed back. His lips quivered, but he could not speak.

She sneered, 'A man would tell him to put the telly on for me.'

Nothing for Prentice to say.

'Tell him to switch it on for me.'

McAnally howled, deep in his pain. 'I only did it for you, for you and the kids . . .'

'Lying sod.'

'It was just for you.'

'You hadn't the balls to go to the Kesh.'

'Because I love my kids.'

'The men in the Kesh are twice the man you are.'

'Because I love you.'

'You're a yellow bastard.'

McAnally hit his wife. He hit her with the flat of his hand across the face.

Goss caught Young Gerard, held him struggling as he tried to get to his father, to defend his mother.

McAnally and his wife clutched for each other. They were both weeping. Their arms were around each other, and the tears were wet on their faces. McAnally buried his kisses in Roisin's shaking, sobbing head.

Goss said to Young Gerard, 'Let's make a cup of tea for your Ma, laddie.'

The watchmender in Monaghan died that evening in the cellar below his workshop.

He was working on a booby trap when a boot kicked in the glass of the cellar's high window, when the petrol streamed down over his work bench, when the match was thrown.

The watchmender in Monaghan had never heard the name of Sean Pius McAnally.

# I I

Because Baby Sean's growing teeth ached in his gums the small child tossed and cried through the night, even when Roisin cuddled his body against her. Coming down the stairs Roisin was withdrawn inside herself and pale-skinned and red eyed, and McAnally had snapped that he didn't have to shave every bloody day and his eyes were puffed and staring strangely. By morning Baby Sean was finally asleep, curled in the centre of their bed.

Goss was in the kitchen, boiling a kettle, looking for tea bags, managing a welcoming smile for Roisin. Prentice drowsed in his hallway chair. Goss greeted Roisin as if there was nothing odd in a woman coming into her kitchen and finding a detective with a shoulder holster worn over his sleeveless sweater rummaging for a teapot. He didn't bother to ask her how she had slept. One thing he had found since he'd come to Palace Barracks was that the woman was the strength of the pair. Whatever happened down the road at Castlereagh with her man, when it came to the home then it was with Roisin McAnally that the minders had to score. Goss reckoned there were never two equals in a marriage, there was one on the top and one on the bottom, and in this family it was Roisin who ruled. If he and Prentice messed with her, then they were scratching . . . and she had walls around her that would take some battering.

She moved around him in the kitchen as if he were an obstruction. With Goss awake and Prentice sleeping it was pretty obvious how they'd spent their night. Staggered duties of sleep and guard. She'd get used to it, she'd have to get used to it, and get used to the pistols worn against their chests, and to the personal radio that was clamped in Prentice's hands.

She had made a small effort to face the day. She wore a smear of lipstick, and she'd combed her hair back to the elastic band. McAnally had made no effort. Not that his cropped hair needed combing and brushing, but the fact that he hadn't washed was clear from the last evening's newsprint stains on his fingers and the sleep in his eyes. Goss sat with them at the kitchen table for toast and tea, and could smell McAnally. Goss's girl, the girl he was to marry, the girl who worked in the Northern Bank, she was a stickler for personal cleanliness. Goss's girl would have said that Andy Goss should pack it in, and get himself something half decent, something where he didn't touch dirt like this. That was another problem, Goss's girl, that was a problem that wouldn't get sorted that morning.

Roisin didn't acknowledge Goss at the table. Goss did not exist. She didn't pass him the toast, nor the butter, nor the jam. She let him pour his own tea, his own milk.

There was a key in the door. Roisin listened. Goss listened. They heard Prentice's voice, and Rennie's, a murmured confidential conversation out in the hall.

'Are we going out this morning?'

'Where?'

Roisin looked at McAnally as if he were an idiot.

'Shopping, for me, for the kids, for the kitchen.'

'Not with me, you're not.' McAnally shovelled toast into his mouth.

'Why not?'

'Because I'm out.'

'Where are you?'

McAnally didn't reply. He reached for more toast.

If it hadn't been so bloody important Goss could have had a big belly laugh. Gingy McAnally wasn't up to telling his Missus that he'd be off to Castlereagh for the morning to do a bit more touting. Gingy hadn't the bottle to chat to the Missus with the happy news that he was spilling through the morning on some more of his mates, and stitching them up for Tens and Twenties.

'So, when you're out, what do I do?'

McAnally poured himself tea.

Rennie came in.

Rennie was like a big bloody bouncing ball. If he was aware of the cut in the atmosphere of the kitchen he gave no sign of it.

'Come on, Gingy ... Start of the working day. Jump to it, lad.'

That was rich, Goss thought, because he knew from the file that Sean Pius McAnally had never held down a job in his life. Urban guerrilla on the dole, freedom fighter on Supplementary Benefit.

'Morning, Mrs McAnally, settling nicely I hope ... Come on, Gingy, shift yourself, we've got a mountain today.'

Goss had to hand it to Rennie. The old cut-throat knew what he was at. Jollying the reptile along was the name of the game, with cheerful, bruising authority. He saw the glance that Roisin gave Rennie. Prentice was well out of it, Prentice was clever to have his head down.

McAnally stood. There was a moment of indecision and then he bent quickly and kissed Roisin on the forehead, and her face seemed to say that if she had known what he was about to do then she would have ducked her face away.

Prentice went with McAnally and Rennie, out through the front door. Rennie led, and Prentice was behind McAnally and close to him.

Goss was watching Roisin. She gazed after them, and then at the slammed front door. He saw the sneer on her face. Now she stood up and walked to the back window.

Goss saw the slimness of her hips, the outline of her shoulder blades.

'It'll get better, Mrs McAnally. There are only two bad bits. This is one of the bad bits, trying to find your balance after what's happened to you. The other bit is when your husband goes into court.'

He couldn't see what sight, out of the window, held her attention.

'There's two bad bits, and a whole lot of good things. Look at it this way ... if Sean had gone to the Kesh for life then you and the kids are wrecked for ever. You're not wrecked now, far from it. You're in good shape and you're in honest hands.'

He saw that he had reached her, that at least she listened to him. Her head jolted back. He fancied her mouth was set in derision.

'The kids have a chance now. The kids have a chance to do something decent with their lives. It's the worst thing with what goes on here that the kids are stained for the rest of their lives with what their parents have done. You don't believe you're in honest hands? We're going to show you that you're wrong.'

She turned to face him. There was a snap of a short smile on her face, and then she looked away.

'I'll be getting the kids up, making the beds.'

She went past him. He heard her tripping up the stairs.

'Tell him you want to play that draughts game.'

'I don't know how to play the game.'

'I'm not caring whether you know how. Tell him to teach you.'

Roisin was at the front bedroom window. She could see the woman from the next house but one and the woman from the house beyond that. They had their overcoats on and there was a push chair and a wheeled shopping basket.

'Gerard, you learn to play the game from him, you be sweet to him.'

'I hate the shit peeler.'

When he was very small she would have ear clipped him for swearing, when he was three or four years old. She didn't any longer. She barely noticed his obscenities.

'Gerard, if I didn't want you to play the game with him then I wouldn't be asking you. Do as I say, Gerard.'

'I have to?'

'You have to.'

Roisin went down the stairs half the flight behind Gerard. Baby Sean was still asleep, Little Patty was in her bed and turning the pages of a picture book. Roisin heard Gerard shyly ask Goss to show him the draughts game. She heard the detective's surprised and pleased reply. Oh, he'd like that, would the detective. He'd like to show the boy how to play a game like draughts. The living room door was open. Goss would be able to see the front door, would be able to watch it even though he was teaching the boy to play the game of draughts. Bloody good kid, that Gerard. Good because he did what he was told without a bloody inquest of explanations.

It was in the night that she had decided what she would do. When she was sleepless, when Gingy had been on his back and moaning his worries, when Baby Sean had been fretting on his teeth, when she had remembered the television.

The kitchen door was locked, and no key. With care she moved the saucepans off the draining board. She climbed easily onto the draining board. Away in the living room she heard the clatter of the draught pieces, and Goss's laughter. She eased the window open.

She dropped out through the window. She pushed the window shut behind her.

There was a cold, wet wind catching at her sweater. She couldn't have put on a coat, too bulky for the narrow kitchen window. She had to pass the window doors of the living room. She couldn't help herself, she peered for a moment into the lit room and saw Gerard on his knees, and Goss leaning forward from his chair and the draughts board on the carpet. She scurried past the windows. Her teeth were chattering.

The side fences separating the small back gardens were waist-high. Her foot sank into the flowerbed as she levered herself up and over the fence and into the next-door garden. The curtains at the back of the house were drawn. She climbed the second fence.

The kitchen door of the house of the woman with a push chair was unlocked.

She went inside. She tiptoed through a polished, scrubbed-down kitchen – house-proud bitch – and into the darkened hallway.

On the low table near the front door, and beside the army dress wedding photograph, was the telephone.

'Remember this, Gingy, he can't touch you. The time that he could hurt you is gone. You go in there and you do your stuff, and you remember that his days for frightening folks are over.'

If Sean Pius McAnally could not confront the Chief with a direct accusation then it was a waste of time, everybody's time, to consider that the supergrass could stand up in court and survive hostile cross-examination. Rennie, pacing near the window, knew that. MacAnally, sitting at the table, knew that. Prentice and McDonough and Astley, standing between the door and McAnally, knew that. Obvious to every man in the room, and unsaid, was the clear fact that McAnally had to be able to level his charge into the Chief's face.

'What's the big deal?' McAnally snarled. 'Who said there was a problem?'

'That's the boy,' Rennie said.

'He doesn't scare me, Mr Rennie.'

'Nice to hear that, Gingy.'

'Where was he when I was with the bloody RPG, close quarters?'

'The Chief hasn't the bottle you've got Gingy.' McDonough swallowed hard, as if speaking made him sick.

Astley said, 'He'd have been playing with himself, Gingy. What he wouldn't have been doing is putting himself up the sharp end.'

Prentice said, 'When you go in there and face him you really kick his balls. You give him interest on what he did to you.'

McAnally's cheeks were flushed. His voice was loud. 'You think I'm scared, don't you? That's what you think, isn't it?'

Rennie smiled. 'Just show us that you're not scared, Gingy.'

If he came through this then he might come through the cross-examination. If he failed this then he would fail in the witness box. Rennie was sweating. Mid-December and the central heating turned too high. He wiped his forehead.

'I'm not yellow, Mr Rennie.'

'It's not his fault, Ma. They've brained him, see . . . You have to tell people that it's not our Gingy they've got. He's like a man I don't know. Ma, I saw what you said on the telly last evening. That's why I've called you. Ma, something'll be sorted out. Ma, I don't know what's for the best. Gingy's all changed, like they've done his mind . . .'

Doggedly Mrs Chrissie O'Rourke repeated the question that had been twice asked and twice ignored. It was the question she had been told to ask until it was answered.

'Where are you, Roisin?'

A long pause, and then a small voice. 'That doesn't matter to you, Ma.'

'Where are you?'

'We have to help ourselves, Ma. You can't help us.'

'I've the right to know where my girl is, where my grankids are.'

Mrs Chrissie O'Rourke stared down at the blank sheet of paper on the pad beside the telephone. She didn't doubt what she was doing. She knew Frankie Conroy to be a decent man. Since he had called the first time to her house she had asked around about him. She had asked Father Francis when he had come to visit and commiserate. She had asked the solicitor when he had come. Both the priest and the solicitor had said that Frankie Conroy was a decent man. No doubts in her mind. She thought the solicitor was flash, but she had a small love for Father Francis. The priest was what any Ma would want of a son. And he never slagged the Provies. Slagged the Brit army, but no-one in the parish had ever heard him slag the Provies. A little bit she trusted the solicitor. Father Francis she trusted all the way. She heard the words spoken in a hush on the telephone and wrote them down.

The policeman had lightly taken the Chief's arm as they came out of the cell and into the block corridor. The Chief shrugged the fist away. The policeman didn't make a big deal of it. All the policemen wore their identification numbers on their uniform tunic shoulders. They could all be identified, and they would all know that the prisoner from the last in the line cell on the ground floor of the block was rated as PIRA Brigade Commander, Belfast. The Chief knew that these were the old sods, those who worked inside at Castlereagh, old sods who had wormed their way out of postings to the front line of West Belfast or South Armagh or the Fermanagh border or Derry. The old sods looked over their shoulders, and thought of the day when a man like the Chief might have his freedom again, and might remember a policeman's face, and put the face to a name, and the name to an address. No big deal for this policeman. He allowed the Chief to walk without his fist in the Chief's sleeve.

In the hours that he had been in custody the Chief had not fathomed the evidence against him. His questioning at the hands of a Detective Sergeant and a Detective Constable had been cursory, and had seemed to involve his daytime movements of ten, eleven days back. Of course, he hadn't answered the pigs. The Chief had set himself to shut his mouth and keep it shut. What puzzled him was that the detectives seemed to think his silence a small matter. Other than the detectives and the escorting policeman he had seen no other person during his time in custody. His stomach growled, the wind bulged like a knot in his belly. They came out of the cell block and through the covered walk way and into the Interrogation Block.

The policeman knocked on the door of the third Interrogation Room on the right side of the corridor. There was an indistinct shout from inside and the policeman opened the door.

The Chief saw the two 'tecs. The same men as the time before, and the time before that. An easy smile from the older one, like they were old friends. The Chief broke wind, and went to a chair at the table. The younger one grinned too. The Chief sat. What had the bastards to smile about?

'Detective Sergeant McDonough ...'

'Detective Constable Astley ...'

'I know your bloody names,' the Chief said. He was sitting, they were both standing.

'Just the rule book,' McDonough said.

Silence ... as if the 'tecs were waiting for something, as if they had no questions. The Chief saw the remote camera, aimed down at him from high on the wall.

Because the Interrogation Room was sound-proofed noises could not escape, and no outside noise could come in. The Chief did not hear the approach down the corridor outside.

The door opened. The Chief looked up sharply. He saw Rennie in the doorway. He had once ordered the killing of Rennie. He knew Rennie from his photograph, the photograph fitted the face in the doorway. The face was expressionless. Their movement had been imperceptible, unnoticed by the Chief before it was completed, but McDonough and Astley were now positioned between the Chief and the door. It was crowded in the doorway. Behind Rennie was another detective, a younger man, and behind him were two uniformed policemen. The Chief blinked. He couldn't help himself. He had seen the face that was half hidden behind Rennie's shoulder. A nervous, peering, gawping little face, Gingy fucking McAnally's face.

Rennie said, 'Get on with it, Gingy.'

The Chief understood. The anger surged in him. His fists were clenched. He saw the hands jump from the pockets of McDonough and Astley.

'Learned your fucking lines, Gingy?' the Chief shouted.

'That man is the Chief of the Belfast Brigade. The man briefed me on the attack on Mr Justice Simpson . . .'

The Chief's voice smashed through McAnally's hesitant recitation. 'Is your bloody wallet full, Gingy? Filled your bloody wallet up, have they?'

'That man explained to me how Simpson was to be taken out . . .'

'You're going to be stiffed, McAnally.'

'He set up the whole attack. I told him that it couldn't be done, but he wouldn't have anything of that . . .'

'You won't live to spend their fucking money.'

'He said that I was the only one he could lay his hands on who had the training to use the RPG without practice.' McAnally was gabbling, charging out his words.

'You've shamed your family.'

'He had the map out, he went over the plan on the map. It was his plan . . .'

'You think you'll ever be safe from us, Gingy McAnally – you, or your woman, or your brats?'

McAnally turned to Rennie. He was pulling at Rennie's coat. 'Stop him, don't let him say that . . .'

'You'll be shot. You'll be pissing down your leg when you're shot.'

'That one, the Chief, he made me do it. Without him I wouldn't have done it . . . You're going down, you're going down for bloody life, you're going to the Kesh, you bloody filth . . . I'll be fucking laughing when you're in the Kesh.'

The Chief saw the hysteria rising in Sean Pius McAnally, saw the saucer eyes, saw the opened mouth from which the shrieking spat. The Chief saw Rennie look away. The Chief saw that Rennie wouldn't help the bastard. 'Course he wouldn't help him . . . If he helped him now then he'd never stand on his feet later, not later when it mattered.

The Chief stood. Not fast, but deliberately. He came round the table. He moved very slowly. His eyes were fixed on McAnally's, he trapped the tout with his eyes. The 'tecs, McDonough and Astley, were shoulder to shoulder, and ready for him if he charged, and behind them was Rennie. He couldn't get at McAnally with his fists or his boots. He could reach the bastard only with his eyes and with his voice. He saw the fear spreading on McAnally's mouth.

'You're dead, Gingy, you're dead for what you've done,' the Chief whispered. 'You're dead in the street, Gingy, before you get near a bloody court. Look at me, Gingy . . . you're dead before you'll spend the bloody money they're paying you.'

Rennie shoved McAnally out through the door.

The Chief saw a momentary flash of the pale white face of the tout.

'You're gone, Gingy. You're gone to a traitor's grave.'

The door slammed shut.


Frankie Conroy smiled a wide and bright smile.

'You did well, Mrs O'Rourke. You've done the best thing that you could have done. I'll get her back to you, Mrs O'Rourke, her and the kids. You done really well.'

Frankie Conroy was hurrying on his way from the back door of Mrs Chrissie O'Rourke's house in the Drive, Turf Lodge, and out over the back fence, and across another garden to his car.

There was no rain now. The clouds had slipped away east over the city that lay scattered and sprawled below the Turf Lodge estate. The light fell on the dark slopes of the Divis mountain above him. Hidden on the wild, rock-strewn bracken covered inclines of the mountain was the arms cache that he would draw upon when he began the process later that day of prising Roisin McAnally away from her husband. He knew the way of the supergrasses. If the woman stayed with the man then the chances of him reaching the witness box were increased. If the woman quit her man then those chances were diminished. With the weapons that were hidden on Divis mountain lay his first and best chance of reaching to the fears of Roisin McAnally.

Palace Barracks, Holywood, wasn't bad for him. Could have been worse. Could have been Thiepval at Lisburn, could have been the camps at Ballycastle or Ballyclare.

He could get close enough to Palace Barracks to scare Roisin McAnally witless. Scare her so that she reckoned she was safer at her

Ma's than she was in the protective care of the squaddys and the peelers.

They had left Prentice to watch McAnally.

They were out in the corridor for the conference.

Through the high small window in the door Rennie could see McAnally in profile.

McAnally sat in his chair, and his hands were tight together around a steaming coffee mug and trembling so that he didn't trust himself to take the mug to his mouth. He lowered his chin to the rim of the mug, and when he drank there was coffee spilling from his lips.

Rennie watched Prentice offer McAnally a cigarette. McAnally took the cigarette. The coffee was smeared on the table, and Prentice wiped it away with his handkerchief, and was trying to laugh as he lit the cigarette for McAnally.

Disgust on Rennie's face.

'That's just one, and he's got to do that thirty more times . . . OK, the Chief's the hardest one for him, but none of them are that different. There are no bloody Volunteers on McAnally's shopping list, they're all Brigade and Battalion. They're all quality, and they're all going to stick our Gingy through the hoop like the Chief did, right . . . and if the Chief can make that sort of mess of him, what state's he going to be in when he's been messed thirty times?'

He was talking aloud but to himself.

Astley didn't care. Astley socked in hard. 'Perhaps we all jumped too fast, perhaps we were running when we should have been walking.'

'What's that supposed to mean?'

'Perhaps we should have charged him, stuffed him away to remand and come back to work on him later, in six months or a year . . .'

'That's bloody hindsight. Hindsight's the biggest load of crap there is in this game.'

'You asked, Mr Rennie.' Astley was now cowed.

'I didn't ask for bloody hindsight.'

McDonough gripped Astley's arm, squeezed hard on it. It was an unspoken instruction from the Detective Sergeant for the Detective Constable to close his mouth.

177

'He's what we have,' McDonough said. 'He's the best we've ever had. He might be the best we're ever going to get. That's how it seems to me.'

'And the best's piss poor,' Rennie said.

'Then he's got to be stiffened, Mr Rennie.'

Astley shook off McDonough's hand. 'Ship him out then. Lose him for a few months across the water.'

'Can't,' said Rennie. 'They're talking about an early preliminary hearing at the Magistrates, getting him into the box good and early. All bloody politics. It's the politicians' pound of flesh they're looking for in return for McAnally's immunity, our boyo in the box filling the front page with evidence . . .' Now he laughed. 'Don't anyone talk about justice, justice has fuck all to do with it. The politicians want success, and their success is McAnally going through his routine at preliminary and then at trial. They want two bites at the bloody flesh. And I've Special Branch queueing for him, and I've got Intelligence waiting in line, and the Army wouldn't mind seeing him . . . So, he can't be lost for a few months over the water . . . a few days, that's all I can get him out for.'

Astley said, 'Then you've a problem, Mr Rennie.'

McDonough said, 'It's not worth considering, Mr Rennie, if McAnally were to fall down on us.'

'It's not worth considering because it can't happen. I'll tell you why it can't happen. The Secretary of State told the Prime Minister that McAnally would be in court. The Chief Constable told the Secretary of State that McAnally would be in court, I told the Chief Constable that McAnally would be in court if I had to bloody carry him there. Got it? Have you got why McAnally can't fall down on us? There are no confessions, from the crowd we've pulled in? There's none of them doing McAnally's job for him?'

'You're joking,' Astley snorted.

'They're none of them opening their mouths,' McDonough said. 'Without McAnally none of them'll go down, and the bastards'll all walk out.'

Rennie stared through the window, and down onto McAnally's sunken head. He saw the shaking in McAnally's shoulders.

'I'm not going to wet-nurse him. He's got to know what he's signed on for. He's to confront McGilivarry and McCreevy this morning, and O'Brien this afternoon.'

'And if he's on the floor?' Astley asked.

'Then we pick him up again.'

'And if he can't stand up?'

'Then we find a different way to prop him,' Rennie said.

Rennie and McDonough went back into the Interrogation Room, both smiling broadly. Astley went to arrange the transfer of Joe McGilivarry, Belfast Brigade Intelligence Officer, from the cell block to the Interrogation Block.

The radio message was brief.

In fifteen minutes Ferris was to rendezvous with his foot patrol at the junction of Whiterock and Glenalina Road for transport that would take him immediately to Springfield Road barracks. Just that.

The junction of Whiterock and Glenalina wasn't a good place to be standing around if the transport was late. But the transport, a Pig, was waiting for them. He'd jumped into the back and they had sped away. It was rare for transport to be punctual. Presumably something of priority required him back at the barracks. He need not have been on the foot patrol. The corporal who had now taken over command could just as well have started the job, but foot patrol enabled Ferris to be out of the barracks, beyond the wire and the fences and the high gates and the sentries.

The Intelligence Officer was waiting for the Pig in the vehicle park.

'We had to search round for you.'

'Bravo knew where I was,' Ferris said tersely.

'You're wanted again. Your friend's crying for you.'

'What's that supposed to mean?'

'Your little Provo friend . . . You don't listen, David, when you're given good advice. That's a weight of a problem you have, not listening to good advice.'

'What advice?'

'Being told not to get involved with Provo shit.'

'I've said it before: nobody asked me if I wanted to get involved.'

'Strikes most of us, David, most of us in the Mess, that you didn't try very hard to uninvolve yourself . . .'

'Who wants me?' Ferris had walked to the Weapons Pit and the IO had trailed him there. He cleared his rifle.

'That thug who's your second friend, the detective. Your game's getting boring for the rest of us. Hobnobbing with scum and policemen. What's with you?'

'I'll tell you what's with *me* . . . What's with me is trying to get this bloody war behind us, not trying just to serve out a four-months tour but trying to tie at least one loose end.' If he couldn't put one on the Intelligence Officer's nose, at least he could spit his words up the wretched man's nostrils. 'What we're trying to do is to put thirty bad men, evil men – am I talking the language you understand – off the streets.'

'Personal conceit's no substitute in soldiering for professionalism.'

'Thirty is more than our Battalion, six hundred of us, is ever going to put away.'

'I hope you don't fall on your face, David. I'd get a pain in the side laughing if you did.'

Ferris walked rapidly to the far side of the vehicle park. He had spotted Rennie's car.

The Intelligence Officer called after him. 'Let us know when your murdering friend's had enough of you, so we can get you back to leading your platoon.'

Ferris stopped and turned. 'Get the fuck off my back,' he shouted.

There were two squaddys working under the bonnet of a Land Rover and listening.

The Intelligence Officer smiled. 'Didn't anyone tell you about my sister, about my sister's fiancé, about the week before they were to be married, about a bomb in South Armagh under a Ferret, about a Hussar who lost his legs and his balls, about a cancelled wedding. Didn't anyone tell you why I'm not fond of people who get cuddly with the Provos?'

Ferris walked on towards Rennie's car.

In the car Rennie pointed to a rug on the back seat and gestured for Ferris to put his rifle under it, to hide it. Ferris shrugged Rennie's overcoat over his military dress, and Rennie handed him his personal pistol to hold at his waist under the coat.

Rennie told him about the confrontations between Sean Pius McAnally and the arrested men of PIRA's Belfast Brigade. It had been bad with the Chief, but better with Intelligence, grim with Operations, and worst of all with the Quartermaster. The Quartermaster had shouted at McAnally in Gaelic and it had been a shambles because Rennie and the detectives with him didn't understand a word of the language. Rennie said it was like a witch handing down a curse in a bad film.

McAnally was in poor shape. Rennie said that Ferris was the only man he knew who could breathe some bottle back into Sean Pius McAnally.

'We're all on the line, David,' Rennie said. 'Understand me, I have to use you. Whether I like it, you like it, you're my only way to him.'

The mortar had been manufactured in a light engineering factory across the border and far away, on the edges of Waterford city. The mortar was precision tooled, and as good as could be obtained when the Organization was unable to lay its hands on the regular military item. The mortar was modelled on the old two-inch variety and could throw bombs a good 250 yards.

Frankie Conroy had yelled himself hoarse to get his hands on the mortar.

'If the men who are in Castlereagh ever get out of there and get to hear that when a mortar was called for it wasn't made available, then you'll be needing plastic in your knees.'

The mortar was a jewel.

'Christ help you, Frankie Conroy, if you don't bring it back.'

In the city, the Organization had never been short of handguns or rifles, never wanting for fertilizer mix in the big bombs, never had to search far for industrial detonators, but the mortar was especially precious.

'Don't you go bloody leaving it where you're taking it. Four bombs you can have ...'

And a man to sight the mortar, and a man to drop the bombs in the tube.

The afternoon light was failing. He had the mortar, and the bombs, and he had two kids out in Andy'town looking for a flat-top lorry to drive away, and he had the men to fire the mortar from the back floor of the lorry, and he had a man with bottle who was touring the small Protestant housing estate between Palace Barracks and the Upper Sullivan School in Holywood who would find him the firing place, and he had three men out in the Falls who were hunting for cars . . . Christ, he needed a bloody army.

He went to the Falls Road offices of Provisional Sinn Fein. He was taken to a back office. The man he talked to had once done time for possession of firearms, and now reckoned there was a career ahead in community politics. Frankie snapped out his requirements, like he was speaking to dirt.

'I want a loudspeaker kit that won't come back. I want to know where I can go and lift one, Public Address that'll be heard for at least two hundred yards clear.'

He was given the address of the firm that rented mobile PA systems to Provisional Sinn Fein.

On the way over Rennie had stopped at an off-licence.

They had arrived with three six-packs of Tennants and a bottle of Rioja, and Rennie had said that if they put the Spanish stuff down the woman's throat at least it would shut her up.

Prentice had laid in the chops and some chips and some peas, and Prentice had made a thing of how it was time for Roisin to have a night off the dishes and saucepans, and he'd cooked, and Goss had minded the kids and sat with Young Gerard and Little Patty on the floor, and Rennie had kept Roisin's glass going.

The meal was finished. The kitchen was cleared except for McAnally and David Ferris. Rennie had contrived it well. One moment the kitchen had been full, like a party time when no-one was in the mood, now there were only the lieutenant and the tout at the table, and the last six-pack in front of them.

Ferris tore at the cardboard wrapping, slid a can across to McAnally.

'It's been a bastard, today?'

'Too right.' There could be a softness in McAnally's voice, as if he lost a bit of hard Belfast when he was down in the caravan beside the canal. 'Right bastard.'

'Every time they curse you, every time they threaten you, think of your kids, Gingy . . . It's all air they're talking. They can't touch you.'

'They said I was dead. Each one of them said I was dead.'

'That's all they can say. They're frightened and they're lying through their teeth.'

'Tom McCreevy said I'd be looking over my shoulder till I was dead, whether it was a month or a year or ten years.'

Ferris speaking earnestly, quietly. 'They have to make believe the world begins and ends with them . . . It's not true, the world's too big for them, for their bullying. You're going to go away to places where they can't touch you, can't reach you . . . you're going to go to places where your kids'll grow up with a better future than time in the Kesh.'

'Ollie O'Brien spoke in Irish – bloody Rennie went mad – Ollie said I'd be called the biggest whore in Ireland.'

'Gingy, you may have been a right little shit when you were in Belfast, but you went out, you learned about a different way of living when you were down south. You saw there was a different way of living than facing up the twenty-five years behind the wire.'

'You know what they are, when they come after you? You think they'll just forget about me?'

'They won't know where to go looking.'

'They'll look till they bloody find me.'

'They won't know where to start . . . You're going to be safe, Gingy, safe with Roisin, safe with the kids . . . Listen, way back the Soviets slaughtered everyone who stood in their way, everyone who turned their back on them. I give you two different men, both Soviets, who went over, defected. One in Canada, one in Australia. If the Soviets had found them they were dead. They lived to be old men . . . they lived long because they had new identities.'

The doubt flickered on McAnally's face. 'And the Commies were looking for them?'

'Looking as hard as they bloody could, and not finding them.'

'You mean it, don't you? You mean it that they'd never get close to us.'

'You'll be where there are no prisons, where kids don't get knee-capped, where Roisin will know when you're coming home in the evening. You'll be where proper people are.'

McAnally dropped his head down onto his hands that were splayed out over the table. 'Shit, I want to believe you.'

The van was in front, once bright red, now battered, the loudspeakers on the roof. Behind the van was the flat-top lorry, nearly blocking the street. Behind the lorry and arse about to it was the Cortina, Frankie at the wheel.

Frankie was following the second hand of his watch. When it crossed the hour he hooted his horn.

'The people you're with now, Gingy, they're not setting you up in a shooting alley. They're going to protect you, they're going to care for you. Get that straight in your mind, Gingy, it's a guarantee of safety. When you've been in the witness box, you're not just going to be chucked out on your own, you're going to be looked after. Believe me . . .'

The building shuddered, the tremors swinging the ceiling light. Then the blast of the sound of the explosion. Ferris sat rooted, the words blocked in his mouth, his mind. McAnally set his throat to scream.

The next blast and after it the sounds of crashing glass, and the curtains over the sink swept back in the draught.

'Don't just bloody sit there.' Rennie had catapulted into the kitchen.

Rennie tore at McAnally's sweater, heaved him out of his chair and dragged him into the hallway. The area under the stairs was open plan. Rennie threw McAnally into the corner, covered him with his body.

Prentice was by the front door with his pistol drawn, crouched low.

A third explosion, nearer than the first, further than the second.

Ferris had watched Rennie's action, had watched the protection of McAnally. He realized he was still sitting at the kitchen table, and there was glass scattered between the Tennants cans, and there was a cold wind hammering through the window. He heard Goss shout that he had Roisin and the kids between the sofa and the interior wall.

Then there was a fourth explosion.

A guarantee of safety.

He slid off his chair and down onto the floor.

# 12

'Gingy McAnally is a lying tout.'

The voice spilled across the length and breadth of the Palace Barracks. The voice carried over the roofs of the old military buildings, through the doors and windows of the modern family quarters. A whole Battalion force and all their wives and all their children heard the denunciation of Sean Pius McAnally.

'Gingy McAnally is a paid perjurer.'

Buried beneath Rennie's huge body, squashed down into the corner beneath the stairs, McAnally heard his name, hugely amplified, echoed out into the night. The explosions were just a memory, a memory that was a minute old.

'Gingy McAnally is a traitor to his people.'

There was distant and sporadic gunfire, one burst from a machine gun and several isolated single shots. Then there were fire bells and ambulance sirens.

'We know where you are, Gingy. We'll always know where you are.'

Ferris ran from the kitchen down the hallway. His rifle was behind the door, still wrapped in Rennie's car rug. Ferris took his rifle, slapped a magazine into its body. He came back to the foot of the stairs. He could see McAnally's head protruding from under Rennie's armpit.

'When we're ready to come for you, Gingy, we'll know where you are, we'll know where to come.'

There was a hard knock at the front door. A clipped military report advised that soldiers were in position around the house, that it was secure against attack. Then a silence around McAnally and Rennie and Ferris and John Prentice in the hallway. Ferris saw the way that Rennie's arm was close on McAnally's shoulders to stifle the shivering. Big, brusque bugger he might be, but he understood a tout's fear. The bellowing voice was gone. The rhythm of the shouts was broken. Instinctively Ferris knew that the attack was finished. He stood up. He stepped over Rennie's legs and went into the living room. The television was playing, and he realized that through the bombardment and the broadcast voice calls he had not heard the television. There was a comedian on the screen and the studio audience was braying with laughter. He went to the settee and looked behind, and down onto the jumble of bodies and arms and legs.

'It's all right now, it's over,' Ferris said.

Andy Goss pushed himself upright. He had a Walther pistol in his hand.

'You can put that away.'

Goss cleared his pistol, made it safe, slid it down into his shoulder holster. Roisin McAnally lay prone over her children. Her face was twisted in cold, controlled fury.

'Are they all right?'

' 'Course they're all right,' Goss barked at Ferris.

Ferris went back to the kitchen. He filled the kettle, put it on the stove.

'. . . It's a guarantee of safety . . .'

He thought of the Mess at Springfield Road, and Sunray presiding at dinner. He thought of Bravo's commander who soldiered in the relaxation of knowing that a thousand Northumberland acres waited for him whenever his father thought fit to retire. He thought of the Intelligence Officer who had briefly, just once, showed the scab of his flesh, and whose friends across the water drove Porsche sports cars or Alfa Romeos. He thought of the Chaplain who drank a couple of bottles of whisky a week and preached on Sundays that God was on the side of 2 RRF. For Sunray and Bravo's commander and the Intelligence Officer and the Chaplain it was all a game with a playing time of sixteen weeks. Christ, but it was a bloody long game for Sean Pius McAnally, and for Roisin, and for her kids. Nothing make-believe in the game of the supergrass and his dependents. Up to that time Ferris had played the Battalion's game, up to the time of the thudding explosions of the mortar bombs inside the perimeter of a fortified army base, up to the time of a mechanical voice jeering into the night that an informer was marked down for execution.

The kettle was whistling.

Ferris heard McAnally's whimpering voice from the hallway.

'How did they know, Mr Rennie, how did the buggers know I was here?'

Rennie, cold and hard. 'Just a random chance, Gingy. They came up lucky, that's all.'

'They knew I was here.'

'Just a guess that proved right, they couldn't have known.'

'You told me I was safe. Mr Ferris said I was safe.'

'Listen to what I say – it was just luck.'

Ferris ignored the kettle. He stood in the kitchen doorway. Roisin had come to the living room's door. She was holding Baby Sean tight against her shoulder. She was white-faced, she was a sleepwalker. Ferris went down the hall, past Roisin, to the telephone. He dialled Brigade Ops at Lisburn Headquarters.

'Lieutenant Ferris, 2 RRF, on secondment to Police Headquarters. There was a mortar bombardment a few minutes ago at Palace Barracks. Holywood. Have any other military installations been targeted tonight . . . Thanks.'

One base only had been hit. The answer was clear on Ferris's face.

'Tell me how they knew.' McAnally shouted into Rennie's face.

Rennie shouted back. 'I don't bloody know . . .' Their faces were inches apart. Rennie dropped his voice. 'I didn't tell them, Gingy.'

McAnally stared at Ferris. He was crying out for reassurance. Ferris couldn't speak to him. He went back into the kitchen to make the tea.

McAnally said, 'You've got to get me out of here.'

Rennie said, 'We're not moving anywhere, not while it's dark.'

Later the owners of Loud and Clear Public Address would report that a van had been stolen from their premises out on the Twinbrook estate, and a haulage company would complain of the hijacking of a flat-top three-tonner on the Glen Road. And when Forensic had eventually finished with the van and the lorry those firms would have their vehicles returned to them.

When the soldiers ventured out from Palace Barracks and retrieved the van and the flat-top lorry there was little for them to examine. The wooden floorboards of the lorry were dented and splintered from the impact of the mortar's baseplate, and wired to the amplification system in the back of the van was an Aiwa cassette player. Neither the lorry nor the van was entered before Felix and his bomb squad had cleared them for possible booby trap devices. The bomb squad officer was always 'Felix' in Belfast. He appreciated his code name, and reckoned that a sense of humour went with the job.

'Shouldn't be too much trouble to identify the miscreants,' he said cheerfully to a Detective Inspector. 'I imagine you'll run a voice print on a hundred thousand Micks, and that'll tell you who the new Sean Connery is. Piece of cake I'd say . . . What's inside?'

'Four firings, all detonated.'

'We'll scratch around in daylight and see what's what,' Felix said.

The blue lights of the bomb squad convoy winked away out of the estate. Detectives moved from house to house in search of an eye witness, and the search was fruitless. Further into the night a burnt-out car was found deep in the trees off the Bangor Road.

After the arrival of a Press Liaison Officer from Lisburn the Commanding Officer of Palace Barracks agreed to meet the assembled reporters at the main gate. The advice that he had been given was not to respond to questions, only to make a statement and ignore interruptions.

'This was a particularly cowardly attack and I can say in all honesty that only incredible good luck prevented the death or maiming of any of my soldiers' wives and children. That no casualties were inflicted was in no way due to the terrorists' aim . . . Without regard for the safety of women and children they sprayed this base with four high explosive mortar shells . . . I'm not prepared to discuss our security arrangements . . . two shells landed harmlessly in the parade ground, thank God. One shell hit the roof of a storage shed. The fourth shell impacted against a garden fence in the married quarters area . . . A tape recording? I know nothing of a tape recording played during the attack . . . The motive of the attack is perfectly clear in my mind, the motive was to kill my soldiers and their families . . . I said,

I know nothing of any tape recording, and that's all I have to say. Good night to you, gentlemen.'

He was flushed and angry as he walked away from the chorus of questions prompted by the reporters' sight of the Loud and Clear van. He had been given no option on whether or not he should play host to a Converted Terrorist and his brood. A bloody headquarters order . . . The Press Liaison Officer, a damned idiot, told him that he had done well.

The reporters went back to the housing estate and filled the pages of their notepads with quotes from the householders on the text of the message broadcast to Gingy McAnally, perjurer, traitor, and tout.

Frankie Conroy returned the mortar tube in person.

'You did well,' the man said shrewdly, 'to know where he was.'

Frankie chuckled, the puckered hole in his neck wobbled. 'They'll need a lorry to carry the bog paper to clear up McAnally's shit.'

'You did well, but you had the luck.'

'We're just starting,' Frankie said.

Roisin's bedroom was on the front of the house, and the glass there was not damaged. She could be alone there with her children. The warming ache of the Rioja had gone from her head with the first of the explosions, replaced by just a pain that needled into her mind.

She had not spoken a word since the 'tec, Goss, had heaved himself off her body, his hand on her hip. She hadn't spoken to Gingy, because she wouldn't have known what to say to him, nor to bloody Rennie, nor to Ferris. By the time that the shouting had died, and the ambulance wail had faded, she had gathered her children to her and climbed away up the stairs. None of the men had tried to stop her going, bloody good riddance on all their faces. In the way, wasn't she? All the bloody men clustered round her Gingy, bloody flies on jam, trying to put some spine in the poor bastard.

How could she have known that this would happen? She had only told her Ma where they were. That wasn't touting, that was for the good of them all, for the good of her Gingy.

In her bed, with Young Gerard against her back, with Baby Sean close against her, with Little Patty's sleeping head close to her eyes, she thought that it was a question of what was worse. Worse to be hunted out in a Brit base, or worse to be at home and amongst her own and to be reviled as a tout's woman.

Into the small hours.

Rennie had gone.

Soldiers had come with hammers and nails and chipboard, and sealed up the kitchen window from the outside.

Goss lay on the floor of the upstairs landing, his face washed by the ceiling light. He was awake and his hand rested lightly across his holster.

Prentice was perched on the chair in the hall, head lolling, but his eyes open.

Ferris and McAnally were in the lounge. Ferris sat cross-legged on the carpet, McAnally lay on the sofa. Mostly Ferris talked, softly, not disturbing the night, mostly McAnally listened.

'They never had a hope of hurting you, not a thousand to one. It was just a gimmick, Gingy, just piss and wind. They're trying to frighten you, and you can't be scared by piss and wind, Gingy.'

There was a flicker of a smile on McAnally's face, a nervous little smile. 'They scared me.'

'What did they do to scare you? They put mortars into a built-up housing estate, an estate full of young women and kids. That's what they were prepared to do to *scare* you. God, Gingy, you turned your back on those people, people who'd do that. They could have killed a couple of kiddies, they could have sliced a couple of women, but that would have been all right if they'd *scared* you.'

'You ever been scared, like I was scared in there?'

'Once, maybe once.'

'You know what it is, when you don't think you can stop yourself pissing.'

'Once.'

'Probably long ago, you've likely forgotten what it was.'

'Pretty recent.'

McAnally brightened. 'Give it.'

'VCP on Divis, a car broke us. We had two bursts on an Armalite. I was a bit scared then.'

'Shit.'

'That was all round me, wasn't in the bloody distance like those mortars.'

'The Armalites didn't have your name on them, the mortars had my name . . . you know the car . . . ?'

'The car in the Divis?'

'I was on board.'

'Didn't you know, because you were in the car . . . ?'

'Know what?'

'That's why you were pulled, because we saw you in the car.'

'Shit . . .' McAnally leaned forward. 'I was on board, it wasn't me on the Armalite.'

'Good to know,' Ferris said dryly.

McAnally grinned, rueful. 'Wouldn't have scared you if I had been on the Armalite, couldn't hit a bloody house . . . RPG's good. You ever fired an RPG?'

'Not our weapon, Gingy. Enemy weapon. We use a thing called a Milan, bigger and better, I've been on exercise when they've fired a live Milan. It's a pretty big bang.'

Gingy mused. 'RPG's right for here. Wouldn't want anything big. And you want it dead simple. When the first one reached here all the stuff about it was in Russian and Arabic . . .' Again the grin. 'That's why we made such a cock at the start. We got better.'

'That's behind you, Gingy,' Ferris said, a sharp cut in his voice.

'What's ahead of me?'

'Everything's ahead of you.'

'Easy enough to say.'

'It's true.'

McAnally swung his legs off the settee. He was crouched down, his eyes level with Ferris's eyes. His hands were groped out ahead of him and Ferris took them and held them between the palms of his own hands. McAnally stuttered for the words before finding them.

'Gingy McAnally, Provo, what's he to you? What's Gingy McAnally to David Ferris, Brit officer? You can't bloody answer.'

'I can't answer.'

'What am I to you? Find an answer for me, you bloody have to.'

'You're a loser, I want to see you win. All the time with the RPG you were losing, all you were getting closer to was three lifers in the Kesh.'

'What's it to you if I *win*?'

'I told you at Springfield. It's still the same. If you win then thirty evil sods get put away. If they go away, you've won. You win, and Roisin wins, and your kids win. I'm going to help you win. I'll put it better, Gingy, I'm going to bloody make you win. I'm going to stand beside you right up till you go into the box, because when you've finished in the box then you've won.'

'I'm a Provo, you're a Brit officer.'

'When you've won, when you've gone from this crap place, it won't matter a shit what you are, what I am.'

'You'll stand beside me . . . If they come for me, would you step in front of me?'

'Yes,' Ferris said.

Ferris saw the wetness in McAnally's eyes. McAnally pulled his hands back from Ferris's grip.

'For a Brit officer you're an idiot.'

'Probably.'

Ferris was exhausted, drained. He tipped McAnally's legs up onto the cushions, and pushed his body over so that his face was against the settee's back. He fetched two blankets and covered him and watched until the pant of his breathing subsided, until he was asleep.

A few minutes past five in the morning, and bitterly cold in the Turf Lodge estate, Mrs Chrissie O'Rourke came out of her house, and Mr Pronsias Reilly closed the door shut behind her. The low gate between the front garden and the pavement was held open by Father Francis. A black dark shivery morning, and Mr Pronsias Reilly was well pleased that Mrs O'Rourke had dressed fast and without complaint. But it was big enough bait to cause her to hurry . . . If you want to see your daughter there is no time like the time now . . . she'd responded well enough.

The solicitor's car was parked in front of the house. His fingers fumbled with the key and the lock. He was nervous, he was taking a chance being this involved. He was further over the line than he would have cared. He heard a car door open from down the Drive and under a damaged lightpost. He heard the footsteps approach quickly. Father Francis held Mrs Chrissie O'Rourke's arm, as if she was in need of protection. Mr Pronsias Reilly saw Frankie Conroy coming close.

'You're set?'

'We're fine,' Mr Pronsias Reilly said.

'Who is it?' Father Francis asked, unable to disguise his anxiety.

'No-one for you to worry yourself with,' Frankie said. He took Mrs Chrissie O'Rourke's hand. 'Do what they tell you, Missus, just as they tell you. Remember what we're trying to do – What we're trying to do is to get your Roisin and your grankids back to you. And, Missus, we're trying to save your family from the shame of touting . . .'

She had just come from the house where there was still some warmth in the pipes, and now she was in the cold, and her glasses were steaming over with mist, and her eyes were bright and blurred and wide behind the lenses, as she looked up into Frankie's face.

'Missus, all I'm doing is for your family . . . Missus, you have to slide something to Roisin, and you have to tell her that it's for Gingy. It's personal from me to Gingy. Gingy'll understand what it is and why it's sent him. It has to get to him, Missus . . . Missus, you have to do it good and quiet. No-one has to see you, Missus.'

He smiled to comfort her, and to strengthen her, and then he winked to her. His hand went to his donkey jacket pocket, and he took out and palmed to Mrs Chrissie O'Rourke a small crumpled tight handkerchief.

'You'll not be forgetting, Missus?'

And Frankie was gone, striding away into the shadow deeps.

Father Francis didn't understand, and the puzzlement bit lines into the youth of his forehead. Mr Pronsias Reilly understood, and he could smile because nothing could be traced to himself. Mrs Chrissie O'Rourke plunged the handkerchief into her overcoat pocket.

Mrs Chrissie O'Rourke was harnessed into the front passenger seat, and Father Francis leaned forward from the back of the big saloon and put his hands on the shoulders of the old lady, and believed in his act of charity.

'Who else'll be there, Mr Reilly?' Father Francis asked.

'I rang the *News*, they'll be there, if the buggers can get out of bed. The *News*'ll pass the word.'

Mr Pronsias Reilly drove away fast from the Turf Lodge estate and out onto the main road that would take them east from the Falls and through the centre of the city. They cut past the City Hall that was to Mr Pronsias Reilly only one more symbol of the old Protestant ascendancy, and past the Magistrate's Court where he earned his living behind the wire fences that protected the building, and he took his right turn opposite the Oxford Street bus station where more than a decade before the Provo bombs had made a Bloody Friday that matched the Brit army's Bloody Sunday in Derry. He took the Albert Bridge over the Lagan, and then left past the nationalist ghetto of Short Strand – he had clients in the dingy and near-derelict warren of Short Strand. Another left, and another right, and he was out onto the open speedway of the by-pass, and the signs at the road side directed him towards Holywood.

When his foot touched the brake, when the car began to slow, he turned to Mrs Chrissie O'Rourke.

'Just as we told you, Mrs O'Rourke.'

Ahead of them, stretching away on the right-hand side, were the perimeter lights of Palace Barracks. They passed the first corner's watch tower. Past the lit main gate, past the length of the barracks frontage onto the main road. He could not park in front of the barracks. He took the right turn into the housing estate, and he saw a crouched soldier beside a front garden hedge, and he cut his head-lights. In front of him the street was sealed with white ribbon, and behind the ribbon were policemen and soldiers and behind them he could see a flat-top lorry and a van. Frankie had given it to him straight, Frankie hadn't told him an untruth. The bastard tout had been softened, and his woman and his kids had been jazzed. He parked. He was well short of the ribbon barrier.

As they left the car, a soldier approached them. The solicitor and the priest each held an arm of the elderly lady.

'Good evening, my son,' Father Francis said politely.

The soldier muttered something, inaudible, and backed away. Another quiet smile from Mr Pronsias Reilly. The Brit squaddys were always impressed by a clerical collar, like a magic bloody password. They went to the main road, and both Mr Pronsias Reilly and Father Francis had tight holds on the slender arms of Mrs Chrissie O'Rourke. They walked past the high wire mesh fences, and the long coiled lines of barbed wire, and the sentry boxes, and the arc lights.

Approaching the main gate, Mr Pronsias Reilly swore quietly to himself. No bloody photographer in position yet.

They came to the gate, the big barrier confronted them. A place as bright as daylight. Soldiers watched them from the front of the Guard House.

'She's in there, Mrs O'Rourke, she's in there with your grankids,' Mr Pronsias Reilly persisted into Mrs Chrissie O'Rourke's ear, and Father Francis smiled courage into her face. 'Just as we said . . .'

She nodded her head. Mr Pronsias Reilly thought she would do them well. She was a frail and pitiful sight. Father Francis thought she would turn the heart of any sinner, even the heart of a British soldier.

They came to the barrier. A corporal came forward.

'What's your business?'

'My girl's inside there, and I've come to see her.'

'Who's your girl?' The first glimmer of confusion from the corporal.

'She's Roisin McAnally, that's her married name, to me she's Roisin O'Rourke. She's with the tout McAnally. She's with my grankids. I've come to see her.'

'You're joking, aren't you . . . ? In the middle of the night, you've got to be joking.'

'I'm not going till I've seen her.'

The corporal shifted his weight from right foot to left foot. Officer's job, this was. 'Who are you, gentlemen?'

'Pronsias Reilly, solicitor at law.'

'Father Francis Kane. Mrs O'Rourke is my parishioner.'

'I'm here to ascertain that Mrs O'Rourke's rights are not abused.'

'I've come to offer any guidance to Mrs O'Rourke that she might seek.'

Definitely a bloody officer's job.

'I'll have to ask . . . You can't stand there, this is MOD property.'

'I'm staying where I am, till I've seen my girl.'

A car pulled up on the far side of the road. A young man jumped from the passenger seat. Mr Pronsias Reilly saw the bag slung over the young man's shoulder, and the camera hung round his neck. The car drove away in search of a parking place.

Mr Pronsias Reilly was smiling.

'You'd better get your officer, corporal.'

Rennie arrived. He was puffed with temper, barging his way into the hall of the house.

In the hall were Ferris and Prentice, and Sean Pius McAnally. Goss was on the landing, leaning over the bannister rail.

Baby Sean was howling from somewhere behind Goss, and there was the clattering of Roisin's feet in the bedroom above the hallway.

'Does she know?' Rennie snapped.

'She knows something's messing us, she doesn't know what,' Prentice said. 'Worst luck, she was already awake to get her packing done when the officer came. Andy has her boxed in the bedrooms.'

'How is she with her Ma, Gingy?' Rennie asked.

'She's as married to her as she is to me,' McAnally said. The sleep was still in his face.

'What's she be like if she saw her Ma?'

'You couldn't depend on how she'd be. She'd bawl, that's certain. I don't know how she'd be.'

'You know the cow's sat down in the middle of the bloody road, and she's a Provo lawyer with her, and a bloody dog collar . . . and she's three photographers and a camera crew. If they don't meet, then I'll have a Habeas Corpus action in court this morning, and if the judge has Roisin in Chambers and she spills that she wanted to see her Ma and was prevented, then we're in deep shit. If she sees her Ma, then that's the end of it, they can't go to the High Court.'

Rennie was thinking aloud. 'It's nothing to do with Roisin needing to see her Ma, Gingy. It's about pressure, it's about Provie pressure to break her away from you. Got it, Gingy? Is she going to stand up to that pressure, Gingy?'

'I don't know . . .' Misery in McAnally's whisper. 'I just want her with me, don't know . . .'

'She's your fucking wife, Gingy . . . How can I know if you don't know?'

'I can't lose her.'

'Give it a rest, for Christ's sake.'

'I don't want them to take her from me.'

'It's a bloody lottery, how she'll react.'

'It's not my fault, Mr Rennie, I didn't tell the Provos where I was, where my family was,' McAnally shouted. 'It wasn't me that told them where to chuck their bloody mortars. It wasn't me that told Roisin's Ma where we was.'

Ferris heard the noise at the top of the stairs. Ferris saw Roisin, and Goss was restraining her, and the kids were round her legs.

'Too late for worrying who told her. The old cow's at the gate and that's the bloody end of it . . .' Rennie's voice cut. He looked into Ferris's face, and followed his eyeline, followed it to the top of the stairs, followed it to Roisin's drawn, devastated features.

'I want to see my Ma,' Roisin said.

Rennie shook his head grimly. The world falling on his shoulders. Was it worth the effort? All the bloody effort . . . No effort at all to have slapped Sean Pius McAnally into the Kesh for three lifers . . . Made the big effort, the big bloody effort for the big bloody success.

'They're just trying to take you from me,' McAnally called to his wife.

'I want to see my Ma.'

'Don't you see, Roisin . . .'

'We're free, aren't we?' she snarled. 'We're not bloody prisoners. I want to see her.'

'You're quite right, Mrs McAnally, you're free,' Rennie had regained control. He spoke carefully. 'You are not a bloody prisoner. Of course you can meet with your mother, of course you can slide back into your bloody cess-pit if you want to, and turn your back on your husband. Of course, you can dirty your hands with Provo work if you want to. You're not a bloody prisoner. You're quite free to chuck up the chance of a new life.'

'She's my Ma.'

'And he's your husband,' Rennie said.

Roisin came down the stairs. She was carrying Baby Sean. The men in the hallway backed away from her, made room for her.

'I'll need my coat,' she said.

The barrier rose, and the Land Rover came slowly out from the barracks. There wasn't much room for the driver, but enough. He was able to bend his way between the photographers and the centre of the road where Mrs Chrissie O'Rourke sat with Mr Pronsias Reilly and Father Francis.

They had done the interviews.

'I'm just here to try to get the chance to see my daughter who was kidnapped out of her house by the Army. I want her to come home to her Ma, to come back with my grankids. I don't want her to be a part of the lies that man of hers is telling, getting good men locked up on his lies. I want the chance to tell my girl to her face that she's to come home, and have nothing of all these lies. Her Da's in bed sick with worry over this. We've always been a good family, there's never been anyone in our family that's not loyal to Ireland, that's what I've come to tell her.'

'It's my belief that Mrs McAnally is being held in these barracks against her will. As a solicitor I'm not prepared to stand idly by and watch the rights of the individual jeopardized in the interests of Show Trials.'

'The O'Rourke family are valued and loved members of my congregation, and that includes Mrs Roisin McAnally. *They* say she's in protective care, with bombs raining down on her in the night. She'd be safer where she belongs, and she belongs back in Turf Lodge.'

On they waited. From time to time flash bulbs lit the darkness, and the soldiers stood with their weapons in a hostile and frustrated line at the Palace Barracks gates.

And behind the soldiers a major stood with his head cocked down to his shoulder the better to hear the message transmitted to his personal radio.

Time slipping by.

And Mrs O'Rourke wondering whether she'd ever get the damp of the roadway out of her skirt.

And Mr Pronsias Reilly thinking of a lost breakfast.

And Father Francis concerning himself that he had made no arrangement for a colleague to take eight o'clock Mass.

A light rain in the air and the wind, and a pastel touch of morning light in the east, above the roofs of the barracks.

And breakfast television came and recorded the litany, and packaged their tape for the studios and transmission.

And the major listened to the message, acknowledged it curtly, and reckoned that soldiering in Northern Ireland was a greater shower of wet shit than he could ever have believed possible. He strode forward, through the line of soldiers, ducked under the painted barrier and came to stand in front of Mrs O'Rourke.

'You are to see your daughter. Follow me, please.'

Mr Pronsias Reilly grinned as he and Father Francis helped the old lady to her feet. Both men made a play of wiping the road dirt from her coat. They walked with her, in the steps of the major, to the barrier.

Mrs Chrissie O'Rourke doubled herself awkwardly under the lowered pole. Mr Pronsias Reilly bent to follow.

'Just Mrs O'Rourke, thank you. On her own . . . If her daughter, quite voluntarily, agrees to meet her, then she hardly requires legal advice and spiritual guidance.'

They watched her go, a tiny sparrow figure beside the major, through the doorway of the Guard House. A minute later a Land Rover backed up hard against the Guard House verandah's steps. The cameras clicked. There were some amongst the photographers who said they had glimpsed the dark long hair of Mrs Roisin McAnally, wife of the tout.

Roisin had taken the baby with her, never without the baby. Little Patty was between Young Gerard and Andy Goss. Goss was reading her a story, a soft-spoken voice heading for a lived-happily-ever-after climax. Little Patty was fine, would cope with whatever, but Ferris bled for the boy. He knew no way to fracture the stolid mask of contempt Young Gerard showed to his father. And Gingy seemed not to notice. He was pacing from room to room. He was passing Ferris. He grabbed at Ferris's arm.

'What you said last night . . .'

'If I said it, then I meant it.'

'You said some daft things.'

'And meant them.'

'Really meant them?'

'You're going to win, Gingy. I promised to help you to win.'

'That's your word.'

'A promise is always binding.'

'You said you'd step in front of me.'

Ferris felt McAnally's clawing through his jacket, to the skin of his arms.

'I promised.'

'When'll I see you?'

'Rennie can fix it. When you shout, then Rennie will make it work.'

The hand loosed from Ferris's sleeve. Young Gerard's head was down, so that he did not have to meet his father's eye. Andy Goss read on, he too would have heard, but he stayed with the momentum of the story of ogres and a shining prince and danger.

From away across the barracks came the thunder of a landing helicopter.

She was crying. There were no sounds to her crying above the crash of the rotors. She was waist-strapped in her seat deep in the fuselage of the Wessex, and she had Baby Sean tight against her chest, and her tears ran on the thin hair of his head. With the RAF loadmaster, Prentice was helping the flotsam family up through the hatch . . . Young Gerard and Little Patty and Sean Pius McAnally, and Goss was passing up the case and the bags. They were a fugitive family.

Young Gerard had taken the seat beside his mother. Without ceremony Goss yanked him out of it, dropping him down on the far side of the fuselage, and pushed McAnally in next to Roisin.

The door slid shut. The engine noise soared, and the Wessex swayed in the moment before lift-off.

'What'd she say?' McAnally shouted.

'For me to go back.'

'What'd you say?'

'That I'd married you.'

'What's that mean?'

'That I'm your wife.'

'Is that why you stayed?'

'It'll do for now.'

She twisted her head so that she could see out through the cleaned porthole windows of the helicopter. They hovered for a moment over the parade ground. She saw the tiny figures of the Brit officer and the 'tec Rennie. They were the men who had trapped Gingy. She couldn't hold the flow of the tears . . . She had met her Ma for four and a half minutes. They had been alone along with the duty roster forms on the wall and the fire buckets on the floor. Her Ma had said that her Da was ill, that if she didn't break with Gingy now she might never see her Da alive again. Her Ma had said she had nothing to fear from coming home. Her Ma had said that Gingy had made his family like lepers. Her Ma had palmed her a crumpled handkerchief, and she had felt the hardness inside the cloth. Her Ma had said to be sure to give the handkerchief to Gingy.

She had to loosen her safety strap to get her hand in her pocket, to reach for the handkerchief. She passed it to Gingy.

She looked out through the porthole at the close-set streets of the city, that gave way to the greens of Ormeau Park, and the greyness of the river, and the red rust of the gasometers across the water.

Gingy screamed. She spun to see him. His eyes were closed, his chin was jibbering, and all the time the howl of his agony. She saw his feet threshing, as if to kick away something on the fuselage floor. The handkerchief was tight in his hands and he struggled for the strength to rip it, shred and destroy it. She saw a moment of light beneath his shoes.

She saw a single bullet.

Christ . . . Christ Almighty.

One bullet, on the floor of the helicopter. A small revolver bullet.

She tried to take his head in her hands.

'I didn't know . . . God knows I didn't know.'

Prentice was crawling on the floor in front of McAnally, one arm on the flailing legs, scrabbling for the bullet. And all the time the screaming of the tout's wound.

'I didn't know, Gingy . . . Believe me. My Ma just said . . .'

Prentice had found the bullet and shouted, 'You're a bitch of a woman.'

She was sobbing into Gingy's shoulder.

'My Ma just said . . . God forgive me, I didn't know, Gingy.'

Her hand was over his mouth to stifle the screaming, and when she had killed the sound then he trembled, like a naked man in snow.

# 13

To most of those who met him John Prentice was a rough, tough policeman, a little of a lout, who would ride his way across people's feelings, a man who didn't give a damn what he said or to whom he said it, a man without the softness of sentiment. Howard Rennie knew better. Rennie had been the older man who had nursed Prentice through his marriage break and his divorce. Rennie knew the man behind the front. On the long weekend drinking marathons, Bushmills and stout, Rennie had discovered the young detective. Rolling, staggering drinking sessions through Saturday mornings and afternoons and evenings in the little hotels on the Antrim cliff coast, had shown Rennie that Prentice had a well hidden caring streak. There if dug for. All the 'tecs drank too much, and better that it was public drinking, far better when the 'tec was falling around in full view. Better than when it was a big bottle in a lonely room, because that was the route to a police issue pistol barrel poking up into a 'tec's mouth. Rennie liked the man, liked his company when he wanted to get pissed, when he wanted to forget Godfathers and widow-makers and mercury tilt time devices. Rennie was proud to have pulled him back from the brink of resignation when his girl gave him the boot.

Prentice had sworn and spat at Roisin McAnally in the helicopter, and had pocketed the bullet, and had known perfectly well that the woman hadn't an idea what she was doing when she had passed the handkerchief to her husband.

He had seen the way she had clung to Gingy for the remainder of the flight in the helicopter. When they had landed at Thiepval in Lisburn, she had hung on his arm, like she'd fall if he didn't lift her, and Goss had been left to carry Baby Sean and Little Patty.

The house was pretty much of a disaster. Thiepval was the old barracks of Northern Ireland Headquarters. By squaddys' standards the quarter was unacceptable, which meant it was God-awful, which was why it was available. The kitchen window was broken, and the rain had come in and cracked the linoleum. The roof had a quota of tiles dislodged and the main bedroom's wallpaper peeled from the wet plaster. The furniture was chipped or torn or frayed, and most of what was portable had long since been 'possessed' by army women. They had been let into the house by an obese captain, who hadn't thought it necessary to apologize for the condition of the premises. The house was in the heart of the old barracks' married quarters, its similarity with the one in Palace Barracks began and ended with its siting at the end of a cul-de-sac. Later that morning the captain had returned with a van-load of crockery and cutlery and bedding and a television, and he had required Prentice to check the items and sign for them on three different forms.

That first morning Goss took McAnally to Castlereagh for a session with the Branch. They went in the back of an armoured police Land Rover, and the supergrass was fitted out in a flak jacket.

Bloody good thing to have got rid of him, Prentice thought. He'd looked bloody helpless amongst the mess in the house. As that morning drifted on Prentice felt he was right in his judgement of the debris family of Sean Pius McAnally: if there wasn't another disaster they just might come through. She hadn't spoken to her husband in the house, but she had held his arm, and when he had gone, and when the van had brought the crockery and cutlery and the bedding, then she had started to work.

Baby Sean fed and asleep, Little Patty with the morning television babbling in front of her, Young Gerard with his mother. She started on the kitchen floor. Prentice found her with a bucket of hot water – there was hot water which was a miracle – and with a brush that was worn down to a stubble. Prentice caught the mood, and he rang the number the captain had reluctantly given him, and demanded plywood to cover up the smashed kitchen window, and portable heaters to blast out the upstairs damp.

More signing of white and yellow and mauve flimsies. The soldiers who brought the three gas heaters and the plywood and the saw and hammer and nails weren't admitted to the house, were packed off with their chitty. Prentice carried the heaters upstairs and lit them, one for each bedroom, and he went outside into the rain and hammered the plywood that he had cut to size over the broken window. She had stopped her scrubbing of the kitchen floor and looked up as he had come through the kitchen door, and she would have seen him lock it after him, and pocket the key. She smiled ruefully at Prentice, and dropped back to her work, and her trousers were tight on her backside, and her jersey had ridden up to show the smooth pale skin at the base of her spine, and Prentice thought she was as good a looking woman as the one who had booted him out of the bungalow in Glengormley.

He found a vacuum cleaner in the cupboard under the stairs, and took the plug off a standard lamp in the living room, and made the vacuum cleaner operational, and he curtly set Young Gerard to work on the carpets upstairs and downstairs.

Prentice laughed to himself when he was upstairs in the small bedrooms. He moved all the beds back from the windows before laying out the sheets. The Provies had blown it. That was his belief. The bullet had been too much.

'You didn't have to do that.'

Roisin was leaning against the doorway. Her hair was streaked down over her forehead, the sleeves of her jersey were pulled up to her elbows.

'The cleaner's out of a museum, but it goes. It's standard police training, getting vacuum cleaners to work,' Prentice said.

She smiled quickly, as if forgetting herself.

'There's no food in the house.'

'I'll get some down here . . . if Gingy's back we'll run you into the supermarket in Lisburn, fill a basket.'

She said simply, 'I didn't know.'

'What was in the handkerchief, I know you didn't know.'

'You called me a bitch of a woman.'

'I think I got you wrong, Mrs McAnally.'

He spread a first blanket over the single bed that filled the room, smoothed it down, and tucked in the bottom and the sides.

When he had finished the bed, admired it, he turned to the doorway for approval. She was gone.

*　　*　　*

Frankie said, 'I can't bloody say what'll happen . . . I just know that last night was bloody good . . . McAnally got himself shaken. He'd have to have had ear plugs not to have heard the tape. His woman ends up in fits of tears with her Ma, 'cos the old lady gives it her thicker than gravy. I don't bloody say it'll happen today or tomorrow, but that woman's his strength, and we've damaged her good and true . . . That's all I can bloody say.'

Sharp, nasal voices swam around the ears of Frankie Conroy.

'You had a hell of a crowd of men out last night, you won't get the likes of that again in a hurry.'

'They put them in the birdie. Who's to say where they've lifted him. Could be to Aldergrove and a flight out.'

'What're you going to do now, Frankie?'

'How're you going to squeeze him, Frankie?'

Frankie sighed. 'I bloody found him and damaged him. I don't know how I'm going to get to him again.'

Opposite Frankie in the private room of the bar in Clonard was a veteran of the movement. He had done time as an Internee in the '56–62 campaign, and again after the '71 lifts, and he had been imprisoned in Portlaoise gaol in the south for membership in '76. He was a man who was listened to.

'You've gone for a big crack, Frankie. You've come in and you've chucked your weight all over. Your crack'll have to hurt, Frankie.'

'Would you be wanting the Chief and thirty others to rot away in the Kesh?'

'Just telling you, that it's best you keep the ideas coming,' the veteran said calmly.

'Is you saying we should forget the Chief, and the Brigade staff, and the Battalions. Forget the Chief and Ollie and Joey and Tom?'

'You don't listen well, Frankie. And don't tell me what you think I'm saying. Listen hard. *You've* got it going, *you* have to keep it going. If you don't keep it going then it's bad for all of us, Frankie, and that's bad for you.'

'Don't fucking threaten me.'

'I didn't threaten you . . .' There was a cold emphasis in the veteran's voice.

Frankie stood. His knees clipped the table skirting, shook the glasses and spilled a sea of beer. The Organization was deep with divisions on the policy of the war. There were those who called for political advancement and ultimately the black saloon cars that would take them to the negotiating table, and there were the fighters. The Chief was a fighter, and Frankie was the Chief's man. In his mind he saw the veteran in his wedding suit, or his funeral suit, smiling at the cameras as he stepped into the black car for a trip to the sell-out table. Soft old bastard . . . There were those who would have dry eyes if the Chief and thirty of his fighters went down for Tenners and Fifteens and Twenties.

Frankie stared out the faces round the table, at the doorway.

'My crack'll hurt,' Frankie said.

Frankie went out and into the street, and he gulped the air, as if what he had breathed in the private room had been poison.

Ferris felt as if he had crawled through a hedge. He felt the dirt on his body and the beard gathering on his cheeks and throat and chin. He should have washed and shaved before entering the Mess, even if just for a fast coffee. Post was always on the sideboard, the sideboard was always his first stop. Bloody good . . . he saw his Sam's handwriting on a smart blue envelope. Big bold writing that could be read across a room, about all they'd taught her that had stuck from school. There was a bank statement and a letter from his mother. His mother wrote every week, about nothing, but had a notion of duty that she should write even if it were only to list the progress of the neighbour's kitchen extension.

He came from the sideboard with the letters tight in his hand, and went to the coffee urn. He heard Sunray's voice.

'You're just back, David?'

'Yes, sir.'

'From your extra-ordinary duties?'

'Yes, sir.' Ferris hovered by the urn.

'And been up all night, with the mortar business?'

'Yes, sir.'

'Your ordinary duties, here, will, I hope, permit you time to bath and shave.'

'Yes, sir.'

'Cook Corporal will keep coffee by for you, so that you can have coffee after a bath and a shave.'

'Thank you, sir.'

The Bravo Company commander and the Battalion Adjutant and the Quartermaster Captain were watching him. Sunray was by the urn, holding his own cup and saucer.

'How's your man?'

'He's fine, sir.'

'The opposition's getting the better of you.'

Pompous arsehole, Ferris thought. 'I hope not, sir.'

'David . . .'

'Sir?'

'I've a few of the locals coming for a drink tomorrow evening, Lisburn's latest on winning hearts and minds is to pour sherry down their throats. You've become very close to the ground, so I'd appreciate your presence, sixish.'

'Thank you, sir.'

He searched out his Platoon Sergeant, heard that a two-vehicle mobile patrol was rostered for mid-day, and cried himself off it. The Platoon Sergeant gave Ferris a fast eyes only inspection, and his face seemed to say that in the state the officer was in they'd be better off without him.

The water was tepid. His towel was damp, which meant bloody Wilkins had used it the previous evening.

He crawled onto his bunk bed. There were three beds in the cubicle, standard for junior officers. No comfort, no privacy, for Ferris and Armstrong and Wilkins. Some idiot would say that it was good for the moulding of character. Junior officers weren't expected to sleep. Junior officers were supposed to be traipsing the streets of Andy'town and Whiterock, keeping the bloody peace, keeping the heathens from each other's throats. He meant to read his mother's letter first, then his bank statement, then finish on a high note with Sam's. Bloody good thinking, bloody poor execution.

Ferris slept for an hour. The Cook Corporal came in search of him with a tray of toast and coffee and found him stretched out, snoring lightly, grinning like a cat, with his girl's letter unopened and lying on his chest. The Cook Corporal let him be. It was a dreamless sleep without trouble. He'd thought of Sam when he'd closed his eyes, it had been his last thought before he crashed out.

There were two teenagers and an older man, past thirty, in the ASU. One of the teenagers, armed with a Mauser handgun, held the widow in her kitchen. The other teenager and the older man went upstairs to her bedroom. The older man carried an Armalite rifle, the other teenager carried a five-gallon petrol can, and a short stave at the end of which had been wrapped a torn string vest and the striped sleeve of a pyjama top. The other teenager unscrewed the top of the petrol can, while the older man, once and briefly, flicked back the window curtain to check his view of the front gates of the Springfield Road barracks.

The widow's bedroom soon stank of the fumes of the can's petrol and the paraffin that had been splashed on the rags around the stave.

Ferris woke.

The long-stay soldiers said it was the mark of a good young officer that he could steal an hour in an army bunk and make it count like a night at the Dorchester.

He felt good. No bloody right to, but he felt good. A bit before twelve. Must have been the combination of the shower and the shave and the shit that had knocked him out. There was a sweet scent close to him . . . Bloody Sam. She'd tipped some perfume on the envelope. He must have smelt like a hanging pheasant before he'd cleaned himself up, why he hadn't noticed Sam's scent.

He read his mother's letter . . . his mother was well, his father was well, the bank his father managed was well, the garden his mother tended was well. They had driven the previous weekend to Windermere and walked on the lakeside with his aunt and uncle, and they were well. When they had returned from Windermere, they had gone to Evensong at St Peter's and St Paul's, and the vicar was well, and had asked after him . . . 'We seem to go to church more often since you went over there. The Rev. Davies knows you're in Belfast and he said a prayer for all "our boys" who are at risk to keep us safe. Your father and I thought he did it very well. We take comfort that there has been nothing on the news since the judge was killed. Your father tells me, and he showed me a map, that you would have been in quite a different part of the city to where the poor man was murdered. Your father says there's no end to it until the army are allowed a free hand. Ernie, you remember our milkman, says Ulster should be given to the Royal Air Force as a bombing range. Ernie always makes me laugh. He hopes you are well. I've been raking the last of the leaves today from the elm, and managed to get a bonfire going, but then Mrs Frobisher put her washing on the line and I had to put a bucket on it. We're playing bridge with her next week, she's not been well.'

He was £98.72 overdrawn. He didn't bank with his father. They'd have to be patient, till after Christmas. Christmas . . . what a thought . . . Christmas in the Springfield Road barracks. Sunray serving up the brown windsor and the yellow turkey for the squaddys, paper hats in the Mess, and the Chaplain trying to pretend that for one day at least there could be hope and love on the streets of Belfast.

There was a biscuit tin in his cupboard. He stuffed his mother's letter into it, and the bank statement.

He sniffed at Sam's envelope. Cheeky girl. He ran his thumb nail under the gummed down flap. He could see Sam's tongue licking the flap down, could feel it if he half tried. Ten weeks gone, six to go. He was certain of Sam, she was the only human being in the world that he was sure of. God, what Sam would have done for the morale of a Spitfire squadron parked out on a field in Kent in 1940. Every pilot, heading for death or glory, would have thought of Sam when it was curtains time and loved her.

'Darling David, it's hells boring here – when are you coming back to me?' . . . Sam was close to being worth a desertion charge . . . 'That hideous little solicitor from Frome has been pestering me to go to dinner, so I told him he should get a commission in the Parachute Reg. and then I'd look at him again, he said I couldn't go through life being flippant, I told him to naff off' . . . he believed her. The solicitor wouldn't have an overdraft of £98.72. The solicitor had a future that stretched further than six more weeks patrolling West Belfast . . . 'The papers have been full of the supergrasses, especially this smelly little turnip they've just roped in. Anyone who has to deal with him must feel like having a good bath afterwards' . . . he saw Sam in the bath, bubbles and nipples and knees, and he saw Gingy McAnally hurrying with his children to the opened hatch of a helicopter . . . 'If you've been without it for sixteen weeks will you be impotent when you come back? I met a doctor at the Mendip Hunt thrash who said that men who had been without for too long sometimes lost the urge' . . . you're a bloody tease, Sam. Fusilier Jones would have a ruder name for Sam. Fusilier Jones wouldn't like to think of a girl in Somerset getting his officer all charged up . . . 'Lots of love, David darling, from your Sam – PS Daddy's dived into a book about the Russian army. He says the Russians wouldn't have let NI go on for so long – finger out, my darling.'

It was the sixth letter he had received from her since the Battalion had travelled. He kept all her letters in a cellophane folder in the breast pocket of his denims. Sam's letters were always with him on patrol in Turf Lodge.

One last time he held the envelope to his nose, then he tore it into small pieces and put them into the black plastic bag that was the room's rubbish bin.

He stretched.

He heard the rifle fire.

He heard the crash of SLRs on semi-automatic.

He heard urgent, shouted orders.

He heard the alarm bell howling through the windowless walls of his room.

Sam vanished. Ferris had slept in his boots. Standard Operating Procedure that officers slept in their boots if they cat-napped in daytime. He plunged off the bunk, grabbed his flak jacket from the nail on the door. He stuffed Sam's letter into his trouser pocket. He took his rifle from the floor under the bed, and sprinted out of the quarters and into the yard where the vehicles were parked.

Bedlam outside. Men running. Officers and NCOs shouting. The Saracens with the big red crosses on them were revving their engines.

Ferris saw the smoke climbing from the street side of the screen fencing round the barracks.

'It's *your* patrol.'

He turned. He saw the Intelligence Officer running behind him.

The gates were open. Ferris ran out into the Springfield in the wake of the second Saracen.

Just down the road, to the right, on the far side, were the two Land Rovers. The lead Land Rover was intact. The follow-up vehicle was a blackened base and above it were climbing flames. Soldiers were kicking in the door of the house beside it. Shots were fired into the upper window. Two black, scorched figures rolled, writhed, in the middle of the roadway, and the stench spread the width of the street.

The medics reached the two men.

An old lady, not an inch above five feet tall, was dragged dumb from the front door of her house.

Sunray was out in the street, and Bravo's Company commander.

Fusilier Jones was kneeling by a lamp post, his rifle at his shoulder and covering the upper windows on the far side of the street. Ferris saw his chin trembling uncontrollably. He went to him, he crouched down beside him. He felt a terrible sense of shame. His men, the men of his platoon, attacked while he was in his pit.

'Tell me, Jones.'

'It's the Sarge and Nobby. Not much to tell, really. Window breaks, a can full of gas and a fire stick came out. That's about it. We pump the window, too fucking late. Sarge's vehicle catches the gas. Harry and Rick get out OK, Sarge and Nobby don't have the luck. Sarge's fucking bad . . .' the young Fusilier looked away from his sighting aim, looked into his officer's face. He was shouting. 'You couldn't see them . . . you couldn't hit the cunts back.'

'Easy, lad.' Ferris's hand rested on Fusilier Jones's shoulder.

Time for a bloody officer to display bloody leadership, wasn't it?

Of course, they couldn't hit back, not with rifles, not with vehicle patrols. Getting Sean Pius McAnally into the witness box was hitting back. Getting him to testify was hitting back at the bastards.

The ambulance Saracen wailed away the few hundred yards to Casualty at the Royal Victoria.

'Take the vehicle back and get a mug of tea,' Ferris said to Jones.

Rennie extricated Gingy McAnally from the Special Branch rooms at Castlereagh.

The Branch were easy on Gingy. Their concern was the structure of the Organization, the morale and thinking of the PIRA Volunteers and Officers, the tactical approach of the movement. An easy ride for Gingy. The big picture was of little use to Howard Rennie. Rennie's job was to get men into court first, to get men into the Kesh second.

Out in the corridor Rennie crowded McAnally up against a wall. He towered over the tout.

'Yesterday was pretty bloody. It won't get better till you make it better. It's in your hands, and the only way you'll make it better is by getting on with it, head down. You have to face them, and you're going to face them, all the men you've named. When you can do that, when you can spit in their bloody eyes, then it's getting better.'

Rennie punched McAnally on the upper arm, hurting him, tensing him.

'Head down, and you spit in their eyes, and you face them.'

McAnally nodded.

'And no pissing me about.'

Again McAnally nodded.

Rennie knew that he could never be certain of a supergrass. Once he had psyched a man right up to the back door of the Crumlin Road Court House, and defence had won a week's adjournment, and the supergrass had gone flat on them, walked out. He'd shouted at him, pleaded with him, threatened him, and the man had walked out on them. Rennie wouldn't risk his life on a supergrass making it to Crumlin Road, hardly depend a bloody toenail on it.

'Is the house all right, the new house?' Rennie asked conversationally. They were tramping the corridors on their way to Interrogation.

'The house is grand.'

Rennie thought McAnally would call a shit house a palace if he thought that would please. He had to find a way of planting some balls in the man if he wasn't to be crucified under cross-examination. He knew all the barristers, mostly Protestants because they'd had the places at the Law Department in Queens, and they wet themselves at the chance of turning over a supergrass in the witness box.

'Don't you bloody dare let me down.'

That afternoon Sean Pius McAnally confronted Fatsy Rawe and Eamonn Bugsy Malone and Damien Dusty O'Hara and Brennie Toibin and Phonsie McGurr and Joey Mulvaney and Billy Clinch. No hanging about, no messing as there had been with Muldoon, O'Brien, McGilivarry, McCreevy. A uniformed Inspector was present as an independent witness. Two detectives to watch the prisoner. McAnally into the doorway, reciting his accusations that were sometimes drowned in the protest shouting or the hissing threats, and out of the door. Rennie never let go of McAnally's arm, not when they were back out in the corridor, not when they were in the doorway in confrontation.

McAnally might have run a mile. He was weakening, he was sagging, and Rennie's hand held him upright, propelled him towards each of his former comrades.

'Can I go back to Roisin?' With both hands McAnally gripped his mug of tea.

'I'm laying charges tonight. You'll go on facing them till you're through your list.'

'Yes.'

Rennie softened. 'Prentice says to me that Roisin didn't know . . . he says she's as buggered by the bullet as you were.'

'She wouldn't have done it if she'd known.'

'She didn't know what she was doing . . . It's not only you that's going through the hoop, Gingy . . . Give her time, laddie.'

'What'll you do with her Ma?'

'Nothing.'

McAnally snorted. 'Possession of ammunition, there's guys doing a Fiver for possession of a bullet.'

'Don't play bloody lawyers with me . . . I'd love to book the bastard who put the bullet in her hand. To send him down I've got to heave her through the courts, as a witness or in the dock. If I do that then you lose Roisin, Gingy. They're not bloody daft, they knew we'd do damn all.'

McAnally dropped his head. 'I'm only here because of Roisin, because I wanted to do the best for her, for the kids.'

Rennie said cruelly, 'And a matter of three life sentences, that little matter too. Let's get on with it . . .'

Back to the Interrogation Block. Back to the snarling, enraged faces of the men accused by Sean Pius McAnally.

Andy Goss escorted McAnally back to Thiepval, same transport, same armoured Land Rover.

Goss wasn't making much of his job as 'minder' during the journey in the dimmed light of the Land Rover's interior. He'd been chirpy enough when Rennie had given him the afternoon to go and see his girl. She'd wanted him with her after the bank closed, for Christmas shopping in Royal Avenue. He'd said he couldn't make it. She'd wanted him at home for lunch on Sunday because her relations were coming up from Dungannon. He'd said there was no chance he could get away this Sunday.

'You're supposed to be engaged to me, not that wretched informer. You'll get known, you know. You can't help but get known. What if he runs out on you, or his wife, then those murdering Provos'll have your name. They'll come for you, to shoot you. That's a hell of a future for me, marrying a man who's a target. You didn't think of me when you walked into the job. God only knows what you were thinking about.'

She'd left him at the door of the bank.

'How did it go today, Gingy?' Goss said.

'Pretty well.' His face was in shadow. Goss couldn't see McAnally's doubt, only hear it.

A long ride to Lisburn, skirting the city centre, and time for Goss to think on what his girl had said, to think of his future if the Provos had his name as a supergrass minder.

The civil servant smiled at the aggravating persistence of the American interviewer. The audience in the United States was considered important. It was believed in Whitehall that if the British 'line' on Northern Ireland were correctly explained then funds for the Provisionals from across the Atlantic would dry up. The civil servant regarded such a belief as nonsense. He reckoned the Armalites and the dollars would still drift over however clean a figure the Secretary of State cut with the American media.

The *New York Times* had come from London.

'But surely you've considered the possibility that a supergrass, like this McAnally, will further alienate the Catholic population, make a bad situation worse?'

He'd come on the early morning flight, taken a taxi round the Falls, then beer and sandwiches with the *Telegraph*, then an ear bashing from an abstentionist Catholic politician, then another taxi to Stormont Castle. Plenty of time to become an expert, the civil servant reflected.

'You have to understand our legal system. I have nothing to do with the law. In the United Kingdom the judiciary are quite separate from the political process. It is for the judiciary to decide whether the supergrass system is acceptable.'

A good straight bat from the Secretary of State, the civil servant thought. The pity of it was that the Americans didn't play cricket.

'Wouldn't you admit that the supergrass system has been widely condemned?'

'The system has been complained about by a particular section of our society here which has shown scant respect for the rule of law, and even less respect for human life. I disregard these shrill protests from groups closely associated with the paramilitary violence that has caused so much misery in the Province.'

'An American lawyer who visited Belfast to study the supergrass system wrote that the use of supergrasses was "an extension of military policy". What do you say to that?'

Excellent . . . the civil servant had given the Secretary of State the right answer to that one. Go on, shove it down his nasty plastic microphone. Typical of the modern times. He didn't see half a dozen journalists a year who could write shorthand.

'We have a maxim here about people living in glasshouses not throwing stones. In the last fifteen years, to my certain knowledge, more than four thousand American citizens – shall I repeat the figure? – have informed on your organized crime syndicates in return for immunity. I'm sure the Mafia have complained, but I haven't read of the complaints of the *New York Times* . . . There's something I'd like to add. If the American people want to show true concern for the community of Northern Ireland, then they should cease providing the terrorists here with guns and ammunition. Do you know that almost every soldier, every policeman, every politician, who is gunned down here, has been murdered with a weapon manufactured in the United States of America? Would you like to go to the police armoury? Would you like to see the weapons we have captured from the terrorists? American-made weapons?'

The civil servant saw the journalist hesitate.

'My flight . . . my next trip, perhaps . . . I'd be happy to. Going back to the supergrass system . . .'

'There are other priorities in Northern Ireland today, which could be of interest to you.'

'Doesn't the supergrass system only alienate middle-ground opinion?'

'You're here ten years too late if you're looking for middle-ground tolerance. Today, the middle ground's gone. How could it have survived? The civilian population of Northern Ireland has been subjected to a peace-time murder campaign of a ferocity unequalled in western Europe this century. The middle ground has been shot and bombed to extinction. There are two camps here. In one camp are those who support paramilitary violence, in the other camp are those who support a democratic rule of law and order. There can hardly be a no-man's land between those two camps with 2500 already dead. I'm talking blunt reality. We are fighting a difficult and cunning enemy – regretfully that enemy has destroyed the middle ground.'

The Secretary of State eased back, drew breath.

'And the prosecution of the war justifies the use of traitors, of Judas men?'

The civil servant saw the flare of anger in the Secretary of State's eyes.

'If you view the Provisional IRA as Christ then the supergrass is indeed a Judas. You won't be expecting me to take that viewpoint.'

'What I was trying to say . . .'

The civil servant stood. 'I think that ground's covered, Mr Broekweicz, and there's your flight . . .'

During the hand-shaking the telephone on the Secretary of State's desk warbled. The civil servant took it, listened, replaced the receiver.

He showed the journalist out, shut the door on him.

'Bloody good riddance. Did I do all right?'

'Perfect, sir.'

'That's no bloody answer, Fred.'

'It'll do . . . Chief Constable was on. The charges are being laid tonight, on McAnally's word. The Chief Constable's rather spare with information. He says that after yesterday's capers McAnally's as well as can be expected.'

'I'm gone, if he retracts.' The Secretary of State stared out of the window, down across the Stormont grasslands. His triumph over Conrad Broekweicz of the *New York Times* had given only short-lived pleasure.

'The Coleraine Development Board are next,' the civil servant advised.

At the door of the supermarket, a huge, basic, covered barn of a place, Prentice palmed McAnally five fivers.

He did it privately, hoping that Roisin wouldn't see. McAnally just passed the folded notes to Roisin. Prentice's effort was wasted. She put the money in her purse.

'Don't you want to get something, Gingy, something for yourself?'

'She'll get all I need.'

'What about the kids?'

'She'll get what the kids need.'

The loudspeakers in the supermarket were playing scratched carols. Prentice reckoned it must be last year's tape, recorded off the previous year's record.

> *God rest you Merry Gentlemen*
> *Let nothing you dismay.*

McAnally was like a lost man, and he held Little Patty's hand tight, and he didn't respond to her excitements and pointings and pleasures that were the shelves. He meandered without purpose, and away from Roisin who had settled Baby Sean in the food trolley's toddler seat, and away from Young Gerard who stayed with his Ma.

What price all the bright tinsel and the plastic holly and the gift-wrapped presents for the family of Sean Pius McAnally? He'd made his bed, the bugger could lie on it. Prentice saw Goss fall in behind the informer, shadowing him as he went between the shelf banks. Himself he went after Roisin; not too close, not so that she would be aware of him, crowded by him.

*Jesus Christ, our Sav-i-our*
*Was born on Christmas Day.*

Always the shoulders and the raven dark hair of Roisin were in his sight.

Rennie came into the Chief's cell. With him were McDonough and Astley and a uniformed Inspector. Astley had his notebook opened. Rennie read from a sheet of typewritten paper.

'Kevin Majella Muldoon, no fixed abode, you are charged that between the 1st day of November 1984 and the 1st day of December 1984 you and others conspired together to murder William Horace Simpson, contrary to section 4 of the Offences against the Person Act 1861. Do you wish to say anything? You are not obliged to say anything unless you wish to do so, but whatever you say will be taken down in writing and may be used in evidence.'

'Nothing.'

'Kevin Majella Muldoon, no fixed abode, you are charged that between the 1st day of January 1981 and the 1st day of December 1984, you belonged to a proscribed organization, namely the Irish Republican Army, contrary to section 21(1)(a) of the Northern Ireland (Emergency Provisions) Act 1978 ... Do you wish to say anything? You are not obliged to say anything unless you wish to do so, but whatever you say will be taken down in writing and may be used in evidence.'

The Chief belched. 'Nothing.'

The Chief turned his head to the wall, and the door shut on his back.

Out in the corridor, to Astley, Rennie said, 'If I lose that bastard you might see me crying, sonny.'

At the next cell door McDonough passed Rennie from a thick sheaf of papers the charge sheet of Oliver Anthony O'Brien.

'I won't just be crying, I'll be blubbering my eyes out, if I lose any of them.'

It would take them more than an hour to work through the charge sheets to be served against the men named by Sean Pius McAnally.

# 14

Mr Pronsias Reilly had a crowded morning schedule to sandwich between the Magistrate's hearing and his attendance at the Crown Court.

He was pleased with his performance before the Magistrate, well satisfied as he was led by a Court policeman down the steep steps to the cells where he would be able to manage ten minutes with the Chief. At the hearing he had established from a reluctant Detective Sergeant McDonough that the evidence against his client was based on the word of Sean Pius McAnally. And he had further established that the same Sean Pius McAnally had been granted immunity in respect of all charges he might have faced. Serious charges? Charges of Murder? Sean Pius McAnally had been granted immunity from charges of triple murder? The solicitor had seen the flickering movement of pencils and biros at the Press Bench. He had scored the points that were there to be taken and had gone on to attack the media for what he criticized as a circus of sensationalism in their coverage of his client's arrest. A good performance.

In the cell he talked to his client within the view, but outside the hearing, of the Court policeman.

'Who's taking care?'

'Frankie Conroy. He's sworn he'll get you out. He's sworn McAnally won't testify.'

'It's one thing to swear.'

'Frankie's sworn it.' There was a quick smile at Mr Pronsias Reilly's lips. 'There's not everyone was prepared to swear the same. If Frankie fails you then you'll be waiting on the judge.'

'McAnally's for killing.'

'Frankie has to find him again.'

'Frankie has to kill him.'

Mr Pronsias Reilly slipped back on the cell chair. It was a new sight of the Chief. This was the hard man of the Organization, and the solicitor sensed the whiff of fear in the Chief's words. The charge of Conspiracy to Murder carried Eighteen or Twenty. There were some of the big men who gave the judge two fingers when they were sent down. Not this one. Bright staring eyes, and the breath coming in little pants.

'Frankie has to stiff him.'

'Frankie's sworn it, he may not get all the help he wants . . . There are some who say there's better things for the Organization to be at.'

'Which bastards?'

'I didn't hear the names.'

The Chief had hold of Mr Pronsias Reilly's hand, squeezed it, hurt him. 'If people turn their arses on me, then they're dead when I'm out; you tell every bastard that who turns his back on me.'

'Frankie knows what he has to do.'


A coasting day for McAnally.

The confrontations completed, the accused in court, a full day with the Branch.

Last night Roisin had cooked a good meal, and cooked for the minders as well, and there had been no talk of the bullet. And she'd washed up with Prentice, and he'd heard her laugh . . . first bloody time. And she'd made something of the house. In a day she'd made the house a home.

The Branch man was an old bugger. Grey hair onto his shoulders, and a leather jacket like he was a teenager, and jeans, and beads round his bloody throat. Proper queer one. Used a cassette tape as a notebook, so they could talk, and they could have a crack and a laugh. Not like taking the statements. Easier this, relaxed, comfortable, and McAnally talking, and the Branch man prompting, and later in the morning the snapshot book came out of a drawer in the Branch man's desk. Bloody incredible photographs. Not mug shots, photos from the long lens cameras. Funerals, street-corner meetings, men into doorways, men out of doorways, men on the pavement, men in cars. Who's that . . . ? Did you ever come across him . . . ? That a fellow you ever met . . . ? Was he ever on your side of town . . . ? The talk was kept light and cool, and McAnally warmed to the Branch man because he had mahogany stains on his fingernails, and dirt under the nails, and he hadn't shaved well, and McAnally could sniff his socks.

McAnally talked through that day. The first time that he had felt good talking. Goss was behind him, in a hard chair, managing to sleep and snoring softly, and McAnally was scratching his mind for memories of the men who had been photographed by the surveillance cameras, and when he could tell a story about a photograph the Branch man told him that he was bloody marvellous.

'He wants to go outside, can he or can't he?' Roisin challenged.

Through the living room door Prentice could see Young Gerard standing in the hall. The boy was silent, but seemed to whine like a dog that needed to get to the front gate and lift a leg. Prentice didn't know the answer. There should have been a woman on the detail, a WPC.

'He's a boy, he's eight and a half, he's been cooped up inside since . . .'

. . . Since the family had been lifted out of Turf Lodge to go into hiding with the breadwinner who was a tout. There couldn't be any harm in the boy going out. He could walk around. He might find some kids to play football with. Prentice hesitated.

'He's not a bloody prisoner, whatever we are.'

If Prentice said that the boy couldn't go out, then he'd be back into the living room, glowering, and park himself across the carpet in front of the television, and bicker with Little Patty.

'Not far.'

'What does that mean?'

'It means he can go out, but he shouldn't be out of sight of the house.'

Roisin stared at him. 'Why shouldn't he be out of sight of the house?'

'Because I say he shouldn't,' Prentice said.

'In a month's time will he be allowed out of sight of the house, in a year's time?'

He didn't know why she wanted to fight. He tried to smile, made a play at not taking offence. 'I said that the boy can go out.'

Roisin shouted to Young Gerard, 'You're *allowed* out, but not out of sight of the house.'

Prentice saw the boy drift down the front path. Baby Sean was sleeping on the settee. He could hear Little Patty scuffling on the floor of the upstairs bedroom, playing.

It was warm in the living room, central heating on full. A side light was lit. Prentice looked across the room at Roisin. She was in the arm chair, a large sagging chair. Her legs were splayed wide. There was a shadow on her face. He couldn't read her expression. He could see her long thighs stretched out from the cushions of the chair.

'You want to screw me, *Mister* Prentice?'

He heard the tinkle of her laughter. He sat on a chair at the table at the back end of the room.

He looked out of the window, into the back garden.

'Only you wouldn't know what I'd do, if you got up, out of your chair. You wouldn't know whether I'd give you a ride . . . or whether I'd scream the bloody roof off. You wouldn't know what I'd do, would you, Mister Prentice?'

He saw Young Gerard's head appear behind the fence at the end of the garden, then move off. He lost him.

'Don't bloody know, do you?'

Prentice stood up, walked through the room and out into the hall. He sat on the stairs.

She came after him, stood in the doorway. She pushed her hair back from her forehead.

'Frightened I'd scream. I might just scream . . . and then I might give you a bloody good ride . . . You're a big bloody disappointment to me. I thought you'd chance it to find whether I scream.'

He was cleaning his nails with a used match.

'Would you be frightened of screwing a Taig woman? Would you be frightened I'd be dirty? Have you ever screwed a Taig woman? Would you know if you had? 'Course you would. Taig women are different to your women, aren't they? Smell different, don't they, and their eyes are closer together. You'd know if you'd screwed a Taig, wouldn't you?'

She came close to him, stood in front of him. Her stomach was in front of his eyes. She jutted her hips towards him. 'Do we smell different to Protestant women?' She crouched so that her eyes were level with his. 'Are they closer together than your Protestant women's eyes?'

'Keep going, if you want your arse kicked,' Prentice said quietly.

'Proper gentleman,' she sneered.

'Proper bitch.'

She sat on the floor. She put her hand lightly on his knee. He took her hand in his fingers. It was a small hand, it would have been a delicate hand before it was roughened from the work of keeping a house while her man was running or in the Kesh or away in the south.

'We're all fucked, aren't we?' she said heavily. 'Me and Sean and the kids, we're bloody gone.'

'That's not true.'

'I forgot myself last night. Because we'd had some drinks, because you'd bought some decent food, I forgot myself. I thought it might bloody work. Idiot bloody thought . . . I thought it would work and Sean came upstairs, all he bloody talked about was the Brit officer. He talked about the Brit officer like he was his bloody friend. The sun shone out of the Brit officer's bum. Sean was a right idiot last night . . . and I'd forgot myself, because I thought that we might have a real life . . .'

He could talk to the tout, he couldn't talk to the tout's woman.

'There'll be a new life.'

'And you'll be doling out the pound notes.'

'Sean'll be got a job.'

'A job . . . Sean's never bloody worked in his life.' Her derision spat into Prentice's face. 'He can't hammer a nail . . . all he can do is shoot people with a fucking RPG . . . You going to get him a job doing that? I'll make a pot of tea.'

Prentice let her hand drop, and she stood.

'We're Republicans, we're Provos.'

'It'll get washed out of you,' Prentice said grimly. 'When you live amongst people who don't give a damn then it'll be scrubbed out of your system.'

'You wouldn't understand.'

'Go and make the tea.'

'You think we're better off, with you, than with our own?'

'Your decision. You should make the tea.'

She went into the kitchen. He eased himself up from the stairs and went to the front door. He looked out, and couldn't see Young Gerard in the gathering darkness of the early evening.

She called from the kitchen. 'I don't think I would have screamed.'

'Your eyes are too close together,' he shouted back. He wondered whether she heard him over the noise of the tap water bubbling into the kettle.

He had seen the patrol approaching, and he had positioned his ambush.

There were five in the patrol and they moved carelessly. They were bunched too close together, and they paid insufficient attention to the parked cars and the dustbins and they chattered amongst themselves, and there was no rear marker walking backwards to cover the way they had come.

The patrol was as sloppy as anything that the urban guerrilla fighter had ever seen. He crouched behind a low hedgerow that had holes enough for him to watch the patrol drift closer. He could hear their voices. He hadn't the experience to recognize where in Britain they came from, and it didn't concern him. They were accents from across the water of the Army of Occupation.

From his hiding place, he studied the faces of the patrol. Cheerful, happy faces, faces without fear. He loathed each of the faces equally. He blamed each of the shock blasts that had entrapped his recent life on the faces of the patrol. There were five in the patrol, and each one of them was a symbol of the disasters in his life. He thought that if he achieved total surprise he could hope not only to smash the smugness of the patrol, but also to capture a weapon. It was more than a week to Christmas, but already the members of the patrol carried shiny, bright weapons.

Young Gerard's weapons were half a brick and the broken corner of a cement building block that filled the palm of his hand. Two of the patrol carried silver chrome cowboy cap pistols. The leader of the patrol had a rifle with a crackling sound for the pulling of the trigger and a battery operated light to flash in the muzzle. The boy behind the leader carried a wooden-made Thompson sub-machine gun, put together by his father who was a Signals clerk at Headquarters. The boy in front of the leader carried an Armalite reproduction, and the butt was reinforced with sellotape because his sister's bicycle had run over it. There were five of them to the one of him, but none of their weapons could compare with the half-brick and the corner of concrete block.

They were bigger than him, every one of them was older than his eight years, but then the British army with all its numbers and tanks was bigger than the strength of the Provies. Young Gerard could understand the war that his father had once been a part of, could understand the imprisonment in the Kesh, and after that the frequent disappearances of his father on active service. After a fashion he could understand, too, his father's move away to the south. He had known that his father would come back, come back and belt the enemy, and he had seen the wreckage of the judge's car on the television. He had understood that his father could be arrested, and he had stood by his father when the bastard army had smashed into their home and taken his father. All that he could understand. The confusions began with his father's return at dawn to their home, and the packing, and his Ma crying, and the drive in the armoured police Land Rover, and the life in the barracks, and the crash of the mortars and the amplified voice, and the helicopter flight, and a bullet bouncing on the floor of the helicopter . . . those were the confusions. Young Gerard could not believe that his father had gone supergrass. A supergrass was the lowest thing that Young Gerard knew of. He thought there must be a motive to what his father had done. He hadn't the age to work out what his father's motive might be, but he had to believe there was a motive because otherwise he was left with nothing to hold.

He was trembling. For a moment he wondered if his father trembled when he held the RPG on his shoulder.

He loved his father. Before his father had come back to their home with the police and the army, he had worshipped his father. Now he could not bring himself to speak to his father. Young Gerard thought that if his attack on the patrol was successful, that then he could talk with his father. He could sit on his father's knee and talk with him, as he'd always talked with him.

Young Gerard rose up from his hiding place behind the hedge. With all his strength he hurled the half-brick at the back of the second boy in the patrol. The brick caught him sickeningly hard between the shoulder blades. As he yelped, he fell. There was a moment of stunned amazement from the boys behind him who saw him topple over, saw his bright little pistol leap from his hand and into the roadway. Before the source of the missile had been identified, Young Gerard thrust himself through the hedge. His target was the boy with the wooden SMG.

He battered the corner of the concrete building block onto the boy's shoulder. He seemed not to hear the scream of pain and fear, again and again he hit the boy with the rough edge of the block. He saw blood, when he hit the boy's ear, and the boy crumpled. Young Gerard grabbed for the wooden SMG.

Too late he saw that the boy had learned from the television pictures of the patrols, that he had copied the technique of looping one end of the weapon's lanyard to his wrist. He was tugging the wooden barrel of the SMG and the boy was being dragged across the pavement, and the blood was pumping from the boy's ear, and onto his anorak, and onto the ground.

Because Young Gerard was too late in releasing his grip on the barrel of the SMG, they caught him.

The leader smothered him onto the ground. The two other boys dived on top, bursting the air from Young Gerard's lungs. They kneed him, bit him, punched him.

He didn't scream. He scratched back at them, hit back at them.

The boy he had hit with the brick was shouting, and the boy with the wooden SMG was shrieking, and Young Gerard tried to cover his head and his stomach from the raining blows and pains.

He thought of his father. He thought only that his father must be able to be proud of him.

He didn't hear his mother's voice, he didn't hear Prentice's pounding feet.

He was lifted to his feet. When the anger mist cleared from his eyes he realized that the minder detective held him by the neck of his collar and lashed the other boy's back, and his mother was trying to free him from the detective, and he kicked with his feet and punched with his hands at the body of the policeman. His fist, small and tight-clenched, hit the shoulder holster under the open jacket. His fingers found the handle of the policeman's pistol and tugged it out.

And suddenly Young Gerard was alone, and Prentice had released him, and the boys were backing and stumbling away from him, and his mother was wide-eyed and staring at him, and he held the pistol in his hand.

Prentice's hand smashed into the side of Young Gerard's head, spun him, dropped him.

He heard his mother cry out.

'You didn't have to belt him.'

'It was armed.'

His mother was kneeling over him, and his hand was empty.

'He's a child . . .'

'It was only on safety, he could have blown us away.'

His mother had her arms around him, protecting him. He felt the warmth and safety of her body.

He heard Prentice say, 'Get him home, Mrs McAnally, just get him back to the house.'

'I fought the Brit bastards.'

He saw that Prentice's shoe covered the pistol, and then the detective bent and picked up the gun, and briefly checked it, and slid it back to his holster.

His mother lifted him up. His enemies were standing back from him, five of them, hating him and frightened of him, as if they wondered if he could still strike once more at them. One of the boys held a red-soaked handkerchief against his ear. His body hurt in every place as he walked away with his mother supporting him. He was close to clinging to her.

'I'm going home . . .' There was a choke in his mother's voice '. . . I'm bloody going home.'

Between the street lamps it was dark in the street. Young Gerard whose father was a tout, and his mother, and the minder detective, went back to the safe house.

\*     \*     \*

230

David Ferris was late for Sunray's evening in the Mess. He had been held up in the Glen Road for an hour with a suspect car bomb, and Felix had been delayed in getting there to clear it. Ferris was in a dismal mood for a party. The guests were local West Belfast. A collection of priests, nuns, school teachers, doctors and principal tradesmen who were to be exposed to what Sunray called the Security Force Point of View.

For the Fusiliers, the Chaplain would be high profile, collar and pealing laugh leading. The Intelligence Officer would be low profile, but flitting and listening because the Commanding Officer believed that there was good intelligence to be gathered. Sunray would greet his guests at the door and then repair to the stove, and his officers would mingle and make small talk and try to cut good figures.

Ferris hadn't changed from his patrol denims. He could smell his own armpits. He was hardly kitted out for winning hearts and turning minds, and he didn't think that the whole bloody thing added up to a row of beans.

He looked around him. He wondered why the guests had bothered to show.

They all looked scared half to death of getting pissed and compromised. After a couple of gins, or a couple of sherries, they were all holding their hand over their glasses, and muttering about taking it slowly. The Mess Orderly found Ferris when he was still close to the door. Ferris took a whisky, and added the measure from another glass on the tray as reinforcement and splashed in a little water. At least the bloody drinks were on the battalion. He saw Sunray at the far end of the Mess, talking to a young priest. Sunray saw Ferris.

'David . . . To me, please.'

The bloody man ran a party as if he had the battalion out on Salisbury Plain.

'On your travels, David, have you come across . . . I'm bad with names?'

'Father Francis, Francis Kane. Have we had the pleasure?'

'David Ferris.' Ferris drained the whisky, looked behind him for more.

'David spends most of his waking hours in Turf Lodge. That's your patch isn't it, Father . . .?'

'Father Francis . . . Yes, Turf Lodge is in my parish.'

'So, you'll have plenty to talk about.'

Sunray was off.

They eyed each other, Ferris and Father Francis. They would have been close to the same age. At once Ferris realized why he disliked the priest. He was used to men in Northern Ireland dropping away from his stare. The hostility of the young priest was overpowering.

'I don't know why you bothered to come.'

'By coming I can understand better you and the likes of you,' Father Francis said.

'I'd have thought that rather than avail yourself of our hospitality, you'd be busy extricating the men of violence from your flock.'

'Extricate yourself from my parish, Mr Ferris, and I'd have no men of violence to contend with. You're the source of the violence, not my parishioners.'

'Nonsense.'

'The principal causes of violence are the presence of a foreign army and a sectarian police force.'

'You believe that?'

'I know that.'

Ferris laughed aloud. 'Do you give that line from the pulpit each Sunday?'

'You're in the wrong place, at the wrong time. Go home, Mr Ferris, to where your efforts are appreciated.'

His whisky was finished. Ferris's voice was growing. He was unaware of the hush around him, of the darting glances of surprise. 'We're forced to stay here because your two communities can't live together in the same cage.'

'What you represent will never succeed here, Mr Ferris. Like all military solutions in Irish history that have been imposed by the British it will fail.' Father Francis smiled sweetly. 'Go home, Mr Ferris. May God speed your journey. And when you go, Mr Ferris, please take with you your tanks and your guns and your concentration camps and your supergrasses and your flag . . .'

Ferris laughed louder. 'That's the one that hurts . . . the supergrass, that's the one that screws your friends . . .'

232

He saw the flush on the priest's cheeks. 'It's an evil system.'

'Because it puts away the men of evil, is that why it's evil?'

Father Francis looked keenly into Ferris's face. He said quietly, 'What's your interest in supergrasses, Mr Ferris?'

Ferris heard the murmur of uneasy conversation around him. 'It's been a great pleasure to meet you, Father Francis,' he said. He felt that he teetered on a cliff edge. He smiled briskly, and shook the priest's hand.

When he turned away he saw Rennie standing near the door of the Mess. Rennie's overcoat was wet on his shoulders, and he was talking urgently with the Commanding Officer. When he saw Ferris he beckoned him, as if Ferris was Rennie's bloody lapdog.

Rennie was speaking urgently to Sunray.

'. . . So if I can have him tomorrow, that's when I need him. That's good, thank you, sir.'

Sunray curtly nodded his consent.

Rennie said, 'She's going . . . Roisin's walking out on him. We're not arguing with her. From tomorrow morning he's to be on his own.'

'But she's all that's holding him on his feet,' Ferris mouthed.

'Then we're in the market for something else to hold the bugger up . . . I'll call for you in the morning at seven.'

Ferris drank the rest of the party away. He felt he had been separated from the family of the battalion. He was thinking of Gingy McAnally and of Roisin and of Young Gerard and Little Patty and Baby Sean when he became aware of the movement of the guests towards the door. He saw Father Francis waiting in line to pump the hands of the senior officers. He saw the smile break on the clean scrubbed features of the priest.

'That was Mr Rennie I saw you speaking with, I fancy. Interesting man is Howard Rennie. Not bad news he was bringing, I hope.'

# 15

At a few minutes after seven o'clock in the morning, Roisin McAnally and her children left by taxi from Thiepval barracks.

It had been the worst night of her life. The arguments were still ringing in her head when she woke, when she dressed her children. The arguments had gone on all through the previous evening, from the time that her man had come back from Castlereagh and found the army nurse and the army doctor patching the scratches and anointing the bruises on Young Gerard's face and body. She had told him she was going . . .

He could have his new life, on his own. He could make his new life how he cared. Her life was Belfast. She had lived in no other city. She was buggered if she was going to exchange what she knew for a new life in company with two detectives and their guns.

When she had first said that she was going home, said it to Prentice as they were bringing Young Gerard back to the house, then she had expected that he would fight her on the decision. He hadn't. He'd not appeared to give a damn. Not a flicker of emotion from Prentice when she had sworn that she was going . . .

Later Sean had come to the locked bedroom door, and tried the handle and found it shut on him, and he had banged with his fist on the door. He had shouted through the door. She had heard the desperation growing in his voice, like he'd told the men downstairs that she was just upset, that if he could speak to her he could change her mind, and she had lain in the bed fully dressed with her children close against her body, and she had squeezed the pillows over their ears to shut out the sounds of his pleading.

She had slept hardly at all.

When she was awake her imagination latched onto thoughts and pictures of a new life amongst soldiers and policemen and shoulder holsters and armoured Land Rovers, a life without friends and without family. When she was asleep fast dreams overwhelmed her, dreams of Sean bleeding in the gutter, and sometimes it was the Sean of today, and sometimes his hair was greying, and sometimes his hair was thinning and white. Always the dreams ended with Sean in the gutter. Whether Sean was shot dead this year, or in ten years, or in twenty years, he was always in the end dead in her dreams. Now she neither hated Sean, nor loved him. She was apart from her man. She was separated by a locked door and by her loyalties. She had chosen Turf Lodge and her family against her man.

In the morning she unlocked the door. From the landing she looked down the stairs to the front door of the house. Prentice was sitting on his chair. To her he seemed fresh, alert, as if he hadn't had trouble sleeping. He ducked his head to acknowledge her.

Prentice smiled up the stairs at her, a grin that gave nothing.

'Would you like some tea, Mrs McAnally?'

'I've not changed my mind.'

'I said, did you want some tea?'

'I'm going home.'

She wondered what sort of home he went back to when he was finished with Gingy McAnally. She wondered what he thought of her, the tout's woman.

'I'd like some tea.'

In the bathroom, she washed her face and hands. The water in the basin was wonderful, hot, and the soap bar was Camay and scented. She had bought the soap in the supermarket with Prentice's money. The shape of the soap was hardly disturbed. She wouldn't have bought soap like that in Turf Lodge, not on the Supplementary Benefit. When she had washed she wiped the soap bar dry with a towel, and took it back with her to the bedroom and put it in her bag.

On tiptoe, hoping that she would not wake her man, she went into the main bedroom. The double bed was empty. She took their suitcase from out of the wardrobe and began to pack her clothes.

'Your tea . . .'

Prentice was in the doorway. She had not heard him on the stairs. He passed her a mug.

'You won't forget anything,' Prentice said lightly. 'You'd hardly want to come back for anything you've forgotten.'

'Where's Sean?'

'Sleeping on the sofa.' Prentice loved to smile. 'He's out on a pill . . . So don't have any bright ideas of talking him into walking out with you. The pill'll last him through till after you've gone.'

'You don't give a shit for him, as long as he's your fucking puppet in the witness box.'

'I care enough to see that you don't take him home.'

'I've the right to talk to my husband.'

'And last night you had the chance, and you turned the key on the chance . . . your tea'll get cold, Mrs McAnally.'

She heard him pad back down the stairs.

She wanted to scream, and she knew that if she screamed that no man would care, that her man would not hear her. She packed carelessly, shovelling the clothes into the case, indifferent to whether they would be creased at the end of her journey.

Back in her bedroom she told the children that they were going home. She told them that they would not be going home with their Da. Young Gerard said nothing, Young Gerard understood, and Little Patty cried and her Ma wanted to hit her. She told her children that they would have their breakfast when they were at their Gran's.

'When'll we see our Da again?' Little Patty's small voice.

'I don't know,' Roisin McAnally lied.

She looked around her. All her possessions were in the case and in two plastic bags. She led the children down the stairs. Prentice was shrugging into an anorak.

'I've rung you a taxi. We'll walk to the gates.'

Goss stood bleary-eyed at the open door of the living room. She stood on her toes and gazed into the room over his shoulder. She could see Sean's head on a cushion on the settee. She could hear the snoring regular breathing of his sleep. Goss stayed his ground, blocked her. She thought she was looking onto the face of a dead man, a dead man in the gutter.

'You bastards, for what you've bloody done to him.'

'Taxis charge waiting time, Mrs McAnally,' Prentice said.

Roisin carried Baby Sean, and she held Little Patty's hand, and Young Gerard walked beside her, and Prentice had taken the suitcase and the two plastic bags. They walked from the married quarters, and away through the administration buildings and came to the main gates. The taxi was waiting, its engine chugging quietly. Prentice opened the door for her, and she slid into the back seat and pulled Little Patty in after her and gestured for Young Gerard to follow, as if she didn't want him to be in the front seat and away from her.

'Pity all your work in the house was wasted, but we're moving on. We'll have him out of here.'

'What's that to me?'

'I'm telling you so that you can tell your nasty friends that Sean isn't in Thiepval.'

'I'm not a tout.'

'Quite the heroine, Mrs McAnally. Just tell your friends that mortar bombs into Thiepval won't touch Sean.'

Prentice slammed the door behind her, and then went to the driver's window and passed him a folded note.

'It'll cover where Mrs McAnally wants to go,' she heard Prentice say.

As the taxi pulled away from the gates she turned and saw Prentice through the back window. He watched them go, didn't wave.

It was a journey of several minutes, from the Lisburn barracks to the Turf Lodge estate. She had crossed a chasm.

The houses in the Drive were still darkened when she came to her mother's home.

She knew the driver was a Protestant because when he stopped he just leaned back and opened the door from the inside, and let her crawl out from it with her children and her baggage, and when she was on the street, he slammed the door behind her and drove fast away.

She walked up the front path and rang the bell of Number 12.

'You'll not have had breakfast – I'm taking you where you'll get a decent breakfast,' Rennie said.

Ferris sat numb beside him. Bloody cold, and he had a headache from the night before.

Rennie eased off the speed once he had crossed the Peace Line, once they were clear of Provo territory and back in the land of the Protestant Ascendancy.

It was unfamiliar ground for Ferris. His knowledge of Belfast was confined to the Housing Executive estates on the west side of the city. They came off the main road into Dunmurry, and the shabby streets gave way to wide tree-lined avenues and modern bungalows and substantial detached houses, and the headlights threw up tended gardens that were stocked from the Garden Centres.

Rennie read him. 'Not all Belfast is Whiterock, Turf Lodge, Ballymurphy. There's another life. People round here don't know there's a war going on. They drive into town, they do their work, they come back here. If they come back in the evening and want a meal out, then they head for the country. People round here have never driven through Andersonstown. There's 25,000 buggers in the Security Forces protecting the people round here, and they don't want to know what we're at or why.'

They turned into a cul-de-sac. It was brightly lit, and the pavement sides were swept clean of leaves, and there were names on the gates. It might have been where his mother and father lived. There was a house at the end of the roadway, front door facing them, and Ferris saw the lights burning above the garage door, and above the front door, and on the front corner of the house, and down the side of the house. Rennie had brought him home.

'Because I live here, every bugger in the road looks under his car in the morning to see if it's wired, to see if they've cocked up the address . . . but in my house you'll get a decent bloody breakfast.'

'How do you live with it, not knowing when, but knowing they'll come one day?' Ferris asked.

An old mirthless smile on Rennie's face. He had brought the car to a stop outside the house. He pointed through his window, down to the black plastic rubbish sacks that were by his gate, and Rennie saw the open cardboard box and the glint from the bottles thrown up by the lights.

'But not before breakfast . . .' Rennie said.

Rennie let himself into the house.

Ferris chuckled, embarrassed, because Rennie had to wait in the open door for him while he cleared his rifle, barrel pointing into the rose bushes, and took off the magazine.

It was a careful, tidy home. There were photographs on the walls of the hall, framed, of police presentations, there were potted plants, and he wiped his feet hard on the mat so that his boots wouldn't carry dirt onto the clean, patterned carpet.

'My wife, Gloria . . . David Ferris, dear.'

Ferris shook hands with the woman who waited for them at the entrance of the kitchen. She wore a housecoat, and no cosmetics and her face was lined and he thought that he had found her before the mascara and the foundation could hide the anxiety of a detective's wife.

There was a rich scent of bacon and sausages and coffee. Breakfast was laid.

'Can McAnally survive if his woman doesn't support him?'

'That's sharp for this time in the morning.' Rennie led Ferris to the kitchen table.

Ferris wolfed the food off his plate.

'He's hooked,' Rennie spoke through his mouthfuls. 'Because he's hooked we didn't make a big deal out of her going. We didn't reckon on going into the counselling business. She was a bloody dead loss. She's a mind of her own, that's why she was no bloody good to us. He wants to get laid, right, we'll get him laid. He doesn't need a woman now, he needs a friend . . . and he needs someone he can trust, and he thinks that's you. David, I'd not be doing my job right if I didn't bloody milk you.'

Ferris stared down at his plate. 'What's to stop him walking out on you?'

'Without our help? He hasn't a chance . . . David, because you're talking to Gingy you should know why he hasn't a chance. I've never threatened him on what'll happen if he reneges on me, but you should know.'

'What'll happen?' Ferris looked up and into Rennie's eyes. They were grey, dark, pitiless.

'A couple of weeks back there was a fire across the border in Monaghan. A man died in his workshop. He was a watchmender.

He did his watch mending when he wasn't making PIRA bombs. It was a bad fire, spread fast, and it trapped the watchmender in his basement. Before we had Gingy we didn't know about the watchmender. The watchmender's down to Gingy McAnally. Believe me, David, if Gingy quits on me then I'd be astonished if some bloody fool 'tec didn't let slip how the watchmender got fried.

'That's foul, that's . . .'

'Grow up soldier.'

'That's bloody murder.'

'You're not a boy scout.'

'Why tell me?'

'So you'll be better at telling Gingy that he shouldn't quit . . . You'll have some more coffee?'

And Rennie was on his feet, and away for the pot, and two teenage girls were in the kitchen and gathering lunch boxes and scattering text books, and Rennie was a father and wanting to know about last night's homework. The faces were a blur and Ferris sagged in his chair. One of the girls had snapped on the radio, and the kitchen was filled with music, and Ferris shook his head, to try to smash down a bad dream.

'What are you doing today?'

'Double biology, English Lit, Maths. There's a hockey match this afternoon.'

'We've got netball . . . What are you doing, Daddy?'

'A day in the countryside,' Rennie said affably. 'I'm taking Mr Ferris and a friend of his for a drive in the country.'

A car horn hooted out in the roadway. The girls fled, leaving their music behind them.

'What are we going to the country for?'

'A scenic drive, where you'll be able to persuade Gingy that he shouldn't quit on me.'

Ferris retrieved his rifle from the floor. Rennie slipped on his raincoat, and shouted his goodbyes up the staircase.

There was no rain, only the low howl of the winter wind as they drove out of the cul-de-sac and away towards Lisburn.

* * *

The tout's family was back in the Drive.

Word spread through Turf Lodge. The supergrass's woman was back, with the supergrass's brats.

The children gathered outside Number 12, because that was where the woman of the traitor and the kids of the traitor were sheltering.

Not a policeman, not a soldier, was seen in the Drive, as the screaming insults flew to the front windows of the semi-detached house.

'Bastard touts . . . they'll stiff your Da, they'll stiff your man . . . How much is they paying your bloody man for his lies? . . . Fucking yellow, that's your man, Mrs McAnally . . .'

Amongst the crowd were relatives of Phonsie McGurr and Brennie Toibin and Fatsy Rawe, and their presence encouraged the crowd, and bricks beat on the front door, and took the glass from the front room windows.

Father Francis came, young and blushing with inexperience.

'Go home, you shouldn't be blaming a good woman. Go home, Roisin's come back to us because she's walked out on the paid perjurer. Roisin has come back to us and turned herself away from the Show Trials . . .'

He cuffed and swiped at a boy who ran forward to get a better aim with a fractured piece of paving stone.

When he came into the house, admitted by Mrs O'Rourke, he found Roisin and her children sheltering on the kitchen floor. She was trembling and red-eyed.

'You took your bloody time,' Roisin spat at the priest.

'I came when I heard.'

'I didn't know it would be like that.'

'They'll be used to you soon and they won't harm you or the children. And now that you are back, there's a man will come to see you and see that all is well.'

'Who will bloody come?'

'He'll be here tonight.'

Father Francis left her, and he went outside and sat down on the front doorstep with his back against the closed door, and the jeering tailed away, and shortly the crowd drifted down the street and dispersed. There were a few of the youngsters who threw stones at the windows of Number 63, only a few because the windows were already broken, and the door was already hanging open, and the inside of Roisin McAnally's home was already wrecked.

'How long will this go on?'

'Till your man retracts,' her mother said.

'I'll go bloody mad.'

'It'll kill your Da.'

Roisin clung to her children. She couldn't gain the strength to crawl up from the floor. Her mother put the kettle on the rings.

'When the man comes tonight you have to tell him what he needs to know.'

'Why?'

'To show that they haven't spoiled you, to show you're still ours.'

She put her hand onto the table, she pulled herself up to her knees.

'I'll help you clear the mess, Ma.'

Rennie was at the wheel, with Gingy beside him and Ferris in the back seat. Goss drove behind them, always on their tail, with Prentice. Across Prentice's knee, and hidden by his anorak, was a Stirling sub-machine gun.

Rennie's scenic drive took them up over the hills from Lisburn and out past the airport, and through Antrim, and past the waters of Lough Neagh, and through Randalstown and Castledawson, and away onto the long open road to the Sperrins, the high rolling moorland mountains. What had been rain in Belfast was sleet out here, with short showers of hail. Ferris had seen that Gingy rarely smoked, but he snatched a cigarette each time that Rennie offered it. Rennie took them off the main road and into the wilderness beyond Lisnamuck and Moneyneany, took them onto the side road that was wide enough for a tractor and a hay load under the summit of Mullaghmore.

It was beautiful, lonely countryside. There were small hill farm buildings of whitewashed stone, and there were barns of rust ochre, set for shelter in the valleys, and on the bare expanses of the hillsides there were the scattered grazing sheep. Between the showers, where there were gaps in the cloud, the sun beamed down with torch pools of light on the fields and moorland.

They stopped in a picnic site lay-by. There were rough cut tables and benches. Christ, Ferris thought, so bloody artificial . . .

Rennie climbed out of the car. He looked pleased with himself. He slapped his hands together against the cold. McAnally was a city man. He followed Rennie out reluctantly. Ferris looked up at the looming brow of Mullaghmore, and then at McAnally's feet, and he saw the Adidas trainers. Shit, and he had his army boots . . . Shit, it was unreal to think of McAnally climbing in winter to nineteen hundred feet in bloody Adidas trainers.

'Get a bit of air in your lungs, Gingy, that's what you need,' Rennie boomed. 'A good bloody hike's what you want.'

If he stayed with them then there would always be someone to tell McAnally what he needed, what he wanted, Ferris thought.

There was a cluster of sheep watching them. 'Come on you young buggers . . .' and Rennie waved towards the summit. 'Goss'll look after your weapon, David.'

They set off on a springy sheep track.

All so bloody predictable. Prentice shouting from his car that he had trouble with his indicator lights, and Rennie saying he'd have to help because Prentice couldn't change his knickers without help and he'd catch them, and Rennie dropping back, and Ferris and McAnally alone on the hillside and trudging away from the parked cars.

In the dips in the ground there were hidden weaknesses in the peat floor, and sometimes McAnally's feet sunk down and were lost in the black mud, and his feet squelched.

Bloody ridiculous, ridiculous even to a moron supergrass.

'You like walking, Mr Ferris?'

'Not a lot.'

'I hate bloody walking.'

'I was at school in the North of England, we used to go for walks, hikes, up in the Lake District, at weekends.'

'You had school at the weekends?'

'Yes.'

'And you had to go, bloody walking?'

'I suppose we had to, nobody ever said they wouldn't go.'

'I walked to school, and I walked home, that's all the walking I ever did.'

'Got you out of the house at weekends. Perhaps that's why we didn't mind.'

McAnally grinned. 'We had the aggro to get us out of our houses. Internment aggro when we put the barricades up, when the Turf Lodge was no go to the Brits. We had the Motorman aggro when they came and pulled them down. Up half the fucking night throwing rocks, half fucking asleep at school. What were you doing when we were doing aggro?'

Ferris thought. ' '71, '72 . . . I was about ten, I was trying to get to the Grammar School; after I'd finished proper school I used to go to a retired teacher two evenings and Saturday mornings for extra lessons.'

'Did you want to do that?'

'I doubt it.'

'But you did it?'

'My father was pretty keen that I should get to the Grammar School.'

'Why didn't you tell him to fuck off? Why didn't you do what you wanted to do?'

'Because where we lived wasn't like Turf Lodge, Gingy,' Ferris said.

They walked on. If they paused and looked back, then the view beneath them was spreading. The clouds were thickening over to the west and Dungiven and Claudy, and there was the grey blue pencil line of the mountains of Donegal. The going wasn't hard for Ferris, but he was anxious for McAnally. McAnally didn't complain. The track wasn't wide enough for the two of them, and McAnally led, as if that were important to him.

'What's your Da do, Mr Ferris?'

'He manages a bank.'

'What does he make?'

'I don't know, I suppose about fifteen thousand.'

'What's that in a week?'

'That's about three hundred a week.'

'Jesus, when I was at home, on the Assistance I pulled in less than sixty.'

'He's been with the bank a long time,' Ferris said lamely.

'Do you get extra if you shoot a Provo?'

'No.'

McAnally turned momentarily to Ferris, his face was cut with disappointment. 'We heard you got extra, that's what we were told.'

'I wouldn't have thought either of us gets overloaded with the truth.'

Three sheep burst from shelter in front of them and stampeded, frightened and clumsy, away from their approach.

McAnally had stopped. He swung round to face Ferris. 'Would Rennie lie to me?'

'What about?'

'I said to him that I'd heard in the papers that a tout was paid fifty grand, he said that was just Provo propaganda. He said that with Roisin and the kids with me I'd get more than a hundred a week. He said that without Roisin and the kids I'd get forty a week. He said that was private, between us, that I wasn't to say about it . . . He said that I'd be found a place to live, that I wouldn't have to pay for anything myself, like the electricity . . .'

Ferris couldn't look at him. Jesus Christ, was that what it was about? Was it about forty pounds a week, and free electricity?

'He said that I'd have people to look after me, after I'd given evidence, and that they'd buy the food, pay for everything. That'd be my spending money, forty pounds a week . . . Would he lie to me?'

'Mr Rennie wouldn't have lied about that.'

Ferris looked at the mud-smear over his boots. Forty pounds a week, the pieces of silver. Touts came bloody cheap.

They achieved a tiny plateau, just a few yards square, and the sheep had cropped the grass short. At the side of this oasis of level ground were old scorch marks of a camp fire. They were open to the wind and to the first spitting pricks of hail on their faces, against McAnally's thin anorak and Ferris's camouflaged tunic. Ferris thought of Rennie warm in his bloody car with the radio on, and probably with a bloody hip flask, and he'd have a bloody great grin on his face as the hail tatooed on the windscreen. He heard McAnally squeal in laughter.

McAnally had bent down, examining something at the edge of the plateau, where it merged into the dead, dropped bracken. Now he stood, and held out between his fingers was a condom sheath.

McAnally was cackling with laughter. He put it to his lips and blew hard and filled it like a balloon and let it go and it soared away into the wind and died and dropped in the undergrowth. Ferris swallowed. He felt sick. Kiss a used Frenchie, and you'd kiss any arse in the world, Ferris thought. McAnally was excited. He patrolled the perimeter of the grass.

He found a plastic football. It was caved in, where it had been punctured before being thrown away.

The storm hit them. The hail pellets whitened the ground. McAnally kicked the ball at Ferris. Ferris caught it, threw it back to him to kick it again. On the middle slopes of Mullaghmore, Ferris and McAnally played football, with a soft ball, and Ferris was the 'keeper and McAnally was the striker.

Ferris was the 'keeper because McAnally had to score – the poor bugger had to win something. Ferris remembered when he had been at Junior School, and they had played kick-about football, and there had always been a line in front of the 'keeper over which the strikers couldn't come, so that scoring should not be too easy . . . There was no line on the mountain slope of Mullaghmore. The laughter was gone from McAnally, his face was closed in concentration and effort. McAnally dribbled the ball towards Ferris. He came forward, across where the line should have been, and no shot. Fuck the bugger, because he was coming so close that he couldn't miss, had to win, fuck him. Ferris dived forward, over the ball, cannoning his shoulder into McAnally's legs. McAnally fell, half across Ferris, and his legs were thrashing to get his toe to the ball that was in Ferris's arms and tight against his chest. And their faces were inches apart, and the fury exploded in McAnally, and his hands surged to Ferris's throat. Eye to eye, mouth to mouth, face to face, and the hail lashing down on them . . . and McAnally sagged away, and his fingers loosened from Ferris's throat. He took the ball from Ferris and punted it away, hard and high, and set off towards the summit, blurred in the hail.

Ferris followed him, trotted to catch him.

'Forget it, Gingy.'

McAnally's head was tucked down onto his chest and he had pulled up the hood of his anorak over his short hair. Ferris spoke up from the side of his mouth.

'Don't be bloody stupid, Gingy.'

They went on in silence. The winds hit them, reeled and crashed against them, as they stumbled forward towards the cairn of stones at the summit. They left the bracken and the grass and scrambled on their hands and knees over the stone scree to the top of Mullaghmore. Neither man would ask the other to turn back, head for the shelter of the cars. They were dripping from the storm, chilled to the skin.

'I'm wrecked,' McAnally said flatly. 'I'm bloody gone.'

Ferris was shielding his face from the rain. They were huddled close to each other, each trying to gain the protection of the squat cairn of rocks.

'You have to go on with it.'

'There was a reason for touting when I had Roisin, and my kids. I did it for them.'

'You asked about lies, Gingy. That's a lie. You did it to stay out of gaol.' Ferris shouted at him across the wind.

'I did it for my wife and my kids.'

'If you're wrecked, Gingy, you've no-one to blame but yourself.'

'Don't fucking shout at me, don't play the big, bloody Brit with me.'

'Facts, Gingy, you did it because you hadn't the bottle to go to gaol.'

'I don't have to go through with it.'

'You're going to give evidence.'

'Smart-arse Brit, you can't touch me, I've got bloody immunity.'

'Try walking out, Gingy.'

McAnally pulled himself to his feet. His hand was on the cairn to steady himself. He yelled down to Ferris, and his arm was waving towards the distant ribbon of the main road. 'I can walk out on you, I don't have to listen to your Brit shit, I can go my way.'

'Go where?'

'Where I don't have a fucking Brit officer preaching at me.'

'Go where, Gingy?'

McAnally said, 'Go anywhere, anywhere I bloody want to . . .'

'You've nothing for a passport, you've nothing for bloody money. How far'll you go without a passport, without money – you've got to earn your precious forty pounds a week.'

'I'll go down south.'

'Like nothing's happened?'

'Like that.'

'But something has happened,' Ferris said.

There was a frost in McAnally's hair, an ice on his anorak from the hail and the sleet. 'I made a statement, others have made statements and retracted. If I walk out, they walk out too – the Chief, Ollie and Joey and Tom McCreevey, they all walk out . . .'

'You told them about a man in Monaghan, a man who mended watches.'

The fear slipped over McAnally. 'What if I did?'

'You named him. He's dead. He burned to death . . . Gingy, you think that you wouldn't get known, you think that Rennie would just wave you goodbye? You think Rennie wouldn't let it be known how they fingered the man in Monaghan? Gingy, don't give me that crap about walking out.'

McAnally slid down to sit beside Ferris. He was shivering and squeezing his arms against his body for warmth.

'Would Rennie tell?'

'You're a big clever boy, Gingy. Do you think he'd tell? You named a man, Rennie passed on what you said, the man was burnt to death. That's Rennie's way, that's how far his claws are in you. That's why you won't walk out on him. Don't ask me if I think he'd tell.'

Ferris pulled McAnally to his feet. Into the teeth of the wind they started down the mountain.

'You made me a promise.'

'I did.'

'You promised you'd stand in front of me.'

'Let's hope it doesn't happen.'

'Was that just bloody words?'

'It was a promise, Gingy.'

Ferris held McAnally's arm, to steady him, all the time of the long descent to the picnic lay-by.

Halfway down the hill Ferris saw the bird that hovered in the driving wind away to his right. The bird was trying to hold a position through the buffeting. He yelled in McAnally's ear, and pointed to the bird. McAnally looked at the fluttering wing beat of the hunting kestrel. He gazed with a longing at the bird, then ducked his head down and pulled Ferris forward.

When they reached the lay-by, Rennie wound down his window. 'I managed to fix the indicator light. You had a good walk?'

They had done a round dozen of bars between the Sperrins and Thiepval Barracks.

Drunk in charge of two cars were a detective chief inspector of the Royal Ulster Constabulary and a platoon commander of 2 Battalion Royal Regiment of Fusiliers and two detective constables and a supergrass. There was a line of parked cars in Antrim that were paint-scraped from Rennie's tail bumper, and a lorry coming away from the airport had done an emergency stop as Prentice cut him up. Otherwise it hadn't been a bad journey, and McAnally had shown that he could sing.

Prentice and Goss manoeuvred McAnally into the house.

Rennie said, 'You chirped him right up. Bloody well done.'

Since breakfast Ferris hadn't eaten and he had drunk twelve Blackbush and he felt sick.

'Thanks.'

'What did you tell him?'

Ferris swayed in his seat. 'I said that if he didn't quit every Presbyterian Minister in the Province and all the Church of Ireland bishops would sing psalms of gratitude for the arrival of Gingy McAnally.'

'Don't pull my pisser, sonny.'

'I said he was better off alive with forty quid a week of yours in his pocket, than with his pockets empty and a Provo bullet packing his head.'

'Is he going to hold up?'

'I don't know – perhaps, perhaps not.'

'I'll drop you back,' Rennie said.

The man filled the doorway.

The ceiling light in the hallway shone over Roisin's shoulder and onto his face. It was a grim face, pocked and without kindness. She saw the hole in his throat where the stitches had knitted the skin back, a blotch on a white throat.

'It's Roisin . . .?'

'Yes.'

'We'll try a few drinks first, then a few words.'

'My baby's in the bath.'

'Your Ma'll do the baby.'

'What's your name?'

'Frankie . . . You'll want your coat . . . Frankie Conroy.'

# 16

There had been singing in the Bar, two young men and a pair of guitars and the amplifiers turned high enough to give them a chance over the talk and the crack.

She wouldn't have chanced her luck on her own, but she'd seen the sour faces soften when Frankie was seen to be her escort. He drank pints of stout, she had three vodka and orange, without ice, because there never was any bloody ice, and he had talked about everything that was nothing to do with Gingy McAnally, her man, going supergrass. Where Frankie sat he held court. Men came to him and nodded to her and then whispered in his ear, and bent their heads down so that Frankie could whisper his answer back. She had known Frankie for many years, since she was young, since before Gingy and the children, everyone knew everyone in the 'Murph and the Whiterock and the Turf Lodge. She had known Frankie when he was a gangling courier of messages for the Organization, when he was a growing man in the Provos, when he came out of the Kesh after the sentence for attempted murder. She had known him as a part of the movement, but she had never before seen the respect that was accorded him that night. The protection of Frankie Conroy was gold dust to her. She recognized that. And she was irritated that she hadn't taken the time to go upstairs at her Ma's and make her face, that she had just slid on her coat and gone with him.

When Frankie took her out of the Bar, he held her arm and steered her between the drinkers. He made a display of her, as if to say that Roisin McAnally had come home to the protection of Frankie Conroy.

He took her out to his car, and drove her away from the estates and up to the slopes of Divis, and he parked in the darkness at the entrance to the rubbish tips. He cut the headlights.

She could hear his breathing, sense the warmth of his body. She stared ahead of her, into nothing.

'How's Gingy?'

'How you'd expect.'

'You did well, telling us where to look.'

'I told my Ma, I didn't know who she'd tell.'

His arm looped behind her and his hand was on her shoulder. He gripped the bones of her shoulder, and if she'd wanted to she couldn't have shrugged him away.

'How'd he take it?'

'The bombs, I didn't see him . . . he was in the hall, I was in the living room . . .'

'How'd he take it, Roisin?'

'I'm not touting on my man. I'm not touting on him just because he's touted on others.'

The fingers bit harder into her flesh, onto her bones. 'How'd he take it?'

The pain was cruel in her shoulder. 'Shaking, frightened.'

'Did he see the bullet?'

'That was bloody evil, how did you . . .?'

'Did he see the bullet?'

'He was pig screaming at the bullet. It was in the helicopter.'

His hands spread over her. A hand tugging up her sweater and her vest from the waist of her jeans, and a hand grappling with the bra fastener at her back. Calloused hands on her skin. And the taste of his beer and his cigarettes on her mouth.

'Is he going to follow you?'

'He's frightened as a dog. He'll come back.'

'How soon?'

'Without the soldier he'd be back now . . .'

He had loosened the fastener. His hands were on her breasts.

'Get your hands off me.'

She was wriggling to be away from him, clawing at the hand that cupped her breast. And he was laughing at her.

'You going to fight me, you going to fight Frankie Conroy?'

'Get your filthy fucking hands off me.'

'Heh, Missus, you start shouting . . . Who's coming to help a tout's woman? Without me you're in bad shit. You be bloody thankful you're with me . . .'

He was huge, heavy, overwhelming her. His hands were away from her breasts and scraping at the zip of her jeans. She brought her knee up sharply into his groin, and he gasped, and sagged away from her. He was staring at her, panting.

'You come near me again and you'd better have a saucepan over it. I'll kick it till it's fucking blue.'

'Without me . . .'

'You don't buy me, Frankie Conroy . . . If I want to get laid, I get laid. But I don't get laid on anyone's say-so. I want to take my trousers off, I take them off, I don't need any lout telling me.'

'You hurt me.'

'Keep your hands under your bum.'

There was a slow smile on Frankie's face that was dimly lit from the dashboard. He shrugged. She leaned forward, and without thinking Frankie refastened the bra catch. Frankie's arm was round her shoulder, but gently. She stared up at the car roof.

'What'll happen to him?'

'We'll try to kill him.'

'If he comes home?'

'He's gone, Missus. To us he's dead. To Turf Lodge he's dead. You walked out on him. He's dead to you.'

Frankie lit two cigarettes, passed one to her.

'Who's with him?'

'Rennie's there . . . There's one called Prentice, one called Goss.'

'Is one of them the soldier?'

'What's it to you?'

'Don't mess with me, Missus. You came back, remember. You came back to your people . . .'

'You want me to tout on my man, so's it's easier for you to kill my man.'

'You help Frankie Conroy and you might just be able to live in Turf Lodge. You mess me and fuck knows where you're going to have to run to. Didn't you think it out, Missus?'

Jesus, that was rich. When was the time to think it out? With the mortars landing, with the loudspeaker, flying from Palace to Lisburn with a bullet bouncing on the floor, bloody good time to think it out. With Young Gerard pointing a loaded pistol at Prentice, with the door locked on Gingy's shouting, bloody good time . . .

'I didn't think it out.'

'You'll think it out now.'

'Yes.'

She had Young Gerard and Little Patty and Baby Sean, and she had her Ma, and she had a house in Turf Lodge.

'Who counts with Gingy?'

A small voice. 'The soldier.'

'Who's the soldier?'

'The one that took him the first time.'

'What's the soldier's name?'

'He's from the barracks at Springfield.'

'What's his name?'

'Ferris . . .'

'Why's he special?'

'He's the one Gingy listens to.'

'His name's Ferris, and he's Springfield? Thank you; Missus. You're back with your own.'

'You don't have to kill him.'

'Gingy? What's he to you now?'

'He's my husband, he's the . . .' Her voice died. She took the hand-kerchief from the sleeve of her jersey and noisily blew her nose. 'He's my man, you bastard.'

He drove her back to her mother's house.

He leaned across her, opened her door for her.

'You don't have to kill him.'

'Might not have to do anything to him.'


Rennie put down the telephone and went back into the living room.

McAnally was on the settee. He was lying on his back snoring and there was a blanket over him. He looked at peace, as if his mind had shut down. Best thing for him, to be pissed and not be dreaming. Goss was feeding himself instant coffee.

Prentice turned from the window.

'Marching orders?'

'You've drawn the jackpot, John. Christmas in a UK army camp. You two, and him. You fly tomorrow morning.'

'About time.'

'Time to make the bugger start earning his keep.'

Prentice looked at Rennie. 'He's got to learn to stand on his own feet, without Ferris holding him up. That's the difficulty.'

'Right now I'm just thankful he's standing. I'm not fussed who's propping him.'

'You can't walk away from the difficulty, Mr Rennie . . .'

He was tired, he wanted to be home. Suddenly Rennie was bored sick with the supergrass, with the 'difficulty' of the supergrass. He exploded, 'So McAnally needs his soldier friend to keep him standing, so he has him, so he will continue to have him . . .'

'He won't stand up without him, Mr Rennie.'

'He will continue to have him.' He savaged the two young detectives with his gaze. Rennie remembered the days when convictions were obtained by evidence. The days of fingerprints, and of identification parades, and the matching of fibres of hairs under microscopes, the days of interrogation. These two detectives were spoiled brats. Their police work was done for them by an informer. Lazy spoiled brats, because all that was asked of them was to keep the informer on his feet until his time came for the witness box . . . The anger evaporated. He thought that he could be a boring old bugger when he tried, and he wanted his bed and his woman's backside against his, and he wanted Sean Pius McAnally out of his mind.

'You don't have to shout, Mr Rennie.'

'I'll see you in the morning, lads, and thanks . . .'

He had the back room of a widower's terraced house off Beechmount. He was a good tenant, paid regular. Bank money and Post Office money, rolled in the south, and changed in the border villages from Punts to Sterling, enabled Frankie to pay his rent on the nail.

It was a small room. Bed, table, chair, and a wardrobe. The widower swept up after him because he paid regularly and he paid above. He drew a hundred a week from the Organization and forty a week from the Unemployment. He was supported by the south's taxpayers and the United Kingdom's taxpayers, and between the two of them they gave him enough for his needs. He would have needed more, of course, if he had had a wife or a steady woman living in. There never had been a wife. There had been a girl who might have been a wife until she went away. The girl was in her eighth year in Armagh prison, pub bombing and Frankie had never been much at writing letters, and worse at visiting.

Lying on his bed Frankie Conroy squirmed with pleasure at the thought of Roisin McAnally, and the thought of what she had given him.

The name of Ferris.

David Ferris of the Royal Regiment of Fusiliers, who were garrisoned at Springfield Road.

In his mind he saw a cripple who moved with the help of a crutch. The crutch kicked away, and the cripple fell helpless, and the crutch was the soldier called Ferris.

He'd not have believed it, that Gingy McAnally would depend himself on a Brit officer.

The Chaplain had come to talk.

The cross on his shoulder flash gave him an access to the officers and men alike that was denied to any other man in the battalion.

From the gap under the door he saw that the ceiling light was on. He eased the door open. He smelt the reek of whisky.

After the night in the Mess he had chided himself for not taking a keener interest in young Ferris. There was no doubt that he *was* bending – not cracking, not yet, just bending – anyone in the Mess and hearing Ferris and the little wart of the local clergy could have recognized that Ferris was bending. He might have left it a few more days, but he had come from the Intelligence Officer's room, and there he had heard the gossip that Ferris had come back drunk from his day out with the police. Word of it had not yet reached the Commanding Officer. Sooner or later it would, and if the Chaplain wasn't quick about it, he would be too late to salvage the record of David Ferris.

He saw on the floor an ugly heap of wet uniform and a pair of muddy boots. Ferris was asleep on the top blanket, in his vest and underpants and his socks. He held against his face a sheet of notepaper, a handwritten letter. Moving carefully, the Chaplain gathered up the clothes, carried them like a housewife to the hot radiator pipes and hung them out.

The Chaplain closed the door and went as discreetly as he had come. No point in waking the poor devil. He knew Ferris's file, knew all the officers' files, he knew of the failed University entrance and the failed Special Air Service application, but for all those failures he was a good young man, conscientious and sincere, a bit of a prig but nothing of a snob. He wanted to do right by Ferris.

He went to Sunray's room, found him pyjama-clad and writing a letter.

'What's your prob, Billy, temporal or spiritual?'

'Young Ferris, Bravo Company . . .'

'Quite wretched behaviour in the Mess. I haven't caught up with him yet.'

'He's under stress,' the Chaplain said flatly.

'Every man here's in stress.'

'His normal soldiering, that's one thing, but his dealings with the police are too much on top. The IO tells me they're using him to hang onto their prize supergrass. That's why he's in a bad way.'

'Have you got him outside?'

'He's out on his feet. He's drunk, I am afraid.'

'God Almighty.'

'Ship him out, sir, if you can, three days, four days, give him some leave.'

'We're a week from Christmas, Billy, we'd all like some leave.'

'He's doing two jobs here, when the rest of us have one.'

'We're all flat out.'

'I'll put it another way, sir . . . You have allowed one of your officers to be manipulated by the police . . . I wouldn't have thought the police will be greatly concerned with young Ferris once they've bled him for what he's worth to them. They'll drop him like he never existed.'

'That's rather bold, Billy.'

'Do you like what he's doing, sir?'

'I wasn't asked.'

'And neither was he . . . What he needs now is help, not a repri-
mand. He's one of your best young officers. He's worth helping. He's
got a lovely girl at home, and when he's done the right thing by her,
as I'm sure he will, he'll lose a few of these sharp edges, and he'll be
a better soldier for it. I'm going to be bolder, sir . . .'

'I'm sure you are.'

'By allowing Ferris to get mixed up in this squalid affair, I don't
think you've done him well.'

Sunray grinned. 'You're bloody preaching, Billy. You're hiding
behind your cloth . . . you'll take a wet?'

'I'll have a drink, if you'll give him three or four days.'

'You'll have to concoct some fool excuse for it.'

'Whisky, please.'


A Wessex helicopter lifted Sean Pius McAnally and his minders
from Thiepval to the Royal Air Force section of Aldergrove Airport.
Rennie didn't take the ride, he contented himself with an early morning lecture to the informer in the front room of the house. He told
him he was saving lives, he told him that whatever he had done in the
past could be wiped out by his evidence. He used thick paint to make
the images of widows and fatherless children. Nothing too sophisti-
cated for a creature like McAnally.

Through the helicopter's porthole windows as it rose above
Lisburn McAnally could see the city in which he had lived all his life
before the escape to the caravan in the south. It was a rare sunny
morning, and the light caught the rows of grey houses that were the
estates of West Belfast, and he could see the needles of smoke rising
from the chimneys before the sweep to the west and the run to the
airport. He sat on his own opposite Prentice and Goss.

There had been no calls for Prentice to make. There was no-one
in his life who would care whether he was out of the city for the holiday. Goss had spoken to his fiancée. He would be away over
Christmas, and it wasn't a bloody holiday, and no, he couldn't say
where he was going.

At Aldergrove they were told they were late, that the Hercules
transporter had been held for them. They were hurried across the
tarmac from the helicopters' park to the aircraft. There were ground

258

crew round the Hercules, muffled against the cold, and they looked with shameless curiosity at the three passengers. They could recognize policemen, something in the manner, something in the walk, but the man between them was the odd man out. Way out. The Adidas trainers on McAnally's feet were still mud-caked, and his jeans were torn, and his anorak was too thin for this cold, and his head was ducked down as if he were fearful of being recognized.

The Hercules was carrying freight. They were found three canvas-bottomed seats forward in the fuselage, close to the bulkhead ladder up to the cockpit, they were shown the piss bucket. They were led to believe they were a bloody nuisance for delaying take off.

Over the roar of the engines revving for power, Prentice said, 'Good case for a Redeye. If any of your friends have a spare heat-seeker lying around then these buggers should be first on the list.'

Goss thought it a hell of a crack. Gingy McAnally didn't laugh, the men in the city who had the rockets and the Armalites and the Kalashnikovs and the Remingtons and the Thompsons were no longer his friends. The men in the city who might one day lay their hands on a heat-seeking Redeye missile would be glad to fire it up his arse.

The Hercules lumbered into the air.

Temporarily Belfast was behind Sean Pius McAnally.


He was tall, he had no belly on him, he always carried a rifle, he was the only officer who came out on foot patrol in Turf Lodge.

That was where Frankie Conroy started. And he built on that small foundation, gathering bricks of information.

He learned that in the mornings the patrols were mostly in open Land Rovers and that in the afternoons they came on foot. You wouldn't be setting a clock on it, but mostly the foot patrols came as the light was going. There was one platoon from Springfield that did the Turf Lodge, it was pretty much always the same platoon. They used the eight-man patrol, four on each pavement. Those that he asked didn't question why the information was required, merely gave him help and closed the door on him.

When he had established the pattern of patrolling in Turf Lodge, cursorily and not at firsthand, he sought out the driver of a delivery van. The van was regular round the Upper Falls and the Whiterock. By the familiarity of its rounds the van had a certain immunity from search, and the driver always had a smile for the troops and the police at road block checks.

'You want a bloody Armalite? What for?'

'For a snipe.'

'On whose say?'

'My say.'

'Brigade has to say it.'

'Brigade's in the Crumlin Road gaol.'

'How long would you want it for, just an afternoon?'

'Four or five days, till I've done my snipe.'

'That's daft, you'll not get an Armalite for that time, not without someone's say-so.'

'It's my say-so . . . when the Chief's out, it would go bad for the man who didn't help with an Armalite to speed him out.'

'To get the Chief out . . .?'

'And all those with him.'

The driver shrugged. 'It's on your head.'

'Your neck if I don't get an Armalite.'

Frankie fixed his rendezvous for the collection of a weapon and a full magazine.

The days and the nights drifted closer to Christmas, and Frankie found for himself the detail of Turf Lodge. Of course he had a map, but a street map told him nothing. For two days he padded the pavements by day, and was a fleeting shadow figure in the darkness of the night as he examined the back entries to the houses and their back fences and their back gardens. Carol singers moved through the estate, and the mothers and children came from the city in the black taxis with arms bulging from shop-wrapped parcels, and the men who were in work laid in drink for the holiday, and a sort of truce invaded the area.

If the sniping of the soldier had been given to an ASU then it would have been simple work. One on the gun, one on the lookout, one with the covering fire, one to drive the getaway . . . But Frankie was alone. He searched in Turf Lodge for a sniping site . . . If an ASU was making the hit then a house could be taken over. That was standard. The family held and the marksman in the front bedroom to while away the hours till target time . . . But Frankie on his own could not hold a family and snipe.

There was a house on the corner of the Drive and the Crescent. The house was derelict. The last woman who had lived there had been prominent in the Peace Movement, and when her windows had been broken and she had gone overseas with her husband and her children the mob had finished inside what they had started outside. The final act had been to pour petrol over the hallway and ignite it. Turf Lodge had hated the Peace Movement women, seen them as Brit stooges, and Prot stooges, and as traitors to the community. When the petrol was poured, when the match was thrown one of the raiding youths had been still inside, and upstairs. It was said later that he had been trying to wrench the taps off the bath. The youth burned to death and in the perverse way of Turf Lodge the death that had been agonized and noisy was blamed on the Peace Movement women. In the lore of the community the house was tainted. It had never been made habitable. It had been boarded up with chipboard by the Housing Executive workmen and abandoned. Frankie reckoned the combination of the first floor small bedroom and the next door bathroom could give him a shot down either the Drive or the Crescent. It had to be a daylight shot . . . None of the street lights functioned within two hundred yards of the junction . . . no bloody way an officer could be identified in darkness, and no bloody way that Frankie would ever get his hands on an Image Intensifier Night Sight.

Frankie Conroy had played the big man in the private room of the bar in Clonard, and he had put his weight around the man who would provide the Armalite. Frankie Conroy had let it be known that he had dedicated himself to breaking Gingy McAnally, and winning the freedom of the Chief and Brigade Staff and Battalion Staff. Frankie Conroy had opened his fat fucking mouth. Easy enough to open his mouth before it was a daytime shot and a charge across the back fences to a getaway car that didn't have the bloody engine switched. Because he had opened his fucking mouth, he was afraid.

He had no woman, he had no children, he was alone.

He drove to the Andersonstown supermarket. He bought a box of coloured lights, and three packets of tinsel glitter, and outside he paid four pounds for a Christmas tree. He went to the Drive, to Number 12.

He carried the lights and the tinsel and the tree to the door, and rapped the knocker.

She opened the door. He had hoped it would be her that came to the door.

'What's that for?' Roisin asked coldly.

He thought she looked bloody awful. She hadn't bothered with her hair, and her face was pasty pale, and there were grey sacks beneath her eyes.

'For you and the kids,' Frankie muttered.

She sighed, her hands were on her hips, sud-covered. 'It's going to be a *great* Christmas . . .'

Inside he could hear Mrs O'Rourke scolding, and Little Patty crying.

'Better here than where you were,' Frankie said.

Without warning, the voice, the foreign accent, belted his ears.

'Good evening, Mrs McAnally . . .'

Frankie spun. He hadn't heard the footsteps of the soldiers.

'. . . Getting ready for the festive season?'

Frankie stared into the young face of the officer. Tall and with no belly and carrying a rifle, and standing by the gate. There was a grin curling the officer's mouth, as if he were teasing a puppy.

'. . . Have a very Merry Christmas, Mrs McAnally.'

The soldiers on the far pavement ran forward, moving away. The officer looked behind him, then trotted off.

'That's him,' Roisin whispered. 'That's your Ferris.'

She took the tree and the lights and the tinsel from him and closed the door on him.

Before there had been a name locked in Frankie's mind. In place of the name there was now a face . . .

'It was all pretty routine . . . I've nothing for you really,' Ferris said.

'You were pavement bashing more than three hours, there must have been something.' The Intelligence Officer sipped at his coffee. He hadn't offered Ferris a mug.

Ferris said, 'It's not my fault if they take a day off from running round with Armalites. Turf Lodge, Whiterock, were just anywhere that's getting ready for Christmas. Bags and parcels and shopping, that's about it.'

'Did you consider that any of those bags and parcels and shopping might be the cover for the movement of weapons, of explosives. Did you open any of those bags and parcels and shopping.'

'I didn't.'

'That's damned lame, David.'

'Well, I didn't.'

The sarcasm spat from the Intelligence Officer. 'Your *especial* knowledge of the PIRA would surely have told you that they don't hang up their boots because it's Christmas.'

Ferris grinned. What a boring arsehole, he thought. On this tour the IO would have put in as much foot slogging as he, Ferris, endured in a couple of days.

He said brightly, 'I saw Mrs McAnally.'

'Did you call in for tea?'

'A chappie was dropping a Christmas tree off at her door, that's all.'

'What did she say to you?'

'I wished her a Merry Christmas . . . she didn't reciprocate.'

'Who was the chappie?'

'I don't know.'

'It's SOP to do a P-check on any man at a Provo house.'

'Well, I didn't,' Ferris said. He wanted to get the hell out. Yes, it was Standard Operating Procedure to do a Person check on anyone calling at a suspect address, and he hadn't.

The Intelligence Officer looked curiously at him. 'You all right, David?'

'Course I'm all right,' Ferris flared. 'Why shouldn't I be all right?'

'Sky pilot's been asking for you.'

Ferris went in search of the Chaplain. He was angry with himself. Of course he should have done the check on the man with the Christmas tree. He found the Chaplain writing a letter for a Fusilier from Headquarters Company. He waited at the door. The little bugger couldn't write his own letter home to tell his Ma that his girl-friend was in the family way, and there'd be a wedding at the end of the tour. Ferris shuddered. If the army was somewhere in between eighteen-year-old Fusiliers who couldn't write and arseholes like the IO then it had to be scratching when it came to solving the bloody Province's problems. Now he snorted . . . Bloody Provo house, bloody load of rubbish. He thought there was more charity waiting for Roisin McAnally in Turf Lodge than there would be in a police safe house. He thought the chappie had looked quite decent, the one who'd brought her the Christmas tree. He thought she might just have been right, doing what was best for her kids, walking out on Gingy. Poor Gingy, he might just have been wrong . . . The trouble with arseholes like the IO, stuck in an office, or in Operations, or in the Mess, was that they saw every male between fourteen years old and seventy as a Provo, and every woman too . . . He had been far away, and the Fusilier was thanking the Chaplain and squeezing past him, and the Chaplain was making nice noises, and carting him off to Sunray.

Hard to believe what the Commanding Officer told him.

'This is a caring battalion, David. We care for our men, and we care for their families. I know you've been to see him a couple of times, but you may not have heard. Sergeant Tunney has been transferred to England for burns treatment. I'd like Mrs Tunney to know that we care for his welfare, and for hers. I think she'd appreciate it if you were to visit him, in England. He'll have Mrs Tunney and his children at the hospital over Christmas. I thought the New Year would be a good time for you to go over . . . I reckoned you'd be away three days. Adjutant'll fix your movements . . . Your policeman rang me. The informer's been shipped out of the country, until his case comes up, I expect. I'm glad that preoccupation's over . . . That's all, David, and never forget that this is a caring battalion.'

Out in the corridor, Sunray's door closed on them, the Chaplain said, 'Firstclass idea of his. Your presence will be of great comfort to Mrs Tunney . . . I like that, a caring battalion . . . You'll be in good voice tomorrow night, Christmas Eve carols in the vehicle park, another of the old man's good ideas.'

'He's not about to join the human race, is he?' Ferris smiled.

Under the cover of darkness, Frankie Conroy entered the house on the junction of the Drive and the Crescent. By torchlight he climbed the damaged staircase, testing his weight on each step. He had prised away the chipboarding on the window.

He preferred to come at night, and he had prepared himself for a bivouac. He carried an Armalite rifle, a sleeping bag and a rucksack in which were two cartons of milk, a dozen slices of ham, a loaf, and a supermarket fruit cake. At the bottom of the rucksack was a can of Harp, for Christmas Day.

The bastard officer better come on Christmas Eve. A fucking good Christmas it would be, stuck in the house, if the officer didn't patrol on Christmas Eve.

On the landing he switched off the torch and groped his way into what had been the front small bedroom.

He laid out his sleeping bag, and made the rucksack for a pillow, and propped the Armalite against the dark, charred, stinking wall, and settled himself to wait. His hands were damp under the rubber kitchen gloves that he wore.

# 17

The patrol moved out.

For a few seconds the gates of the Springfield barracks were opened sufficiently to permit the soldiers to squeeze through. As the gates swung shut on them they sprinted away up the Springfield Road. Ferris had taught his platoon always to run for the first fifty yards from the barracks' gates. He had learned that at Crossmaglen on the South Armagh border. At XMG the squaddys came out of the barracks like it was the Greyhound Derby, like they thought there was a chance of catching the hare. The departure from the barracks, and the return, were the two most vulnerable moments for the patrol, and Ferris had drilled the message into the heads of his platoon.

They dashed for their first cover, for a lamp post, for a doorway, for a parked car. They seemed to scatter without cohesion, but when those first crouched hiding places were found the patrol had established its pattern. Eight men, four on each side of the road, and the officer on the right-hand side and third in the 'brick', and Fusilier Jones behind him and walking backwards because the protection of the officer's back was his first priority.

It was a few minutes after three o'clock in the afternoon. There were no clear-cut shadows for them because the sun hadn't been seen that day, and there was a light mist rain. The cars and vans had their side-lights switched on already.

Sometimes trotting, sometimes walking, sometimes stationary and watching, the patrol covered the Springfield Road. They passed the Kashmir Road and Cupar Street entrances to the Nationalist enclave of Clonard; a bad place, a place to be wary of if you hadn't celebrated your nineteenth birthday and you were wearing the beret and the red and white Fusilier hackle of 2 RRF. Past the Mackie's factory gate, the pride of the Protestant engineering industry, where the squaddys relaxed. On towards Nationalist Ballymurphy, and past the barricades across the Springmartin Road that were in place to frustrate the attack routes and the escape routes of random sectarian assassins, whether they were coming from Protestant Springmartin to prey on Catholic Ballymurphy, or vice versa.

On and into Ballymurphy. Off the wide Springfield Road, and into the estate, into Divismore Way and Glenalina Road, and heading for the Ballymurphy Bullring. They'd have liked to have had a bloody British squaddy alone in their bullring, liked to have tossed knives and swords in his guts, and stoned him till he was bleeding . . . Christ, and it was Christmas Eve, and he didn't usually think like that, didn't usually loathe the natives, one and all, and lump them together as if each and every bloody one was a Provo-lover.

'Been a sight better off in the Rovers, sir.' Behind Ferris came the bleat from Fusilier Jones.

'You'll be back in time for the carols, Jones.'

'That wasn't what's bothering me, sir.'

'Chilblains playing up?'

'Bloody footrot's playing up.'

'Footrot won't be your problem if you don't open your eyes and shut your mouth, a bloody bullet up the arse'll be your problem.'

'Just so, sir.'

Hard enough to drill into the soldiers the need for patrolling, and harder still to persuade them that foot patrolling was more effective than riding in the Land Rovers. Ferris reckoned that he and his squaddys could see and note twice as much when they were on foot as they could from a vehicle. The bloody police were never out of their Land Rovers. The squaddys each had a sheet page of photographs for the week, to memorize. Mug shots of the top men on the wanted list who might frequent these West Belfast estates. The photographs were pretty awful, and they'd all have grown beards or cut them off, but at least it was bloody trying . . . Men wanted for the Maze escape, and for the kidnapping across the border, and for all the little jollies that kept them busy.

They were in the Bullring. They were surrounded by the grey walls of the estate's houses, and the grey roofs, and the aerosol graffiti of Provo power ... The thought was a recurring tick in Ferris's mind. If he had lived in Ballymurphy, or Whiterock, or Turf Lodge, and the British army had come through twice a day with their cocked rifles and their swagger, then would David Ferris have been a Provo ...?

There was a pretty girl coming past the patrol on the far pavement. She'd be fifteen, she still had her looks, she'd have faded in a few short years, she'd be bloody ancient at twenty if she stayed in the Bullring, Ballymurphy. He heard the banter of the squaddys as the girl came past them. Crude little sods, David Ferris's squaddys.

'Will you bloody shut up,' Ferris shouted. He saw the faces of the soldiers spin to him in surprise that gave way to resentment. 'Just bloody concentrate on what you're doing.'

Because he had shouted at them in the hearing of the girl and the woman who was banging her front mat on the garden gate post and of the women who were talking beside the leaning lamp post, they were coldly angry. But their eyes were back on the rooftops and the upper windows, back on the street corners, and on the car reversing on the far side of the Bullring.

'Do as your teacher tells you,' the girl cackled. 'Do as he tells you, or the Provies'll get you.'

It had started to rain more heavily. The girl had gone her way, but her shrill laugh hung around the patrol. It would be the talk of the Bullring, that an officer had shouted at his men.

The patrol came out of Ballymurphy and into the Whiterock Road. Two police Land Rovers passed them, the rifles jutting uneasily from between the rear doors. The squaddys ignored the Land Rovers, but each man was pleased to see them after the loneliness of the estate. The Land Rovers seemed to say to them that they were part of a larger brotherhood.

The rain ran from Ferris's beret down onto his nose, down across his mouth. It would rain, but it wouldn't snow. Not cold enough for snow.

He wondered where Gingy was and why Rennie hadn't telephoned him or called for him. Bloody silly, to feel as if he had been stood up by a girl, because Rennie hadn't called by, and he didn't know where Gingy was ... he reckoned that Gingy McAnally's would be a black bloody Christmas, snow or no snow.

At the top of the Whiterock, the patrol P-checked a group of youths. They gave their names. The names were radioed back to Springfield Road Ops Room, and fed to the computer. Every name was clean.

The pace of the patrol quickened as they came to the northern end of Turf Lodge. Downhill, halfway through the bloody patrol.

He was almost certain of it. If he had been brought up in Ballymurphy or Whiterock or Turf Lodge, he would have been a Volunteer.

They hurried past the big Christian Brothers Primary School before swinging back into the narrow streets of the Turf Lodge estate.

He had been in the house for twenty hours.

In the night a tramp had come and rattled at the back door to see whether it was fastened, and not found the place where Frankie Conroy had made his entry and replaced the chipboard window cover. Other tramps had been in the house, the smell told him, and the slime he had slid on at the top of the stairs. In the morning he had eaten a little of his food. He had been hungry and cold in his sleeping bag, but had eaten only a little of the food because he had been determined to wait for the officer, for as long as it took. Difficult to eat in the gloves that hid the points of his fingertips from anything he touched. At lunch time he had heard two young voices outside the kitchen door, and giggling, and after a few minutes he had seen a girl slip away into the Crescent tucking her blouse into the waist of her skirt, and a boy followed her a minute later.

When he crossed between the small front bedroom and the bathroom he walked on his toes, and with whatever care he took the boards creaked, and the sounds seemed to him to scream in the empty house. From daybreak he had been continuously on the move, between the two rooms, searching down the Drive and then down the Crescent, hunting for the patrol.

It was the half light now, the light that he wanted, the grey light. It would be right for him if they came at this time. He checked his watch. If they came within ten minutes, fifteen minutes, it would be good for him. Not after fifteen minutes. He wouldn't have the half light after fifteen minutes.

Backwards and forwards, between the two rooms, Frankie Conroy watched and waited for his target. He could come close to the broken glass of the windows, where the chipboard had rotted in the weather, because he had smeared his face with blackening from the damp charred beams at the top of the stairs. His features merged with the darkness of the interior of the derelict house.

Each day since she had been back, her Ma had told Roisin that she should get herself down to Gingy's people. On the afternoon of Christmas Eve she had exhausted her excuses, which had nothing to do with her dislike of them at any time and her unwillingness to speak to them at this time.

Mrs Chrissie O'Rourke had persisted. The McAnallys had the right to see their daughter-in-law, wasn't their fault that Gingy had done what he had.

Her kids didn't need her for an hour, her Ma didn't need her in the kitchen, she had no reason not to go.

The tree stood well in the living room, the lights twinkling into the gloom behind the drawn curtains, and the tinsel was bright and glittering, and the fire was lit and the kids had the telly and were watching BBC with the bloody Brit accents and were sticking the links of a paper chain, and weren't arguing. Her kids didn't need her. Her Ma was baking, and the kitchen wasn't big enough for two to be working there.

Her Da was coughing upstairs. Her Ma said that her Da might get up for Christmas lunch and try some breast of chicken.

She couldn't take her Ma lecturing. It was easier to go and see the McAnallys than scratch another excuse together, and fight.

She had to walk the length of the Drive, almost to the junction with the Crescent. She had to walk past her home. There had been workmen there the previous day, making a start at sealing the broken windows. They'd come to her Ma's and then they had gone down the Drive to Number 63. After the holiday she'd have to find out when they could get her furniture back. She couldn't live with her Ma, not permanent. She'd have to get back to her own home after Christmas.

It didn't look like her own home, not with the wood sheets guarding the windows and broken glass up the front path. But if she didn't go back into her own home after the holiday then the house would be lost to her, would become like the house on the junction with the Crescent that had been burnt and abandoned.

There were never any bloody men to be seen in the Drive, always only the women. There were two women struggling along the pavement, loaded with their shopping, dropped by a black taxi on the Glen Road. They neither of them noticed her, though she had to get off the pavement to let them by. They, neither of them, looked at her, smiled at her. Bitches . . .

Frankie Conroy took me out the first night I was back, isn't that fucking good enough for you? Bitches . . .

And it would bloody go on. If she had a legal separation from Sean, if she had a civil divorce, she would still be known in the Drive as the tout's woman, and he'd be across the papers for the Magistrate's court, and he'd be on the telly with his Crown Court evidence. She'd be bloody known for ever as the tout McAnally's woman. The women with their shopping wouldn't look at her until they were past her, then they'd bloody look at her. They'd look at her back.

They lived at Number 97.

The aerosol heroes had been active. The walls beneath the front windows were all sprayed.

'Touts will be stiffed.'

'Provos Rule, Not Traitors.'

'No Show Trials. No Paid Perjurers.'

It was like a house where there had been a bad death. There were good deaths and bad deaths. There were deaths that were natural. It was like a house where there had been a bloody awful death.

She knew Sean's father as a big man, bigger than his son. He had shrivelled. She had never seen his shoulders gone before, not when his son was off to the Kesh, not when he was running, not even when he quit and went down south. Sean's father seemed to thank her with his eyes for coming.

'You'll have a cup, we'll put the kettle on.'

Sean's mother smiled at Roisin vaguely, from the kitchen door at the back of the hall. She understood the look, she knew what the

Valium did, or the Librium, or whatever new pill it was that the doctors were peddling. She was shown into the front room. She looked straight for the mantelpiece. She saw the photograph frame. She had given them the photograph frame for Christmas three years earlier to hold the photograph of Sean in his confirmation suit. She saw the frame was lying face down. She saw that his father and mother couldn't look at the face of their son.

Sean's father blurted, 'I'd kill him myself, God forgive me, but I'd kill him . . . Does he know what he's done to us? . . . When we went to Mass, the Sunday after he'd gone supergrass, do you know that no-one would sit near us, not in our row, not in front of us, not behind us . . . You seen his mother, you wonder she's like that . . .'

'I tried to tell him.'

'Why . . . his mother keeps asking me why he did it . . . So he got himself caught, but there's plenty of fellows get caught, the Kesh is full of them, but he didn't have to do this to us.' Sean's father pleaded for the answer. 'Will he change his mind?'

'He doesn't have a mind any more, not of his own,' Roisin said.

Sean's mother came into the front room. She was carrying two mugs of tea and her hands were shaking, and the tea was spilling from the mugs.

'You didn't bring the little ones,' Sean's mother said. 'You haven't brought our grankids for us to see.'

'They'll be round tomorrow . . . You'll find Young Gerard a bit funny, you're not to take notice of him. You mustn't mind him . . .' Roisin gulped down her tea, scalded her throat.

The patrol came down the Crescent.

They were soaked, they were on the home run, and Ferris wasn't bothering with any more P–checks. Showing the bloody flag would have to be enough for Christmas Eve.

He saw the one he wanted. He couldn't fail to see him.

Taller than the men in front of him and behind him. Not ducking and weaving like they were. Like they were scared and this one wasn't. Frankie Conroy eased the Armalite up to his shoulder. The hard steel of the extended stock pressed back into his shoulder. Hold it tight, the bread delivery man had said, lock it against the bone of your shoulder. Have your fingers fast on it, the bread delivery man had added, and don't bloody tremble, and don't bloody think what it's for and what's going to happen.

Hard not to tremble. Frankie Conroy was on one knee. The anti-flash cover and the needle sight on the forward end of the barrel protruded three, four inches through the gap in the rotten chipboard at the window. The officer was a hundred yards from him, coming down the Crescent steadily. The officer would be forty yards from him when he fired, but already Frankie Conroy was lining his aim.

He had listened well to the bread delivery man. There was nothing in his mind about what it was for, what would happen, no crap like that. No troubles in his mind, that sort of shit, about taking the life of a British soldier on the day before Christmas. What concerned Frankie Conroy, waiting and watching, aiming through the half light, was whether he could hold the barrel steady, whether he could put the bastard down first shot.

There would only be one shot, the first shot.

He was sweating. The wetness was clinging on his skin. And he couldn't take his hands from the Armalite to wipe his forehead or smear the dampness out of his eyelids.

It was to save the Chief from the Kesh that the officer would be blown away with a high velocity bullet. That's what it was for, that's what would happen.

The barrel was steady. The leaf sight and the needle sight met on the chest of the officer.

The officer seemed to be talking to himself. Frankie Conroy could see his lips move. He heard only the soft slither of the patrol's boots on the pavements, and the moan of distant traffic. He couldn't help himself, he wondered what the bastard was saying to himself.

His finger was on the trigger, round it, starting to squeeze on it, like the bread delivery man had said he should.

The barrel traversed, followed the officer to the corner of the Crescent and the Drive. He'd fire at forty yards.

He was trying not to think about Sam. Thinking about Sam was too damned dangerous when strolling in Turf Lodge. He was going to ring Sam in the morning, Christmas morning, to tell her that he was coming across the water, to try to fix something with her. He'd have to spend a day with his parents in Lancashire, and then there was the day with Sergeant Tunney at the hospital, but he should be able to manage the last evening with Sam before the long bloody trek back, and if he was really bloody trying he might just make a night with Sam . . . He reckoned it would be New Year's Eve. Sam was hardly going to be sitting round on New Year's Eve waiting for poor old Ferris to give her a bell from Belfast. He should have rung her straight off, as soon as Sunray had told him he was going cross-Channel . . . Arseholes . . .

'Arseholes . . .' Ferris said out loud.

'Beg your pardon, sir,' Jones said cheerfully, from behind.

That was the moment Ferris turned to smile at Fusilier Jones.

It was the moment of the shot.

The whip crack of the shot belted Sam, New Year's Eve, every bloody thing out of Ferris's head.

He was spinning, couldn't stand, the blow turned him like a top. Lost the control of his legs, and the pavement was rising to take him, and he couldn't hear anything after the shot.

The pavement smashed into his face.

Frankie charged down the staircase. One step broke under him, and he was close to losing his balance, and he careered through the kitchen and put his shoulder into the chipboard masking the window, and he climbed out into the late afternoon murk and the back garden of the house.

He'd seen the officer twist away at the moment he'd fired.

There were shouts in the street, the wrong side of the house from him, panic shouts, squealed shouts in the bloody Brit accent.

He went over the garden fence, and into the back path that went to the garages, and he ran till the wind sobbed in his throat.

He reckoned he'd done pretty bloody well because he had seen the officer twist and go down.

And the shouts were far away, and behind him.

\*    \*    \*

Roisin stood in the opened door of the McAnallys' house.

Over the top of the hedge she could see the backs of the soldiers as they bent low. She could hear the frantic, frightened cursing. Past the hedge where the gate was open, she could see the boots and legs of a squaddy on the ground, but not his face. She could hear the atmospheric and staccato replies of their radios.

'What's happened?' The call was from behind her, far back in the hall.

'A soldier's been shot,' Roisin said over her shoulder.

'Are you coming back to your tea?'

She closed her eyes, she shook her head. She closed the door on the street.

She turned to Mr McAnally. She smiled brightly. 'I have to help my Ma, but I've time for another cup.'

His hearing was back.

The carols out in the vehicle park were a pain in his ears, and the MO's voice was an agony.

The MO swabbed at the blood round his nose.

'No Purple Heart for you, Mr Ferris, but by Christ there's someone up there with a sense of the festive spirit and smiling on you . . . do you know that the incoming round *actually* hit the mag on your SLR, not full-face of course, but glanced it, and the mag was enough to richochet it. Head butting the pavement wasn't sensible, giving yourself a nose-bleed doesn't exactly fit the hero slot . . .'

'They didn't get the shit,' Ferris said bleakly.

'Didn't even get a shot back, too much powder in their bloody tea . . . you've got leave, haven't you? Well, don't expect a good time with the crumpet, not with the way your hooter's looking . . . bloody great excitement here when the Contact came over the air, your lads must be fond of you, they were half hysterical, bellowing for an ambulance, the way it sounded at this end the Sky Pilot was reaching for his beads and prayer book . . . You'll dine out on that one, your mag getting in the way. You'll bore the pants off your grandchildren . . . There you are, laddie, perfect though not pretty.'

Ferris straightened on the surgery couch. 'I'm clear?'

'Free to get pissed. You'll have an expensive night in the Mess.'

Gingerly Ferris touched his face. 'It feels a bit wretched.'

'Not half as wretched as the bugger who sniped you . . . Your bill of health'll put him right in the mood for Christmas. He'll be boasting to all his mates, till News At Ten. Merry Christmas . . .'

Ferris went out to the vehicle park. He was in time to join the singing of the final two carols.

He had cut his knee when he had stumbled in his flight over a rusted, scrapped bicycle frame.

Frankie Conroy sat on his bed in the room that he rented from the widower, and he had pulled his trouser leg up to his knee, and he held a handkerchief against the wound to staunch the bleeding. His door was open. He could hear the television downstairs, in the widower's front room.

'. . . the Cardinal concluded his statement by saying that he hoped that all members of the community would examine their consciences during the Christmas holiday, and remember the true spirit and meaning of Christmas, and renounce the ways of violence.

'In West Belfast, an officer in the 2nd Battalion the Royal Regiment of Fusiliers had an extraordinary escape when a sniper's bullet glanced off the magazine of his rifle. The officer, leading a foot patrol, was unhurt. An army spokesman described the escape as a "miracle".

'In Part Two, we will be seeing how they are getting ready for Christmas on an oil platform in the North Sea, and we'll be reporting on Pope John Paul's visit to a young people's reformatory in Rome. Join us again . . .'

He could have bloody wept, because he had seen the officer go down.

He could have bloody screamed, because he had seen the face of David Ferris over the leaf sight of the Armalite.

The train rocked and rolled through the outer London suburbs.

The lights were on in the back rooms of the houses. When the curtains hadn't been drawn across Ferris could see into the warm homes. The food was being laid out for parties in the dining rooms, and there were aproned women over their stoves in the kitchens, and upstairs there were youngsters in their bedrooms preening themselves in front of mirrors, preparing for the celebrations at the year's end ... All so bloody safe, and so bloody relaxed. Hundreds and hundreds and hundreds of safe, relaxed, warm homes, that were the homes of families who were far from the front line of David Ferris's war.

He wasn't in uniform. He wore a grey suit under his anorak, and his other civilian clothes were in the canvas grip between his feet. There was nothing about him to show that he was a soldier. He was any young man who was going to visit a friend in hospital, any young man who was then going to meet his girl and celebrate the passing of an old year.

His newspaper was discarded on the luggage rack above his head. He had gutted it for news of the war, and found nothing. He knew that he had made the newspapers, one paragraph after Christmas, and no name, but a few words about a miracle, and he knew that it had been reported on the box. An 'escape' had to be pretty miraculous to make the papers and the box when a death couldn't guarantee getting a column inch or a few seconds of airtime.

The previous day he had travelled from Belfast on the ferry to Liverpool, and he had taken the train to Preston and his parents' home. He hadn't told them about the stunning impact of a high velocity round against the magazine of an SLR. No bloody point. He had told them, and made a laugh of it, that he had slipped on an icy pavement and clipped his nose on the kerbstone. They'd accepted the explanation, because they knew nothing of the grey world that was Turf Lodge. There had been some of their friends invited round for supper, and the talk at the table had been about everything but Northern Ireland. They wouldn't have discussed cancer or incurable leukaemia at the supper table, and there was no reason why they should discuss Northern Ireland. His mother had watched over him and seemed to wonder why her boy drank so often and so deeply. After the guests had gone when his mother was in the kitchen, his father had sidled close to him and asked if 'things were all right' over there, and David had said they were 'all right'. There was a sharp nervous smile on his father's face as he had supposed that his son didn't see much of the 'difficulties', and David had said that he never seemed to see anything of the 'difficulties'. Not their war, they hadn't volunteered for warfare across the Irish Sea. His father had made a play of seeming satisfied.

He had travelled down to London that morning, and crossed London by underground, and taken a stopping train to a station near Roehampton. It wasn't a bad day for the last of December, quite a bright sun. Until he had gone through the front doors the hospital had seemed a fairly decent sort of place. Not that there was anything wrong with the inside of the buildings, it was the people inside that bruised him. They were all of his age, the men who were learning to walk with artificial limbs, and on crutches, and on sticks, and the men who were learning to get themselves down a corridor when their eyes were shaded with dark glasses.

'Why didn't you tell me earlier?' Rennie snapped into the telephone.

'I thought we could get over it, and I was wrong . . .' Prentice's voice was faint on the line.

'Have you taken him boozing?'

'He's pissed every night.'

'Get him a woman.'

'He'd run a bloody mile – that's not his problem. His problem is that he's talking about scratching out.'

'He knows what'll happen to him?'

'I've told him, Goss's told him. He's not in the mood to be told.'

'Have you talked money with him?'

'Like we're a couple of investment brokers. It's not about money.'

'What in Christ's name is it about?'

'He's lost his balls.'

'If he ever had any,' Rennie muttered.

'Come again, Mr Rennie . . .'

'I said that it's your job to lift him.'

'We can hold him up, Mr Rennie, Goss and me'll hold him up till he's in the box. When he's in the box and we can't hold him then he'll fall flat on his bloody face.'

'Will he get better?'

'My opinion only, but he'll get worse. My opinion, you have to get him through the Magistrate soonest, it might show there's nowhere else to go but the Crown Court. Doing his act at the preliminary hearing might just toughen him, steel him – but I wouldn't put money on it – it might just fold him. We're in a bad way.'

'If you let McAnally through your fingers . . .'

'You've no call to be threatening me, Mr Rennie.'

Rennie sat in his office. The telephone in his hand was sheened with the sweat from his palm. New Year's Eve, and the end of the week when he had come near to forgetting Sean Pius McAnally. New Year's Eve, and he had been hoping to take Gloria to the rugby club for the dinner dance. Just about cleared his desk, when Prentice had rung. He shouldn't have been doubting Prentice. Prentice was as good as any he had. Prentice had been nursing the problem, hoping it would go away.

'John, give it me again.'

'I told you all of it, Mr Rennie.'

'Just give it me again.'

'We let him ring home on Christmas morning, mid-morning. It couldn't have been worse. His little girl had gone down to McAnally's parents, just down the Drive – this is what Roisin told him – she was chased by some kids. Bloody Christmas morning, and they chased her, they were shouting "Tout's brat" at her, something like that . . . she ran into the road. There was this car, it swerved in time. It didn't hit the girl, it frightened the wits out of her. The car hit a hedge. His Missus came out, she was screaming up and down the road, that's what she told Gingy. The girl wasn't hurt, but she could just as well have been killed . . . Gingy caught the lot of it. She'd just got the girl indoors when he rang, she was still hysterical. She told Gingy that if Little Patty had been killed then her blood would have been on his head . . . I don't think she meant it, it was just bad luck he phoned when he did.'

'Fucking animals . . . right, that's Christmas Day.'

'Next day we let him ring again – we reckoned she'd have calmed down. The boy, Gerard, picked up the phone. Gingy said who he was and the boy cut him, just cut the call. They must have left the phone off after that, because Gingy tried twice more and it was engaged both times.'

'I see your problem,' Rennie said heavily.

'We gave Gingy the chance to call again last night, late, after the kid would have been in bed. Gingy dialled it, he went pretty white, he just put the phone down. A fellow answered it . . . Gingy won't say who it was . . . he just went to pieces then. Look, this morning we were trying him with his evidence. He was awful. If he were like that in court, up against Counsel, he'd be massacred.'

'You took your bloody time telling me.'

Rennie pondered. He was bleak-faced. He was searching his memory, recalling his last conversation with the Commanding Officer of 2 RRF. He remembered what had been said about David Ferris.

'John, where are you tonight?'

'Some awful dive that Andy's found.'

'In the town?'

'Yes.'

'For midnight?'

'Yes, we've a hell of a lot to celebrate.'

'What's it called?'

'The Midnite Club – you coming over, Mr Rennie?'

'Don't fuck me about, boy . . . You be in the Midnite, you better be there.'

'That the lot, Mr Rennie?'

'It'll be the lot for now.'

Rennie put down the telephone. He began to search in his book for the direct line to the Commanding Officer of 2 RRF.


Alone in his cell, the Chief brooded on what he had learned on that day, the last day of the year. His lunch tray was on the floor in front of him, untouched.

Mr Pronsias Reilly had made, in the late afternoon, a solicitor's call to his client.

'You'll not credit it of Gingy McAnally, but the word is that he's under the thumb of a Brit officer, that the officer's got him wrapped round the finger. The officer's what's holding Gingy up . . . So the name of the officer was learned . . . Frankie Conroy had the name. Frankie went for him, set up a snipe on him, and hit his bloody rifle. Without that officer, McAnally's gone, and Frankie hit the officer's rifle. That was Christmas Eve, and the officer hasn't been seen since.

We've lost track of Gingy, most likely he's across the water, but the officer was the way to him, and he's not been seen since the snipe . . . If you're to break the charges then Gingy's got to lose that officer. That's about all there is, but I reckoned you'd want to know.'

The Chief had access to newspapers and to a pocket transistor radio. He knew the war was scaled down in his absence, and the absence of the Brigade Staff, and the absence of the Battalion Officers, all in the cells alongside him, there on the word of Gingy McAnally. The Organization always hit hard before Christmas, and then allowed a lull, and came back kicking the New Year in.

'Why Frankie? Why that donkey on the rifle?' the Chief hissed out of earshot of the watching prison officer.

'The only one who was interested,' Mr Pronsias Reilly muttered.

'There's plenty of men who wouldn't have hit the rifle.'

'None of them interested enough to try.'

'Only Frankie?'

'Who you'd depend your freedom on? Only Frankie.'

'He's useless.'

'He's what you've got.'

The Organization was stagnated. It was castrated without the influence of the Chief and his Brigade Staff and his Battalion Officers. He hated to lie on his cell bunk because then his head was close to the whitewashed wall and the cell seemed to close around him, and his ears seemed to ring with the crash of closing doors, and the scrape of bolts, and the tinkle of the key chains. He hated to lie on his bed blanket with his head close to the wall because then the knowledge of the months and years in the Kesh seemed to overwhelm him.

He sat on his bed, and he stared at the door, and he cursed, because the only man who would champion him was the donkey, Frankie Conroy.

He spent an hour and a half with Sergeant Tunney . . . for David Ferris it was a hard hour and a half, and he tried not to look too often at the scorched raw flesh of the sergeant's face and hands. He told the sergeant what had happened to him, out in Turf Lodge, and he lied a bit and said they might have hit the bugger with return fire,

281

because that would please the sergeant. He told him about Christmas Day, and Sunray serving soup for the Fusiliers, and the 2 i/c carving the turkeys, and the Adjutant dropping a two-dozen tray of cans and the beer foaming when the rings were pulled and making a hell of a mess, and Fusilier Jones losing a tooth filling on a 5p piece in the Christmas pudding. When he left, when he touched gently onto Sergeant Tunney's shoulder, he thought there was the dribble of a tear at his platoon sergeant's eye. He couldn't shake the sergeant's hand, so he had to touch him on the shoulder, and he couldn't be sure whether it was tears or not because there was so much mucus and ointment on the sergeant's face.

'You give the fuckers hell, Mr Ferris, when you get back.'

'We'll leave a few for you, Sergeant Tunney, for when you're with us again.'

He smiled with as much confidence as he could muster, and he walked out of the ward.

The sergeant's wife was sitting on a hard bench in the corridor. She looked away from him, and he pretended that he hadn't seen her. He thought that each of the days of the year the Ministry should bring the cameras into the wards and the corridors of this hospital to record what his father called the 'difficulties' of Northern Ireland. Let the people, the voters, see the real price of keeping the peace in the Province. Let them see the men without legs, without stomachs, without sight, without skin on their faces and hands. The sergeant's wife had the right to look away from him.

'David . . .'

She was coming down the corridor towards him. His Sam, his girl. A full swinging skirt. Shined Italian boots. A suede coat open over a cashmere sweater. Long hair darting golden over her face. His Sam, coming towards him with excitement loud on her cheeks. She was light in darkness. She was love in a place of misery.

He saw the wide open newspaper that hid from him the face of the sergeant's wife. He was meeting his girl, he was whole. She was waiting on her man, he was damaged. Fucking Northern Ireland, fucking Belfast . . .

'Sorry I'm late, David darling, bloody traffic, God knows where it all comes from. Heavens you look well. Got your business done?'

She came into his arms. He was embarrassed, Sam wasn't. Sam hugged him, kissed him. Sam didn't see the newspaper of the sergeant's wife.

He felt the tackiness of her lipstick on his mouth, on his face. He felt the warmth of her coat on his neck. He felt the shape of her pressed against his chest.

'It's wonderful to see you,' Ferris said, into her ear.

'Too damned right it's wonderful. You finished?'

'Yes.'

She was still kissing him.

'Let's get the hell out. It's got the smell of death, this place.'

His voice would have carried across a parade ground. They walked away together down the corridor, and from Mrs Tunney.

'We're well fixed up – Christ, you didn't give me much time . . . We're going to someone called Penny's for supper – we were at school – lives in Farnham – then we're going dancing. We're staying at Penny's. All right?'

'Brilliant.'

'Penny says she's dying to meet you. She says any man that keeps me celibate must be worth meeting. She's married to an accountant, so no army talk . . .'

He pushed open the rubber doors at the end of the corridor and they came out into the Reception hallway of the hospital. He kissed her forehead, she kissed him back on the mouth.

'Who were you seeing in there?'

'My platoon sergeant.'

'What's his problem?'

'He's just a bit ill.'

'You've got to go back tomorrow, to Belfast?'

'Got to.'

'Wouldn't you desert for me?'

In the centre of the Reception hallway, David Ferris held Samantha Forster. Held her, squeezed her, buried his head in her soft, scented hair. He didn't see the nurses, nor the visitors, nor the doctors.

The voice in his ear was respectful, even quiet.

'Excuse me, it's Mr Ferris, isn't it?'

He turned. A receptionist was beside him. He nodded.

'There's a telephone call for you, long distance.'

There was a frown on his forehead.

'Not the bloody army . . .' Sam said.

'They're holding on for you.'

He let go of Sam. He thought she sounded quite amused, himself he felt bloody furious. He walked after the receptionist to the front desk. The telephone was lying beside its cradle. For one moment he considered ignoring the call. It was a short moment. He looked round at Sam. She was lovely, she was pulling a face at him.

'Hurry it up, David, Penny'll be pouring the gin by now.'

He picked up the telephone.

'Ferris . . .' he said curtly.

'Thank Christ for that. It's Rennie . . .'

It was a good line. Ferris could hear Rennie clearly enough to sense the relief.

'Happy New Year's Eve, Mr Rennie.'

'This isn't a secure call, so watch what you say. I know it's New Year's Eve, I know you're on leave, I know you're with your lady – and I'm making no apologies. We're in deep shit, David. The word I have is that our friend is likely to walk out on us . . . Don't argue, just listen. If it wasn't important I wouldn't have tracked you . . . David, the boys say that our friend's going through the floor – doesn't matter why, but he's in maggots. Don't tell me you've got plans for tonight . . . David, you're in Roehampton now. Before midnight I want you in Aldershot . . . Before midnight I want you in Aldershot . . . Before midnight I want you at a club in Aldershot. Our friend's going to be there. He's got to be lifted, he's got to be helped. David, if you don't lift him, then the whole thing's over. Got your pencil, I'll give you the address.'

Ferris gripped the telephone between his ear and his shoulder, and reached in his pocket for a pen.

He met Sam's eyes.

'I'm dying for that drink. Hurry up, darling.' Sam blew him a kiss.

He wrote the address.

Rennie said, down the long line, that if David Ferris ever did the decent thing by the girl that he'd buy them a wedding present, and in the meantime a Happy New Year to both of them.

*   *   *

It was an hour before midnight.

Sam was bloody extraordinary. He'd thought she might have ditched him, might at least have gone acid on him. She had shrugged, said that it might be fun, said that Penny's accountant was a boring pouf, said that they might have a good laugh out of it. He'd just told her that it was something to do with his work, that there was a man he had to meet.

They'd eaten Penny's dinner. He'd drunk three gins and the best part of a bottle of wine and he hadn't a lot to say for himself, and Sam didn't seem to notice and had rabbited about school days, and the accountant had watched him morosely each time he'd filled his glass. Sam didn't seem to mind, and there was a double bed waiting upstairs, and turned down, and Sam's nightdress on the pillows.

He was holding her hand and they were walking past shop windows. He heard the disco music.

'Sam, don't ask me who this man is. Please just help me cheer him up, just make a fuss of him. All we've got to do is give him a bloody good evening.'

'And have one ourselves.'

Some bloody chance.

There was a muscled bouncer on the door. The place called itself the Midnite Club, and there was a pound surcharge because it was New Year's Eve, and fancy dress was optional, and denims weren't.

'It'll be full of Other Ranks, Sam, sorry . . .'

'Don't be so pompous. You're worse than bloody Daddy.'

She tugged him to the door, smiled sweetly at the bouncer, and won a bow. Ferris paid them in.

They went down the stairs inside and thoughts of Sean Pius McAnally, supergrass and cracking, were blown clean out of his head by the explosion that was the music.

# 18

The lights flashed from the ceiling through revolving prisms over the dancers. They were early. Jackson and Boy George pounded their ears. He'd looked around him as soon as they were inside. There were tables and chairs around the edge of the dance floor, but the action was middle-stage. The minders and the supergrass hadn't shown. There was a bar, but Sam said that she had to drive, and she didn't want him falling over and he didn't need any more to drink, and she'd come to dance. She took his hand and led him to the centre of the floor. Now, for the first time, she joked about his damaged nose and he gave the same lie that had stopped his mother's fussing, and the lie was good enough for Sam as well.

She wore a full black skirt, and she showed her glorious legs when the tempo was going hard and she twirled from the ends of his fingers. She wore a tight-fitting polka dot blouse, and he felt the warmth of her against his shirt when the music was slow, loving. And she told him he was a damned heifer when he scraped her toes and that he wasn't that bad close to, and she nibbled his ear and chewed his lobe.

He was a prisoner who had escaped. For twelve weeks he had been incarcerated in the Springfield Road, and he had bust out. Belfast was ancient bloody history . . . There was nothing in his mind of the Turf Lodge, or of a hidden marksman, or of Sunray or the IO. The present was Sam, and the sweat streaking the fair strands on her forehead, and the damp lovely warmth of her, and her hips that were swinging and drifting against him. She was a bad bloody woman, and she knew it, and he thought he might just love her for it.

Sam kept Ferris to the centre of the dance floor, and she grinned because her elbows made room for them to dance without being buffeted by other couples. And the Midnite Club was ORs' territory, and ORs and their girls gave space to an officer and an officer's woman. Obvious she was an officer's woman when she didn't care that his cheek had lipstick smears, when she wore a string of pearls at her throat, when she didn't give a damn who saw her thighs. Ferris thought that Sam was the best-looking woman in the Midnite Club.

They didn't talk. The bedlam of the noise was too much to talk across. He no longer looked every minute or so to the entrance steps. He was close to forgetting what he was there for. Her hands were locked on the nape of his neck and her lips nuzzled under his chin.

Midnight was closing on the Club. The floor was emptier as the dancers struggled to reach the bar and gain the refills for the twelve o'clock toasts. Ferris and Sam danced on. Ferris heard nothing around him but the gentle breathing of Sam. He danced as if he were unaware of the music, he moved in the world that was Sam and himself. And Sam was lovely, the loveliest.

The voice rabbit punched him.

The accent carved through the music, through Ferris's preoccupation with holding Sam tight to him.

The accent rasped in his mind for recognition.

'If we's wants a bloody drink, we'll have a bloody drink.'

He could pinpoint the accent. The accent was Gingy McAnally's.

'So get your fat arse out the way, so's we can get a bloody drink.'

The accent was drunk.

Ferris had stiffened, he no longer moved with the music. He felt Sam pulling him, trying to drag him back to the dancing steps. There was a puzzlement in her face, merging with annoyance.

'Where's the bloody bar? . . . and it's your bloody shout, Goss.'

He turned slowly, towards the door. He saw McAnally shove himself past the bouncer, and as the bouncer reached to grab him, then Prentice's arm was out and restraining, and Goss was grimly flashing his warrant card. The bouncer backed off. On the edge of the dance floor McAnally seemed to lose his footing and he careened into a girl who was dancing, and half tripped her, and the girl's fellow was squaring up when again Prentice's hand dropped on the arm. At the bar McAnally tunnelled for space and service and Prentice and Goss were hard in behind him.

'Scotch for me, Goss ... whatever you's having, Scotch for me.'

It was ten days since he had seen McAnally, since they had walked on the mountain of Mullaghmore.

'Shift your arse ... three Scotches, he's paying.'

The man was devastated. There was a new suit on him, three-piece Burtons' in the High Street, but that couldn't conceal the devastation, nor could the centre-parting hair salon job hide the damage.

'Come on, Goss, for fuck's sake, show her your fucking money so's we get served.'

McAnally had put on half a stone that bulged his waist under his unbuttoned waistcoat, and his shirt tail was out of his trousers, and his tie of brilliant green was loose at his throat. His face was a blotched red mess, and his eyes blinked as if to focus on his nose, and a cheroot cigar hung from the side of his mouth and jerked when he shouted. Prentice was bent over his shoulder, whispering in his ear.

'Don't tell me to shut up, Prentice.'

The drink from Goss was in his hand, and swigged.

'Piss poor measures they give here.'

Prentice had him by the throat.

'Don't tell me to behave ...' McAnally drained his glass. 'Goss, keep shouting, same as before.'

Ferris shuddered. The sight of McAnally appalled him. He understood why Rennie had tracked him down.

'Sam ...' Ferris spoke softly in her ear. 'I'm sorry, you should go back to Penny's. I'll catch you there.'

She stared at him, astonished. 'I'm not going anywhere.'

'Please, Sam.'

'We're in this ghastly place to meet your friend who hasn't come. So we enjoy ourselves. I'm not going anywhere.'

'Come on, darling.' He tried to gently pull her off the floor.

She held her ground. 'It's five to midnight, David.'

'I don't want you to stay here.'

'Because a drunk's making a bit of noise, don't be so wet ... I'm not going at five minutes to midnight and neither are you.'

She kicked him sharply on the ankle. As he hopped she swung him back into the rhythm of the music. As he danced he twisted his head, always watching McAnally. She tweaked his nose, hurt him.

'What's special about the drunk?'

'Don't ask,' Ferris said.

'Why not . . . ?' She was laughing happily into his face. 'Is *that* your friend?'

'I said, don't ask.'

'You can't *actually* know him.'

'Sam, be quiet.'

'Aren't you going to introduce me?'

'When I bloody have to, not before.'

The disc jockey, an excited sallow youth with a purple streak in his hair, was calling for the floor to be filled, the last spin of the old year. Sam danced mechanically, distant from Ferris.

He heard McAnally's voice.

'There's no bloody offence meant, so's you needn't be taking offence.'

He heard Prentice's voice.

'Just close your hole up, Gingy, do us a bloody favour.'

'I was just telling the man that there's no offence meant . . .'

'He got your message.'

Goss was trying to pour water from a jug into McAnally's new whisky, and McAnally's hand was wobbling, and the water had flowed into the lap of a lady, and her husband was on his feet and remonstrating. Ferris reckoned the husband to be at least a colour sergeant and an evil little toad whatever he was, the sort of little toad who'd break the bottom off a bottle.

'Apologize, you silly shit,' Prentice shouted.

'No offence meant, that's a bloody apology.'

The man was apparently satisfied.

His lady was standing and squeezing the water out of her frock.

Ferris closed his eyes. A bloody nightmare.

The disc jockey was on the countdown. The dancers were shouting the numbers with him. Ferris looked at Sam, she wasn't shouting, she was staring straight ahead, at Sean Pius McAnally, fascinated.

'I'm sorry . . . Sam, I'm sorry.'

He tried to kiss her lips and she turned her head away and his mouth brushed her cheek.

'It's a bit different to what Penny had in mind for us, and that would have been bloody boring. You're a right laugh, darling.'

'Happy New Year . . . Happy New Year . . .' the disc jockey shrieked.

'Happy New Year, Sam,' Ferris said softly.

'Happy New Year yourself,' she said, from the side of her mouth. 'Level with me. Are we here to meet that drunk?'

The dancers linked arms, made a long bent line that circled the dance floor.

Auld Lang Syne on the turntable, and everyone singing, and Ferris singing and trying to wake up from a bad dream.

The line stamped across the dance floor, squashing itself together. Bodies barged together, elbowed each other, kneed each other. He held tight onto Sam's hand. The faces in front of him were blurred, blurred as the noise of the singing.

'It's the fucking officer . . .'

He saw McAnally. McAnally was in the line opposite him, pinioned by Prentice and Goss.

'Look, you daft bugger . . . look, Goss, it's our bloody officer.'

The line swept back. Across the floor McAnally's feet scrabbled for a grip on the boards as Prentice and Goss hoisted him away with the motion of the line. McAnally's eyes were locked on Ferris.

'Don't you see? It's bloody Ferris . . .'

Sam jabbed her elbow into Ferris's side.

'Who is he?'

'He's nothing you need to know about.'

McAnally leered across the floor.

'That's a great bit of fanny, Ferris,' McAnally shouted. 'You're on a better bloody promise than I am . . . You've got a right looking raver, I've got these jerks . . . I hope it's a promise, hope it wasn't her that did your nose.'

Prentice was laughing, and Goss was trying not to look pained, and McAnally was laughing with Prentice and giggling with Goss, and leaning on their arms, and the singing died and the arm chains broke.

'Is this some crack of Rennie's?' To Prentice it was a hell of a joke.

'Did Rennie put you up to being here?' Goss, embarrassed, trying for his answers. 'I mean you're hardly in this dump out of choice.'

Ferris turned his back, he turned away so that he faced Sam.

'He's Belfast,' Ferris said simply. 'He's nothing to do with here.'

'What is he in Belfast?'

'He's ... Sam, I can't plead the bloody Official Secrets Act with you.'

'What is he?'

'He's ...'

He felt the fingers grappling with the shoulder of his jacket. He spun, McAnally was hanging to his clothes, and he stank of Scotch and the cheroot was still in his mouth. Prentice and Goss were holding McAnally upright.

'Mister bloody Ferris ... Happy New Year, a fucking happier New Year than the last one was ... You've forgotten your Gingy, haven't you? You wouldn't be thinking about Gingy when you've that fanny with you ... aren't you going to introduce us? You're friendly enough with Taig filth, with Gingy McAnally, when you're 'cross the water. Aren't you going to be friendly now?'

'I'd *love* to meet your friends, David,' Sam said, and she rolled her south-of-England accent, and Ferris thought she might have winked at the minders.

Ferris said unhappily, 'Sam, this is Sean McAnally, and this is John Prentice, and this is Andy Goss ... gentlemen, this is Samantha Forster ...'

'Please to meet you, Mr McAnally.'

'Fucking pleased to meet you, Samantha.'

'Watch your foul mouth, Gingy ...' Prentice snapped.

'You're talking to a lady, Gingy ...' Goss snapped.

'Good-looking fanny, and all ...' McAnally belched.

'I hear you're a friend of David's, Mr McAnally.'

'Prefer to be your fucking friend, lady ... Get some drinks, Goss, for my friend and his fucking lady ... Piss off and get the drinks.'

'Gingy ...' Ferris's voice was cold, quiet. 'You are behaving like a silly shit, Gingy.'

' "A silly shit, Gingy",' McAnally tried to mimic Ferris. 'Not good enough for the officer, are we? Not good enough when he's going to get laid by this lady . . . Where're those drinks, Goss.'

She was laughing. Her head was back, her hair was back. She was laughing through her open mouth, her open lips.

'If I was you, Mister officer, I wouldn't be hanging round the likes of us when you could be laying that lady.'

The laughter was pealing in Ferris's head.

Ferris smashed his fist into the right-side cheek of Gingy McAnally's face.

The fist slapped into the soft flesh of the cheek, crunched against the jaw bone. Ferris had never before hit a man with the bare knuckles of his fist.

There was a moment of bewilderment spilling over McAnally's face, then his mouth screwed tight with the pain.

'He's only drunk, there's no call . . .' Sam shouted.

'You daft bugger,' Prentice growled.

McAnally's knees buckled. He crumpled down onto the floor, down amongst their feet.

The bouncer piled into the knot of Prentice and Goss and Ferris and Sam. When he pulled Goss's jacket the button cotton snapped and the jacket came open and the bouncer saw the shoulder holster and the wood handle of the PPK Walther, and he backed away. The music soared around them, and the dancers cocooned them.

McAnally held his hand over the right side of his cheek.

The bewilderment was past, and the pain was overcome, he was suffused with fury.

'I tell you what, Ferris, I'll tell you this . . . if I ever had any doubts, I've no doubts now . . . I'm out, I'm gone. You get on the phone to Mister bloody Rennie, and you tell him from me, tell him that Gingy McAnally's on his bike. He can stuff his fucking immunity, he can shove his evidence up his arse . . . You tell him that, you tell Mister bloody Rennie that Gingy McAnally's not part of his bloody plans, not any more . . .'

Goss bent to placate McAnally, and was shoved away.

'Don't play the bloody soft soaper with me. I'm gone . . .'

There were tears welling in McAnally's eyes. He gazed up at Ferris.

'All the bullshit about friendship . . .' He tried to imitate Ferris's accent. 'I'll stand beside you, I'll step in front of you – horseshit. I'm scum to you, to you I'm just a Taig tout. I'm not a person. I'm just a Taig informer to be pissed on . . .'

A crack in Sam's voice. She rounded on Ferris. 'Is he a supergrass?'

'He's a fucking supergrass, lady, he's a fucking stoogie.' McAnally choked out the words, smeared his sleeve across his eyes.

'You're mixed up with people like this?'

'Didn't he tell you what shit he's mixed with, doesn't he tell his fanny?'

Ferris saw that Prentice's fists were clenched, that Goss was poised to come forward.

McAnally crawled onto his knees, pushed himself up, and stood in front of Ferris.

'I'm out, I've quit.'

For a few steps McAnally staggered, then he seemed to regain his balance, and he spun to the exit light. His head was down on his shoulders, he seemed not to look ahead of him as he ploughed through the dancers.

'That was hell's clever,' Prentice said.

'You could have walked away,' Goss said. 'Or did Rennie send you to cheer us all up. If he did, haven't you made a bloody good job of it?'

Prentice sighed. He set off to follow McAnally. Ferris looked from Sam away to the back of McAnally's head that was bobbing on the steps to the exit. He muttered something, he didn't hear his own words and Sam wouldn't have heard them, it was something of an apology.

Ferris ran across the floor, and he pushed Prentice back from the door, back down the steps. The bouncer was shouting in his ear that it was a respectable club, that his behaviour was a bloody disgrace.

The night air hit him. He tripped on a dustbin, clattered the lid off. He was in an alleyway at the side of the club. He ran up the alley to the main street. He looked right, then left, when he looked left he saw McAnally.

There was an oath from the alleyway behind him. He knew that Prentice had found the dustbin.

McAnally was holding onto a lamp post, and was vomiting. And he was crying, and Ferris could hear his sobs. A couple, arm in arm and in fancy dress, crossed the road to avoid contact with McAnally.

He walked towards McAnally. McAnally would have heard his footsteps, and he looked up and saw Ferris closing on him.

'I said I'd bloody gone, I said I'd quit,' McAnally shouted. The vomit gleamed on his shoes. He turned and shambled away up the street, and Ferris followed.

Ferris reached him at the traffic lights. McAnally stood, listless and with his head shrunk down into his shoulders, and waited for the lights to change. They crossed the road together. He smelt the vomit on Gingy's waistcoat. Just as the comedians said, it was always diced carrot. They walked past the shop windows, past a patrolling police-man. In silence they walked until they came to a park. There was a bench that was too near to the street and the lights for the couples who shivered and sought warmth from each other's hands. Gingy had fought back the tears, Ferris no longer heard the sounds of his crying.

Gingy sat on the bench. Ferris sat beside him.

'I said I was quitting.'

'It was pretty daft what happened in there.'

'I was going to quit, what happened inside's not to do with it.'

'I'm sorry I hit you,' Ferris said simply.

'I was pissed . . . shit . . .' McAnally found the vomit on his hands. 'It was the drink I'd taken.'

'I didn't have to belt you.'

'I'd have fucking belted me, if I'd been with the bird . . .'

'So it happened, so it's history.'

'Did you walk out on your bird?'

Ferris took his handkerchief from his pocket and wiped the mess from Gingy's mouth, and took his hands and cleaned them, and he threw the handkerchief behind him into the Corporation's flowerbed.

294

'I meant it, what I said, that I'm quitting.'

'They'll wreck you, they won't let you walk out. They'll put the mark on you.'

'You get so's you don't bloody care.'

'Rennie'll let it be known that you named the Monaghan man. He burned to death, there'll be no love for you after that's known.'

'Don't you listen, you get so's you don't bloody care.'

'What happened, Gingy?'

Sean Pius McAnally told David Ferris about the telephone calls.

'There's nothing any of us can do about it,' Ferris said.

'That's a bloody good help.'

'I mean it, Gingy. You stayed in, she didn't.'

'She's my wife, they're my kids.'

'It was her decision not to stay with you. She might change her mind.'

'She's never changed her mind yet,' McAnally laughed shrilly. And the laugh was killed. Bright eyes staring at Ferris. 'You want to know what it's like here?'

'Tell me.'

'I'm never out of their sight. It's all pals, isn't it? It's all Gingy and Johnny and Andy, it's all like we're bloody muckers in it together . . . That's a lie. They say they're close on me because I need protection . . . bollocks, they're with me so's I don't quit . . . but they can't stop me quitting . . . I'm a bloody puppet to them. They tell me I need some clothes, so's we're out to the shops. I don't choose this suit, Prentice chooses it. Prentice goes down the line and he decides what I'm going to wear . . . I hate this bloody suit. Nobody asks me if I like the bloody suit. I'm not to open my bloody mouth, I'm just a parcel of shit that has to be tarted up. They don't want Gingy the way he is, used to be. They want him so's he's theirs. They want the old Gingy buried, they want him like a bloody puppet, that they can sit on their knee, that they can talk through. What do you call that?'

'They call it a ventriloquist's dummy, Gingy.'

'That's what they want, Gingy for a dummy. I'm not having it . . . They want to put the mark on me, let them . . . We're in a para barracks. The cover is that we're 'tecs over for a course. No sod's buying that. We're in a flat, top floor, end of corridor. The door's always locked. They put me to bed, like I was a kid. I can hear them when I'm in bed, I can hear them bloody laughing. The bloody walls are like cardboard, every time they bloody laugh I hear them. We go out each night, go on the booze, and if I come out of the room after I've gone to bed, for a leak, then the laughing stops. There's never any bloody laughing when I can get myself close to them.'

Ferris shuddered in the cold, and Gingy's teeth were chattering, and he was gushing out his talk, as if speaking kept him warm. When he looked behind him he saw the outline of Prentice sitting on a low wall of the park, fifty yards from them, sitting and watching a man who was blown out.

'I'm not a bloody fool, I know what they're at. They're at taking myself away from me, they're at changing me. The clothes is changing me, and the bloody haircut's changing me. . . . We went to church on Christmas morning, the local RC. They looked a bit nervous, and they was watching everyone else so they'd get the movements right. I said I wanted to go to Confession, that was a morning after Christmas. I didn't really want to go, I was chancing, but they said no, that I couldn't . . .'

'What would you have confessed, Gingy?'

'That's not your business.'

'Would you have confessed that you were an informer?'

'Confession's not for blabbing about, not to the likes of you.'

'Or would you have confessed that you'd killed a judge and two detectives?'

'Not your business.'

'Or that you were running scared?'

'What do you know of running . . . you've a bloody great army behind you. You're not on your bloody own. If you were ever on your own, against them, then you wouldn't give me talk about running scared.'

Again Ferris looked behind him. Prentice would have seen his face, white from the high street light. He saw Prentice raise his hand in acknowledgement. He knew that Prentice wouldn't approach. He knew Prentice would leave him to do the graft alone, to bend McAnally once again back on course . . . bastard.

'What else have you been playing at, Gingy?' Ferris asked briskly.

'Rehearsing, isn't that your word?'

'Could be the word.'

'They've brought my statements over. We've been taking a morning on each statement. Today it was what said about Phonsie McGurr, yesterday it was Dusty O'Hara, day before was Fatsy Rawe. It's Brennie Toibin tomorrow . . . wrong, not Brennie Toibin, because I've quite . . .'

'How do you rehearse the statement.'

'I have to be able to speak the statement without looking at it. They start shouting at you, trying to interfere with what you're saying, and they tell you you're a liar, that you're making it all up.'

'Like it would be in court?'

'That's what they say it would be like in court – only I'm not finding out what it's like in court, I'm quitting.'

'That's what you said, Gingy.'

'And meant it.'

'What'll you do?'

'When I've quit . . . ? I'll lie up for a bit, then I'll put the word out, that I'm looking to go back . . .'

'Go back?'

'Go back home.'

'You'll be dead before you get a mile off the boat.'

Gingy seemed not to hear him. 'If the word's right I'll go back home.'

'What's home.'

'Home is Roisin, home is the kids.'

Ferris breathed the cold air deep into his lungs. 'She'd not have you back.'

'Don't mess me,' Gingy snarled.

'You know a big man . . .'

'I know a hundred big men.'

'Do you know a big man with a bullet scar in his throat?'

Gingy hesitated, he was trying to read Ferris and could not. 'What if I do?'

'Do you know him?'

'I know Frankie Conroy, so what if I do?'

'Does he know Roisin?'

'She might know him.'

'Does she know him very well?'

'She's no reason to.'

'Does she know him well enough for him to be calling with the presents and the tree for Christmas and the lights, does she know him that very bloody well?'

Gingy's head dropped into his hands. His shoulders were shaking, his face was hidden from Ferris. His voice was muffled through his fingers. 'Do you know what the fear is? Does a Brit soldier know that?'

'Yes.'

'You'd not have the chance of knowing.'

'We had a sniper, when I was out on patrol last week, we were hit by a sniper, that was pretty scary.'

'One of your squaddys got hit, you wondered how you didn't?'

'I was the target,' Ferris said. 'I just stopped, I can't remember why, I must have broken his aim as he was on the trigger. His bullet glanced off the mag on my rifle, the impact put me down on the deck, which is why my nose isn't healthy, wasn't Sam. Knowing the rifle had been on you, the aim on you, that was pretty scary. Knowing that you'd been chosen, out of eight and he'd chosen you. I suppose it was because I was the officer . . .'

Gingy shook his head, he looked up from his hand. There was pity for Ferris in his eyes. 'You know fuck all of nothing.'

'He'd taken a derelict house, on the corner of the Drive and the Crescent in Turf Lodge, he had food there and a sleeping bag.'

'Don't go back,' Gingy said hoarsely.

Ferris smiled, sadly. 'Have to go back, and lightning never strikes twice.'

'How many snipes in your platoon area, the last month?'

'No snipes, not in the last month.'

'Not in your Battalion?'

'Not one, we had a petrol attack . . .'

'And it's the first snipe, and it's you that's the target . . . and Roisin's gone home, and Frankie Conroy's sniffing at her fucking door . . . You think you were bloody random?'

Ferris gazed at Gingy, open-mouthed. 'Roisin would have . . . ?'

'They've got you down as the way to me. Don't go back . . . 'Course Roisin would have, you're her fucking enemy, you're the enemy of every bastard in Turf Lodge. You're the friend of the supergrass . . . If you go back you know fuck all of nothing. You tell me if I go home I'm dead. I'm telling you that if you go back you're sniped.'

'I have to go back. Because I said I'd stand beside you, and I will.'

'You're bloody mad.'

'I'm going to go back, and you're going to give evidence, Gingy.'

'What's you going back going to get you?'

'Gingy, believe me, me going back is going to get you into the witness box.'

'You're all crap, Ferris.'

'We're going back, you and me, Gingy . . .'

'You'll be in the bloody gutter.'

'So you can put the bastards away.'

'You'll be in the gutter and the kids'll be jumping round you, fucking clapping.'

'Not you, not me, neither of us are running scared from the bastards.'

Ferris stood up, and Gingy McAnally followed. The light from the street lamp beamed onto their faces. Ferris managed a sharp smile, and Gingy grinned and then shook his head. Their hands were clasped for a moment.

'What'll have happened to your girl?'

Ferris walked away.

He passed Prentice, who nodded curtly, and further down the street he saw Goss who was lolling head back and asleep in a parked car.

He thought of a man waiting in the upper room of a derelict house with his food and his sleeping bag and his Armalite rifle, and the face of David Ferris in his mind. He thought of a gutter in Turf Lodge, and he thought of the children's feet jumping before his fading sight, and he thought of their shouts in his dying ears. He thought of his father who was embarrassed to speak of the 'difficulties'. He thought of Sergeant Tunney who wanted a few left for him and who would never again wear a uniform over his re-grafted skin. He thought of the Chief of the Belfast Brigade, pulled from a hiding place under a bed. He thought of the faces of Turf Lodge, all anonymous, all without names, all joined in their loathing of David Ferris, friend of Gingy McAnally.

The door of the Midnite Club was padlocked. The windows were darkened. He looked both ways on the street, and didn't find her.

He went to the car park, where she had left her car. The car park was empty.

He walked the eight miles from Aldershot to Farnham, and revellers who were returning to their homes hooted at him and swept past.

He walked into the estate of new Wates houses. He walked up the cul-de-sac to the accountant's home. He saw Sam's car, parked with the near front wheel among the pruned roses.

He walked round the side of the house, and looked up at the back room where the double bed was, and shouted Sam's name.

When the kitchen door opened, when she stood in her nightdress in the doorway, he saw that Sam who had laughed in the Midnite Club had wept in her friend's bedroom. She clung to him, he clung to her. Big, bold Sam, crying like a baby.

'I so wanted you to come back here . . .'

'You're going to be mine, Sam, I'm going to be yours. Soon as I'm out of that dreadful place.'

'Promise.'

She was smiling and she was crying. A rainbow in the night, crying and loving.

'I promise.'

'Thank God you came back . . . That creature, is he really your friend?'

'I have to be his friend. If I'm not his friend then he's had it.'

'You promise you'll come back to me.'

'Promise, Sam.'

She kissed him all the way up the stairs, all the way to the back bedroom.

# 19

The Land Rover was waiting for David Ferris in the car park outside the Customs hall. It had been a rough night on the boat, force eight, he had hardly slept in the hard seat in the passenger lounge. Since they had sighted land, a blur in the dawn light, he had been on deck, leaning on the rail, watching the coastline. He was chilled from the sea's climbing spray.

The faithful Jones, with two squaddys to ride shotgun, had brought the Land Rover to meet him.

Ferris was unshaven. He wore the same shirt and socks as in the Midnite Club. His suit trousers were holed from the collision with the dustbin, the skin on his right knuckle was bruised.

Fusilier Jones arched his eyebrows. 'A good leave, sir?'

'Excellent,' Ferris said.

'How is Sergeant Tunney?'

'In good shape, Jones, looking forward to getting back so he can bawl your arse off you.'

'You gave him our love, sir?'

'I told him you were all wetting your beds because he wasn't there to tuck you up each night . . .'

They drove through the city that was awakening from the Christmas and New Year holiday. They queued in the traffic lines, and saw the files that were waiting for the Sales doors to open on Royal Avenue and in Donegal Square. All the greasepaint normality of Belfast was on show for his homecoming, all the fraud that pretended this was just another community in the United Kingdom lurching back to life. In the cars around their Land Rover were the civil servants and the representatives and the bank clerks and the insurance men, and on the pavements beside the Land Rover were the housewives and the secretaries and the shop girls who were late and running, and none of them would care a shit for Ferris's war and the supergrass's war.

And then they were on the Falls. He had Jones's rifle across his knee, and he had cocked it. He saw the bomb sites and the graffiti, and the end of terrace wall that had long ago been painted white so that a passing patrol would show up for a marksman's aim, and he saw the bar that was caged in wire against petrol bombs, and the Housing Executive office that was protected by concrete dragon's teeth against a close-quarters car bomb, and he saw a cruising RUC mobile, and a foot patrol of Charley company. His eyes were on the rooftops, and were searching for the missing slates, and for the darkened holes in bricked-up doorways. He was watching the gable walls that would give a sniper cover until the moment he was prepared to fire. He watched the dustbins that could be the hiding place for a pack of explosives linked to a command wire. He watched the Falls as he had never watched it before.

He remembered Gingy McAnally's warning and the clasp of McAnally's fingers on his, and in that moment he thought he might throw up because he was so bloody scared to be back in the Falls.

The Land Rover swung through the gates at Springfield.

Jones cut the engine. 'I'd get yourself changed, sir,' he said confidentially, 'and get your face scraped . . . I'd do it soonest, sir.'

Back in uniform, with his face burning from a new razor blade, he went to the Armoury and drew out his rifle and signed his name for two magazines of 7.62 mm ammunition.

On his way to Bravo's Ops he met the Intelligence Officer.

'Have a good leave?'

'Fine,' Ferris said.

The Company Commander greeted him like a malingerer.

'How was your leave?'

'Fine.'

He passed the Chaplain in a corridor.

'Nice to see you back, David. A good leave I hope.'

'Very good, thank you.'

He went to the Commanding Officer's room.

'What shape's Tunney in?' Sunray asked.

'Firstclass, sir, raring to be back.'

'Damn good. You had a good leave?'

'Very good, sir.'

There was what they wanted to hear, and there was what they didn't want to hear.

The Battalion area, Ferris learned, had been as quiet as a cemetery during his absence. The locals were still sleeping off their New Year's liquor intake. He had missed nothing, so he was told.

They met in the city centre and went together into Boots on Royal Avenue.

Mr Pronsias Reilly had set up the meeting with Frankie Conroy, scrambled it into his lunch break from the Crown Court. He preferred to meet among the crowds of the Belfast shopping area, rather than risk himself against the hidden electronic surveillance systems that operated on the Falls and throughout Nationalist West Belfast. He would have preferred Frankie to have used his bloody loaf, to have dressed with a little more care, not to have appeared as if straight off an Assistance queue. They made a rare pair – Mr Pronsias Reilly, suit and black overcoat and blue shirt and white collar, and Frankie Conroy, mud-scarred Docs and jeans and donkcy jacket and a wool cap – working their way past the cosmetics counters and the garden tools and the hardware electricals.

'They're galloping, they're rushing into court,' Reilly said quietly.

'What does that mean?'

'They're going for an early Preliminary hearing in front of the Magistrate. They've delivered the prosecution statements, they're going ahead in a week or so . . .'

'Normally it's bloody months.'

'They're going to get McAnally into court, get the boys committed for trial, then they'll put him out to clover for a year, then we'll have the main show.'

'Why're they rushing?'

'Perhaps because he's going to be better sooner rather than later . . . there's fuck all the defence can do about it, whatever the reason.'

'I've lost him,' Frankie said simply.

'Lost who?'

'Lost his *friend*, lost the Brit officer who holds his hand.'

Since St Stephen's Day, the day after Christmas, Frankie Conroy had trudged the streets of Turf Lodge, looking for the officer whose face was drawn in his mind. He had seen the mobiles and the foot patrols, and the VCPs and the P-checks. He had been out early in the morning, and in the late afternoon, when the patrols came. He had wondered whether the television and the papers had lied. They had said the officer wasn't hurt, that the magazine of his rifle had deflected an aimed shot. He had wondered whether that was a bloody lie. He had recognized some of the Brit soldiers from Ferris's platoon, but their officer had never been with them.

'You promised . . .'

'There's fuck all I can do if he's not out on the streets.'

'I told the Chief you were taking care of him.' The ferret eyes of Mr Pronsias Reilly gleamed in anger. He should never have gone in so bloody deep. Direct association with the Organization was walking him out of his depth, too bloody deep.

'He's not where I can get at him.'

'You bloody said you'd get at him.'

'I can't bloody ring up the barracks and ask . . .'

'You said you'd stiff him.'

'If he's not on the streets, I can't get him.'

'Then you keep looking for him, laddie, because the Chief's waiting on your word.'

They went their separate ways. Mr Pronsias Reilly walked back to the Crown Court and the canteen and a sandwich, and Frankie Conroy took himself off in search of a black taxi and a ride to Turf Lodge.


Rennie rang Aldershot.

In staccato sentences he spelled out to Prentice what he had achieved with the office of the Director of Public Prosecutions.

The Preliminary in court opening in a week, two days for the Prosecution counsel before the weekend. McAnally to come in on the Friday, and be ready to perform on the Monday.

'We reckon he'll be in the box for the rest of the week. He has to see that through . . . you've got a holiday after that. It's fixed that you're for Cyprus once he's past the Magistrate. You're bloody lucky.

Prentice, sunshine and cheap plonk to calm down with. You'll have forgotten what bloody Belfast is by the time you get back. You'll have him ready?'

Prentice said he would have him ready.

'How's his chin?'

Prentice said that Sean Pius McAnally's chin was mended.

'He'll be all right?' No more certainty from Rennie.

There was an age-long pause on the line, like Prentice had gone away to have a leak.

'I'll have him ready, and his chin won't look like he's been scrapping. He'll know his lines, he'll know what to expect, but that's all I know for sure. He doesn't talk to us any more. He's inside himself. Ferris talked to him, you know that. I don't know what he said because McAnally won't tell me, and because Ferris isn't around to be asked. McAnally's gone inside himself so's I can't reach him. As I said, Mr Rennie, he knows what he has to say, but whether he's going to say it I just don't know. You won't know whether he's going to deliver right up to the time he goes in the box.'

'You mean he might fall down on his arse.'

'I just don't know.'

'You're a bloody comfort. I'll have his friend on ice for him.'

'You do that, Mr Rennie.'


'Not good news, David, I'm afraid,' the Adjutant said. 'Cast your memory back. The day you were shot up in the Falls, the McAnally fellow, that business. You were running down to Hastings Street RUC because there'd been a complaint from a newsagent chappie or something, about your apes wrecking his place. We thought the peelers had forgotten about it, seems they haven't, seems you're required in the afternoon for your statement.'

'I'm supposed to be patrol leading.'

'If your chaps can't manage without you then you're a pretty poor platoon commander. Most mortals would be grovelling thanks at the thought of spending time in the cop shop rather than pavement bashing . . . You all right, David?'

\*   \*   \*

Frankie Conroy had a bicycle and a ladder and a bucket, and he smear-wiped front windows in Turf Lodge, and didn't ask for money, and those that didn't know thought he was a fucking eejit, and those that knew him saw the way that his head was most of the time twisted away from his work and watching the Drive and the Crescent and the Avenue.

And still no officer with them when the patrol came through. And there was a biddy at his shoulder, shouting that the glass was dirtier than when he'd started.

In a corner of the Mess the Bravo Company commander collared him.

'You're in luck, David. Sunray's got it into his head that the Battalion's short of range firing. You're going down to Ballyclare tomorrow, you and 2 platoon from Alpha. I don't want Henry crowing over me that my lads can't shoot. If Alpha put one over us, I'll kick you where it hurts . . . Well, don't look so damned miserable.'

Ferris went back to his chair and the dog-eared *Illustrated London News*. The pages were bouncing in front of his eyes. For another day he was spared patrolling. He had stiffened himself to accept that in the morning he would be on the streets of Turf Lodge, a target. There was no-one he could tell . . . he couldn't ask for a desk job, or a transfer, or to be shipped out. His pact was made with Gingy McAnally. It was the third time that he had tried the page and the report of last season's Calcutta Cup match. He couldn't read the words, and couldn't absorb the photographs. He was obsessed by the narrow streets of the Falls, and by the estates of Whiterock and Ballymurphy and Turf Lodge.

'If you saw Frankie then you'd know he was trying.'

Mr Pronsias Reilly was hunched over the interview table. The Chief's face was a few inches from his. The lawyer saw the licking nervous strokes of the Chief's tongue against his lips.

'Frankie's doing his best, but his man's off the face of the earth.'

'What else is there?'

'There's nothing else, there's only the officer.'

'Without the officer . . .'

'Gingy might retract.'

'With the officer?'

'They're going ahead, rushing it, because they reckon he won't retract if they can get in fast. If he's got the officer . . .'

'What if he's got the officer?'

'Then it's bad for us, that's all I can say.'

'Why isn't there anything else?'

'Because there isn't.'

'What about his wife.'

'Wouldn't matter a shit to him.'

'What about his kids?'

Mr Pronsias Reilly gazed into the face of the Chief. He felt the fear tremor in his belly. He knew of Mattie Blaney's boy . . .

'I didn't hear that,' he said. 'If one of those kids is harmed – so help me, I'll stand in court and cheer when you go down. I'll cheer if you go down, for twenty—'

The Chief grinned. 'I didn't make a threat.'

'Then be careful with your words.'

'The Brit officer's different?'

Mr Pronsias Reilly shuffled together his papers. Finally he said, 'I'll do my damndest to see you walk out a free man, but not if the McAnally kids are harmed.'

'You get that officer, you and Frankie.'

'I put it to you, McAnally, that you have told a tissue of lies.'

He said stubbornly, 'I've told the truth.'

'I put it to you, McAnally, that you have lied for one simple reason, to save your skin.'

'No.'

'You are a man with a violent criminal record, a record of murderous terrorism, for which you deservedly faced a life sentence of imprisonment, and now you're lying to wriggle clear of that sentence.'

Prentice walked the room. McAnally sat on a hard wooden chair, and just behind him and cross-legged on the carpet was Goss.

'I'm telling the truth.' McAnally swung to face Prentice, his control was sliding. 'It's not lies.'

Goss's hand came up to McAnally's shoulder. 'Never turn and face them, it's to goad you into facing the dock, facing the relatives. You just look in front of you, just at the Magistrate.'

'Would it not be correct to say, McAnally, that by naming names you have won immunity from prosecution for a number of serious crimes?'

Gingy's hand, clasped tight, slapped down onto his thigh. 'It's all bloody rubbish this . . .'

'Just answer my question. I am suggesting that you concocted events to go with the names of quite innocent men.'

Gingy had turned again to Prentice. 'I know what happened, I know what I've got to say.'

Goss gestured for Prentice to hold off. He spoke quietly, urgently, in McAnally's ear. 'Gingy, I've told you every bloody day, and I'll tell you again. It's your word against their word. What it comes down to is this. They are going to try to destroy you, to cut you up in little pieces.'

Gingy sighed dramatically. Prentice caught Goss's glare of annoyance. Prentice didn't hold back. There was no requirement for him to mollycoddle the supergrass. His requirement was to toughen him, strengthen him, so that when the barristers got their hands on him, he'd have some defence, some armour.

'You say that you were brought back from the south against your will.'

'Yes.'

'And you were then dropped at your home?'

'Yes.'

'I put it to you, McAnally, that if you had been brought back from the south against your will, that when you were dropped at home, you were then perfectly free to return to the south.'

'You don't understand . . .'

'I suggest to you that you were a willing member of a murder gang, who when arrested plucked names out of the air and signed a statement which was traded in for immunity from a life sentence of penal servitude.'

'That's a bloody joke . . .'

'Try, Gingy,' Goss hissed. 'Try and help yourself.'

'Is that what they're going to say to me?'

'That's what they're going to say to you,' Prentice said. His voice had roughened, lost the court-room gloss.

'Jesus . . .' McAnally had slumped forward in his chair, his hands covered his face.

'Do you know what's happening now, if this was the court?' Prentice crowded close to McAnally's chair.

'What's happening?' The reply muffled from behind McAnally's fingers.

'Defence are on their feet. They're pleading there's no case to answer, that it doesn't even go to the Crown Court, because the witness is a half-wit, and they might just get away with it . . . and the Chief's cracking a bloody smile, because he might be walking down the steps of the Crumlin in half an hour's time. And if he's walking out then he's thinking bloody well of Gingy McAnally. And if the Chief's out, then out with him are Shay and Dommy and Fatsy and Bugsy and Phonsie and Dusty, and they're all talking bloody well of Gingy McAnally, tout . . . Don't be a pathetic bastard, McAnally.'

Goss waved Prentice back. McAnally's shoulders were shaking, convulsing, and his hand couldn't steady them. His mouth was against McAnally's ear. 'We have to do this, Gingy, it's for your own good. By hurting you now, we're trying to make sure they don't hurt you in court. You sit in the box, you don't turn round, you take your time.'

'I didn't know . . .'

'. . . it would be like this? We're teaching you because it's better you find out now, than find out when you're in the box.'

'I can't . . .'

'I don't know that bloody word,' Prentice shouted.

'I gave you your statement. I'm not going through with being ripped.'

'Your statement didn't buy you immunity.'

'Where's Ferris?' McAnally's head jerked up. He stared at Prentice.

'Back in Belfast,' Prentice said warily.

'He's really back there, no bloody lie?'

'He went back to Belfast, back to his unit.'

'He's not transferred out?'

'He's back on the Springfield Road.'

'You know that? You're not lying to me?'

A puzzled frown cut Goss's forehead. 'Why, Gingy?'

'You wouldn't lie to me?'

'He's with his unit, soldiering. That's certain. Rennie rang him. We're going back on Friday, right. We're staying up the coast of the Lough for the weekend. Rennie's called him out for a piss-up on Friday night, that's how I know that Ferris is in Belfast.'

'Could he sit in court?'

'Christ, Gingy, what for?' Prentice stalked away from McAnally's chair.

'Where I could see him,' McAnally said quietly.

Goss summoned a little gentleness, didn't bloody know where he found it. 'I'll get it fixed.'

'And he went back to Belfast?'

Prentice leaned against the wall behind McAnally. He said keenly, 'Why shouldn't he have gone back to Belfast?'

McAnally stared at the carpet pattern between his feet. He pursed his lips in concentration and he drove his fingers through his hair, and he lit a cigarette, and drew deeply onto the butt.

A calm settled on his face, and his shoulders no longer shuddered.

Without warning, he smiled, and shrugged.

'Can we go over that again?' McAnally asked.

Goss shook his head at Prentice, nothing for either of them to say. He went and sat at the table. He was to the left of McAnally's eyeline, but McAnally could see him if he was staring straight ahead. He sat where they would fix for the officer to sit.

Prentice stated, 'I suggest to you, McAnally, that you were a willing member of the murder gang, who, when you were arrested, plucked names out of the air and signed a statement which was traded in for immunity from a life sentence of penal servitude.'

McAnally gazed at Goss who sat in front of him. He seemed to see the officer, and he saw a mountainside and the rain was lashing from the officer's face, and he heard the words of the officer, quiet and caring, in his ears.

'What I said is the bloody truth,' McAnally said.

*     *     *

310

In the early morning dark the patrol slipped out of the Springfield barracks. Eight men, shadowed and silent figures, jogging between the doorways, crouching in cover. And raining over West Belfast.

The Brave company officer had suggested that the patrol should be a Mobile. Ferris had requested that they should be on foot. The company commander had cocked his head in surprise, but made no objection. Each day that he had not been out on patrol had been worse for Ferris. There had been the Hastings Street visit, and then the day on the range where he'd shot like a blind pig, and there had been the day when the local scribbler from the North East had come to Springfield to write 'home town stories' of the squaddys and she'd been fifty and fat and thought it a bloody adventure to get as far as the barracks. The police station and the range and the minding of the reporter had kept Ferris off the streets. Each day had been worse than the one before.

On his upper body were his vest and his shirt and his heavy knit sweater and his camouflage tunic and his flak jacket, and he was shivering. In the first sprint across the Springfield Road from the gates he had nearly dropped his rifle, and he had stumbled down into his first cover and torn the skin from his knees. If a squaddy had come to him and said he was shit scared of stepping outside the barracks' perimeter, Ferris would have played the good officer, and slapped him cheerfully on the shoulder, and told him there was nothing to fear, and that he was a member of a highly trained group of young men, that his back was always covered, and not to talk such crap. If an officer was afraid then he was a case of LMF. You couldn't hide Lack of Moral Fibre. All the Battalion would know that David Ferris had been categorized as LMF. Right down to Fusilier Jones they'd know. His mother and his father would know. And Sam would know.

David Ferris didn't think he had the balls to go to the Commanding Officer and request a transfer, on the grounds that he was a possible specific target. So he led his foot patrol out into the warren of West Belfast, and each time he was stationary the foresight of his rifle flickered on the rooftops and the chimneys and down the dark unlit alleyways.

He didn't think of Sam. He didn't think of Gingy, nor of Rennie who had telephoned to request his presence at a hotel bar on Friday evening. He didn't think of twenty-one more days in Belfast before the Battalion up-sticked for home.

Dangerous to think of anything but the shadows of the doorways and the marksman's possible hiding places, and the plastic bags and the dustbins and the lengths of discarded piping.

The patrol found two youths acting as though they were about to teach themselves a lesson in larceny, and over the radio they whistled up a police wagon, and handed the brats over along with their bag of tools.

They were almost into Ballymurphy when, high on the Springfield, there was the crash of a single shot. Ferris was aware of his men flinging themselves to the pavements, crawling towards shadow. Outgoing, from one of his own. And then the swearing from across the road, and the section corporal giving out, and then running across the road to where Ferris lay.

'That silly cunt Conville, Mr Ferris. Tripped over an old push chair, and his thumb flicked off the safety. Accidental Discharge . . .'

Ferris hauled himself up. He tried to keep his voice flat and calm. 'Thank you, corporal. Make a note of the details. It'll have to be reported.'

'Wouldn't have thought so, sir,' the section corporal said easily. 'There's a few rounds spare from the range . . .'

'Don't know what's the matter with the bugger, mind you keep your eyes on him. And mind you make up his ammo.'

'Best way, sir. Wouldn't want 3 Platoon knowing, never hear the bloody end of it.'

When the shot had been fired he had been terrified. He banged the sharp corner of his magazine into his knee-cap. Pain was preferable to fear.

The morning was coming, the light was hazing through the streets as the patrol entered Turf Lodge.

She slid her legs off the bed and reached for her dressing gown and slipped it over her shoulders.

Frankie was on his back, snoring, the blankets lying low on his bare stomach.

It had been Roisin's first night back in her old house. The workmen had been the previous morning and finished the repairs to the windows and the door, days bloody late and a piss awful job they'd made of it, and the van had come in the afternoon with her furniture. Not one of the neighbours had stirred a fist to help her move her furniture, and she'd been struggling on her own, and with Young Gerard, when Frankie had appeared on his bicycle. He'd parked the bicycle round the back, with his bucket and his ladder, and he'd shifted the furniture with her.

And his bicycle and his ladder and his bucket were still round the back, against the kitchen wall.

She'd surprised herself because it hadn't seemed that important to her, going up the stairs with Frankie Conroy, him going to bed with her and settling onto Sean's side like he had the right to be there. She'd reminded him of what she had said in his car. Nobody took her trousers off her, she took them off when she wanted them off. She'd thought she wanted Frankie Conroy in her bed that night. Not that important, not a big deal, when she'd carried Baby Sean out of her bed and put him down with Little Patty. He was a clumsy sod, and he wasn't clean, but he'd been good to them. God knows where she and her Ma would have found the money for the Christmas tree and the lights. They'd have been without if Frankie hadn't showed. And he'd bought the supper that night, before she'd taken him up the stairs. He'd given Young Gerard the money to run down to the chipper van, four cod and six chips. They'd had a good crack round the table, and even Young Gerard had smiled. Young Gerard liked the big fellow. And there wasn't a man who she should be keeping herself for, not since she'd taken the taxi and her kids away from Thiepval Barracks.

It was good to be back in her house even if the workmen had made a bloody awful job of it. It was good to have a man in her bed even if he bloody snored.

She pulled back the curtain.

The soldier crouched by her front gate, and he must have seen the curtain move because his rifle swung to aim at the window. She saw the grin explode on the soldier's face and pulled the dressing gown tight around her. Then saw Ferris.

'Sean's friend,' she said, to herself out loud.

'What's you say?' Frankie propped himself up on his elbow.

'I said, it's Gingy's friend.'

She spoke her husband's name flatly, as if he were gone from her, as if he had never been part of her.

She saw Ferris's face, and his hollow deep-set eyes, and the way his rifle barrel traversed over the roof top above her before he went away up the road, a loping loose stride.

Frankie was beside her, white-skinned, naked, bulging his stomach against the window sill. Together they watched the officer's back until it was gone from their sight.

Frankie left her at the window. He dressed fast.

'What's your bloody hurry?' She didn't turn to look at him.

'I've got to be away.'

'Where to?'

'Limerick . . .'

'Down south?'

'I'll call by when I'm back.'

She heard him go down the stairs and into the kitchen. She heard him open the back door. She heard the squeaking of his bicycle and the ring of his bucket in the hall.

Frankie Conroy rode away down the Drive, away from the patrol, wobbling on his bicycle because he balanced his ladder on the handlebars, a shadow figure in the early morning light.

Thursday, early. January's wet low cloud hovering on the Crumlin Court House. They had to be in the Crumlin for the Preliminary because the city centre Magistrate's court on Chichester Street didn't have the capacity to hold so many defendants.

A few minutes before 10 a.m., the prisoners filed into the dock. They'd had to squeeze their way up the stairs from the basement cells, because there was a prison officer flanking each of them, and more prison officers waiting for them in the dock, and the dock itself was ringed by uniformed policemen. There were policemen at each corner of the courtroom, and two cradled their carbines, and some rested their hands on the handles of their holstered handguns.

As each of the prisoners came up the steps, appeared at the back of the dock, there was clapping from the public gallery where the friends and relatives were herded close together. More policemen in the public gallery. The prisoners were at this moment stars greeted by their faithful admirers.

The barristers and solicitors and clerks gathered together in the sectarian knots of Defence and Prosecution, and talked earnestly and quietly and seemed to make the pretence that this was an everyday occasion, not special. Every seat taken on the hard wood benches of the journalists, their sharpened pencils laid out with new shorthand notebooks.

The prisoners talked loudly amongst themselves and waved back to the public gallery. All except one made a show of cheerfulness and bravado and cameraderie. The Chief was alone. The Chief didn't look up to the gallery, didn't acknowledge the particular ripple of applause that greeted his entry into the dock. The Chief allowed his chin to be on his chest and his shoulders to droop.

It would be different on Monday. There wouldn't be the clapping and the applause and the waving on Monday. On Monday all eyes would be on the small low door at the back of the courtroom through which the witness would come. There would be a tension and expectancy on Monday, because Sean Pius McAnally must come through that door on his way to the witness box to supergrass on the Brigade and Battalion officers of Belfast's Provisionals.

There was a straight-backed wooden chair, not taken, against the wall of the courtroom, to the left of where the Magistrate would sit and below his raised dais.

# 20

Ferris had the billet to himself. Armstrong was on early stag in Ops, Wilkins was taking his turn on the range.

Soft disc jockey patter and the easy music through the ply-board partitions that separated this billet from half a dozen like it.

He lay in bed, the notepad on his pillow, writing to Sam.

My dearest Sam,

It's been a pretty soft week. I've had masses of time to think about you, to think about us. I want us to make the announcement as soon as I can get you to a shop and get you the RING.

I've got a really soft week coming up. From Monday I'm going to sit in court and hear the supergrass give his evidence. They've got some daft idea that if he can see me while he's in the witness box he'll have the guts to go through with it. He's flying in tonight from England and I'm being taken off for a few drinks with him, which means I'll be dumped back here legless. If you didn't know what he'd done, you'd say that he's quite a fair chap really. He's wrecked himself. I shouldn't really have got involved, but you get no choice.

I was talking to our Sky Pilot, and he put in a bid to do us in the Depot chapel – we'll talk about it. I showed him your picture – he said you had child-bearing hips! See you soon, Sam, see you at home, see you away from this awful place. Look after those hips.

Lots of love,
David

He put the single sheet of paper in a coarse brown envelope, licked down the flap and addressed it.

He shaved carefully that morning, as if there was to be a special purpose for the day. He thought his face was that of an old man. He saw the worry lines when the razor was close to his mouth, and he saw that his eyes were sunken. He shouldn't have recognized the bloody face in the mirror. He had to shave with great care because the blade was new and his fingers shook.

He went to the Mess, and at the mahogany table he hid himself behind a newspaper and drank three cups of coffee.

'David, jolly good, glad I've caught you.' The Adjutant breezed towards him. 'What are you on today?'

'Rennie, the detective, is picking me up this evening – he cleared it with you.'

'This evening . . . what about today?'

He said heavily, 'I've a mobile going out in the morning, in the afternoon I've two sections for foot patrol.'

'Excellent . . . you're out yourself this afternoon.'

He hesitated. 'I'm not sure yet . . . I've got Rennie coming.'

'Rennie's this evening. Whatever you do this evening kindly remember that for today you are a member of 2 RRF. You won't need a whole day off to ready yourself for junketing with the police.'

'I'll probably be out with one of the foot patrols, probably not out with the mobiles.'

'That's more like it. I've a couple of Scots Guards in. They take over from us. It would thrill the pants off them if you take the lieutenant on walk-about, show him the ropes, give him a feel of things.'

Ferris swore to himself. No bloody chance of quitting foot patrol now.

'Be a pleasure.'

'That's grand . . . nothing wrong is there, David?'

'Never been better.'

'Excellent. What time do you want him?'

'Ops Room at fifteen hundred.'

The Adjutant tramped noisily away, whistling.

Ferris finished his breakfast and went off to beg a stamp from the kitchen corporal.

'They said you was a tout.'

'And I never was.'

'I know you was never a tout.'

Frankie smiled down at the pinched defiant face of Mattie Blaney's boy. The boy was the last of the cogs for the wheel trap that he had fashioned in the fifty hours since he had seen the officer from the window of Roisin's bedroom.

The boy supported himself with a metal stick. He was mobile, after a fashion. He was as agile as any of the others who had had the plastic knee-cap fitted at the Royal Victoria Hospital.

'Does it hurt you much?'

'Not so's I'd notice,' Mattie Blaney's boy lied.

'You can stand on it?'

' 'Course I can stand on it. Standing now on it, aren't I?'

'Could you stand on it a long time?'

'I could.'

'Like two hours?'

'If I wanted to I could. Why should I want to?'

'They made a mistake with you.'

'I was never a tout,' the boy blurted.

'You was blamed for something you never did.'

'Right I was.'

'We think you're too good a kid to walk away from us. We think you're still one of us, even after what we did to you.' Frankie gave the boy a cigarette, and struck the match for him, and watched the boy choke on his first inhalation, and cough the smoke out of his mouth. 'There's been a hell of a row about what happened to you . . . I still trust you, boy.'

'Wha's you want from me?'

'Not what I want from you, it's what the Organization wants from you. We want you to mind something.'

'What do you want minded?'

'You don't ask questions, not when you work for us. We're trusting you. We's saying you wasn't a tout. No bugger'll ever again say that Mattie Blaney's boy touted.'

'You know what they did to me?'

'They was wrong to do it, they'd no cause to do it.'

'They burned me with a fag . . .' The boy held the cigarette close to Frankie's nose, close enough for him to feel the ash heat. 'They put the boot in on me, then they hooded me, then they shot me fucking knee off . . . I told them I was never a tout.'

'If any man says you're a tout, he'll have to say it to my face, if you's help me.'

Mattie Blaney's boy wasn't much more than a child. He was a thin little scarecrow. He wore running shoes split at the toes, and jeans that were knee-patched, and a sweater that had come down from three brothers. Mattie Blaney's boy nodded his trust to Frankie Conroy. When they walked away Frankie had to curb his impatience because the boy hobbled awkwardly after him.

Frankie took him from the Drive into the narrow footpath that divided the gardens of 50 and 52. They could just walk side by side. The alley was wide enough for a running man, or for a man on a motorcycle. He felt bloody tired. It had been a hell of a drive to Limerick, and he'd had to find the cottage out on the Clare side of the city. And when he'd found the man the bastard had said that for that sort of work he needed clearance from Army Council, and he needed permission from the Quartermaster General for the gelignite and for the detonator. They were funny bastards down south when it was joining-up time with Northern Command or Belfast Brigade. Frankie had pleaded that he didn't have the time to wait on the authorization, and the bastard hadn't been easy to twist because he'd wondered who'd dropped his name. Frankie had said that the name came from the Chief, and that was true. The bastard had been suspicious as a virgin nun, and hard bloody going because Frankie couldn't understand all the Clare accent chatter, and the bastard blinked at the Belfast talk . . . What did Frankie want? Frankie wanted the same as the bastard had done before . . . Four hours of talking, and a half-bottle of Paddy, and finally the bastard had said he'd do it.

Frankie had gone to sleep in the chair by the fire. The bastard had woken Frankie in the chair and handed him the cardboard box, and the bastard had told Frankie how it should be done. He had come back over the border on an Unapproved Crossing. He hadn't met a block. He'd been wetting himself all the way towards the border in case he hit a block and the cardboard box was opened.

The rough back road at the end of the alley that served the pre-cast concrete garages for the residents of the Drive and the Avenue was rutted and pot-holed. He was certain it would work. Frankie

Conroy had to be certain. It was down to him. Fucked if he was going to sit in another bloody house with an Armalite and wait for a patrol and for the officer. He thought that with his plan he could guarantee that the officer would come. Guarantee? ... that was bloody rich. Christ, he was doing his bloody best.

He led Mattie Blaney's boy to the third garage in the back road. The doors were old and sagging, but there was a new padlock on the clasps. He had the key and he opened the door. He checked both ways and saw nothing and nobody to disturb him. He pushed Mattie Blaney's boy in ahead of him, into the dark interior of the garage. The boy hadn't gone easily. Frankie wondered if they'd done his knee in a place like this. The garage was empty ... there were few enough cars owned in the Drive or the Avenue, if a bugger had a car then he kept it in front of his windows, where he could see it. He went to the back wall, to a heap of plastic sheeting. He pulled back the sheeting and displayed to Mattie Blaney's boy two Suzuki 125cc motorcycles, blue painted, identical. He bent down and pointed behind the far wheels of the motorcycles, showed the boy two black mouth-guard crash helmets. He unwrapped a strip of sacking and stood back to let the boy see two Luger pistols.

Jesus, and hadn't he worked since he had flogged back from Limerick ... worked to 'loan' the motorcycles, worked to 'borrow' the helmets, worked for the Lugers, worked to 'acquire' the garage, worked to find the trap for the officer.

He covered the pistols and laid the sheeting back over the motorcycles.

The boy watched him. There was no awe on his face, no admiration.

'He'll have to be a right fool,' the boy said coldly.

'Who?'

'Who you're going for.'

'Why's he have to be a fool?'

There was almost a sneer at the boy's mouth. 'They did this two years ago, the INLA did it. The peelers'll know this one.'

'It's not for the police,' Frankie said angrily.

'If it's for the Brits it might work. The Brits isn't permanent here like the peelers, they mightn't know about it.'

Frankie smiled and tried to be the boy's friend and patiently explained to him what he wanted.

The tunnel corridor echoed to the crack of the warder's shoes.

The Chief thought that the shits always shod their shoes with metal, toe and heel, as if it gave the shits some authority. Each man in the long file was escorted by a warder down the steps from the gaol, through the tunnel corridor under the Crumlin Road, up the steps and into the basement of the Crown Court.

He felt the winter dampness on the prison walls. The younger men in the file looked to him for leadership, for defiance, and he had nothing to give them . . . Shay and Eug and Dommy looked to him, and Fatsy and Bugsie and Dusty and Phonsie. They looked to him as if he had some bloody magic . . . and when he turned to them suddenly, when they hadn't expected it, he could see their resentment, their belief that he was to blame for having called back Sean Pius McAnally from the south.

Beneath the court he was locked into a cell by himself.

The Chief sat on a wooden bench. There were names scratched and biroed and pencilled on the walls. He saw names that he knew, the names of the men who were his contemporaries as he had come up in the Organization, men who were rotting in the Kesh on Tenners and Fifteens and Lifes.

There was a rattle of keys. The cell door opened, and Mr Pronsias Reilly bobbed inside. The Chief smelt the aftershave and the talc powder.

Mr Pronsias Reilly came close to the Chief.

'Frankie's going this afternoon, going for bloody broke. If you're a praying man, you should be bloody praying the sun's shining on Frankie's arse this afternoon . . .'

The saloon bar of the big road house on the A 31 beyond Guildford was empty but for them.

Goss leaking in the jacks, and McAnally at a corner table with his back to the wall and trying to pretend he could read a newspaper, and Prentice drumming his fingers on the counter and waiting for the skimpy girl to take time off from glass polishing. Rennie had said that McAnally should arrive pickled, and stay pickled through Friday evening, and through Saturday, and they'd dry him out on Sunday and give him a bomb to get him to sleep, and bounce him into court on Monday morning.

He reckoned they'd managed to get McAnally quite respectable. The suit had been dry-cleaned, and unless you looked hard you couldn't see the vomit stains. Not that the runt was saying much, so the sooner the pickle was inside him the better. For himself, he wasn't fussed about getting back to Belfast, but Andy was. Andy was bloody fretting over his lady. He'd learn. When the door was slammed in his face, he'd learn.

'Two halves of draught lager, love, and a large Scotch.'

Fine for McAnally to be pissed on the flight, not so fine for Goss and himself. Goss came to him at the bar as he was paying. Goss was staring along the bar at McAnally.

'He's a horrible little turd, isn't he?'

Prentice laughed out loud. 'Did you expect a bloody saint?'

'I was standing in there, having my pee, and I thought – up your zipper, Andy, on with your smile, and go back out there to that horrible little turd.'

'Like I said, he's no more than you'd expect,' Prentice said quietly.

'You know what I hate about him? He's never been one bloody bit sorry for what he did. You ever heard him say that he regrets blowing away an old man and two young coppers? Have you hell.'

'It's your bloody job, Andy,' Prentice said.

'Then it's a rotten bloody job.'

Prentice took his glass of lager and McAnally's Scotch and walked to the corner table. He saw Goss drain his glass and head for the door. He'd have gone to sit in the car. No-one said it was easy, cuddling up to a supergrass. He thought that he didn't care who he was cuddling with. He thought he was a good bloody 'tec for a rotten bloody job. And in the evening it wouldn't be John Prentice who'd be cuddling up to the supergrass, it would be the Brit officer, and John Prentice would be at the bar, and getting well pissed.

A warm smile gathered at Prentice's mouth.

'Double Scotch, Gingy, what the doctor ordered. Crack it down you, lad.'

'What's with him?' McAnally gestured towards the door.

'Something about the car. Get it down, Gingy, then we've time for one more. We'll not get any more once we're with the Air Force . . .'

'What was he saying to you?'

'He was saying the car had a rotten bloody engine. Myself, I don't care. If the engine gets us where we want to go then I'm happy. I'm not fussed as long as we get where we want to go. You understand me, Gingy? Another of the same won't see you wrong, right?'

He was still smiling when McAnally drained the Scotch and belched, and he went back to the bar to get the glass refilled.

He had been in the pub, and he'd tried to pee away the pints that he had drunk while Mattie Blaney's boy waited outside with a packet of crisps and a chocolate bar. It was a cold afternoon, but Frankie Conroy was sweating. He thought now that he might have been better on an Armalite, that what he'd managed was too bloody elaborate, but he had got it, and he was stuck with it.

He pushed the motorcycle down the alley and into the Drive, and the boy came after him with the crash helmet under his arm. He took the motorcycle fifteen, twenty yards down the Drive from the entrance to the alley so that it couldn't be seen by a man standing at the top of the alley at the garages.

The two pounds of industrial gelignite were strapped to the inner top of the helmet, with the detonator and the bicycle lamp battery that provided the power to explode the gelignite when the circuit was tripped. Frankie had the coat collar of his jacket turned up and he wore his wool cap low down on his forehead as if for disguise. He laid the Luger pistol on the pillion seat of the motorcycle and placed the crash helmet carefully over it, and lifted the tinted visor so that when he looked through the space he could see the weapon. There was a single, short length of fishing line hanging from the helmet. Irritably, because he was frightened, he waved the boy back from him, not for the boy's safety, but because he needed the light to complete the arming of the booby trap. He fingered the line down to the iron bar underneath the padded pillion seat, and gently inserted it round the bar, and tightened it so that it was taut. He was breathing heavily. He had seen the six-inch steel nails that were held round the gelignite with binding tape, as he knotted the line.

If the helmet was moved, lifted, picked up, then the line would be tugged, then the power circuit would be opened.

He wiped the sleeve of his jacket across his forehead. The boy watched him, detached and unexcited. The boy watched him as if Frankie were a craftsman mechanic. He was angry that the boy had to see him when he was sweating.

He told the boy that Mattie Blaney, in the Kesh, would be proud of his son. He repeated his instructions to the boy, stabbing with his finger for emphasis.

When Frankie had gone, the boy lowered himself down onto the pavement and sat beside the rear wheel of the motorcycle. There were no scratches on the vivid blue paintwork and on the chrome finish to the engine parts, and he could see his own face reflected and distorted on the curve of the crash helmet. And when he looked through the opening of the helmet he could see the Luger. The idea wasn't new, but it might work on the Brits.

The motorcycle stood outside Number 46. After Frankie had gone, the woman came out from 46 and asked the boy what he was at, and the boy told her shrilly not to ask, and that she'd be better in the back, in her kitchen. She went into her house to fetch her man. The man came close to the motorcycle and the boy waved him away with his steel stick, and the man went back into his house and drew the curtains of the living room and of the upstairs front bedrooms so that he would see nothing.

Two women, with their push chairs and their older kids around their skirts, came towards the boy, and the kids ran ahead and wanted to touch the motorcycle because it was new, expensive, shining. The boy flailed at them with his crutch, and the mothers saw the cold determination on his face, and gripped the hands of their kids and dragged them on down the pavement.

All those who looked from their windows, or who paused to stare out from their front door, or who walked past the motorcycle, saw Mattie Blaney's boy guarding it and taking care of the crash helmet on the pillion seat, and they knew what was planned. There were telephones in some of the houses, but none of those who knew even considered ringing the confidential number at Police Headquarters. Hadn't a wee boy been shot dead by the peelers in Short Strand the week after Christmas, and him taking sugar to his Gran, and him claimed by the peelers as a gunman, and him not fifteen? The man in Number 46 systematically removed the family china from the mantelpiece above the fire in his living room and stacked it on the kitchen table.

Half an hour after Frankie had left Mattie Blaney's boy there were no children playing on the pavements of the Drive. A silence had crawled over the street, a silence of waiting.

Within minutes of their meeting Ferris had been told that the Scots Guard lieutenant liked to be known as 'Roddy', being an abbreviation for Roderick. He was a veteran of the hike to Port Stanley. He was hating the prospect of four months in Belfast because he gathered that he wouldn't get to a decent party all the time he was there. He was disappointed to hear that they would be going on foot.

Ferris didn't say much.

Ferris said less when they were out on the Springfield, when they were clear of the covering fire of the barracks' perimeter.

Roddy ambled beside Ferris. He seemed unimpressed with the sudden charging runs of the squaddys, and didn't take part in the frequent dives for cover behind the base of lamp posts and the privet hedges and in the doorways. They were at the top of the Springfield, hemmed in by the estates. In front of Ferris a squaddy sprinted, bent low, across the road, causing a black taxi to swerve to miss him. Ferris was crouched down on his haunches, his rifle at his shoulder rotating over the roofs and upper windows. Roddy stood beside him. He had been issued with a Browning automatic pistol, and the strap of the holster was still fastened down. Ferris's face and the faces of all his section were blacked with camouflage cream, Roddy's cheeks were pinkly fresh.

'Do you always behave like this?'

'What do you mean?'

'All this scampering about . . . I'm not a bloody general, you don't have to impress me. If it's for my benefit . . .'

'It's not for your benefit,' Ferris muttered. From the corner of his eye he saw the flash of a movement at a chimney stack ... and a seagull flapped itself airborne.

'Well, you're hardly impressing the natives. If I lived here – what do you say this place is? Bally what? Whatever the place is called – if I lived here then I'd say the British army is half scared to death. You're like rabbits bolting out of a cornfield. When we were in the Falklands ...'

'Shut up,' Ferris said quietly, too faintly.

'... In the Falklands we *dominated* the Argies. Didn't have manpower superiority or logistics superiority, but we dominated them, enough for them to crumble.'

'Belt up,' Ferris snarled.

'Did I hear you right ... ? Please yourself. If one can't make an observation ...'

'When you're in charge you can walk up here in fucking red coats. For as long as you're with me, for Christ sake, shut up.'

Ferris ran across the street, and Roddy loped after him. Ferris saw the surprise beetling the Guards officer's brow. Jones came after them, grinning hugely.

'Wipe that off your face, Jones, and concentrate,' Ferris said.

Roddy said, 'Where are we?'

'Coming out of Ballymurphy, going into Turf Lodge.'

'What's Turf Lodge?'

'Turf Lodge is the enemy – just like Longdon and Tumbledown were the enemy, only you won't see any bloody white flags because we don't have any Argie conscripts here.'

Ferris could have kicked himself. The Guards officer would go back to his depot and report that the Fusiliers had the wind up.

'Listen, I'm sorry for shouting ... every doorway, alleyway, dere-lict house, is danger. You get used to that and that way you stay alive.'

His apology was acknowledged. Roddy ignored him as he would have ignored a bore at Sunday morning drinks.

Over his radio Ferris reported his position to Ops, and then he waved the section forward, into Turf Lodge.

McAnally stumbled down the steps of the Hercules. Prentice hung to the collar of his jacket.

Rennie was by the cars. He nodded with approval to Prentice as the minders brought McAnally to the transport.

Prentice said softly to Rennie, 'I wouldn't bet on him, sorry.'

Rennie seemed not to hear. A big jovial smile for McAnally.

'Welcome back, Gingy . . . They've not been force-feeding alcohol down your throat, I hope. You'll need to have left a corner, we've a bit of a thrash tonight. I'm dropping you off, then I'm going for David.'

The doors snapped shut on them. Rennie and his driver in the front, McAnally sandwiched between Prentice and Goss in the back. Behind them was a back-up. They swept away for the forty-minute drive to the seaside hotel on Belfast Lough.

Roisin was on her knees in the kitchen. It was the third time she had scrubbed the kitchen floor since they had moved back. When she was close to the linoleum, when her nose was near to it, she could smell what the mob had done on the floor of her kitchen.

'Ma, have you been out the front?' Young Gerard was in the kitchen doorway, excited and bubbling.

'How've I been in the front when I'm on my knees out here?'

'They're going to do a fucking Brit, out in our road.' It was her son that spoke, her child. Roisin shuddered.

'Honest, Ma, they're going to do a Brit, the Provies are.'

Young Gerard didn't speak of his father any more, not after he'd put the phone down on him. She had tried, twice, three times, haltingly, to make an excuse to the child for what his father had done, and Young Gerard had walked away from her.

She wiped her hands on her apron.

Young Gerard ran in front of her to the front door. As his hand was on the latch she caught him, swung him behind her. She opened the door, she looked out. She looked right and the Drive was deserted. She looked left and she saw the bright blue of the motorcycle and Mattie Blaney's boy standing beside it.

'Look, Ma . . . the bike, Ma . . . that's for the Brits.'

She remembered the hunting keen glare on Frankie's face when she had called him to the window, pointed down to the street for him to see the officer who was Gingy's friend.

She swore at Young Gerard that she'd half bloody murder him if he followed her out.

She slammed the door shut after her. She was wearing her slippers and her apron and she had her hair tied up in a scarf.

She walked to the motorcycle and Mattie Blaney's boy. The boy watched her coming and his eyes were alive with suspicion, dislike.

'What's happening here?'

'It's nothing to you, what's happening.'

'Don't give me lip.'

'You'd be best in your house, Missus.'

'What's special about the bike?'

'Wouldn't be telling you, wouldn't be telling a supergrass woman.'

'What's the bike there for?' She was shouting at the boy.

Mattie Blaney's boy was coldly calm. 'You wouldn't need to know.'

She took a step nearer to the motorcycle, and the boy raised his stick, and its tip pointed at her stomach. She walked round the motorcycle, out of the range of the stick if the boy lunged for her stomach. Through the visor space of the crash helmet she saw the barrel of the pistol.

The light was beginning to slide. The afternoon was falling fast away. The patrols always came in the grey half light. Usually she saw the officer in the dusk patrols.

'They'll stiff you if you tout, Missus,' Mattie Blaney's boy said. 'And they'll burn the roof off over the head of your brats.'

She turned, very slowly, and walked back to her house.

She took Young Gerard and Little Patty and Baby Sean into the kitchen, and she locked the door on the inside and put the key in the pocket of her apron, and worked with the brush and the bucket at the linoleum flooring.

Frankie sighed the air deep into his lungs.

He kicked down the support leg of the motorcycle, left it gleaming blue and chrome with the engine ticking. The crash helmet was a tight fit on his head, awkward, hard for his face to twist behind the tinted mask. He took the Luger from his pocket, cocked it, and ran towards the doorway of the Post Office.

He cannoned through the door. His voice reverberated inside the helmet as he screamed for money. It was dark in the Post Office, and he saw women cringe away from him, indistinct shadowed figures. He fired twice into the ceiling, and the pistol shots were muffled. The Post Office on the Glen Road was hit regularly, five times the last year. The Post Master was protected by a bullet-proof glass from counter to ceiling. Frankie waved his Luger at a woman and fired into the wall, over her head as she knelt on the floor. The woman was weeping. The woman was Mrs Deasy, and he'd been to school with her twins. The Post Master thrust a bundle of notes into the sliding tray under the counter glass. Frankie grabbed for the money, dropped some, pocketed some, and ran for the door.

The Suzuki roared to life. Every man and woman and child walking in the Glen Road on the southern edge of Turf Lodge saw the motorcycle and its black-helmeted rider career away towards the roundabout and the junction with Kennedy Way and the Monagh by-pass.

He cornered on the roundabout, and the grin split his face pressing his cheeks against the glass. He saw the grey toad shape of a police Land Rover coming circumspectly down the Monagh by-pass. Fucking good . . . It was more than a hundred yards from him. Still turning on the roundabout, he fired twice at the Land Rover's windscreen. Fucking liven up the pigs. He accelerated back down the Glen Road, the siren in his ears, piercing the helmet. Now the air waves would be jumping.

Twice he turned to check that the Land Rover was in sight, in touch with him, then he turned off, skidding and fast, into the Crescent of Turf Lodge.

'BRAVO 41 . . . BRAVO 41 . . . COME IN . . . URGENT YOU COME IN BRAVO 41 . . .'

'Bravo 41 . . .' Ferris said into the radio mouthpiece clipped to his tunic collar. Around him the patrol had sunk to cover and defensive fire positions. Roddy's face was misting with a flicker of interest.

'BRAVO 41 . . . GLEN ROAD POST OFFICE ROBBED BY ONE ARMED MALE. DESCRIPTION IS BLACK JACKET, BLACK CRASH HELMET. ESCAPED ON BLUE MOTORCYCLE INTO TURF LODGE. POLICE MOBILE IN CHASE. YOUR POSITION? OVER.'

'The Avenue, Turf Lodge.'

329

'WAIT OUT . . .'

Ferris shouted, 'Post Office on the Glen Road. One armed male. Black crash helmet. Blue motorcycle.'

He saw his squaddys checking that their rifles were armed. He saw Roddy groping numbly for the fastening strap of his waist holster.

Frankie sped down the Crescent. As he swung into the alleyway linking the Crescent to the garages, the police Land Rover was reaching the entrance to the Crescent. He bounced down the alleyway, and swerved among the ruts to get to the garage entrance. He heaved the door open, drove inside, cut the engine. He shed the crash helmet and tossed the Luger into a corner. He went out and closed the garage door behind him and fastened the padlock. He crossed to a back garden and climbed over the fence and was gone.

'BRAVO 41 . . .'

'BRAVO 41.'

'POLICE MOBILE'S LOST HIM. WENT DOWN AN ALLEYWAY BETWEEN TURF LODGE CRESCENT AND TURF LODGE DRIVE. POLICE MOBILE NOT KEEN TO FOLLOW ON FOOT. GET YOURSELF THERE AND SWEEP. OUT.'

'Out.'

The section came fast into the Drive.

Oldest bloody trick in the book, Ferris thought, as he pounded up the pavement hill, using a motorbike to get down an alley that was too narrow for a Land Rover to follow.

There was something hostile about the street, something that he couldn't finger, something about there being no-one on the street.

'What are you going to do, David, what's your procedure?' Roddy was at his shoulder, heaving. His questions snuffed out Ferris's thoughts.

Roddy was panting as if he hadn't run two hundred yards since he crossed East Falkland island. For Christ's sake . . . it wasn't a bloody chat-up in the Mess. This was hunting an armed man. There was something . . . Shit, something, and he couldn't find it.

He saw the boy limping down the hill of the Drive towards him.

He saw the boy with his stick. The face of the boy was familiar. He had seen the face in torchlight when it was screwed in pain, and he had seen the face in the headlights of the vehicle park as the boy was lifted into the ambulance. He felt the weight of the boy in his arms.

'Hello, you won't remember me . . .'

The boy stared up at Ferris, no sign of remembering him.

'I took you down to hospital when you were . . . when you were hurt.'

The boy looked away from Ferris. He seemed to wait for permission to walk on.

'Have you seen a man on a blue motorcycle, with a black crash helmet?'

The boy gestured with his stick behind him.

'Is that where you saw the man and the bike, lad?'

Again the boy pointed.

'How long ago?'

'No time ago, mister.'

The section ran forward, and the boy lurched away.

There was a shout from a squaddy on the far pavement to Ferris. A shout of triumph and success.

Ferris saw the motorcycle. Ahead of him, in the failing afternoon, the motorcycle was stood at the side of the road, against the gutter of the pavement, and there was the shine of a crash helmet that was placed on the pillion seat. Ferris didn't have to tell them, the squaddys had fanned out on either side of the motorcycle, and his corporal had taken one squaddy and gone up the alleyway to secure the rear of the homes on the side of the Drive where the motorcycle was parked. Ferris looked ahead of him, and behind him. No sign of the boy, and the Drive was empty. He looked at the windows of the houses and there were no lights lit, and there were no pale faces staring out at the patrol.

There should have been . . .

'That's a good show, latching onto it so soon,' Roddy drawled.

'Please don't talk to me,' Ferris snapped.

'You don't have to be scratchy. It's not the Maze break-out, it's only a Post Office . . .'

'Don't you see something's wrong . . .?'

Ferris's voice tailed into the quiet of the Drive. His squaddys were watching him. Jones was at his shoulder, and his lips were narrow and his finger white against the trigger guard. A cat scurried from under a car, and from instinct four rifle barrels followed it over the first yards of the dash.

He walked to the motorcycle, and Jones walked behind him, backwards and covering his officer, and Roddy went with them and thanked the Lord they didn't have the likes of this one in the Guards.

Ferris stood at the side of the motorcycle. His thighs were within a foot of the rider's seat. He crouched down and the dome of the crash helmet was level with his eyes.

Something was wrong.

Ferris laid his rifle on the tarmac. He slipped to his knees. He edged the fingers of his right hand forward towards the engine parts. The tips of his fingers hovered over the metal work, feeling for heat. A slow smile spread on his face. He dropped his fingers onto the metal, and felt nothing, no warmth. He had found the something that was wrong. Jones was looking down at him.

Ferris winked at Jones.

He depressed the 'Speak' button on his radio.

He spoke quietly, privately into his microphone. 'Bravo 41, Bravo 41 . . .'

'COME IN BRAVO 41 . . .'

Roddy strolled to the far side of the motorcycle.

'Bravo 41. Clever games in the Drive. We are outside Number 46. We have a blue Suzuki motorcycle like the one in the Glen Road, we have a black crash helmet, and the engine's cold. This machine hasn't moved anywhere . . .'

'Take a peep at this,' Roddy called.

'. . . There's not a soul on the Drive. It's never like that, not at this time . . .'

'Here's his shooter, David.'

'I'm requesting the help of Bomb Disposal. In the meantime I'm going to have my hands full evacuating the nearest houses. I'm not in much of a position to mount a search. Over.'

'BRAVO 41 . . . WAIT OUT.'

Ferris turned to the Scots Guard officer. 'Sorry, what was it?'

'He left his shooter here.'

To prove his point, to display the Luger, Roddy lifted the crash helmet from the pillion.


Rennie came into the bar.

They were playing cards. Prentice and Goss, Gingy, McDonough and Astley. They were playing poker for pennies.

Gingy saw him first. Gingy saw that Detective Chief Inspector Howard Rennie had been weeping, crying his bloody eyes out.

# 21

In the rain, the crowd stood on the pavement outside the cream and honeysuckle majesty of the Crown Court. They were mostly women in the crowd, and some had brought their toddler children, and some held placards that had been made and given them by the Sinn Fein workers. Mostly they were from the families of the accused men. There were the wives and the mothers and the cousins of Fatsy Rawe and Bugsy Malone and Noel Connelly and Brennie Toibin and Joey Mulvaney and Dusty O'Hara and Billy Clinch and Ollie O'Brien and Joey McGilivarry and Tom McCreevy. There was the brother of Mrs Oona Flaherty. There was the aunt of the Chief . . . Waiting on the pavement outside the Crown Court building was someone who was family to each of the men named by Sean Pius McAnally, the supergrass. They had been on the pavement since dawn, just as they had waited all through the previous morning, the Monday morning, before the word had spread that the Prosecution had sought and obtained an adjournment of a day. On the Monday morning the crowd had been raucous in its denunciation of the Show Trials and the Paid Perjurers to the microphones of the television crews and of the BBC radio and downtown. Then, running from the Court House, Mr Pronsias Reilly brought word that the Prosecution had won an adjournment. The word was that the Prosecution didn't have their tout to crawl into the witness box. And the word, spoken quietly, was that the death of a Brit officer before the weekend had shattered the resolve of the informer.

Amongst the Sinn Fein workers and the local journalists who knew the habits of the police, it was said that the supergrass was always brought early in the morning to the Court House in an armour-protected saloon car with a back-up behind and hurried into the building through a side door at least two hours before the court was due to sit. Some of the workers and some of the journalists had been at the main gates of the Crumlin court since six in the morning. They said that McAnally was not inside. They said that they would swear that McAnally had not shown. The Magistrate had come with his bodyguards, and the Prosecution had come with the detective who had been assigned to him for the duration of the Preliminary hearing, but of the star and the centrepiece of the Prosecution case there was no sign.

The camera crews and the journalists were no longer interested in the relatives and their slogans – yesterday's news, yesterday's chip wrappers. There was a growing excitement amongst them, a feeling of anticipation. If the supergrass didn't show, if the Prosecution collapsed, if the accused walked free, then that was one hell of a story, that was front-page, that was the lead on the lunchtime bulletins.

Suddenly there was movement. The cameramen jerked their heavy equipment onto their shoulders. The crowd of relatives surged towards the gates and the stone-faced policeman.

Mr Pronsias Reilly skipped down the steps of the Court House and jogged to the gate. The crowd pushed round him, and the cameramen jostled for vantage views of his beaming face, and the microphones were clustered under his chin.

'I have just come from the meeting in the Magistrate's room, a meeting which was called for by counsel for the Crown. The Prosecution asked for a further adjournment. I can tell you that I and my colleagues objected strongly to further delay and pointed out to the Magistrate that this case was being heard with considerable and unusual speed at the demand of the Crown. His Worship has compromised. The court will sit at two this afternoon, and if the Prosecution are then unable to produce their witness, then their case is over, finished. I hope for a satisfactory outcome at two o'clock this afternoon . . .'

The wife of Ollie O'Brien kissed Mr Pronsias Reilly wetly on the cheek, and repeated it for the photographers who had missed the first time.

\* \* \*

The Secretary of State said, 'You know what I should be doing now, Fred? I should be emptying my drawers, piling my papers in the middle of the carpet, and setting fire to them. Isn't that what a general does when he's in full retreat?'

The civil servant said, 'Not your fault, Minister. It shouldn't be your head.'

'The Prime Minister rang this morning, before I'd even had breakfast. The Prime Minister said that as a result of my advice, the Cabinet had been led into a cul-de-sac from which it could not escape without humiliation. McAnally not showing in court, that's humiliation in the PM's book . . . God, this bloody place . . . I'm not prepared to wriggle over a resignation. I'm going to get it over with.'

'I'd leave it until after lunch if I were you, sir,' the civil servant said.

'To what purpose?'

'Only that the ending of a political career is not something to be rushed . . . Now, Confederation of Industry's outside, you've an hour with them. Security meeting's at eleven. Lunch is with the GOC and the Chief Constable . . . Oh, and the flowers you wanted were sent.'

The wind blustered round the flowers, and the rain burgeoned on the petals. The colour bloom would be short-lived in the cemetery in winter. He could not see the grave because his view was obscured by the ranks of the umbrellas and the backs of the Honour party. There was the volleyed crash of blank cartridges. His own flowers, a bunch of early daffodils, were buried beneath the carpet of wreaths. He thought it was a good turn-out, considering the weather. He thought it was the same sort of turn-out that he would have had if he'd been blasted when he was with the RPG, when he was hitting 'Tenner' Simpson. The Last Post was played, and the face of the young bugler quivered. One by one the mourners left. He saw David's father and mother, and he saw his Commanding Officer who walked crisply with his hands clasped behind his back inside a knot of the Battalion's officers, and he recognized the girl who had been at the Midnite Club who wore a black silk coat and who held a crumpled envelope in her black-gloved hand. When the people had gone, when the troops had marched away, when the gravediggers had had their fags and set about their work, Rennie came to his side. For the service at the graveside, Rennie had stood away from him, behind him, with Prentice and Goss. He was looking at the flowers, at the love that had brought the flowers to the cemetery.

'Your decision, Gingy . . . Your choice,' Rennie said.

The wind was on his face. The rain was on his suit jacket.

The wind of the slopes of Mullaghmore. The rain of the summit of Mullaghmore.

When Rennie had come into the bar, and ignored his soft swollen eyes, and told in a stern hard voice of the explosion in Turf Lodge and the casualties in Turf Lodge, then Gingy had fled to his bedroom in the small hotel. He had cried the night away into his pillow. It was Gingy who had asked to be brought to the funeral, and Rennie had made the arrangements. Over the weekend, during the flight to Manchester, through the evening in the hotel outside Preston, Rennie had never asked Gingy for his intentions.

'I can't force you, Gingy . . . I can't be twisting your arm,' Rennie said.

He watched the men who shovelled earth onto the coffin. He gazed over the flowers. He didn't feel the wind, nor the rain.

He turned to Rennie, he nodded. It was Gingy's decision, it was his choice.

They drove fast to the airport with a siren escort of the Lancashire police.

They by-passed formalities and were last on board the British Airways flight.

They were met at Aldergrove by a convoy of unmarked police cars.

They came through Ballysillan and Ligoniel and past Ardoyne, they came down the Crumlin, and there was a Smith and Wesson revolver in Prentice's hand, and a Stirling sub-machine gun on Goss's lap, and Rennie was glancing at his watch and talking into the car radio to announce their approach. Gingy was hunched down between his minders, but he could see the gate towers of the gaol and the high painted walls of the Court House.

They were seen by the crowd, and the women threw themselves at the linked arms of the policemen, and a placard hit the roof of the lead car, and the line of policemen bulged, and held. And Gingy, low in his seat, masked by the minders, heard the cat-calls of abuse that were hurled at the bullet-proof windows. And he covered his face from the photographers and their flash bulbs.

He was hustled into the side of the Court House, and they pounded him up the back staircase to a second-floor room. He was breathing hard.

'Your decision, Gingy,' Rennie said.

Goss detached the magazine from his Sterling, clattered it down onto the table.

There was a light knock at the door.

'It's straight in, Gingy. Good luck, lad.'

He stood alone. They were all watching him. The knock came again at the door, sharper. Rennie and Prentice and Goss were watching him. He straightened his tie. It was the tie of brilliant green that he had worn to the funeral.

'It's not for you,' Gingy said. 'I'm not doing it for you . . . just so's you know that.'

After the darkness of the staircase and the corridors he blinked when he came into the courtroom.

He heard the growl of interest as he was seen. He hesitated, he seemed to those who craned to see him to freeze, then the weight of Rennie shoved him forward. He looked straight ahead of him. He saw the Magistrate whose body was huge under the black gown and he knew that the Magistrate wore a bullet-proof vest. He saw an RUC constable in the corner ahead of him, expressionless, and holding his carbine. He saw the barristers and the solicitors and the clerks peering at him shamelessly. He saw beyond the witness box an empty straight-backed wooden chair. As he came forward he locked his eyes into the empty straight-backed wooden chair as if it were his talisman.

No longer the growl of interest. The shouts from the dock bleated into his ears.

'Filthy traitor, McAnally.'

'Sold out your country.'

'A disgrace to your people, McAnally, that's what you is.'

'McAnally, you're in your fucking grave.'

338

The hate spat down at him from the dock. The prison officers fingered their truncheons. The policemen ringing the dock tensed themselves to prevent an attack on the supergrass. He didn't turn to see the faces of the prisoners. He never saw the loathing and the anger and the bitter twists on the mouths of the men who had been his comrades in arms. He didn't see that the only man who was silent in the dock and who hadn't stood to shout and finger-jab was the Chief. Rennie and Prentice and Goss were close on him, breathing to him.

'How much did they pay you, McAnally, thirty pieces of silver?'

He seemed to stumble and Prentice and Goss were reaching to hold him, and when he felt their hands on his arms he shook them away.

He walked through the floor of the court. He didn't look behind him, nor to his side. The shouting from the dock had died. A great silence slipping on the courtroom. He looked ahead to the empty straight-backed wooden chair against the wall.

He stood in the low-sided witness box. He felt the blood pumping in him, he felt the stampede of his heart.

'You are Sean Pius McAnally?'

The clerk was in front of him.

'Yes.'

The clerk passed him a worn bound bible. 'Repeat after me . . .'

After he had spoken the words of the oath of truth he was told to sit by the Magistrate.

He stared at the empty straight-backed wooden chair. He tried to find the face of the man who had been his friend. He prepared himself to give his evidence.

THE END

339